Praise for *The Nature of Witches*

"*The Nature of Witches* is unlike anything I've read before. With its wholly original take on witches, thought-provoking commentary on climate change, and a swoony romance I would die for, Griffin has crafted a magnificent debut that will have readers on the edge of their seats. To put it simply—I'm obsessed with this book!"

—Adalyn Grace, *New York Times* bestselling author of *All the Stars and Teeth*

"The forces of nature and magic blend perfectly in this masterfully told story. *The Nature of Witches* is one of the most well-developed magical worlds I've read in a long time. I couldn't love this book more."

—Shea Ernshaw, *New York Times* bestselling author of *The Wicked Deep* and *Winterwood*

"*The Nature of Witches* is a love letter to the earth. This lush, atmospheric book charmed me with its magic system, captured my heart with its swoony romance, and stole my breath with its gorgeous words. I want to wallpaper my home with Rachel Griffin's sentences."

—Rachel Lynn Solomon, author of *Today Tonight Tomorrow*

"*The Nature of Witches* is a timely, thoughtful tale of the responsibilities we have to our planet and to one another. Griffin's well-developed world building and complex main character make for a read that will resonate deeply."

—Christine Lynn Herman, author
of the Devouring Gray duology

"Seasonal magic abounds in this addictively thought-provoking tale of love, loss, and self-identity."

—Dawn Kurtagich, award-winning
author of *The Dead House*

"I could have stayed lost in the pages and magic of *The Nature of Witches* forever. Griffin's lush prose and evocative imagery adorns and compliments the thoughtfully designed world, and the well-drawn characters triumphantly carry the story from beginning to end. A stunning and timely debut."

—Isabel Ibañez, author of *Woven in Moonlight* and *Written in Starlight*

"A bright, fresh read from a glowing new voice, *The Nature of Witches* is both timely and stirring. Griffin's emotional writing that cuts to the heart will make her a new YA favorite."

—Adrienne Young, *New York Times*
bestselling author of *Fable*

"Vibrant and magical, *The Nature of Witches* is an achingly beautiful exploration of love and hope perfect for fans of Shea Ernshaw and Taylor Swift's *Folklore*. This book is a ray of sunshine."

—Rosiee Thor, author of *Tarnished Are the Stars*

"In her debut, Griffin ties the story of a witch learning her strength to the raw power of nature and places it in a world decimated by climate change. It's new, different, and well worth a read."

—*Booklist*

Praise for *Wild Is the Witch*

"A contemporary fantasy brimming with tremendous empathy for the natural world and all its creatures. The moody Pacific Northwest is the perfect setting for this book, a romantic adventure mixed with some of the cleverest magic I've read in a long time. Iris, Pike, and MacGuffin the owl stole my heart. I loved getting lost in the woods with them."

—Rachel Lynn Solomon, *New York Times*
bestselling author of *See You Yesterday*

"This fantasy novel draws readers into an atmospheric trek... bound to engage readers with its warmth, vivid portrayals of outdoor settings, and romantic spark."

—*School Library Journal*

"A strikingly tender enemies-to-lovers romance told in the cozy love language of warm fires, s'mores, and small acts of kindness, juxtaposed with wild magic and a treacherous hunt through the ethereal woods of the Pacific Northwest. I devoured every word of this rich and emotive novel."

—Julia Ember, author of *Ruinsong* and
the Seafarer's Kiss duology

"Griffin is a masterful storyteller who uses all five senses to draw the reader into a rich emotional landscape. Using the Pacific Northwest as a backdrop, Griffin never forgets to remind you of the magic of nature as Iris and Pike figure out the truth about each other. *Wild is the Witch* is magical, romantic, atmospheric, and beautifully written, all things we are learning are the hallmarks of Griffin's work."

—Kristin Dwyer, author of
Some Mistakes Were Made

"Rachel Griffin is, without a doubt, one of YA's greatest new auto-buy authors. *Wild is the Witch* is a deeply atmospheric and emotionally raw story about forgiveness, vulnerability, and learning to move forward through pain. Griffin's books feel like slipping on a cozy sweater and settling in to enjoy a cup of tea on a foggy day. Even the darkest and most vulnerable scenes are filled with a profound sense of hopefulness that has become such an intricate part of the author's brand. Everyone should add this to their TBR, stat."

—Adalyn Grace, *New York Times* bestselling
author of *All the Stars and Teeth*

"The narrative balances both action and emotion, anchoring familiar elements of survival stories... The driving force here is the romantic relationship between Pike and Iris, and readers will root for their enemies-to-lovers journey to have a happy close."
—*The Bulletin of the Center for Children's Books*

Praise for *Bring Me Your Midnight*

"Prepare to be bewitched. Achingly beautiful, devastatingly romantic, and deliciously atmospheric, *Bring Me Your Midnight* casts a powerful spell. Readers who pick up this book will feel the sea spray of the ocean, the heart pounding romance, and the impossible choices that Tana must make."
—Stephanie Garber, #1 *New York Times* bestselling author of *Once Upon A Broken Heart*

"Darkly enchanting and lush, *Bring Me Your Midnight*—with its forbidden romance and gorgeous atmosphere—is sure to cast a spell on you."
—Kerri Maniscalco, #1 *New York Times* Bestselling Author of *Kingdom of the Wicked*

"*Bring Me Your Midnight* will sweep you away on a tide of atmosphere and romance. It's a sensitive exploration of what we owe to our communities, ourselves, and the Earth."
—Sara Holland, *New York Times* bestselling author of the Everless and Havenfall series.

Also by Rachel Griffin

The Nature of Witches
Wild Is the Witch

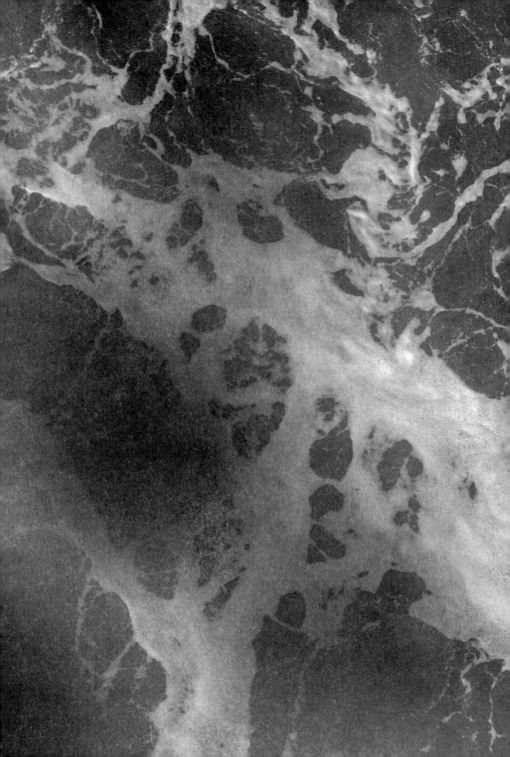

BRING
ME YOUR
MIDNIGHT

RACHEL GRIFFIN

sourcebooks
fire

Published by Sourcebooks Fire, an imprint of Sourcebooks
P.O. Box 4410, Naperville, Illinois 60567–4410
(630) 961-3900
sourcebooks.com

Cataloging-in-Publication Data is on file with the Library of Congress.

Printed and bound in the United States of America.
LSC 10 9 8 7 6 5 4 3 2 1

For Dad.
Thank you for teaching me that my
happiness matters,
and for reminding me when I forget.

one

My mother once told me I was fortunate I'd never have to find where I belong. Being born with the last name Fairchild on a small island due west of the mainland meant I had already found it before I even knew to look. She's right, the way she is about most things, but I've always thought that if I needed to find my true north, I'd find it in the depths of the sea.

The piercing cold of salt water and the thick silence feels more like home than the ornate five-bedroom house perched just two blocks from the shore. The water welcomes me as I wade in and submerge myself, the sounds of the island fading away until they are swallowed whole. My long hair floats out in every direction, and I push off the rocky bottom and swim, keeping my eyes open. The currents are getting stronger, and I watch for any signs of restlessness or agitation, but the sea is quiet.

For now.

I float on my back. The sun rises above the horizon, chasing away the dawn, and the hazy gray of early morning is replaced with rays of golden light that sparkle on the surface of the water. I'm the only one out here, and I can almost fool myself into believing I'm insignificant, a tiny speck in an impossibly vast world. And while the latter is certainly true, insignificant I am not. My mother made sure of that.

I roll over and dive toward the seafloor, deeper and deeper until the water cools and the sunlight fades, entirely unreachable. I pause close to the bottom, reveling in the way expectation and duty can't follow me here. Reveling in the way my life feels like my own. My chest aches and my lungs beg for breath, and I finally relent, kicking toward the surface. The sea ejects me, and I gasp for air.

It's still early, but the Witchery is coming to life in the distance. Many of us rise with the sun to take advantage of every minute of magic we can. The days are getting shorter as winter draws near, and the long nights of our northern island mean we will soon have even less time with our magic.

I take another deep breath as soft waves lap against me. I've already spent too much time out here, and I turn toward the shore, but something draws my attention. It looks like a flower, light and delicate as it rises through the water to greet the sun. I swim toward it and watch as it surfaces, gently floating an arm's length away, inviting me to reach out and take it.

I blink, and the flower vanishes. I scan the water for any sign of it, but there is none, and I realize I must have imagined it. My mind is hazy with the upcoming ball, playing tricks on me in my favorite place. But it's enough to undo the peace of the morning, and I swim back in, knowing there is too little time to recover it.

When the bottom is close enough to scrape my knees, I stand and trudge up the rocky beach, fighting the urge to look for the flower one final time. I wring out my hair and grab my towel from my bag. Salt clings to my skin, so familiar that I no longer rush to rinse it off. I slip into my sandals and twist my hair back in a low bun, then gather the rest of my things.

"Better hurry, Tana," Mr. Kline calls from the sidewalk. "Your mother is on her way."

"Already? She's a half hour early."

"You weren't the only one up with the sun today."

I give him a grateful wave and rush toward the perfumery, thoughts of the ball and the stress of being late mixing in my stomach, turning it sour. I should already be in the shop, getting ready for the stream of morning tourists, but the first ferry doesn't dock for another forty-five minutes, and I've never revered the schedule the way my mother wishes I would.

I turn onto Main Street, where dozens of magical shops line the cobblestone road like wildflowers in spring. Storefronts in baby pinks and sky blues, soft yellows and minty greens stand out against the often-overcast haze that blankets the Witchery, inviting people in, gently reassuring them that magic is as sweet and delicate as the colors of the doors they walked through. In an hour, this strip will be full of tourists and regulars from the mainland who visit our island for perfume, candles, tea, baked goods, natural textiles, and anything else we can infuse with magic.

Dense green vines climb stone walls, and clusters of wisteria hang above doorways, every detail meant to convey that this place is special, but not threatening. Peculiar, but not frightening. Enchanted, but not dangerous.

An island so lush and lovely, one might forget it was once a battlefield.

Large daphne shrubs encircle bronze street lanterns, their strong floral scent filling the air with more magic than we ever could. I sprint over the cobblestones until the perfumery comes into view on the corner. My best friend is waiting for me, leaning against the door with a cup of tea in each hand.

She raises an eyebrow at me as I bend over and rest my hands on my knees, trying to catch my breath.

"Here," Ivy says, shoving the tea in my face. "It's our Awaken blend."

"I don't need your magic," I say, ignoring the tea. I push my key into the lock and open the door, ducking under a waterfall of lavender wisteria.

"Really? Because you look terrible."

"How bad?" I ask.

"There's seaweed in your hair and salt crusted in your eyebrows," she says.

I grab the tea from her and take a long sip. It feels good as it slides down my throat and settles in my stomach, its magic working instantly. My mind clears and energy moves through me. I rush into the back room and change out of my wet clothing and into a simple blue dress.

"Sit down," Ivy says, and I give her a grateful look. Her dark brown eyes glimmer as she moves her hands over my face. I feel the salt lift from my skin and light makeup settle in its place. I don't have a talent for makeup the way Ivy does; mine usually comes out too dramatic for my mother's taste, but Ivy gets it perfect every time. As she works, I tame my hair, drying it instantly and letting it fall in loose waves down my back. Ivy holds up a mirror.

My dress brings out the blue of my eyes, and my chestnut hair doesn't look quite so plain with curls in it. Nothing about my appearance reveals that I was recently in the water, and while my mother will be pleased, I like the way I look when touched by nature and slightly disheveled, a person instead of a painting I'm afraid of messing up.

"Thank you for your help," I say.

"How was your swim?" she asks.

"Not long enough."

The small bell on the door rings just then, and my mother flits into the shop.

"Morning, girls," she says as she walks into the back room. I sit up straighter when I see her.

"Good morning, Mrs. Fairchild," Ivy says with a smile.

My mother looks polished as always, her blond hair pulled back into a simple knot, her tanned skin glistening with whatever new makeup she's trying from Mrs. Rhodes's skin care shop. Her lips are stained pink, and her blue eyes are rich and vibrant.

Always put together. The perfect new witch.

The floor is wet and littered with seaweed, and my mother

looks down. "Ivy won't always be here to cover up your failings, Tana. Clean this up," she says, leaving the room.

I grab a mop from the closet and wipe up the mess, ignoring the sting of my mother's words. I throw away the bits of seaweed that followed me into the shop and make sure the tile is dry before putting the mop away. Magic is tied to living things, and unfortunately, that doesn't extend to the floor.

"We almost had her," I whisper. "Thanks again."

"Anytime," Ivy says, taking a sip of her tea. She's always put together as well, never late for work at her parents' tea shop, never disheveled or groggy when she arrives. Her brown skin glows without magic, and her dark curls bounce lightly over her shoulders as she moves.

I grab a bunch of dried lavender from a glass jar on the wall and take out a mortar and pestle from the cupboard beneath the island. My dad and I made the work surface from a large piece of driftwood we found on the shore, and I run my hand over the smooth wood grain.

Early morning sun drifts in through the store's front windows, stretching into the back room and illuminating all the varietals of plants and herbs. Ivy enjoys her tea as I create the base of a bath oil, closing my eyes and picturing how it feels to fall asleep, the heavy calm and gentle sinking of it. I let the feeling tumble into the lavender until the petals are drenched. Practicing magic is my favorite thing to do, and though I'm creating an oil to calm others, it has the same effect on me. This is when I'm happiest, when I feel most at home.

The bell rings again, and I reluctantly open my eyes. I recognize Mrs. Astor's voice before I even look up, a regular from the mainland who comes to the Witchery for two things: magic and gossip.

"Good morning, Ingrid," she singsongs to my mother, taking her by the hand, a gesture of friendship my mother likes to remind me is only possible because of the sacrifices made by the generations of witches who came before us.

"How are you, Sheila?"

"I should be asking you the same question," Mrs. Astor says, giving my mother a significant look. "There are rumors circulating on the mainland, as I'm sure you're aware."

"Oh?" my mother asks, busying herself with some glass bottles on the counter.

I turn my back to the door and try to focus on the lavender.

Ivy nudges my arm and nods toward the woman. "Listen," she whispers.

"Don't play coy with me, dear. Something about your daughter and the governor's son?"

I hold my breath, waiting to hear how my mother will respond. The rumor is true, of course, but timing is everything, as my mother says.

"You know as well as I do that I don't like to share anything unless it's settled."

"Can we expect a... *settlement* anytime soon?"

My mother pauses. Then, "Yes, I should think so."

Mrs. Astor lets out a tiny shriek, then congratulates my mother and gushes as she buys two new perfumes.

I quietly shut the door to the back room and rest against it, closing my eyes.

"News travels quickly," Ivy says.

"News travels as quickly as my mother wants it to," I correct her.

I just swam, but I want to run from the shop and dive into the sea, silencing Mrs. Astor and my mother and the expectations that weigh on me.

Ivy sips the last of her tea and hands me mine. "You should finish this."

I take it from her and drink it down.

"Before I go, how are you doing with all this? It was one thing when your mom decided it was time to start your courtship with Landon. It's another thing now that it's truly happening."

"This is huge for us," I say. "It would be the most high-profile marriage between a witch and a mainlander in history. It would completely solidify our coven's place in society."

Ivy rolls her eyes. "I didn't ask how your mom persuaded you. I asked how you're doing."

I exhale, moving closer to her. "Did you read any articles about the dock fire?"

The words are so quiet I'm not sure if Ivy heard me, but after a moment, she slowly shakes her head. "Only what was in the paper here."

"I went to the mainland and read every newspaper I could find," I say, watching the door to ensure my mother doesn't walk in. "And you know what? There was hardly anything."

A look of confusion settles on Ivy's face. The fire happened one month ago, when a mainlander who didn't trust magic or witches rowed to our island in a wooden boat and set our docks ablaze, trying to destroy the ferry route between the mainland and the Witchery. Trying to cut us off. As soon as my mother learned the details, she said it was time to begin my courtship with Landon.

"Why did you go there?" she asks me.

"I don't know. I guess I just wanted to see how the mainland felt about it, how strongly they would condemn it. It never occurred to me that I'd find just three short articles that never even called it what it was. I know it's a small subset of people who feel that way, but things like this will continue to happen until the mainland takes a firm position on the Witchery, and what better way to do that than the future ruler marrying a witch? It's the most powerful statement they can make. If Landon and I were already married and the mainland had officially written their protection of the Witchery into law, would our docks have been burned? We don't even know how harshly the man who did it is being punished, if at all. It's easy to feel like we're protected with the sea separating us, but we aren't."

Ivy nods along to my words. "Mom locked our doors that night. It was the first time I could ever remember her doing that."

"It's time for Landon and me to announce our courtship. I'm ready."

The truth is that the fire only affected the timing. My life has been mapped out for me since the day I was born. This is my role—keeping my coven safe by cementing our place among the mainlanders. It's a role I'm proud to play, even though it isn't up to me.

"Well, then," Ivy says, wrapping her arm around my shoulders, "I suppose it's a good thing he's handsome."

"He most certainly is," I say, laughing.

Ivy takes my cup from me and walks toward the door.

"Thank you for asking," I say. She turns. "It's nice to be asked."

"I'm glad you feel that way, because I'm going to keep bringing it up." She grins and walks out the door, saying goodbye to my mother as she leaves.

I've known my parents' plan for this wedding since I was a little girl, and Landon is a good person. He's decent and kind. We will formally announce our engagement on the same day as my Covenant Ball, when I will bind myself to my coven for the rest of my life. It's the same ritual every witch must go through, a choice that can never be altered, can never be undone. I must choose my coven or the outside, seal it with magic, and never look back. Without that choice, magic becomes volatile and dangerous.

Even magic needs a home.

In many ways, I've been preparing for the ball for nineteen years. It makes sense to share it with Landon.

My mother has never sat down with me to ask my thoughts on the plans my grandparents set in motion, to find out if I would be okay with leaving the Witchery and becoming part of the mainland's ruling family. If I would trade my magic for jewels, my swims for social calls.

Every so often, I think it would be nice if she asked, if only so

I could look her in the eye and tell her with absolute certainty that yes, I'm committed to this path we're on.

I love my parents and my coven with my whole heart. I love this island with my whole heart. And I will do whatever it takes to secure our place in this world, even if it means marrying a man I don't love in order to protect all the things I do.

two

I always take the long way home. I like to breathe the salty air and feel the rocks under my feet, listen as the waves roll onto the shore over and over again. The eastern edge of the Witchery disappears into the Passage, giving way to the arm of the sea that separates us from the mainland.

The mainland rises in the distance, countless buildings and crowded streets stark against the horizon. A large clock tower anchors the city, and while we can't hear the bells this far out, its presence is undeniable. It's an impressive sight to behold, and from the shores of the Witchery, it looks almost fanciful, like something from a book.

It's hard for me to picture what my life will be like when I marry Landon and live on the mainland. The Witchery is my home, with its rocky beaches and cobblestone roads, old stone buildings and plants that cover every inch of them. I love it here. And even though the mainland is only an hour-long ferry ride away, it feels too far.

I'll still come here, of course. I'll help my parents at the perfumery, and I'll be here every full moon for the rush, but I want these moments of walking home, stopping on the beach, looking out at the mainland in the distance.

I don't want to look at the Witchery in the distance instead.

I shake my head. It's not that I don't want it, I tell myself. It's just that I'll need to get used to it. I take comfort in knowing the earliest witches lived on the mainland, that they moved only to preserve their magic. If they could build lives there, so can I.

Sunset is in one hour, and the last ferry out will leave several hours after that. The island will rest, breathe in deep after a long day of busy streets and eager tourists and delicate magic. Magic that can't meaningfully change a person's life or even make much of a difference, in the grand scheme of things.

Magic that is only a shadow of what my ancestors practiced. But that's the price of being accepted in society, of having our hands shaken instead of bound, our cheeks kissed instead of slapped, our island celebrated instead of burned.

I've never known more than the gentle magic of the Witchery, but I've heard rumors about what our ancestors were capable of. Controlling the elements. Cheating death. Compelling others. Sometimes it scares me, knowing the same magic that ran through their veins runs through my own, that there is something inside me far stronger than the perfumes in our shop or Ivy's most potent tea.

I sit down on the shore, not caring that my blue dress will get damp and dirty, not caring that my mother will comment on my appearance when I arrive home, the way she always does. She wants me to be more put together, more polished, more presentable.

More like her.

But she doesn't see what I see: the most beautiful things are wild.

I push my fingers into the rocks and sand, feel the jagged edges and rough grains. Our shore is smaller than it used to be, the angry currents carving away at it, carrying it off to other parts of the island or swallowing it altogether.

My mother says I spend too much time worrying, that she and the other coven leaders have things under control. But the currents are getting stronger, and it won't be long before they snatch a boat from the surface and pull it to the bottom of the sea.

We'll see how fully the mainlanders accept us when our currents drown one of their own.

But once I'm married to Landon, his father will extend the government's protection to us, not only in promises spoken at fancy parties but in written law. There will be no going back after that, not even if a ship sinks in our waters or our currents grow more violent.

This is the kind of security my ancestors only dreamed about, the kind of security that not even moving off the mainland could afford them. Because as soon as the witches made the island their home, fear among the mainlanders ran rampant. The only thing more terrifying than seeing our magic on their streets was not seeing us at all; we could be doing anything on the island.

At first it was an idea born of pure desperation, that magic could be something to delight in instead of something to fear.

That this island could be a place mainlanders wanted to visit instead of a hideaway for witches and evil. Out of sheer force of will, my ancestors created an entirely new order of magic, softening their power and tending to the island so they could survive. They only practiced magic in daylight, never hiding it in darkness. They gave up the terrifying parts of magic and magnified the wondrous parts. They were kind to the mainlanders who monitored the island, smiling when they really wanted to curse them to the depths of the sea.

And it paid off.

The waves are coming quicker now, rolling up the shore and licking at my legs. I close my eyes and listen, let the rest of the Witchery fade away as I imagine myself under the water. Most silence is unbearably fragile, stolen by a single voice, a shattered glass, a muffled cry. But the silence underwater is thick and sturdy and impenetrable.

The sky is turning orange and pink, as if Mrs. Rhodes has taken her brightest eye shadows and smeared them across the horizon. I'll be scolded for more than just my appearance if I'm not home for dinner, so I push myself off the ground and stretch.

I take one long, deep breath and let the salty air fill my lungs, but I stop when something in the water catches my eye.

A flower, exactly like the one I thought I saw this morning.

The world is getting darker by the minute, but I'm sure of what I'm seeing. Without thinking, I rush into the waves and dive under, swimming toward the bloom that bobs and sways with the rolling of the sea.

It stays put as I get closer, as if it's anchored to the bottom somehow. The waves still and the flower comes into sharper focus, my entire body tensing as it does. I gasp and thrash backward.

It can't be real. I've never seen one in person. My heart slams into my ribs, fear seizing me.

The flower rocks side to side, only unfurling with the arrival of evening or in the presence of a witch. The trumpet-shaped bloom has stark white petals that almost shimmer, reminiscent of the moon at its fullest.

Moonflower, deceptively beautiful and fatal to witches.

It doesn't look threatening, though, with its long, white petals tightly curled together. It looks beautiful.

But I suppose we're meant to think the most dangerous things are lovely.

The flower slowly unfurls, opening up to me as I shake with terror. The sea is stirring, and my breath catches when the flower gets caught in a current and swirls around in the water, going faster and faster until it's finally sucked below the surface. I kick my legs and shoot my arms out in front of me, pulling with everything I have, trying to create some distance between the current and me. I swim as fast as I can and beg the shore to meet me halfway.

Land is getting closer, and I reach for it, stretching my arms as far as they'll go. I finally touch the bottom and pull myself the rest of the way up the beach, ignoring the jagged rocks that cut up my knees.

The moonflower is gone, but I'm certain it was there, so mesmerizing that I can't quite bring myself to see it for what it is: a harbinger.

Before the witches moved here, the island was used solely for harvesting plants and herbs, and only rarely. Endless fields of the poisonous flowers made it a perilous task, but when the mainland outlawed the use of magic, the witches chose to move to the island, a refuge just beyond the reach of the mainland's laws. It took years to get rid of the flowers, and I wish I could go back in time and tell the witches who came before me that one day the mainlanders would help us get rid of the deadly blooms, help us create a home here after all but banishing us so many years ago. And they would do such a good job of it that there would be a generation of new witches who would never see a single moonflower in person.

Until now.

A sharp, prickling sensation begins at the base of my neck, crawling all the way down my spine. I turn my back on the water and run the whole way home. Every light is on in the two-story house, the tall glass windows framing my father cooking dinner and my mother pouring a glass of red wine.

She puts the glass to her lips and closes her eyes, creating her own kind of silence.

I walk around to the back of the house and quietly slip into the mudroom. As soon as I'm inside, I pull my soaking-wet dress up and over my head, wrap a towel around me, and quietly walk up the back staircase.

"Tana," my mother says behind me. I jump. "Where have you been?"

She asks the question even though it's obvious where I was. "I thought I saw something in the water," I say. My dress is dripping on the hardwood steps, and I roll it into my towel to stop the mess.

"I told you to come straight home and help your father with dinner. Why were you there in the first place?"

I don't answer because nothing I say will satisfy her.

My mother sighs. "Go get cleaned up, and then you can tell me what you saw in the water." Her wine sways from side to side as she turns and walks away.

I hurry upstairs to dry off, shuddering as I catch a glimpse of the sea. The sea is my safe place, my refuge, my haven. But tonight, it was dangerous.

"Just in time," Dad says when I walk into the kitchen. A dish towel is thrown over his shoulder, and he holds a wooden spoon up to his mouth, tasting the stew simmering on the stove.

"I'm sorry I wasn't here to help," I say.

"I'm sure you had a good reason." Dad winks at me and motions to the silverware drawer. "Why don't you set the table?"

I grab what we'll need and set the table for three, just like my mother taught me. Tonight's is a casual dinner, but I know how to set a table for a twelve-course meal, a skill I have yet to use but that my mother assures me is important all the same.

When we all sit down, I place my napkin in my lap and take a long sip of water.

"Try to get a good night's sleep tonight," Mom says, eyeing me over her glass. "You want to be well-rested for the ball tomorrow."

It's a celebration for Marshall Yates, Landon's father, marking his tenth year of governing after the late Marshall Yates Sr. could fulfill his role in title only, no longer able to keep up with the demands of ruling. It will be big and loud, with many eyes watching Landon and me.

"This is your first outing since the mainlanders heard there might be something going on between you and Landon." She says *heard* as if she isn't the one who spread the rumors. "We need to play this carefully."

"Tana will play it just right," Dad says, turning to me. "Landon is eager to see you—that's all that matters. And I suspect you're eager to see him as well."

I am eager to see my future husband, but I'm more eager to cement our union, to see the faces of the eldest in our coven when they hear the news. "Of course," I say, taking a bite of my stew.

Dad smiles at Mom, but she doesn't look convinced. We sit in silence for several minutes before Mom puts her glass down and looks at me.

"You will love him one day," she says with a nod of her head. Certain.

I want to believe her. Landon has been just an idea for so long, something to wonder about as I drift off to sleep—what he will be like, what our life together will be like. But he is no longer an idea, no longer a distant point on the horizon, and I want the reality of him to match the picture I've been painting in my head all these years.

The irony is that if we hadn't formed the new order, my parents could simply concoct a perfume that would make me fall helplessly in love with him. But that kind of magic doesn't exist anymore.

I smile at my mother. "I'm sure I will."

She nods in approval. "Why don't you tell us what you saw in the water?" she says, changing the subject.

The question makes me tense and my palms begin to sweat. My fear from earlier returns, grasping at my nerves, but I suddenly doubt myself again. Maybe it was some kind of cruel joke; there are still many mainlanders who hate magic, hate that our island is here at all, and perhaps one of them thought they'd get a good laugh out of making the witches believe moonflowers had returned to the Witchery.

My mother is the leader of the new witches, and if I tell her I saw the flower, she will be required to look into it. I'm torn over what I should do; I don't want to make a big deal out of nothing, but if it *is* something, she needs to know.

I walk the shores every day. If I see one again, I'll tell her.

"Nothing," I say, trying to calm my racing heart. "Just a flower."

She watches me for several moments before nodding. "Well, please stay out of the water tomorrow. It's a big night for you."

"It's a big night for us all," I say, and that brings a smile to her face.

I take another bite of my meal, my mind wandering as I do, but it keeps catching on the flower. There are plenty of explanations that make far more sense than a moonflower appearing after all these years, and yet I can't help the dread that blooms in my center, spreading outward, invading everything else.

three

The currents never used to be a problem. I remember swimming as a young girl, letting go of my father's hand and rushing into the water without hesitation. He'd read a book on the shore, talk with our neighbors, even doze off if the sunlight hit him just right. The Passage was calm back then, with clear water and gentle waves that caressed the beach as if they were lovers. It wasn't until I got older that my father stood at the edge of the water as I swam, close enough to run in if needed, wary of the restless sea.

Then one day, it was needed.

I was fourteen years old, testing my father's patience and my own insolence when I swam out farther than I knew I should. My father called for me from the shore, but I pretended not to hear him, fully submerging myself instead of keeping to the surface and swimming back in. My eyes were open, and I noticed the sand on the seafloor had been disturbed, swirling around in a violent spiral that reduced my visibility to nothing. By the time I realized what was happening, it was too late.

The current found my arm first, pulling me under with such strength that it forced the air from my lungs. I don't remember much after that except the desperate need to breathe and the sheer terror of knowing I couldn't.

My dad pulled me from the water, pushing down on my chest and giving me breaths until I ejected the salt water from my lungs. I thought he'd be mad at me, furious for what I'd put him through, but it wasn't me he was mad at. That night, after I'd gone to bed, my parents had their worst fight ever. My father doesn't yell, never raises his voice or speaks with aggression, but he yelled at my mother that night.

I couldn't make out all the words, but I heard enough to piece together that he was blaming the currents on her. Until that moment, I'd thought the currents were a natural part of our complex Earth; I didn't realize they were our fault, a consequence of our rushes where we expel our excess magic into the sea. I couldn't sleep that night, trying to make sense of what I'd heard when my bedroom door creaked open and my mother quietly walked to my bed. I kept my eyes shut, not wanting her to know I was awake. She sat down on the bed and gently began to stroke my hair, her hand shaking, her breaths shallow as if she was fighting back tears. But the next morning, she was calm and collected, scolding me for swimming too far out.

I tried to ask my parents about what I'd heard, to understand how my father could blame such a thing on my mother, but I never got an answer.

I have tried many times since with the same result.

It took months before my parents let me in the water again, and it was only after seeing how miserable I was without it. They were shocked I wanted to go back in after almost losing my life, but I never saw it like that. I have only ever seen the sea as perfect. They set strict parameters around when I could swim, for how long, and where. I push the boundaries every so often, but for the most part I stay within them.

When I think back to that day, I don't think about the current or the fear or the horrible tightness in my chest. I think about my dad yelling at my mom, blaming her for something that couldn't possibly be her fault. And I think about my mom, hand trembling, fighting back tears as she stroked my hair.

"Tana?" My mother's voice brings me back to the present, and I realize I've been staring at the large oil painting of the Passage that hangs behind the counter of the perfumery. "Mrs. Mayweather asked you a question."

"My apologies, I must have been somewhere else," I say, smiling at the woman in front of me. She's about my mother's age, and she has a daughter on the mainland who attended secondary school with Landon. She has become a regular visitor of the Witchery in recent weeks, and I can't help but think it's because of the whispers that have started about me.

"Probably thinking about the ball tonight," she says with a knowing smile. "Can we expect your presence?"

I look to my mom, and she gives a single nod.

"I think that would be a safe assumption," I say, mimicking

the tone I've heard my mother use a thousand times when she wants to seem modest about something.

"Then I will look forward to it even more." Mrs. Mayweather grabs her ivory bag from the counter, says goodbye, and leaves.

I slip into the back room before another customer can stop me, itching for my magic, for the way it calms my nerves and quiets my mind. In this room, surrounded by flowers and herbs and empty glass jars, everything else seems to recede. I know my ancestors gave up a lot to create the new order, but I can't imagine anything better than the tender magic that fills this space. It isn't a sacrifice, this life; it's a gift.

I gather fresh rose petals and pile them high in my mortar. I'm not as polished as my mother, and I don't always know the right words to say to people, but magic is one thing I don't have to try at. I don't have to do several test batches to get things just right or continually tweak my spells until I've achieved the desired effect; magic comes naturally to me, the way leadership comes to my mother and sincerity comes to my father.

I want a special perfume to wear tonight, one that feels like a spark, like that perfect moment when you see another person and your insides start to vibrate. I imagine it as the final note of a masterful concerto or the first bite of cold when entering the sea, surprising and delicate and exhilarating.

It's what I hope I'll feel tonight when I see Landon at the ball.

The rose petals eagerly soak up the magic, and I put them in a jar, add the base, and gently swirl the bottle.

"Is that Tana back there?" I hear a customer ask, peering through the crack in the door.

I sigh, capping my perfume and putting a smile on my face before stepping back into the shop.

"Hi, Mrs. Alston." She's a regular from the mainland, with several bags hanging from her arms and her warm beige skin glistening with a recently sprayed perfume.

"Hello, dear. Excited for the ball tonight?" It's her way of asking if I'm attending, and after a pause, I reply.

"I am."

Her eyes widen just slightly, and a large smile spreads across her face. "I'll see you there," she says, paying my mother and breezing out of the perfumery.

Mom waits until the door shuts fully before she turns to me. "Why don't you go home and start preparing for the ball?"

"But it isn't even noon yet," I say. "I don't need the whole day to get ready."

"No, love, but you don't need to be bombarded with questions all day, either. Go home, and I'll handle the store on my own." Her tone is sweet, but it's clear her mind is made up.

"Okay, Mom, if you think that's best."

"I do." She kisses me on my forehead, and I walk out the door just as a new wave of customers enters the shop. I hurry outside and hear my mom's warm greeting as the door shuts behind me, welcoming patrons as if they're the oldest of friends. While I sometimes think how exhausting it must be to hold herself to such high standards, the truth is that I'm in awe of her.

It's an overcast day, and the cobbles are slick with rain. I lift my shawl above my head and make my way down Main Street, trying to avoid eye contact so I won't have to talk with anyone. Up until now, it's been my mother whom most people recognize, so I haven't had to worry about mainlanders stopping me on the street unless they're regulars. But I suspect that will change after tonight.

When I pass Ivy's tea shop, the Enchanted Cup, she knocks on the glass and waves me in. I look back toward the perfumery to make sure my mother isn't watching, then duck inside. The Enchanted Cup is one of my favorite shops on Main, and not only because it belongs to Ivy's family. The walls are a dusty rose pink with deep gold chair rails and matching crown molding on the ceiling. Candle sconces fill the space with delicate light, Ivy's parents opting for candlelight even after the island was electrified because they wanted the shop to retain its original charm. But the real centerpiece is the grand chandelier in the middle of the room with twelve teacups hanging from gold chains, each holding an ivory candle. All the chairs are shades of pink velvet, and each table is set with gold stirring spoons and lace napkins.

"Where are you off to?" Ivy asks, clearing a table in the far corner and motioning for me to sit.

"Home. I was being bombarded with Landon questions this morning, and I don't think I was fielding them as well as my mother would have liked."

"No one fields questions like your mother."

"I know. The bar is unbearably high."

"I was just about to take my break. Want to sit with me before heading home?"

"Definitely. My mom seems to think it will take me the rest of the day to prepare for the ball tonight."

Ivy laughs. "What does she want you to do? Individually curl each strand of hair on your head?"

"I'm sure she would love that," I say, draping my shawl over the back of my chair.

"I'll be right back. Want anything in particular?"

"Surprise me."

I settle into my seat, and Ivy returns a few minutes later holding two teacups. She sets them down on the table before sitting across from me. As usual, she won't tell me which tea she brought—she wants me to guess.

I take a few sips. It's a black tea with hints of cinnamon and orange, and it feels bold and robust as it moves through me.

"Well?" she asks.

"Confidence?"

"You're close, but no."

I think I see my mother out of the corner of my eye, and instead of trying to make myself smaller so she won't spot me, I sit up taller and lean forward. The woman turns, giving me a better look at her, and it isn't my mom, but I think I know what Ivy gave me. I laugh and look at her.

"Bravery?"

"Yes! For tonight," she says.

"Why would I need to feel brave?"

"Well, for starters, you hate being the center of attention, and this is the first time the mainlanders will see you in their world, so they'll be watching. It's also kind of your debut as a couple, *and* you'll be expected to dance. In front of everyone. It's a lot."

I take another sip of tea, much bigger than before. "You know, I wasn't actually nervous until just now, so thanks for that."

"No problem." Ivy smiles and brings her teacup to her mouth.

"What are you drinking?" I ask, but before Ivy can answer, a teacup shatters on the ground. I look up and see an older woman standing at the marble counter, yelling at Mrs. Eldon, Ivy's mother.

"This is too strong," she shouts, shoving her pointer finger in Mrs. Eldon's face. "I can feel you trying to compel me! No one drink the tea," she says, turning to the other patrons in the shop. The room falls silent, all the conversation and clatter sucked up by the woman's words. Ivy stands and goes to her mother's side.

"I can assure you that all the tea in this shop adheres to each and every standard of low magic," Mrs. Eldon says. "If you don't like the particular blend you were given, we'd be happy to replace it with something more to your liking."

"I'm no fool," the woman says, her long gray ponytail swaying from side to side. "The problem isn't the tea, it's the magic. There is dark magic here, I can sense it." She practically spits the words, and murmurs break out around the room. I'm shocked that she would be so bold. Dark magic hasn't been on the island in years; it was all but eradicated with the new order.

Mrs. Eldon takes a step closer to the woman, her expression turning from patient to stern. "You are not to say those words in my shop. If you don't like what we're serving, you are free to leave, but I will not stand here and tolerate your disrespect."

"All of you are being brainwashed. Each and every one," the woman says, looking around the room. "You should be protesting the existence of this island, not putting silver in their pockets!"

"That's enough," Mrs. Eldon says. She walks to the front of the shop and holds open the door. "It's time for you to go."

"This place is an abomination. You should all be ashamed of yourselves." The woman pushes past Ivy's mother and out onto Main Street, leaving behind a heavy silence.

Mrs. Eldon takes a deep breath and closes the door, then turns to the other patrons. "I'm terribly sorry about that," she says.

"For the record, I wish my tea was stronger," says a man on the other side of the shop, and it's enough to break the discomfort that had settled in the room.

People laugh, someone says, "Here, here!", and then the rest of the customers raise their teacups in agreement, drinking to the idea of more magic, not less.

Mrs. Eldon smiles and walks back to the counter, but I see the way the confrontation weighs on her, the way her shoulders are drawn and her eyes are heavy with thought. Ivy and I haven't seen many encounters like this—people come to the Witchery because they *like* magic. But our parents, and especially our grandparents, remember more frightening times when the majority of the mainland sought to get rid of magic altogether. They tell us the stories, remind us of how fortunate we are, but hearing it and seeing it are different things.

Ivy wraps an arm around her mother and whispers something in her ear. Mrs. Eldon nods, then excuses herself to the back room.

"Are you okay?" I ask, walking to where Ivy stands behind the counter, her eyes wet.

"I'm fine," she says, wiping at her lashes. "These are angry tears. Seeing someone talk to my mom like that..." She trails off, unable to finish her sentence.

"I know," I say, grabbing her hand. "Why come here if you hate magic?"

It's easy to fall prey to the belief that the entire population of the mainland is like the regulars who visit the Witchery, but it isn't true. How many people are on the mainland, looking across the Passage to our island, wanting it to go away? How many people still want the eradication of all magic? It's scary, knowing that where there is one, there are others. And if those people got the ear of the governor, that would be terrifying.

I don't believe there are many people who want us truly cut off from the mainland, who would be willing to burn our docks under the cover of darkness, but it's becoming clear there are people who don't want to live in a world where magic is accepted. Even magic ruled by the new order, gentle and mild, is too much for some. But in order to do away with magic, they would have to do away with us.

The memory of the moonflower surges back to me, and I swallow hard.

"What are you thinking about?" Ivy asks, taking a deep breath. Her eyes are dry, and any trace of her anger is gone.

I sigh, then down the rest of my tea in one gulp. "That I need to be flawless tonight."

"Then you better go," she says. "You've got a lot of hair."

four

The night is clear. I spent the entire ferry ride looking for signs of a moonflower, but there was nothing. My legs feel weak as I walk up the shore of the mainland, and I jump when an automobile rumbles down the road. We don't have them on the Witchery, and I take a breath, letting the rhythmic lap of the waves calm my racing heart. The governor's mansion towers in front of me, lit up from bottom to top, and the band's festive music floats out into the night.

Several people are leaning against the balcony rails on the second and third floors, fancy drinks in crystal glasses in their hands, silk dresses and loose updos blowing in the breeze. I hug my arms to my chest.

My pale pink dress is wrapped tightly around my ribs, making sure my lungs and heart stay put. The bodice gives way to flowing layers of sheer fabric that brush the tops of my satin shoes, and short cap sleeves cover my shoulders. I wanted to wear something gray, reminiscent of the way the fog looks in the early mornings on the Witchery, but my mother overruled me, insisting the pink was more appropriate.

My makeup is subtle and my long hair is curled, falling halfway down my spine.

My parents begin their walk up the large stone steps, and I follow behind them, tugging at my white evening gloves.

"You're going to do great," Ivy says, falling in step beside me.

"I'm so glad you're here. Thank you for coming."

Landon told me I was welcome to bring a friend if it would make me feel more comfortable, and I'm thankful for the gesture. Ivy is confident and sure of herself, effortlessly slipping into conversation with whomever she happens to be standing near. A daffodil-yellow dress hangs from her shoulders and stops short of the ground. Her lips are painted a soft pink, and three strands of pearls are wrapped around her neck.

I turn my head and take one more breath of cool, salty air before we step inside and breathe the hot air of hundreds of other bodies.

"I'm glad I'm here, too," she says, "but if you dive into that water right now, I swear—"

"Relax, I'm just taking a breath." I turn back to face her. "Shall we?"

She loops her arm through mine. "We shall."

We walk through the open double doors, and the breath I took just moments ago drains from my lungs.

A large marble staircase rises from the center of the room and splits at the top, each side feeding a different wing of the house.

A crystal chandelier catches the lights and shimmers overhead, casting rainbows around the room. Colorful flowers sit in dense arrangements on cocktail tables, and the walls are painted a soft mint green that's as lively as the music.

Ornate woven rugs in bright colors with golden tassels lead us into the ballroom, where my parents have already disappeared into a sea of people. A string quartet is playing on a stage, and I immediately recognize them from the Witchery. No wonder everyone seems to be having the time of their lives—with each note the musicians play, they send waves of excitement and happiness into the room.

It makes me sad for a moment that the mainlanders think they need magic to ensure they have good time. But it's the resentment I feel that startles me. Witches are forbidden from practicing any form of magic after the sun goes down, but the governor asked for an exception that my mother approved. She never would have approved it for anyone else.

And I can't help but think what a waste it is to make an exception for *this*.

The stage backs up to the gardens, and I look longingly out the window.

"Don't even think about it," Ivy says. "You weren't invited here so you could stand stoically in the garden."

"But I'm so good at that."

"I'm not disagreeing, but there will be plenty of time for that later. I'll go get us some drinks before we make the rounds."

Sometimes I think how much better things would be if Ivy

could take my place. I'm a direct descendant of Harper Fairchild, the witch who formed our coven and created the boundaries of low magic. Because of that, my mother is the head of our coven, and forging a bond between the most powerful family of witches and the most powerful mainlanders is the strongest declaration we can make.

But Ivy's family is one of the original families, and as I watch her glide around the room and see the eyes that follow her as she moves, I can't help but feel this life would suit her very well.

Ivy hands me a drink and clinks her glass to mine. "To getting through the night."

"I can drink to that."

I take a long sip and look around the ballroom. Large sheer curtains hang from golden rods and move with the breeze from the open windows, and multiple chandeliers glisten overhead. The room smells of candle wax and brine, and arrangements of white roses and greenery sit on crystal stands around the perimeter. It's grand and impressive and nothing like my life on the Witchery.

My parents are at the front of the room, talking with Marshall and Elizabeth Yates. They all look comfortable and easy, as if enjoying each other's company is a given. As if we didn't have to earn it.

And then there he is.

Landon.

He walks around a large marble pillar, scanning the room. He's tall, and his navy suit pulls just slightly across his broad chest. His skin is smooth and tan, and his dark brown hair is cut short. He holds himself as if he owns the place, as if he owns the whole world.

I stare for a single breath before his eyes find mine. A smile tugs at his lips, one that seems genuine, and it brightens the room, a smile that would make me believe he was indeed gifted the whole world.

I stiffen next to Ivy, realizing I have no idea how to greet my future husband. "Tana, you may want to indicate that you're happy to see him," Ivy suggests under her breath. "Because right now it looks like you might launch yourself through the window and swim the whole way home."

I can't help but laugh. "Very helpful feedback, thank you, Ivy."

"Of course."

I take a sip of my drink, but what I could really use is Ivy's Bravery blend from earlier. I close my eyes for just a moment and think about how it feels when I drink it. It feels the way Landon carries himself, like I deserve to be here. My spine straightens and my chin lifts. I roll my shoulders back, and when I open my eyes, they lock right on Landon. I give him a shy smile and tilt my head, beckoning him over.

He can't hear the way my heart races beneath my too-tight dress, the way my lungs can't quite find enough air. Being brave and feeling brave are two very different things.

"Tana," he says when he reaches me, taking my hand in his and placing a soft kiss on my skin. "You look lovely."

"Thank you," I say.

"Ivy," Landon says, straightening his stance. "It's nice to see you again." He doesn't take her hand, making sure this entire room knows his sights are set one person tonight: me.

"Likewise," she says, offering him an easy smile that touches her eyes.

The music fades, and the room erupts in applause. The musicians bow slightly, then settle in with their instruments and begin playing again. This song is slower, a waltz, and Landon holds out his hand to me.

"May I have this dance?"

I pause, knowing a dance will change things, that I will no longer have the luxury of going unnoticed. I take a deep breath, hold it in my chest and count to three, then let it out. "I would be delighted," I say.

I give Ivy my drink and let Landon lead me to the center of the room. The crowd parts, eyes following us as we turn to face each other, my right hand holding his, my left resting on top of his shoulder. He hesitantly places his hand on my back, his fingertips brushing the skin above my dress. My breath catches, and I finally raise my eyes to his. We watch each other for one, two, three beats, and then the music picks up and we're spinning around the room.

Landon is a skilled partner, leading me smoothly even when I miss a step or become too focused on the way his fingers feel on my skin. His eyes never leave mine, his gaze confident and assured.

I thought dancing in front of so many people would be terrible, that I'd feel their eyes on me the whole time, but every part of me is focused on Landon, on the way he holds my hand, the way his touch remains just a whisper on my back, the way his breath mixes in the air with mine. Dancing is such a common part of his world, but it feels entirely intimate to me. This is my future husband, and the first time I've ever felt his touch on my skin is in the presence of an audience.

"Are you enjoying yourself?" he asks, not seeming to notice the way the rest of the room watches us.

"I am, thank you."

"Tana," he says, his amber eyes never leaving my face, "I'm asking because I genuinely want to know."

I'm so aware of his touch and the smell of citrus on his breath, and he's carrying on a conversation as if it's nothing.

I laugh, quiet enough that only he can hear. "It's a little overwhelming," I admit. "I'm not used to being the center of attention." I don't move my eyes from his because I'm scared of what I'll do if I see the way people are watching us, whispering to one another. I don't want to see the proud looks on my parents' faces or the envious looks of the mainlander girls. I try to take a calming breath, but my dress barely lets in enough air to keep me conscious.

"You'll get used to it," he says. "This is all for show, anyway. For our parents. How about this: once the song ends, we'll go sit in the garden. Our parents will love it, but we'll keep our backs to the house. I could use some fresh air, anyway."

My heart beats faster, and I wonder how this man I barely know has somehow said the perfect thing. "I'd like that."

"Me too."

The song slows, and Landon twirls me once more before tightening his hold on me. He lowers me into a gentle dip, and my head floats back, my hair almost grazing the polished floor. He leans over me, his face mere inches from my neck.

"I love your perfume," he murmurs, slowly pulling me up, his hands not releasing me even after the music fades. I wait for the spark, the vibration, the final note in the concerto, but it doesn't come. I suppose it wouldn't, surrounded by all these people, and I tell myself there is time. It will come later. Landon leans close and whispers, "Quite a show, Miss Fairchild."

I smile at that, a shy smile that barely tugs at my lips, but it's enough. Applause breaks out all around us.

Suddenly I'm dizzy, and I grip Landon's back and rest my forehead on his shoulder to steady myself. He doesn't pull away, waiting patiently as I regain my balance. His pointer finger finds a section of my hair, and when I let him go, he carefully tucks it behind my ear. "That earned us at least two songs in the garden, I'm sure."

He winks at me and leads me off the dance floor. Ivy is waiting for us at the bar, her back against the marble ledge, elbows propped up as if she's never been more comfortable in her life. She hands me my drink, an amused expression on her face.

"That was some dance," she says.

"I was just telling Tana that I believe it earned us some time in the garden."

She studies Landon, and her features relax, an expression I recognize as relief. Relief that this man I've been betrothed to since before I could even speak understands enough about me to know that a break in the garden is exactly what I need. We exchange a glance before Ivy looks back at Landon.

"I think you're right," she agrees.

"Would you like to join us?" I ask.

"Absolutely not. I didn't get dressed up like this to hide myself in the garden."

"May everyone here look upon you with wonder," I say.

She bows her head. "Thank you."

Landon takes my hand and leads me outside. The cold night air sends goose bumps up my arms, and I shiver, but it's the best feeling. I can hear the water again, the waves lapping against the rock wall, and my whole body relaxes.

We walk to the far corner of the garden and sit on a stone bench that looks out over the Passage. Lights from the Witchery flicker in the distance, and my heart aches, knowing this will be my daily view not long from now.

Landon slips out of his jacket and drapes it over my shoulders, bringing me back to the present.

"Thank you."

He nods, and we sit in comfortable silence. I've never been one to enjoy parties, but I love being on the outside of them, close enough to hear the notes of the music and the murmur of voices, far enough away that the sounds fade into the background, quiet enough that I can still hear my own thoughts.

I love knowing people are having fun and laughing and making memories that will stay with them for years to come. I like imagining the conversations and the shy glances and the way it feels to dance with someone you like for the first time.

"What are you thinking about?" Landon asks me.

"How much I enjoy knowing people are having a wonderful time inside."

He looks at me then. "You're a really good person," he says, surprising me.

We don't love each other. We hardly know each other, but as the night goes on, we're each discovering things about the other, and there's so much relief in knowing that the person you have no say in marrying is *good*. It isn't a masterful concerto, but it's something.

Maybe my mother is right. Maybe I will love him one day.

"I have a gift for you." He pulls out an emerald velvet box and hands it to me.

"What's this for?"

"It's a promise," he says, looking me in the eye. "A promise that I will get to know the real you. Not the person your parents or my parents want you to be, but you, exactly as you are."

"Landon," I begin, but his name is the only word I can manage.

A breeze rushes off the water and sends my hair out behind me. My fingers shake as I open the box. Sitting in the center is a single piece of sea glass, and I smile as I take it out and feel it in my hand. It hasn't been polished down; it's rough, exactly as I'd find it on the beach, turquoise and jagged and perfect.

"Your mother told me that you love the sea. I must admit I've only ever thought of it as an inconvenience, but it's important to me to know the things you love so that those things can follow you here after we marry."

"An inconvenience?" I say, unable to believe that anyone would look upon the Passage with anything but awe.

"Of course. It separates me from my intended."

I look at him then. This union is as important to him as it is to me, and instead of finding comfort in that, I can't help but wonder if there's something in it for him and his father that I'm unaware of. I look down, scolding myself; my mother has been open with me about the terms of our agreement. They want more eyes on the Witchery, on our magic, and they want a share of our silver. We want protection. It is beneficial for us both.

"I don't know what to say." I grip the sea glass tighter, let the weight of it anchor me in this moment. "Thank you."

"You're welcome."

My hands are shaking, and I'm not sure if it's from the cold or something else entirely. Landon hesitantly touches his fingers to my knuckles, and when I don't pull away, he takes my hand in his. The shaking stops, and I look down, wondering how much of this is for show and how much is real, wondering if he, too, is hopeful we might one day love each other like my mother says.

A new song begins in the ballroom, and Landon stands. "I believe we owe the room a final dance," he says.

This time, his touch isn't enough to stop me from noticing the way every person in the ballroom turns toward us when we enter. My heart races, but I keep my head high, leaning into Landon.

"Then let's make it count."

He smiles at that and leads me through the crowd, never once letting go of my hand.

five

The ferry is quiet as it takes us across the Passage. Mom and Dad are talking in excited whispers, beside themselves at how well the night went. Ivy is sleeping, her head resting on my shoulder, her hem brushing against the floor around her feet. There are no other passengers, a stark reminder that, apart from the musicians, we were the only witches in attendance tonight. I'm tired, slouched in my chair, but my mind is too active to sleep.

Ivy shifts and slumps down in her seat. Her head lolls back, and I take the opportunity to escape to the bow. I have the entire deck to myself, and I walk to the railing and close my eyes as the wind whips through my hair, sending chills through my body. The Witchery is mostly asleep in the distance, my perfect island quiet and dark after a busy day. It looks so peaceful.

"You did great tonight," my mother says behind me.

I turn to look at her. Her shawl is wrapped tightly around her arms, and the wind seems to avoid her, going around her completely rather than risking messing up her hair, which is still in a tight updo, every strand in place.

She looks pleased, and it fills me with warmth.

"Thanks, Mom. I'm glad you're happy," I say, because I am. That's all I really want, for the people I love to be happy.

Happy and safe.

She nods. "I am. So is your father."

"That's good."

"Things are right on track for your Covenant Ball. Announcing your engagement to Landon that night will be perfect."

"I think so, too. I can't wait."

"Really?" she asks, studying me.

"Really." I smile and turn back to the sea. The waxing moon plays hide-and-seek with the clouds, coming into view and glistening on the surface of the water before disappearing again.

I've been looking forward to my Covenant Ball my whole life, so eager to bind myself to my coven in front of all my friends and family. If I'm being honest, that's the part I'm most excited about. I worry that announcing my engagement that night might take away from my Covenant, but my mom is sure it won't.

I suppose it makes sense. I'm marrying Landon to protect my coven; binding myself to them and protecting them all in the same night has a beautiful harmony to it.

Most of the witches are just starting to hear rumors about Landon and me, just like the mainlanders. My mother has kept the secret of our betrothal for most of my life in case it fell through, and the witches will be overwhelmed when it's announced.

I turn around, but my mother is gone. A lullaby jumps into my mind unbidden, and I hum it softly to the sound of the waves.

Soft like magic, calming tea,
give your power to the sea.
If they should turn,
come after you,
your weakness will ensure your doom.
Soft like magic, easy glee,
you cannot stop this violent sea.

I've always wondered who wrote it, where the words came from. It's clear it was written as a warning, likely from the witches who refused to give up their dark magic and adhere to the new order. There was only one coven who refused, a small subset of witches who would rather have put us all at risk than convert to low magic, but no one has seen or heard from them in many years.

It's as if they vanished.

The prevailing belief among new witches is that they eventually died out—it was a small coven to begin with, and as time went on, there probably weren't enough of them to sustain the group. No one wants to practice dark magic when it means you have no security, no safety, no home. When it means you could die in a jail cell on the mainland.

Still, the words dance through my mind, but they don't scare me the way they used to. The mainlanders can't turn on us once I'm married to the governor's son.

A shrill sound comes from somewhere in the distance, and I jump back from the railing. I squint into the darkness, looking for the source of the cry, and find a sea lion thrashing in the water, trapped in a current.

One of our currents. My heart aches as I watch the animal helplessly, wishing I could do something but knowing I can't. There is nothing to do.

The sea lion swirls in the water, roaring as it goes around and around and around. The sound is awful, tearing at my insides, sending bile up my throat. I run to the railing in case I get sick, and I swear the animal looks right at me. My eyes fill with tears, and I want to tell it I'm sorry, so sorry that the currents we caused are taking its life.

Ivy rushes over to where I'm standing, grabbing my hand as if she's afraid I might dive in.

"There's nothing we can do," she says. I'm leaning over the edge, as far as I can go without falling over, and Ivy gently pulls me back. We watch as the animal turns in the water, wailing into the night.

Then it's pulled under the surface and the sound abruptly stops. Eerie silence.

Tears stream down my face, and I take a deep breath and try to regain my composure. The currents are getting worse, eroding our island and killing our sea creatures. Hurting the things we love.

My mother says they're under control, that the coven leaders are taking care of things, but watching a sea lion be drowned by its home is not control.

It's failure.

I think back to that night five years ago when I almost drowned, to my father's angry voice as he blamed it on my mother. What will he say to her tonight in the safety of their room, in whispers that can't get past the door? Will he blame this on her as well, or were his words unfounded, brought on by the terror of almost losing his only child?

"I'm so sorry," I whisper.

The boat slows as it approaches the docks on the Witchery, and Ivy and I walk inside together. She leans against the wall of the ferry, and I rest my head on her shoulder and exhale.

"You okay?"

"I'm okay," I assure her.

"The currents are getting worse," she says.

"I know." I pause and lower my voice. "Ivy, what if that had been a person? A mainlander? It's only a matter of time before that happens, and if Landon and I aren't married when it does—"

My mother walks over, and I cut myself off, but I don't miss the worry in Ivy's eyes.

"Let's get you girls home, hm?" she says. We walk toward the exit, and she wraps an arm around each of us. "Tonight was an incredible success. Well done."

We follow my father off the ferry, over the rickety bridge and onto the dock. The clouds are getting heavier, concealing the moon and the stars. Everything is dark.

We stop at Ivy's house first, and I give her a tight hug before she heads inside.

"Do you really think that's a risk?" Ivy whispers as she hugs me back. "What you said about the currents drowning a mainlander?"

"I think we've got time before that happens," I say, not wanting to make her worry more than I already have. "Mom says the council has it under control." I squeeze Ivy tight, and she nods and heads inside.

My parents are walking slowly, their arms around each other, delighting in the memories of the night. I follow behind them, the lullaby still playing in my head, punctuated by the sounds of the sea lion slipping away.

I grip Landon's sea glass tightly in my palm, its sharp edges digging into my skin.

When we get home, my mother walks to the kitchen and pours two glasses of wine while my father lights a fire.

"Would you like to join us, Tana?" she asks.

"I'm tired," I say.

"Of course. Get some rest, sweetheart."

I nod and head up the stairs, the sound of my parents' happy laughter following me as I go.

I love that sound.

My room is dark, and I set the piece of sea glass on my dresser. I don't bother turning on the light before I unzip my dress and fill my lungs for what feels like the first time tonight. I walk into my bathroom and wash my face, pull my hair up, and brush my teeth.

I'm about to crawl into bed when a dim light outside catches my attention. I pick up the sea glass and open the window, inviting the sound of the waves into my room. I sit on the window seat and roll the glass around in my hand, watching the world outside.

My head rests against the wall as I look out into the black night. The light gets brighter and brighter, coming from the lawn, a small brilliance against the darkness. I rise up on my knees and lean my head out the window, trying to focus on the light, and that's when I see it.

A single moonflower, hanging contentedly over the perfectly trimmed grass.

A shiver crawls up my spine.

"No," I whisper. It isn't possible.

I blink and look again, but it sits there as sure as the clouds in the sky and the chill in the air. A flower so lethal that a single touch of its petals can kill. And it's illuminated by a light source I can't find.

If they should turn...

My grip on the sea glass tightens.

come after you...

The sharp edges cut into my skin as I stare at the flower in disbelief.

your weakness will ensure your doom.

It isn't until a trail of blood runs down my wrist that I realize I've cut myself. I drop the sea glass and it clatters to the floor. I rush to the bathroom and run my hand under the faucet, and when I'm cleaned up, I go back to my window.

But the light and the flower are gone.

six

I know it's time to tell my mother about the moonflowers, but when I get downstairs the next morning, she's already gone. A child was born last night, and it's tradition for the highest witch to welcome a newborn into the coven with ritual blessings.

Dad has made me a sprawling breakfast of fresh fruit, eggs, scones, and cinnamon rolls, and it's almost enough to make me forget about the white flower.

"What's all this for?" I ask, setting the table and steeping some of Ivy's Awaken blend tea.

"Does there have to be a reason?"

I raise my eyebrow and Dad laughs. "I won't always get to make you elaborate breakfasts, that's all."

The comment makes an ache start in my chest; we're both realizing things are about to change, that soon breakfast with my dad will no longer be a given.

"A truly unfortunate part of adulthood," I say.

We sit down at the table, and I take the largest cinnamon roll. "How did you make them this big?"

"Magic," he says, winking at me.

I laugh. Dad usually refrains from using magic in the kitchen—he thinks he'll lose his edge if he does. But every once in a while, he makes an exception.

"Good call," I say.

"You and Landon looked great last night." He says it casually, but I know he's bringing it up to see how I'm doing. Dad understands the importance of the path I'm walking, and he supports it, but I think he feels guilty that I don't have much of a choice.

When he met Mom, they fell in love quickly. He said it was as if he'd been living in black and white and meeting her turned his world to color. It was passionate and exciting and right, and I know he wishes I could experience the same thing.

I want to tell him I hope for those things, hope that one day I'll see Landon and a vibration will take over my stomach. But I don't want Dad to think I'm unhappy, so I shove the words aside.

"Landon's a good man," I say instead. "I'm glad we've gotten to spend some time together. He'll treat me well." They aren't the exact words I want to say, but I'm confident they're true, and letting them out eases something inside me.

Dad takes a sip of his tea. "He will," he agrees.

"He gave me a piece of sea glass last night. He said it's important to him that the things I love still have a place in my life after we're married." I smile at the thought, but the memory sours when I think about the sea glass lying bloodstained on my bedroom floor. My fingers find the cut on my palm, and I wince.

"Thank you for sharing that with me," Dad says, clearing his throat.

"It was a really lovely gesture."

He nods, and I realize he doesn't trust himself to speak without getting emotional. I'm going to miss this so much when I move to the mainland, and I suddenly find that I don't trust myself to speak, either.

We finish our breakfast, then put our dishes in the sink and clean the kitchen together, a rhythm we have down after many mornings like this one.

"Mind if I join you on your walk to the perfumery? I'd love some fresh air," Dad says once I've put the last dish away.

"I'd like that."

When I open the front door, I jump back at the sight of a blossom on the doorstep. I frantically scan the lawn for the moon-flower from last night, but there's nothing. I bend over to pick up the flower, a single rose with a handwritten note attached.

> I saw this rose in the garden this morning—
> the same color as your dress. Thank you for the
> dances.
>
> —Landon

My heart stops racing, and I smile to myself and hold the rose close to my face, inhaling deeply.

"What's that?" Dad asks, and I turn and hand him the flower. The same relieved expression I saw on Ivy's face at the ball last night settles over my dad now as he reads the note.

"I wonder how he got it here," I say, walking back into the house and filling a small vase with water. Dad cuts the stem before putting the rose in, and we leave the house together.

"He's the governor's son; I imagine he had plenty of options for how to get it here."

Dad automatically takes the long route to the perfumery, walking along the beach so I can get my fix of the water. I scan the surface for flowers, but it's a foggy morning, and I can see only a couple of yards past the shoreline.

The thick fog follows us as we turn onto Main Street and walk down the cobblestone road. The coffee shops, tea rooms, and bakeries are all bustling with morning crowds, but we open the perfumery later on Sundays. Especially in the winter, it's nice to have some daylight to ourselves before work begins. Otherwise we'd lose all our magic hours to the shop.

I put the key in the door and turn on the lights. Dad follows and helps me get set up before heading back out.

"What are you up to today?" I ask.

"We're low on lavender and sandalwood. I'm going to the fields, then the cottage to extract oil. I'll be back later today to refill our stock."

"Happy hunting," I say, and Dad smiles before kissing me on the top of my head and leaving.

There's a steady flow of customers throughout the day,

and I'm surprised by how many of them ask me about Landon. Thankfully, my mother arrives an hour after opening and steps in, giving me a much-needed respite.

I watch in amazement as she answers smoothly, always with the perfect amount of mystery. She doesn't trip over her words or look at the floor when she speaks. She knows the right thing to say in every situation and has no desire to run from the shop and dive into the sea.

On some days, it makes me feel like something's wrong with me, this overwhelming frustration that I can't do what my mother and Ivy seem to do with such ease. But today I'm thankful for it.

For her.

At six o'clock sharp, we lock the door and switch our sign to CLOSED. It's a full moon tonight, and we have to get ready for the rush. The tourists make their way to the docks, catching the last boat out.

Only witches are allowed on the island when we drain our excess magic into the ocean.

The one problem with low magic is that it leaves a buildup of unused power in our bodies that we aren't meant to carry. If it isn't expelled, it can kill us. So roughly every twenty-nine days, on the full moon, we shut down the island and rush our leftover magic into the sea.

It is, ironically, the most powerful spell we do, and the only one that is allowed at night.

It's a raw, forceful display of magic that would terrify the mainlanders if they saw it, and as such, it's become something the coven is ashamed of, a taboo ritual they'd give anything not to have to participate in.

Which is why it isn't talked about. We don't mention the rush leading up to it, and we don't talk about it for the following twenty-nine days.

I think that's what bothers me most about it—we're ruining our island and harming our sea creatures and killing our crops for a ritual the witches *hate*.

I've never said it aloud, but I look forward to the rush. I feel powerful when that kind of magic is flowing through me. I don't feel ashamed or disgusted—I feel alive, connected to my magic in a way I can't replicate in the shop. I only wish I could use all that power for something good instead of casting it into the sea, where it will continue its violent tear through the water.

"All set, Tana?" my mother asks.

I nod and grab my bag, following her out of the shop. The fog has cleared, and a light drizzle is tapping the island, making the cobblestones slick and the shrubs heavy. The moss that lines the rooftops somehow looks greener in the rain, and I inhale the perfect scent of petrichor.

The last ferry pulls away from the dock, and I watch as it gets farther from the Witchery. I can practically feel the island relax as the weight of hundreds of eager tourists sails away, settling into itself and taking a breath.

"I have a quick meeting with the council, so why don't you head home and I'll meet you there?"

"Sure. Is everything okay?" Their regularly scheduled meeting was last week, and it's rare to have another so soon.

"Of course. I think there are some members who feel they deserve a briefing on the governor's ball."

"You mean on me," I say, instantly regretting the words.

My mother stops in the street and lets the rain wash over us as she looks at me.

"It isn't just about you, Tana. What you're doing, it's for all of us. It's for our children and our children's children. Don't you think the council has a right to know that after generations of uncertainty and fear, it's almost over? That the mainlanders will finally accept us and we will no longer have to worry that a single misstep could cost us our freedom? Our lives?"

I look down. "I'm sorry. I didn't mean to sound like I was only thinking of myself."

My mother relaxes her stance and sighs. She puts her arm around me, and we begin walking again. "I know, baby. It doesn't feel as tenuous to you because things have been stable for a while. But don't forget that we are on this island because those who came before us were forced here to preserve their magic, and they were given none of the necessities or comforts they were used to on the mainland. Having permanent safety and freedom is something the generation before you, and certainly before me, could never have dreamed of."

"I understand. I'm sorry," I say, thinking of the woman in Ivy's tea shop. Thinking of the fire.

Mom gives me a tight squeeze before letting her arm fall, but

I feel unsettled. It isn't Landon or the impending marriage that's bothering me. It's the urgency. Landon was nothing more than a spot in the distance not three months ago, and now he's all my parents are talking about, and the council is meeting about him.

About me.

About us.

It makes me wonder if the fire was just an excuse to hasten the timeline, but guilt moves through me as soon as I think it.

"See you at midnight," my mother says, referencing the time we meet to avoid uttering the phrase *the rush*.

Mom heads toward the village hall, and I walk along the shoreline toward home.

I slow my steps, going over my mother's words. The council doesn't want a recounting of the governor's ball. They want to know exactly how long it will be before they can expect an engagement, an alliance between the witches and the mainlanders.

They want to know when they'll be safe.

And if they want to know when they'll be safe, it's because they're afraid.

I hum as I walk along the water's edge, then abruptly stop.

Your weakness will ensure your doom.

Your doom.

Your doom.

seven

It's midnight. The full moon is unobstructed in the black sky, its light glinting on the surface of the sea and casting the beach in a faint blue glow that makes it possible to see the witches around me.

There's a large white pillar on the beach with a copper bowl sitting on top.

I pull a strand of hair from my head and place it in the bowl, then prick my finger and let a single drop of blood fall in after it. Smoke rises from the bowl, and the strand and blood vanish.

I walk onto the beach, and the witch behind me goes through the same attendance procedure.

Once we have all checked in, the rush will begin.

None of us is strong enough to rush our magic on our own. Magical perfumes and teas and pastries are wonderful—they're how we support our lives here and why the mainlanders began to accept us—but they don't require a lot of magic.

The combined force of all of us together is the only thing that makes the rush possible.

We all wear identical white rushing gowns, loose, light garments that hit at the ankles and look like nightdresses. The eldest witches stand spread out in a row along the shoreline. Behind them, my parents' generation stands, and behind them, the youngest of us. None of the witches speak. We look out at the water or down at the rocky beach. Shame is a powerful weapon, convincing every person on this shore to turn away from each other during a ritual that is part of who we are.

Sometimes I think it is the shame, not the fear, that will ensure our survival as a coven. The rush is a pillar of the new order and what enabled us to begin a productive dialogue with the mainland; they didn't stop trying to eradicate magic until we proved to them that the new order was not a threat. In many ways, the rush should be a celebration of survival and courage, of sacrifice and wit. But another pillar of the new order is a complete and utter disavowal of dark magic, and over many generations, that disavowal has turned from conviction to shame. As soon as dark magic became something to be ashamed of, no one wanted to practice it any longer.

And it has stayed that way.

We're on the western edge of the island that looks out onto the open ocean. We would never rush on the eastern shore that faces the mainland; even with the Passage as wide as it is, knowing the mainlanders could never see us from so far away, it would still feel too vulnerable. So instead we make the trek to the western edge, turning our backs on the mainland for one evening per month. Just one.

I jump when the copper bowl behind me goes up in flames, signifying everyone is here.

"Let's begin," my mother says, her voice carried on a wave of magic so everyone can hear.

In unison, we wade into the water, the eldest witches going out the farthest and the younger witches following. Those not old enough to rush their magic are held by their parents, the spell powerful enough to coax what little unused magic is in their systems out to sea.

The water has just touched my ankles when something catches the corner of my eye. I turn. It's a small circular light identical to the one I saw outside my bedroom window, hovering above the ground, illuminating a moonflower.

I look around, but no one else notices it, focusing instead on the water.

The light gets brighter, and I can no longer ignore it. I carefully back away from the water, checking over my shoulder to make sure no one is watching. The actual rush won't happen for at least twenty minutes, and it doesn't take me as long to prepare as some of the others.

As quietly as possible, I hurry up the beach and around a dense patch of flowering bushes, following the light. I'm no longer in view of the shoreline, and I move faster, chasing the glowing sphere.

But the closer I get, the faster it moves away from me.

I keep running, following it into an inland field, long grasses blowing in the nighttime breeze. They nip at my skin as I push my way through, and I keep my eyes on the light as best I can.

It comes in and out of view, then goes out entirely. A shiver rolls down my spine.

I run toward the last place I saw it, relying on the light of the full moon to guide me, and slam directly into another person.

I fall to the ground, shocked and disoriented. The wind is knocked clear out of me, and I clutch my middle and groan, rolling onto my side. No one else should be here—everyone is on the beach.

"What the hell?" The voice is coming from a few feet away, and I push myself off the earth and frantically look around.

The light is long gone by now, but slowly, another person rises from the ground. A person I've never seen before. I take a step back.

"Did you miss the ferry?" I ask, wondering how I can possibly get him off the Witchery before the rush happens.

"You ran right into me," he says, ignoring my question. "Where the hell are your manners?"

I'm completely taken aback, and I stare at him with my mouth open.

"Well?" he asks. His dark hair is unkempt and falling into his eyes, the light of the moon casting his pale skin in a faint blue glow. The set of his jaw is hard, and he looks at me as if he's irate, as if I killed the thing he loves most in the world instead of accidentally running into him.

"I'm sorry," I say, trying to keep my voice even in case his parents are people of importance on the mainland. "I should have been paying closer attention."

He scowls at my answer, like he's disappointed in me.

"Did you see that light?" he asks, and my heart picks up speed. "You saw it?"

"Several times now," he says, shoving a hand through his hair. "I can't figure out where it's coming from."

"Me neither," I say.

The light went out right where we're standing, and in the span of a breath, the earth groans and a single moonflower rises in the space between us, sprouting large, heart-shaped leaves.

I jump back and take several steps away, putting enough distance between the bloom and me, but I'm not willing to run from it. Not this time.

The boy raises his eyebrow and looks at me with an amused expression.

"It's a moonflower," I say.

"I know what it is." And with that, he picks it from the ground and touches it to his lips.

He stretches his hand out, offering me the flower, and I move even farther away from him. "Don't come any closer."

"They say these flowers are poisonous to witches, you know," he says as he looks at the flower, twirling it between his fingers.

A sick feeling settles in my gut, and every impulse I have tells me to get out of here. I break out in a cold sweat, wondering who this person is, wondering if he hates witches enough to throw that flower at me. I should run, need to run, but for a reason I can't explain, I stay where I am, frozen.

"One touch can be lethal." He looks at me then and smiles, and for one terrible moment, I think he might be here to kill me. "I'll tell you a secret, though," he says, leaning closer. "It isn't true."

I swallow hard. Sweat beads on the back of my neck, and I shiver. "I don't know who you are, but you need to leave. *Now.*"

"Why would I do that? I live here."

"That's not possible," I say.

"Of course it is," he responds. "Anything is possible."

He moves his right hand through the air, back and forth, and the previously light breeze picks up into a gale force wind, slamming into me, sending my hair and my dress every which way.

Then, just as easily, he moves his hand down, and the wind calms.

I know what I'm seeing, know what I feel on my skin, but there's only one explanation for it, and I can't make myself believe it. I close my eyes and shake my head, trying to clear my mind of the two words screaming inside me, but they won't go away. They get louder and louder until I'm forced to acknowledge what I saw: a perfect display of dark magic.

Goose bumps rise along my arms, and I take another step back.

"No." It's all I can say.

"No?" he asks, quirking his brow and raising his hand again. The wind picks up, and I rush over and slam his arm down to his side.

"That magic is forbidden, and I will not have it on my island."

"Our island," he says. "And where I come from, it most definitely is *not* forbidden."

Our island. What he's saying doesn't make any sense. I've lived here my whole life and have never once encountered a wielder of dark magic. If what he's saying is true and he does use dark magic, then—

"You're from the old coven," I say, more to myself than to him, my voice barely audible. I can't believe the words have left my mouth. A chill moves down my spine.

"Wolfe Hawthorne," he says, holding the flower out once more. A large silver ring adorns his right hand, glinting in the moonlight. "And yes, I'm a member of the old coven."

I stare at him, unable to speak.

"You know, it's customary to reply to an introduction with one of your own," he says.

"Tana," I reply in a kind of trance. "Mortana Fairchild."

"Well, Mortana, I can assure you this flower isn't poisonous. Take it."

I stare at the flower, feeling an undeniable pull toward it, a desire so strong I can't ignore it. I've never felt anything like it, and for a moment, I wonder if I'm being compelled to take it, to reach for my own death. I can't fight it. It feels as if I'm outside my body, watching myself from high above as I extend a shaking hand to accept the moonflower.

I take hold of it.

And nothing happens.

It doesn't hurt. It doesn't burn. My heart is still beating and my lungs are still breathing.

I slowly bring the flower to my face and inhale.

The petals brush my skin, and I remain unharmed. Every text I've read has described the pain as instant, followed quickly by death, but I feel normal. I'm trying to work through what I'm experiencing, knowing full well it's impossible, but no explanation comes to mind. I'm at a complete loss.

"Did you put a spell on it?" I ask.

"How could I have done that if it's poisonous to witches?"

I shake my head, staring at the bloom. I don't understand, and I'm distraught that I don't. Moonflower is the first plant I learned to identify because it's so crucial to know what it looks like. So imperative to our survival. And here I am, holding one in my hand as if it's a common lupine.

I scramble for anything that will make it make sense, that will tie up the threads unraveling in my mind, but I come up short.

A drop of sweat rolls down the back of my neck. Then, all at once, I come back to myself and realize what I'm doing and who I'm speaking with.

I drop the flower and jump back. My heart is beating so hard it feels as if it could crack my ribs.

"The old coven is *gone*," I say.

"Now, how would you know that?" His voice is casual, taunting even, and heat rises to my face.

"I don't know who you think you are, but this isn't funny. The old coven doesn't exist anymore." This must be some kind of joke, some elaborate prank to humiliate me. But then I think back to the way the wind picked up, the way it felt on my face, and I know it's real. I look at the flower on the ground and can't stop the questions that cascade through my mind one after another. The loudest, most incessant one of all—the one that should be simplest to answer and yet feels as if it's threatening everything I've ever known—repeats over and over again:

Why didn't it hurt?

At that moment, a raw, guttural roar comes from the shoreline as the witches rush their magic in unison.

I whip around toward the sound. Dread moves through me in a slow, steady crawl.

No. This can't be happening.

The sound gets more crazed the longer it goes on, and all I can do is stare in the direction of the sea, stunned. Then all at once, it stops.

The silence of the night takes over again, and my entire body begins to shake with terror.

I missed it.

I hear the waves of the ocean and the rustling of grass, the wind in the trees and the hoot of an owl. Then I remember the boy.

I slowly turn back around, but he's gone.

My head falls into my hands, and I close my eyes, wishing with every part of me that I could go back in time to twenty minutes ago and ignore that damned light.

I can't believe I missed it.

My legs finally react, and I run toward the shoreline and hide in the shrubs, watching as the witches wade out of the sea. The rush takes an enormous amount of energy, and they walk as if in slow motion.

No one can know I missed it. Not with my upcoming engagement and my mother's place on the council. I wait until the eldest witches are past my hiding place, then run into the water and soak my gown. The fabric clings to my legs as I trudge up the shore. My parents are on the sidewalk, leaning into each other, and I slowly make my way to where they're standing. We walk home together, but I can't stop the shaking that has taken over my body.

The only person in recent memory who ever missed a rush was Lydia White almost twenty years ago.

She died ten days later from the excess magic building in her system.

No one has missed a rush since. We find a way to get everyone to this shore, no matter how difficult it may be.

My eyes fill with tears, and I take several breaths, not wanting my parents to see. Even if I told them what happened, there would be nothing for it. The only reason the rush works is because we use our collective power to make it happen.

An overwhelming sadness moves through me. My eyes burn, and it feels like shards of glass are lodged in my throat every time I try to swallow.

I can't believe I missed it.

But I'll fix this. I have to.

I start a countdown in my head: ten days. I have ten days to figure this out. If I don't, my fate will be the same as Lydia White's, and everything my coven has worked so hard for will be lost.

eight

I lie awake in bed, unable to sleep. The rush, the boy, the moon-flower—it all swirls in my mind like a hurricane, threatening to destroy everything in its path. Landon's sea glass trembles in my hand, dried blood still caked on the edges. I'm not sure why I didn't think to clean it off.

The house is quiet. Dark. My parents will sleep in—the Witchery is closed the day after every rush. We simply don't have the energy to run the island, and a day for recovery is necessary.

I replay the events of the rush over and over in my mind, but all I can focus on is the fact that I don't want to die. I don't want to be eaten alive by the magic I love so much. And I'm scared. Everything I know about Lydia White's death points to a pain-ful, excruciating ten days, and my palms sweat as I try to imagine what that might feel like.

I'm so angry at myself and so angry at that boy I had the utter misfortune of running into.

I know I'll have to deal with him, figure out who he is and where he came from. But that can wait until after I've rushed my magic and saved my life.

I quietly get out of bed and place the sea glass on my night table, then slip back into my rushing gown. I open my bedroom door and sneak down the back staircase, though I know my parents will sleep through any noise. They're spent, just as I should be.

When I'm out of the house, I stick to the shadows and run as fast as I can to the western edge of the island. I don't see a single soul.

It has only been a few hours since the rush, and if the magic is still close to the shore, still swirling in the shallows and buzzing in the air, I can try to harness it to rush my own. It's the best chance I have at fixing this.

It has to work. It's the only way.

I trip as I splash into the waves, scraping my hands and knees on the beach. I stand back up and press on, wading out until the water touches my ribs. Hints of microcurrents form around my legs, and it's the only time I've ever been happy to feel a current—it means I'm not too late, that the power of my coven is still in this place, waiting to set me free.

Please.

I raise my hands in front of me, palms up toward the full moon. I close my eyes and steady my breath, my heart slamming into my rib cage as a sharp pain starts in my chest.

I imagine myself in the back room of the perfumery, infusing magic into the dried flowers and herbs that make up our scents, small spells for calm, joy, excitement, confidence, assertiveness, all things our magic can summon and the mainlanders will pay for. I see myself hunched over the worn wooden island gathering lavender and sandalwood oil, lilac and wisteria. Magic swirls in my belly and rises, but I don't let it go yet. I need more.

I go through the routine over and over, acting as if it's just another day at the shop, as if I'm making the perfumes and candles I love, working as hard as I can to reach as much magic as possible. Magic has always felt like a natural extension of myself, something I don't need to work at the way most others do, and I'm counting on that innate ability to help me.

The air around me vibrates with the energy the witches left here earlier, their excess magic agitating the sea, forming stronger currents that pick up speed. I widen my stance to keep my balance and take a deep breath.

This can work.

It's going to work.

Water rises around me, sloshing in every direction, strong and cold and full of the power I so desperately need. When the water reaches my chin and I taste the salt on my lips, I begin my rush. I shoot my arms straight up to the sky and roar into the silent night, calling forth every ounce of magic I can.

My eyes are squeezed shut and my muscles are tense, magic pouring out of me like wine from a bottle. It rushes into the sea and joins the building currents, swirling around my shaking body. I give myself over to it, awed and terrified by the way it feels to have this much power moving through me.

Then all at once, it stops.

It's so abrupt I sink into the water, as if my magic was the only thing propping me up. I thrash around and force myself to stand, choking on the salt water I swallowed. I find my footing again, then reach my arms toward the sky and start over.

I frantically call up images of being in the perfumery, reaching for the way it feels to pour magic over bright florals and the spicy scent of the earth, but it's no use.

The currents release my body and begin to dance farther out into the sea, taking the power I need with them. The air around me stills, and the shore is unbearably calm.

I beg my magic to come back, but I can summon only a small amount, enough to make one batch of perfume, maybe two.

I can't reach the rest of it. I'm not strong enough.

I scream into the night sky and punch my fists into the water, angrier at the sea than I was the day I nearly drowned. Tears stream down my face, and I try one more time, a futile attempt to draw more magic from my core.

But nothing comes.

It's over.

I don't know how long I stand in the water. Dawn is beginning to break by the time I force myself from the sea.

I'm dripping wet as I walk up the beach, and I take the long way home, wandering through open fields and wooded trails, breathing in the scents of the island I love so much.

Taking advantage of the energy left at the shoreline to produce my own rush was my only idea, and now I'm at a total loss. I don't know what to do, if there even is anything to do. I wonder how my parents will react when they find out, what Ivy will say, if Landon will want to see me one last time.

I think it would be nice to see him again.

My house comes into view, and I take the exterior spiral staircase all the way up to our rooftop patio. I don't bother to change out of my rushing gown. I just sink onto the couch and wrap myself in a thick wool blanket. Now seems like a good time to watch a sunrise. I have only nine more chances to watch one, after all.

The dawn is chased away by vibrant oranges and soft pinks, the rays of the sun bursting over the horizon and drenching the ocean in golden light. If this were any other day, I'd be waking now, excited to use my magic after the long night.

And suddenly, I'm angry. This magic I've had my whole life, that I've risen with the sun for each and every day, has let me down. It's eating me from the inside, and soon it will kill me.

The ultimate betrayal.

Once the entire sky is painted blue, I go inside and peel off my damp clothing. My parents are still asleep, and I grab the sea glass from my night table and crawl into bed.

My eyelids finally get heavy, and my hands still.

Then the boy from the field comes to mind, and I sit up.

Wolfe Hawthorne. If the old coven really does exist and he really is a member, he knows dark magic. I remember the way he called the wind as if it were nothing, the way he held the moonflower with ease.

He can help me.

He *has* to help me. This is his fault, and though the thought of seeing him again fills me with fury, I refuse to die because of him. If dark magic can summon the wind and heal the sick, it must be able to help me rush my magic.

But as soon as I think it, I reprimand myself. That magic is forbidden, and more than that, I'm terrified of it. It goes against everything my coven stands for and everything my ancestors worked so hard to protect.

I've heard stories of what a life infected by dark magic looks like, the ways in which it poisons a person. When the new witches gave up that kind of magic for good, our bodies forgot how to wield it, instead acclimating to the gentle magic we practice today. Illnesses ran rampant in the old covens, and witches went mad with power. Those things all but stopped when we switched to the new order, and it was only then that our ancestors realized they never should have been practicing dark magic to begin with.

It's pure evil, rotten the whole way through.

I can't do it. If anyone ever found out, I'd be banished from my coven for life.

But I wouldn't be dead.

The thought invades my mind, startling me. I shove it aside. Asking for help from Wolfe Hawthorne, a boy I don't know and certainly don't trust, would be an affront to every witch who sacrificed a part of themselves in hopes of creating a better future.

But as I lie back down and let my eyelids close, I see the boy from the field extending his hand, offering me a moonflower that didn't hurt to touch.

nine

When I wake up, the fresh pain of remembering the night before pierces my chest and takes my breath away. I sit up in bed and pull my knees to my body, hugging them close. My parents are downstairs, and I don't know how to face them.

They'll see it in my eyes, hear it in my voice. They'll know something's wrong.

The thought of their faces when I tell them I missed the rush is what makes the decision for me. I can't put them through that, not unless I've exhausted every option to fix it.

I'm going to find Wolfe Hawthorne. And when I do, I will force him to help me.

I don't know where to find him, but he said this was "our" island, so he must be close. I roll out of bed, get ready, and pack a bag.

When I get downstairs, my parents are both nursing cups of tea. They're still in their pajamas, sitting on the couch together, sharing a wool blanket.

Dad yawns. "Want some tea, Tana?" he asks, moving the blanket from his lap.

"No thanks, I'm fine. Don't get up," I say. "I'm just going to eat a quick breakfast before heading out."

"Where are you off to today? Everything's closed."

"Just for a walk," I say. "It's nice to have the island to myself without all the tourists." I try to keep my voice casual, but it sounds eager and loud.

My mother looks up at me. "You okay, hon? You should probably rest after last night. I don't want you overdoing it."

I fight to put a smile on my face. "I'm fine. I'll take it easy; I promise."

"I suppose it's okay, then. Have fun and be back before dinner."

"I will," I say.

I grab some fruit from the kitchen and hurry out the door before they change their minds. There's a bite in the air, and I wrap my arms around my chest as I skip down the stairs and head toward the western edge of the island. That seems like the best place to start.

The sky is overcast, a low blanket of gray covering the Witchery. I can barely make out the shore before the water is swallowed by the clouds, and if this were any other day, it would put me at ease not to see the mainland in the distance, to pretend it's just us here, safe to practice magic however we want.

Just us. Just us and this island and our magic.

But I can't enjoy it. An ache has settled deep in my belly, or maybe the ache is blooming from the excess magic that's killing me.

75

I'm not sure.

Rocky beaches encircle the island, but dense woods and over-grown fields make up the interior—evergreens so tall they fade into the clouds, thousands of green giants watching over us. They sway in the breeze as if they have their own magic, and the thought makes me smile. If flowers and herbs, trees and fields, oceans and mountains aren't magic, I don't know what is.

The salty air feels good in my lungs. Healing. If I didn't know better, I'd believe that if I just breathed in long enough, I'd be okay.

By the time I get to the western edge of the Witchery, I'm no longer worried about running into anyone. All of our shops and homes are on the eastern edge, leaving this side of the island wild. The founders of the new coven made the choice to build up the Witchery on the east coast—they thought we would be more motivated to maintain the new order of magic if we felt the main-landers were always watching.

And even though the mainland is far enough away that details are impossible to see, it's always there in the distance. Always reminding us of the power that lies on the other side of the Passage.

But the western side is free from mainlanders. Here the grass is long and the shrubs are dense. There are no manicured gardens or carefully placed cobblestones, no pastel doors or sparkling streetlamps.

Everything is wild.

The wind is getting stronger, and it blows my hair and nips at my skin. The sound of the waves rolling onto the shore follows me as I cut through the trees and toward the field where I met Wolfe. It makes sense to start here, but my footsteps slow as the reality of what I'm doing sets in.

Part of giving up dark magic meant relieving the mainland of the notion that we were powerful enough to change the course of things. If that sort of magic existed, there would always be someone who wanted to use it for their own gain. No one is meant to have that kind of power, so we got rid of it entirely.

Or rather, we thought we did. If what Wolfe Hawthorne said is true, there is still one coven left practicing it.

It hurts to imagine telling my mother what I've learned, that we've all been tricked into believing the old coven is present only in our history lessons and myths, that they live right here on this island, poisoning it with their magic. But that will come later.

Long blades of grass poke at my skin as I walk through the field where I first encountered Wolfe. I brush them out of the way and move toward the place where we collided, finding it easily enough—the grass is bent toward the earth where we fell, and the single white moonflower is still on the ground, wilted.

"You," a voice behind me says.

I jump and turn around. Wolfe Hawthorne stands several feet away from me, an annoyed expression on his face, as if he owns this field and I am nothing but a trespasser.

"What are you doing here?" he asks.

"I could ask the same of you."

"I came back for the moonflower. If people knew it was on the island, there would be a lot of panic."

"Understandably. They haven't grown on the Witchery in decades."

"Is that what they told you?" he asks, an edge creeping into his voice.

Coming here was a bad idea.

"I told you why I'm here. Now it's your turn," he says.

I pause, unsure whether I should answer or get far away from him. I know what I *should* do, but I want his help. I stay where I am and look at him. His jaw is sharp and his eyebrows are pinched together, and I wonder if he always has such an unpleasant expression or if it's somehow related to me.

I swallow hard and force myself to meet his eyes. My heart beats wildly, but I don't let him see how scared I am. "I need your help," I finally say.

He cocks his head to the side. "My help?"

"Yes. If you are who you say you are."

He laughs, but it sounds mean. "Implying I'm a liar while asking for my help is an interesting approach to take."

I sigh. "Can you practice dark magic or not?"

"High magic," he says.

"What?"

"Tell me, Mortana, what kind of magic do you practice?"

It takes me a moment to respond, unsure what he's asking. "Low magic, of course."

"Its full name."

I exhale, frustrated. "Low tide magic. What does this have to do with anything?"

"Everything," he says, bending to pick up the wilted moon-flower. "And where do you think that name came from?"

"It's named for the tides," I say, impatience lacing my tone. "For the gentle nature of low tide."

"And how do you think the new coven came up with that name?" He twirls the moonflower between his fingers, drawing out his point as if it's molasses, unbearably slow.

"I don't have time for this," I say, my voice rising, too aware that every moment we spend talking is a moment we could be rushing my magic.

"Do you truly believe our ancestors referred to their own magic with the same disdain the new coven does? Obviously not. Before the new coven was formed, our magic was called high tide magic," he says, his words sharp.

I stare at him, shocked. I don't understand why I've never heard the term before now, and it pulls at another thread in my mind.

"For the powerful nature of high tide," he adds, mocking my words from earlier. Anger flares inside me. "Don't they teach you anything over there?"

"I—" I start to speak, wanting nothing more than to refute his words, but I don't know what to say. I wasn't taught that. Why wasn't I taught that? I close my mouth, dropping my gaze to the ground.

"To answer your original question, yes, I can practice high magic." His tone is smug and condescending, and it makes my stomach twist with ire. Still, if what he said is true, it's a part of our history I should have known.

I shove the thought aside for now, taking a deep breath and working up the courage to ask for what I need. "I'm in trouble," I finally say. "I missed the rush last night, and if I don't get rid of the excess magic in my system, I'll die from it." I'm amazed that I manage to keep my tone even and strong, amazed I'm able to speak at all through the fear.

"Yikes."

My jaw drops. "Yikes? Seriously?"

"Yeah. Yikes." He brushes his hair out of his eyes and looks at me. I feel myself withering beneath his gaze, and I make a point of standing tall and rolling my shoulders back. I raise my chin and meet his eyes.

"You know, if you 'new witches' practiced high magic, this wouldn't be an issue." He practically spits the phrase *new witches*. Utter disgust.

"Well, we don't, and it is. Will you help me do my own rush or not?"

Wolfe looks up and to the right, then rests his chin on his fingers as if what I've asked requires a tremendous amount of consideration. Then he drops his arm to his side and meets my gaze.

"No."

My heart beats faster, and I struggle to maintain my composure. "No?"

"No," he says with finality.

"And why not?" I demand. "It's your fault I'm in this mess in the first place," I say, my voice rising.

"My fault? You're the one who ran into *me*."

"You are infuriating." The words come out in a growl. "You know, you actually have a chance to use your dark magic for something good."

His eyes spark at that, and he stalks toward me until he's standing so close I can feel his breath on my skin. I force myself to stay where I'm standing.

"You have no idea what I use my magic for."

We stare at each other for several breaths, neither of us speaking. I didn't notice last night, but his eyes are a marbled gray, the color of the sky as a storm approaches. "Please," I finally say, the word nothing more than a whisper, so quiet he wouldn't hear it if not for his nearness.

"No," he says again, softer this time.

"Why?" My eyes sting with the threat of tears. The word is a plea, a prayer.

He takes a step back. "You really want to know?"

I nod, unwilling to speak and hear the way my words tremble.

"Then come on." He shoves the moonflower in his pocket and grabs my hand, dragging me to the shore.

I stumble behind him, trying to keep up. His hand is rough, and his grip is tight but not unpleasant. It's urgent.

When we get to the shore where the rush happened last night, he drops my hand and points to the sea.

"That's why," he says, his voice angry, but all I see is water.

"I don't understand."

"Your rushes are destroying this island. You're killing the animals and ruining our crops, and our shores are getting smaller by the day. Your currents will eat up our entire island before you do anything about it. And who knows what will happen when they start taking down boats and drowning people. Witches are stewards of nature, and look what you're doing to it." His voice gets louder and his words come faster, flying through the air like an attack, and they hit me right in my chest because he's right. "So no, Mortana, I won't help you with a rush."

I nod and look out at the sea I love so much. There's nothing for me to say; I agree with his reasons. They are sound and good.

"You're right," I say quietly. "I can't argue with any of that."

I shift my bag on my shoulder and look away before the tears break free and roll down my cheeks. I start walking up the beach, wiping my eyes and hoping the boy behind me doesn't see.

"That's it?" he calls after me.

I stop walking and slowly turn to face him.

"You're just going to let yourself die?" He still sounds angry, and I don't understand.

I look at him but don't respond. What else is there to say? I asked for his help rushing my magic and he refused. That's it.

He walks up the beach and stops in front of me. "There's another way," he says.

I blink and fight the hope that rises in my chest. "There is?"

His eyes glint, and a small smile tugs at the corner of his lips. "I can teach you a few spells, enough to get the magic out of your system. You won't die, and you won't make the currents any stronger."

He watches me intently as I process his words. "You mean dark magic. You'll teach me dark magic."

"*High* magic," he says with annoyance. "And yeah, I'll teach you enough to get your excess magic out."

"Why?" I ask, suddenly aware that there's nothing in it for him.

He pauses and his expression changes. His jaw tenses, and the way he looks at me sends a shiver down my spine. "Because you insulted me when you called me a liar and said I don't use my magic for good. I want you to have to go back to your fancy house in your protected coven and know with every rise of your chest that the only reason you're alive is because of the magic you've been taught to hate."

I'm stunned. I open my mouth to speak, but nothing comes out.

"If you want my help, meet me here at midnight. I won't offer again," he says.

Then he's gone.

t e n

It isn't as hard to get through dinner with my parents as I thought it would be. Certainly not as bad as it would have been had I chosen not to do anything to fix my situation. For better or worse, my mind is made up, and I haven't second-guessed myself since my walk home.

I want to live, and I don't think that means I'm disrespecting my magic or the values with which I was raised. I think it means I'm human.

Landon is coming to visit the Witchery tomorrow, and my parents are busy deciding what we should do, where we should go, who we should see. It will be our first public outing on the island, a very strong signal to the other witches that things are about to change. They won't see us as two young people falling in love for the very first time, star-crossed and shy, hopeful and self-conscious.

They will see us as a walking alliance. A safety net. A vow of protection.

They will see us as the brilliant end to a game we started playing generations ago.

A game we're about to win.

"A picnic," I say, cutting off my parents.

Mom pulls her lips from her glass, and Dad looks up from his plate.

"What?" my mother asks.

"Landon and I will go on a picnic. I'll tell you the beach ahead of time, and you can spread that information however you like. Landon and I will be out in public for all to see, but in a place that *feels* private, with our backs to the island. We need to be able to talk and get to know one another without feeling like we're being paraded around. This may be about attracting attention for you, but it's my life."

My mother nods along until I say the last sentence. Then she opens her mouth to speak, but Dad cuts her off.

"I think that's a great idea, Tana. We can definitely work with it."

Mom clears her throat and swallows whatever she was going to say. "Yes, we can work with that."

"Great."

I shove back from the table and carry my plate to the kitchen. I rinse it and put it in the sink before filling my glass with water and heading upstairs.

"You're going to bed already?" Dad asks. He and Mom are still at the table, plates in front of them, drinks half full.

"I'm sorry, I'm just exhausted. It was a long day."

"It probably wasn't a good idea to go walking after last night. Get some rest, sweetie," Mom says.

I nod and walk up the stairs, my parents' conversation about my picnic with Landon in full swing before I reach the top step. I go to my bathroom and wash my face and brush my teeth, then crawl into bed and anxiously wait for midnight.

My heart races as I sneak down the back staircase and quietly slip out of the house. This is the most defiant I've ever been in my life. I don't feel guilty about it, though, and I'm not sure why.

Tomorrow's visit with Landon will bring whispers and watchful eyes, and I'm glad I'm doing this tonight, before everything changes.

When I get to the western shore, Wolfe is waiting for me. My heart beats faster when I see him, fear and adrenaline coursing through my veins, and I force myself to close the distance between us.

"I'm impressed," he says. "Glad to see you have a survival instinct after all."

"Do you always have to be this unpleasant?"

"That's hardly fair. I brought you a flower and everything." He takes one step closer to me and pulls a moonflower from behind his back.

His eyes sparkle in the moonlight, the color of the waves that crash into the shore. My breath catches, and my hand reaches for the blossom independent of my command.

But he shakes his head. "Not to hold," he says.

My long hair is blowing in the wind, and Wolfe gently brushes it back, tucking the flower behind my ear.

"There," he says. "Queen of the dark."

My hand drifts up and brushes the soft petals. *Queen of the dark.*

"Are you making fun of me?" I ask, the words quiet. He hasn't moved back, and we watch each other, close enough to touch.

"It was meant as a joke, but it...it looks nice." He clears his throat and takes a step back.

My cheeks burn and I hope he can't see the heat that's spreading across my skin. The petals feel like velvet against my fingertips, and the question I haven't been able to let go of since last night tumbles around in my mind. *Why doesn't it hurt?*

I bring my hand down to my side, ignoring the question for now. There are more pressing matters.

"Can we just get this over with?" I ask, forcing my voice to stay steady.

"Whatever my queen commands," he says, bowing, his tone ensuring I know I'm being made fun of this time. I shake my head.

"What do I need to do?"

"I thought we'd play with the tides," he says. It's impossible to miss the way his eyes light up when he says it, the way his voice lifts in anticipation. He's disagreeable, his face nothing but hard lines and sharp edges, his voice constantly laced with annoyance, and yet beneath it all is a boy who deeply loves his magic.

I suppose that's one thing we have in common.

"Will that cause more damage to the sea?"

"No," he says. "Why do you think you'll die if you don't use your magic?" He doesn't wait for me to answer. "It's a gift, and it's meant to be used. Spells and charms burn away the magic once they're cast. The reason your rushes are so damaging is because the magic is just sitting in the sea, restless and edgy. That's why the currents are getting so much worse." He's back to being angry, his words pointed and accusatory.

"I understand," I say.

"Do you?"

His question hangs in the space between us, and I breathe it in, let it settle in my core. Then I level my gaze at him. "Yes."

"Good. Let's get started." He takes off his shoes and walks toward the shore until the waves roll over his feet. I do the same.

"High magic is all about balance. It requires respect and patience from the one who wields it. It requires discipline. The only time you ever come close to using a significant amount of magic is during your rush, a ritual that fully takes over you. But you can't lose yourself in high magic the way you do during a rush. You have to constantly assess how the world around you is responding to the energy you're using. It's rhythmic, just like the tides. If you learn only one thing tonight, let it be this: magic isn't about you. It's about the Earth."

He lets his statement hang in the air, and I'm shocked when the words cause something in me to stir, as if that truth has always been inside me and I'm just now realizing it.

"Let's start with something easy," he says.

My heart slams against my rib cage, so loud and fast I wonder if Wolfe can hear it over the sound of the waves.

"Do you feel the breeze coming off the water?" he asks.

"Yes." Fear has stolen my voice, making the word sound rough and quiet.

"It's easier to work with things that already exist around us. Much easier than creating something from nothing. Now, close your eyes," he says.

I watch him, wary and nervous, scared and uncertain. I don't think I can do it.

"You're safe," he assures me. "You're not doing anything unnatural. As much as you want to resist it, this magic—what we're doing tonight—lives in you. Close your eyes."

I want to argue with that, but he's trying to help me, so I take a deep breath and close my eyes. I can still feel his stare on me in the emptiness of my stomach and the hammering of my heart, the goose bumps on my skin and the heat of my neck.

"We're going to let the wind carry us above the water."

Levitation. My eyes fly open, and I shake my head. "Absolutely not," I say. "I can't do that."

"Why?"

"Because... because it's so obviously..." My words trail off.

"It's so obviously high magic?"

I nod.

"Yeah, well, that's what we're here to do. Just think—if you're successful, you'll never have to use it again." Something changes in his expression when he says it, as if he thinks it's the saddest thing he's ever heard. Then he takes a step closer to me, and another, and another, and another, until he's so close I can smell the spicy scent of his soap, see the moonlight glisten off each strand of hair. "What should scare you most about tonight isn't that you're about to use high magic, Mortana. What should scare you most is that you're going to want to use it again."

I stare at him, my palms beginning to sweat. "You're wrong."

"Not about this," he says. He watches me for another moment, then speaks again. "Moving on. You're inherently connected to every living thing on this Earth. That is our role, and as soon as you learn to recognize that connection, you can start practicing high magic."

I nod along to his words. When I'm working in the perfumery, I don't have to spend time wondering which flowers or herbs will work best with the kind of magic I'm infusing into them. I just know. My hands reach for the things I need and leave the things I don't. It isn't something I think about. It's something I do.

"Close your eyes and concentrate on the wind. It will pull at something inside you, and all you have to do is let it."

I nod again and do as he says. I focus on the way the air cuts through my hair and across my skin, the way I could almost feel it inside myself if I were still enough. I instinctively spread my arms out and turn my palms toward the sky. I tilt my head back and breathe deeply.

Magic rises in my belly as if it wants to touch the breath in my lungs.

"Just like that." Wolfe's words fuel me, and as I breathe more of the wind, more magic rises to touch it.

After several seconds, it's no longer clear to me where the air ends and my magic begins. We are connected, just like when I'm working in the perfumery. Except instead of dried herbs and flowers, it's *wind*.

"Let yourself fall backward and tell the wind to carry you," Wolfe says.

It sounds so absurd, so easy, so harmless when he puts it that way. I'm scared, but if I fall, I know the water will catch me, so I do what he says.

I focus on the connection and fall back. "Please catch me," I whisper into the night, and as I do, the world responds.

I gasp as my body rises out of the water and into the air. Magic comes alive in every part of me, as if it's dancing through my veins, as if it's been waiting its whole life for this.

My eyes fill with tears, but I keep them shut, terrified of losing the connection.

"I can't believe it," I whisper, unable to keep the emotion from my voice.

"Pretty incredible, right?"

I open my eyes, and Wolfe is right beside me, floating in the air, his back to the water. He's looking at me in a way I can't describe, the hard lines of his face softer now, the sharp edges sanded down.

He's beautiful.

I startle as soon as the thought enters my mind, losing my thread of magic and falling into the water below.

Wolfe looks down at me with a smirk, then joins me in the waves.

"You were doing so well. What happened?"

"I got distracted," I say, completely mortified.

"That was good for your first time. Let's do it again."

It's easy to find the connection now that I know what it feels like, and within seconds I'm back in the air. Magic rolls around inside me and pours into the night sky as I rise higher above the water. My whole body relaxes as the magic leaves my system, as if with each passing moment I'm reclaiming another year of my life.

I'm not going to die in nine days.

Silent tears roll down my face, and the cool night breeze dries them on my skin. I stretch my arms out and revel in what it feels like to float. To live.

"Come back down, Mortana," Wolfe says, his voice far away. I look down and see how high up I've drifted, but instead of feeling panic, I feel pride.

"What, can't keep up?" I call down to him.

I hear him laugh. "You really shouldn't have said that." With a wave of his hand, the breeze stills, and my connection to it is lost. I scream as I plummet toward the water, such a long way to fall.

I brace for the harsh impact, but just before I hit the water, a current of air slips underneath me and gently cradles me above the surface, right where Wolfe is standing. He looks down at me, his expression unreadable. We watch each other for several breaths, then he gently slides his arms underneath me and places me back on my feet.

"That was good," he says. "You're catching on very quickly." He says the words as if he's puzzled by them, and for some reason it makes me nervous. I turn away from him and shake my head, try to erase the feeling of being up in the air, because if I don't, I'm terrified I might realize that this is the most fun I've ever had. That this is the most alive I've ever felt.

"No," I say out loud. None of this is real. It's just the exhilaration of doing something I know I shouldn't be doing. It's the relief of knowing I get to live. That's all.

"What was that?" Wolfe asks.

"Nothing," I say, turning back to him. "Are we done?"

"Done?" he says, laughing. "That was just a warm-up. Ready for the main event?" His eyes don't move from my face, challenging me, daring me to follow wherever he wants to take me.

I shiver and push down the fear that turns in my stomach. I can do this. And if I do this, I can live.

"I'm ready," I say.

eleven

The ocean spreads out in front of us, reaching as far into the darkness as I can see. The tide is low, and we walk far enough out that there are fewer rocks and softer sand. The shore is wet and shines in the light of the moon.

The water seems infinite.

"Don't you think manipulating the tides feels a little extreme? I mean, can magic even do that?"

Wolfe raises an eyebrow. "Our magic can."

I don't miss the disdain in his voice. The judgment.

"You act as if you're better than I am because you practice 'high magic,' but you're not. The only reason you're even able to practice that magic is because the new witches have convinced the mainlanders it doesn't exist anymore."

Wolfe takes a step toward me. He's several inches taller than I am, and I have to look up in order to meet his eyes.

"We convinced *you* we don't exist anymore. We live on our

own, hidden from view, so that we can maintain our way of life. We have to live in the shadows because your weak, fear-driven ancestors were all too willing to give up who they were to appease the masses. You're all a bunch of cowards." His voice is low and rough, and his eyes never leave mine.

I lean closer to him. "If we hadn't created the new order, your ancestors would have been killed and you would never have been born. You owe your *life* to us."

"I owe you nothing."

"Then why are you here?" I demand, daring him to answer. We stare at each other, breathing heavy and red with anger. Then he shakes his head and shoves a hand through his hair before taking a step back and turning away from me. I have so many questions, want so badly to understand his life on this island, but what I need now is to focus on surviving.

"Do you want to live or not?" he finally asks.

"I want to live."

"Then let's get rid of that magic."

I follow him in silence, trying to swallow my anger and questions so I can get through the night. The next nine days.

When we reach the water, he turns to me. "This requires a lot of magic. It's an intermediate spell that I don't expect you to be able to perform. But trying something this intense will require a steady rush of magic, and we'll work at it until you're safe again."

"Thank you."

He nods once and turns back to the sprawling sea. "Kneel down. It will help you form a stronger connection to the water."

I sink down into the sand and put my hands in the ocean. Wolfe kneels beside me and does the same.

"I want you to concentrate on the feel of the water. Its temperature, its viscosity, its grittiness. Breathe it into your lungs and taste it on your lips. This water is in you—find it and bind it to the water around you."

It's an extension of what we did earlier with the wind, what I do every day in the perfumery. It should be easy, connecting the place I feel most at peace to the magic inside me, but the ocean is so vast. It's so powerful.

"I can feel it inside me, but I don't know how to tie it to the sea."

"Imagine that your body is totally permeable. The water isn't going around you; it's moving through you. It isn't outside of you, it's in you. Speak your intentions out loud and invite it in."

I never speak when practicing magic; the new order is softer and doesn't require the power of words. I suddenly feel self-conscious, and I sit up. "I don't know what to say."

"It's like a prayer," he says, and something about the way he speaks the words forces my insides to shift around, as if making space for them. "You can say it aloud or think the words to yourself. It's up to you. But you need to ask the sea to rush into you and seek out your magic."

"What's it supposed to feel like?"

"When you feel it, you'll know." He watches me, and even though I'm kneeling in cold water, heat spreads through me.

I start again. "Please seek out my magic," I say. "Please help me."

I keep my eyes tightly closed, my hands tense in the water, but nothing happens. I don't feel magic pouring through me; all I feel is a creeping dread that this isn't going to work, that it is foolish to even try.

"It has to be genuine, Mortana," Wolfe says beside me. "You have to approach it like it's something you want, not something you need."

"But I don't want it."

I open my eyes, and he's suddenly so close to me, his thigh almost touching my own as we kneel in the water. "For just one night, give in to it." His words are quiet, but my entire body responds as if he'd shouted them at me.

Give in to it.

I gently place my hands back in the water, turning my gaze away from Wolfe before closing my eyes. I take a deep breath of briny air and hold it in my lungs for several seconds. Then I speak.

"Ocean around me, ocean within, touch one to the other, let the magic begin." I don't know where the words come from, but they feel natural as they pour from my lips, and I chant them over and over again.

And as I do, the magic inside me wakes.

I'm flooded with relief as magic releases into the space around me, giving the cold night air an energetic buzz, making the water around us stir.

Everything is coming alive.

I am coming alive.

My words get louder and louder, and soon my whole body is filled with power, the way I feel right before the rush.

"Gentle tide, waters low, rise to us now, send us below." The words fall from my lips of their own accord, and soon my magic follows, flowing out of me with a power I've never known. It's exhilarating and terrifying and confusing, but I keep saying the words because it feels as if something inside me will break if I stop. My body is shaking, and I'm unsure if it's due to fear or the magic roaring through me.

I am being rewritten, the water around me and the magic inside me carving new paths until the map of who I am looks different.

"Mortana!" Wolfe shouts, grabbing my arm.

I open my eyes just in time to see the water rise and surge toward us. The ocean slams into me, knocking me back. It rushes over my head and I gasp, filling my lungs with salt water. The tide grows higher and higher, and I try desperately to reach the surface, but I can't.

My chest burns with the need for air, but my body is being tossed every which way, and I can't get my bearings. I start to choke, and I'm instantly reminded of the time I was caught in a current made by magic, when my father told my mother she was at fault. And now here I am again. It's a different kind of magic, but drowning feels the same.

I thrash in the water, clawing for the surface, but I don't know which way is up. I'm frantic for air, but I can't find it. My muscles are tight and cramping, and my body suddenly feels heavy. So heavy.

I can't keep fighting. I'm absolutely drained, an exhaustion more intense than after my most powerful rush. Slowly, my muscles relax and I let my eyelids close.

If the sea wants me, it will have me.

My lungs ache for another breath. I can't get to the surface.

It will be over soon.

I sink lower and lower, the water in my lungs pushing me to the bottom.

I hit the sand, and then an arm wraps around my waist and my eyelids drift open.

Wolfe is holding me against his chest, kicking his legs. Kicking and kicking. I try to move, try to help, but I can't. Everything goes dark.

Total silence.

Then suddenly I'm choking. I'm sprawled on the beach on my back, water spouting from my mouth like a fountain.

"Good, get it all out," Wolfe is saying, gently holding up my head.

I keep coughing until I'm sure my lungs will end up on the rocky shore. But eventually the coughing stops, and a powerful fatigue moves through me. I don't think I will ever stand again. Wolfe gently lets go of my head, and I lie back on the sand, staring up at the stars. He crouches next to me, stiff, as if he can't decide if he should stay or go. Then, slowly, he lowers himself to the ground next to me.

His body is close to mine. If I moved my arm a single inch, it would rest against his. If I stretched my hand out, my pinkie would find his. I've only ever been this close to a man when dancing with

Landon, but this feels different. I'm aware of myself in a way that's entirely new, not out of self-consciousness or modesty, but something heady. More intense.

Everything about this night is new.

I suppose it's normal to feel a pull toward him. He did save my life, after all.

The moon is starting to wane, and the stars are shining brightly overhead, thousands of sharp pinpricks in the curtain of night.

"Mortana," Wolfe says beside me, keeping his eyes on the sky, "do you know what you just did?"

"I'm sorry," I say. "The spell got away from me; I don't know what I was saying."

"No," Wolfe says, suddenly sitting up. He helps me into a seated position, and I watch him. "You pulled in the tide. On your own. Your very first time using high magic."

Something like dread settles in my stomach.

"I've never seen anything like it," he says.

"I've always loved to swim," I whisper. "It's like I'm bonded to the sea. I've always felt that way."

"You're incredible," he says, so low I barely hear it.

"I'm incredible?"

He swallows hard and looks away. "I mean, what you did. What you did is incredible."

You're incredible.

I banish the words from my mind. "I don't think I'm strong enough to stand," I say, clearing his words from the air.

"That's good," Wolfe says. "That means you got enough magic out. You're going to be fine."

I can feel that it's true. My body is even weaker than it is after a rush.

I'm going to be fine.

I'm going to live.

"Thank you for what you did."

Wolfe searches my eyes for several seconds, then turns away. "You're welcome."

We sit in silence for a long time. The sky turns a deep velvet blue, and I know I have to get home before my parents wake.

"How do you do it?" I ask. I should leave, but for the first time in my life, I want to extend the night.

"Do what?"

"Stay hidden. What kind of a life is that?"

"It's a full one," he says. "It isn't perfect, but it's ours."

"But how is it that we don't know about your coven? How is that possible?"

He shifts next to me, as if he's trying to decide how much he wants to share. "The home we live in is protected by magic," he says. I wait for him to elaborate, to explain how magic can shield them like that, but he doesn't. "We're pretty self-sufficient. We grow a lot of our own food, and the island provides for us in many ways. When we need to go into town, we use a spell that allows us to be perceived as tourists. Nobody gives us a second glance."

"Have you seen me before?" I ask, the words whisper-soft.

He turns away from me and looks at the ocean. I don't think he'll answer the question, but then he lets out one tense word: "Yes."

"Have we spoken before?"

"No."

I nod, dozens of questions entering my mind, but I can't find the words to ask any of them. The night is quickly slipping away. It's time to go home, and Wolfe helps me to my feet, his ring reflecting the moonlight. He catches me when I sway a little. I steady myself. "I'll be fine."

I tuck a strand of hair behind my ear, and my fingers brush the moonflower Wolfe gave me, somehow still in place after everything. I take it off and hand it to him, knowing I can't go home with it no matter how much I might want to.

Wolfe walks me up the shore until we reach the road. "You saved my life," I say.

"It seemed like a good use of a Monday night."

"Don't lessen it." I wait until his eyes find mine. "Thank you, Wolfe Hawthorne."

"You're welcome, Mortana Fairchild."

We look at each other for a long time, and for reasons I can't explain, taking even the first step toward home feels impossible.

Absolutely impossible.

"You better go," he says. The words come out strained.

"Will I see you again?"

He pauses before answering. "Do you want to?"

"Yes." The word slips through my lips before I have a chance to think about it, before I can come up with the right answer, which is, of course, *no*.

"Do you want to see me again?" I whisper.

He's quiet for so long that I think he didn't hear me, which is probably for the best. His jaw tenses and relaxes several times, like he's grinding his teeth. He looks at me as if it pains him to do so.

"Yes," he finally says, but the word is angry. Frustrated. As if it's the wrong answer for him as well.

And it is. It's the wrong answer for both of us.

And yet the word slides down deeper and deeper inside me, where it settles in my core, heavy and meaningful.

Do you want to see me again?

Yes.

twelve

I wake with a horrible headache. My entire body is sore, and I feel as if I could sleep for the rest of the year, as if I combined all the rushes of the past twelve months into one single night. But I'm going to live, and I'm all too aware that it's Wolfe and his dark magic that saved my life.

Just like he wanted.

The scent of Awaken blend tea drifts into my room, and I roll over and prop myself on my elbows.

"Good morning," Ivy says from the sky-blue upholstered chair in the corner of my room.

I rub my eyes and groan. "Let me guess—my mother felt I could use a little help getting ready for my date today." I collapse back on the mattress and stare up at the ceiling.

"She did. And it was either her or me, so I took it upon myself to make the choice for you."

I reach for the tea, but Ivy holds it back and quirks her head to the side. "There's sand in your hair."

"There's always sand in my hair."

"There's a *lot* of sand in your hair." She walks over to the bed and pulls down the quilt. "It's everywhere, Tana. What did you *do* last night?"

I want to tell her. I want to recount every single detail, explain the way it felt to be cradled by the wind and connected to the sea. I want to tell her about Wolfe and how he lay in the sand next to me, how the sharp edges of his face didn't seem so sharp when he looked at me in the moonlight.

I want to tell her how scared I was, how I thought one night of dark magic would make me feel tainted in a way I'd never be rid of, a way that would stain me forever.

I want to tell her I was wrong.

Ivy always asks me how I feel about things, how I'm doing, how I'm meeting my own needs when my entire existence is meant to meet the needs of others. And I never know how to answer.

But I know exactly how I feel about last night, and what worries me more than anything is that I don't feel traitorous or evil for using the dark magic we've been taught to fear. I feel thankful to be alive.

"I went swimming," I say.

"Clearly. Did you also burrow into the ocean floor? Wrap yourself in kelp when you were done?"

"I met someone," I say, the words so quiet Ivy leans toward me.

"What now?"

I grab the tea from her and take a long sip. I can't tell her who he is or what he showed me, but Ivy is my best friend, and I have to tell her something. "A boy. He was on the beach. He swam with me."

Saying it out loud, telling Ivy about him, makes him real. It's comforting to know that as I move on from the events of last night, he won't exist solely in my memory. He will be a living, breathing secret between Ivy and me.

"You met a boy. On the beach. In the middle of the night. And he swam with you." She repeats everything back to me in short, staccato sentences.

"Yes."

Ivy looks bewildered. "Who is he?"

My palms begin to sweat and I drop my gaze to my quilt. I should have known this would be the first thing she asked, and while I hate the idea of lying to her, the alternative is worse. Far worse.

"He's from the mainland. He missed the last ferry and was camping out on the beach."

Ivy stares at me, and I'm sure she can see right through my lie, see the dark magic snaking through my veins. Then one side of her mouth pulls up and she stands. "Well, that's going to require another cup of tea, isn't it?"

Before I can respond, Ivy is out the door and rushing down the stairs. I hear her in the kitchen, and then she's back in my room. She closes the door behind her and climbs onto the bed, curling her legs beneath her and pulling her tea to her face.

"I'm ready," she says.

I laugh and take a sip of my own tea. I tell Ivy all the details I can without giving away who Wolfe is or what kind of magic we practiced. I only tell her what it was like to be in the water with him, but it's enough. Ivy drifts closer to me, and by the end of the story, she's hanging on each word as if it's a lifeline.

When I finally finish, she's quiet for several seconds.

"Damn."

"That pretty much sums it up," I say. I pause before speaking again. "Last night was the first time in my life I can remember making a choice solely for myself, without thinking about what my mother would say or how it would affect the coven. And it worries me because—" I cut myself off. There are certain things that should not be spoken aloud.

"Because it felt good?"

I look at Ivy and nod, ashamed of myself.

"That's nothing to worry about. I'd be more concerned if you didn't enjoy making choices for yourself. *Of course* it felt good. You carry a lot of responsibility, and it's heavy." Ivy's brown eyes are filled with so much love for me, so much understanding. She reaches out and grabs my hand, squeezing tight. "I'm so glad you had a night when things didn't feel quite so heavy."

"You are?" I ask.

"There's something beautiful about it. Even though so much of your life has been mapped out for you, you still had this night that was entirely unscripted. Entirely your own."

I'm embarrassed when my eyes fill with tears. I turn away from her and wipe my face, taking a deep breath.

When I've regained my composure, I look at Ivy and offer a

smile. "Thank you for saying that." I lean into her, and when we've finished our tea, I take our mugs and set them on my dresser.

"Okay," I say, standing in front of her and spreading my arms. "Make me presentable for my future husband."

"Tana," Ivy says, her voice chastising, "there's only so much magic can do. Go shower."

She watches me for several seconds, and then we burst out laughing. I do as I'm told, running the shower as hot as it will go. Scalding water pours over my head and down my body, washing away any trace of Wolfe, any trace of our night together.

I turn off the shower, watching until the last drops of water swirl down the drain. Then I get out, dry off, and prepare myself for Landon.

I begged my parents to let me come down the stairs before Landon arrived, but no such luck. My mother wants me to make an entrance.

I can hear my parents doting on him, and I nervously look at Ivy. "Think they'll scare him off?"

"I suspect he's used to involved parents," she says.

"Thank you for this morning." I take a final look in the mirror, but I know I look perfect for the occasion. Ivy's magic erased any trace of last night. My makeup is subtle and fresh, making my blue eyes pop and my lips look as if I've just licked them. I used my own magic to blow out my hair and smooth it back into a classic chignon my mother will love. I'm wearing a camel-colored shift dress, a string of pearls around my neck, and nude leather shoes with a square heel.

It isn't what I would have chosen for myself, but I look put together and classic, and most importantly, I look like someone who belongs by Landon's side.

"You're welcome," Ivy says, handing me my shawl.

I give her a quick hug, then take a deep breath and walk toward my bedroom door.

"Tana?"

I turn and look at Ivy.

"Enjoy yourself."

I nod and open the door. When I come around the bend in the stairs, I see Landon waiting at the bottom for me. He smiles when he sees me, and much to my surprise, I smile back. Relief floods me as I realize it's nice to see him.

He's wearing a white collared shirt with a tweed jacket on top, and I suddenly get the feeling that we're playing dress-up, wearing these clothes that are meant to portray a level of maturity that I, at least, don't feel.

But I suppose if I'm going to play a part, there are worse people to play with than Landon.

"Tana, you look lovely," he says when I get to the bottom of the stairs.

"Thank you," I say. "So do you."

My parents are watching us, and I'm thankful when Landon asks what I have planned for the day.

"A picnic. We'll choose our food from some of the shops on

the Witchery, and then I thought I'd take you to one of my favorite lookouts to eat."

Landon's smile is easy and generous, and it looks like he's truly excited. "Sounds perfect," he says.

I grab the basket and two blankets from the table and say goodbye to my parents, and then we head to the door. Landon opens it for me, but just then I hear Ivy sneak down the stairs, and we both turn to look at her.

Something like gratitude settles on her face when she sees us together. Ivy, my best friend, who has known about this arrangement almost as long as I have, is still struck by the magnitude of it. I blink several times and look away, trying not to get caught up in the emotion of the moment.

"Have fun, you two," my mother says.

Ivy clears her throat, and I give her a small smile before walking out the door with Landon.

"Thank you for coming out here," I say to him.

"I'm glad to be here. Thank you for planning such a great day—it will be wonderful to see the island through your eyes."

"I really love it here," I say, falling in step beside him.

"Will it be difficult for you to leave?"

I pause and look at him. "Yes," I answer honestly.

He nods. "Then we'll have to create many reasons for you to visit."

It's a kind thing to say, thoughtful and sweet, but it still doesn't feel like enough. And that's when I realize my life with him might not be enough. It will be so many things: good, important, monumental, safe.

But it might not be *enough*. And I have to learn to be okay with that.

"What are you thinking about?" Landon asks me after I've been quiet for too long, looking out across the water instead of responding to his comment.

"Our life together."

"What about it?"

"I was thinking that if I'm not going to have a lot of say in who I spend my life with, I'm glad I'm ending up with you."

"And why is that?"

"Because we believe in the same things. We value family and duty and progress; many marriages have been built on far less."

"That's certainly true," he agrees. "Do you think you ever would have chosen me on your own?"

The question catches me off guard, and I pause before answering. "I've always known I didn't have a choice," I say. "But maybe I would have." I can see myself loving Landon one day. I can see that spark appearing. Maybe under different circumstances, I would have chosen him for myself. "What about you?" I ask.

"I've never given it much thought. But under any circumstance, I would choose to honor my family. And my family has chosen you."

It isn't romantic or transformative or even sweet, but it's honest. And that's the most we can offer each other right now.

We start walking again, and I point out parts of the island as we go. He's interested, stopping to ask questions and get a better look at things. He cares. And it's satisfying showing him around, showing him the place I love more than anywhere else in the world.

"Is that the only church on the island?" Landon asks, stopping in front of a small stone building with a steeple on top. Ivy crawls up the sides, the leaves turning red with the autumn chill.

"It is."

"But how do you all fit inside?"

"We don't," I say simply. "Do you not think it a narrow view that meeting God in the confines of a room is more likely than under the cover of the trees or in the open air of the fields?"

Landon pauses, considering the church. "Yes, I suppose it is."

He looks at the building for another moment before falling in step beside me. We turn onto Main Street, and I watch as the charm of it washes over him, brightening his eyes and pulling at the corners of his mouth.

"Landon, are you ready to experience the best cheese of your life?" I ask.

"That's a lofty statement, Miss Fairchild."

"I stand by it," I say.

Landon tips his head to the side, considering me. "I'll be the judge of that."

The bell rings as we enter the Mouse Trap, and Mrs. Cotts runs out from the back to greet us. Her eyes widen and her smile spreads as she takes in the sight of the island's highest daughter and the mainland's most powerful son together.

Landon takes my hand, a confident smile settling on his face.

And so it begins.

thirteen

Once we've filled our picnic basket with meats, cheeses, bread, and rose water, we make our way to our last stop on Main Street: the perfumery. Wisteria hangs from the top of the stone storefront, filling the air with its sweet fragrance, and we walk inside to a group of mainlanders who look up as we enter.

Silence creeps through the store like fog through the trees.

I instinctively look down, but Landon keeps his head high. He turns to me and lowers his mouth to my ear. "Don't let them off so easily. It's rude to stare," he whispers, so quietly only I can hear. "Let them know it."

I look back up and make eye contact with each of the mainlanders, and each one looks away as if I've caught them stealing.

It feels good, letting them know I've noticed their scrutiny.

Finally, they begin chatting again, keeping their voices low as they walk out the store and leave us to ourselves.

"Scaring away our customers?" Dad asks with a wink when he walks out of the back room.

"Something like that," I say.

"Well, I'll leave you kids to it. I'll be in the back if you need anything." Dad gives me a soft smile before disappearing.

"So, this is your family's shop," Landon says as he looks around the room. It's bright and airy, with wooden shelves the color of honey and white wallpaper walls printed with delicate ferns outlined in black. Dozens of plants sit on the shelves between rows of glass bottles, and a small chandelier with crystal lights in the shape of rosebuds hangs from the ceiling. Votive candles are nestled on the shelves, and small glass bottles filled with coffee beans sit beside them.

Dad is humming in the back, and it somehow adds to the charm of the perfumery.

"It is," I say proudly, looking around the room.

I love it here.

"It's something special," he says. I look up at him and smile.

"I think so, too." I lead him to the shelf that holds our more earthy, spicy colognes. "I'd love for you to pick one to take home with you."

"Really?" he asks, his eyes drifting over the labels. He looks delighted, and it fills me with happiness.

"Absolutely," I say.

He sets our picnic basket on the ground and takes his time gently removing lids to smell each scent, pausing often to sniff the coffee beans and clear the prior fragrance.

In the end, he chooses our Driftwood scent, magicked with a subtle calm that puts anyone around the wearer at ease.

"Great choice. It's one of my favorites," I say.

He presses the top once, and the briny, fresh scent fills the space between us.

"I love it," he says, putting the cap back on and gently placing it in our basket. "Thank you."

"You're welcome. Ready for our picnic?"

"I am."

I feel my father's eyes follow us out of the shop, and it feels good to breathe the cool autumn air. An easy breeze picks up around us, and it instantly makes me think of Wolfe.

Floating above the water with him.

Being pulled to the surface by him.

Lying in the sand next to him.

I shake my head and dispel the images, dislodging them as if they're debris in a gutter.

I lead Landon to a beach on the eastern shore so we can see the mainland in the distance as we eat. Most mainlanders like to see their city across the Passage—just another way to make them feel more at ease with us.

I spread one of our blankets on the sand, a perfectly chosen spot that backs up to a dune with long grasses and shrubs. It gives us some sense of privacy, and I settle onto the blanket as Landon empties our basket. He pulls out a bundle of fresh lavender, studying it.

"How are the flowers here always in bloom?"

"Magic," I say. "How else could we keep our shops open year round?"

"Fascinating." He sets the flowers down and sits beside me. At first we're stiff, each hugging our own edge of the blanket, but as the autumn sun glides across the sky and the tide goes out, we relax. The space between us begins to feel like air again, not an invisible wall we dare not climb.

I take a sip of rose water and look out at the mainland. It will be my home after the Covenant Ball, and this picnic will be nothing but a memory, a moment in time that slipped by me too soon.

Landon offers me the last bit of cheese and leans back onto his elbows, staring out across the Passage.

"I was skeptical, but I have to say, that was undoubtedly the best cheese of my life," he says.

"I wouldn't steer you wrong." I blot my mouth and place my cloth napkin back in the basket.

"No, Tana, I don't believe you would." His voice is laced with a seriousness that wraps around my insides. He looks at me then, his amber-brown eyes fixed on my own, and it is suddenly difficult to turn away.

We stay that way for several moments, and my heart speeds up as he inches his face closer to mine. I'm frozen, completely still, unsure of what to do.

Part of me wants to close the distance between us, to press my lips to his and let myself get lost in the moment. I wonder if dragonflies would erupt in my stomach, if a fire would start in my core and spread to the rest of me.

I wonder if I would want to keep kissing him over and over till death do us part.

But the rest of me is scared, because if dragonflies don't take flight and a fire doesn't spark, I'd rather not know until after we make our vows to one another. It wouldn't change anything, of course, but it's nice to believe that there's the possibility of passion.

Landon pauses at the halfway point, but I don't move closer to meet him. His eyes search mine, and something like understanding seems to pass over his face. He nods and pulls away, creating enough space for me to breathe again.

"Tana," he says, his voice quiet, "will you promise me something?"

"Yes."

"If at some point you'd like me to kiss you, will you let me know?"

I wish I knew why he wants to kiss me—if it's because he feels a pull toward me, a spark, something more than the duty that has brought us together, or if it's because I'm his future wife and that's what's expected.

"I will," I say. "It isn't that I don't want you to kiss me, though. I'm just not sure I'm ready yet."

"Understood," he says.

He watches me for another moment, then looks out toward the mainland again. I follow his gaze, and we sit like that for several breaths, both quiet, contemplative.

"We're going to be okay, aren't we?" I ask, letting the sound of the waves on the shore settle the unease that has started in my stomach.

"I've asked myself that same question a lot," he says.

"And what have you come up with?"

"I can't think of a more worthwhile pursuit than that of duty. Our names will be remembered for generations to come; we are the beginning of a new day. How could we not be okay, knowing the importance of our union?"

Disappointment spreads through my gut, and I wish I could make it stop. What he's saying is true; I've told myself the same thing many times. But I want more than that, more than talk of duty and honor. Those things may be what brought us together, but they aren't the only things we have room for in this alliance. I have to believe there could be more.

I've been quiet for too long. Landon looks at me, and I finally respond. "It is a remarkable thing to think about. But surely duty isn't the only thing ensuring our happiness. Surely we can hope for other things as well?"

Landon furrows his brow, and it's the first time I've seen a break in his confident composure. "I'm not sure what you mean."

"Duty is why we're together, but we don't have to limit ourselves to that, do we? We could find true enjoyment of one another. We could find passion, even love. Why not hope for those things?"

"Hope is too fickle a thing."

"Why?"

"Because it's too broad. Hope paves the way for wanting things that were never part of the plan."

His words take my breath away because he's right, because wanting something more than what's before me is entirely too dangerous. And I hate that I know that.

I must look upset, because Landon gently lifts my chin, forcing my eyes to meet his. "Don't misunderstand me, Tana. I believe we're going to have a remarkable life. I believe it will be satisfying and enjoyable. But I can't promise you love. I can promise you many other things, stronger things that can bear the weight of shifting emotions and familial obligations. I can promise you that not only will we be happy, but we will also be fulfilled, the kind of fulfillment that can only come from something far more stable than love."

I nod and try not to let his words hurt, try to accept them for what they are: forthright. "Thank you for being honest with me."

"There are many things that are out of our control. Being honest with each other isn't one of them."

"Then let me be honest with you, too. I understand your position, and I know you're right, but hope is not something I'm willing to give up. You don't have to promise me love, but I would ask that you stay open to the possibility of building a foundation on more than duty alone."

He nods. "You have my word."

"Thank you." I turn back to the sea, and my insides relax just slightly. We heard each other, we listened, and that means something. I built Landon up so much before we met, had so many dreams and visions of what our life together might look like, of how he might make me feel, and I hoped for them right away. But we are just two people getting to know each other, and I have to give him the space and time to get there. I have to give myself the space and time to get there.

"Tell me something, Tana," Landon says, the heaviness gone from his voice. "What would you be doing right now if I weren't here?"

"You go first," I say, still stuck on his previous admission.

"There are stables about an hour's journey east of my home, and my father and I visit often. We ride the horses through the woods and discuss political matters if needed, but often, we simply talk. It's a nice respite from the normal pace of things."

"That sounds wonderful," I say.

"Do you ride?"

"I don't, but I'd love to learn." There are horses on the island, of course, but I've always preferred to walk.

"Then I will teach you."

When I think about the mainland, I picture an endless city, brick and concrete as far as the eye can see. I'm so glad to know it isn't true, that there is a haven Landon visits, that I can visit as well.

"Your turn," he says. "What would you be doing?"

"Swimming."

"Swimming? In the ocean? In autumn?"

I laugh at his response. "I love to swim. It's when I'm happiest."

"What do you love about it?"

"Everything," I say. "But the thing I love most is the way the entire world quiets when I'm underwater. It's as if nothing can reach me there. No expectations or worries or insecurities. I get to just be."

"I don't think I've ever noticed that," he says. "Will you show me?"

"Just name the time."

"How about now?"

I look down at our clothing, at our outfits that make me feel like we're playing dress-up, and I can't think of anything I'd rather do than drench them in salt water.

"It's cold," I say.

"I can handle cold." He unties his shoes and slips them off his feet, then pulls off his socks and helps me up.

"My mother will kill me for this," I say, removing my shawl and dropping it to the ground. I shiver and catch the way Landon's eyes linger on my bare shoulders.

"You can blame it on me." Landon slips out of his jacket, then takes my hand and pulls me down to where the waves rush onto the shore.

"I will absolutely be blaming this on you," I say, taking off my shoes and wading into the water. My heart begins to race, and I quickly scan the surface, looking for a moonflower, but there isn't one. Being in the water with Landon in the light of the day makes the flowers seem so distant. Not real, somehow. And yet my questions about them still linger. I'm too scared to ask them aloud, to hear answers that don't fit into my world. I don't want to tell my mother about them and see how the information shifts her world, either. So I push it all out of my mind and focus on the person beside me, the person who matters far more to our way of life than a near-extinct flower does.

When we're in up to our knees, Landon looks at me and says, "One."

I smile. "Two."

"Three," we say together, diving into the water and swimming away from the shore. When we surface, Landon is breathing heavily.

"You weren't kidding about the cold."

"You'll get used to it." I swim next to him and take both his hands in mine. "Ready for the best part?"

"Ready."

We both take large breaths, then descend below the surface of the water. I watch Landon as he opens his eyes, squinting at first, then getting more comfortable with the salt.

And then I see it—the exact moment he understands what I told him, the way he feels the quiet as if it's a living thing.

His eyes widen, and he looks around with an awed expression on his face. His short brown hair sways on top of his head, and bubbles rise from his mouth as air escapes from his lungs.

We look at each other for as long as we can stand it, suspended in the perfect silence, hair and limbs spread out around us.

When my chest is aching, I let go of Landon's hands and swim to the surface. I gasp for air when I pop out of the water, drinking it down like my mother drinks her wine.

Landon surfaces moments after me, and we tread water next to each other as our breathing slows.

Then we do it again, but something catches my attention as we move into deeper water. Seaweed rolls around, violently spinning until it's pulled away, out into the middle of the Passage. The sand on the seafloor is stirring.

We have to get out of here.

I catch Landon's gaze and point up, and we both swim to the surface.

"We need to swim back," I say, already moving toward the shore.

Landon follows, and it isn't until we're safely on land that I meet his gaze.

"What was that about?" he asks, looking out over the water.

I catch myself before telling him about the currents. I don't know if the mainlanders are aware of the damage we've caused to the sea, and I don't know how my mother would react if I made them aware.

"Nothing," I say, trying to sound casual. "I just don't want the governor's son to catch a cold." I say it playfully, but Landon is watching me. He knows that there's something I'm not saying, something I'm not being honest about. But it isn't in my control.

We head back to our blankets and wrap ourselves up, shivering and wet and cold. Wolfe's angry words enter my mind, accusing my coven and me of destroying the island we're supposed to be stewards of, and I hate that he's right. I hate that there's nothing we can do about it.

What good is magic if we can't use it to protect our home, the very thing it's meant for?

As soon as I think it, I try to shove away the thought, forget it, wipe it from my mind. But it takes root, weaving through the paths and alleyways of who I am, burrowing in. It finds a home in me, and against my better judgment and every impulse inside me screaming that danger lies ahead, I let it.

fourteen

News of my date with Landon spreads through the Witchery like kudzu vines, fast and invasive. The perfumery sees an influx of customers, and my mother acts like my bodyguard and personal assistant, all rolled into one unfathomably put-together woman. She coyly steps around the questions she doesn't want to answer and demurely responds the ones she does.

I haven't been to the shop for several days, but I can't avoid it forever.

I take a detour on my way to the perfumery, visiting the western shore and the field where I met Wolfe. I take my time gathering grasses and blades of kelp, then cut through the woods in the center of the island and make my way to Main Street. It's so quiet on this side of the island, overgrown and untouched. It's a shame we only use it for the rush. Then again, if we used it more, it would lose the qualities I love most about it.

I turn onto Main Street and am almost to the perfumery

when Mr. Kline stops me. His white hair is blowing in the sea breeze, and his weathered skin crinkles around his eyes. He takes off his wool cap and holds it in his hands.

"Hi, Mr. Kline," I say, hugging my basket close to my body. "How are you?"

"I'm well, Miss Tana, thank you."

"Glad to hear it," I say. I'm about to start walking when Mr. Kline says my name again. He's rolling his cap in his hands, and he looks at the cobbles as if he's nervous. When he raises his eyes to mine, they're wet.

"I wish my parents were alive to see this. They always believed it would happen one day. 'Just stay the course,' they used to say to me."

"Landon is a wonderful man. I'm very lucky." I smile as I repeat the words my mother told me to say, and Mr. Kline's eyes widen as I confirm the rumor he heard. He takes my hand and pats the back of it.

"Landon is the lucky one," he says.

"Thank you."

I gently pull my hand away and give Mr. Kline another smile before stepping around him and walking the rest of the way to the perfumery. But when I get there, I stop. The storefront is clogged with people, and I can't make my feet move, can't force myself to go inside. I take several steps back and turn away before anyone sees me, then round the corner and walk down the path behind the building. I slip into the back room of the perfumery and breathe out in relief, thankful that the door leading into the retail space is closed.

I hang my coat on a hook and set my basket on the island, taking out the things I gathered from the shore and the field.

The sounds from the shop fade into the background as I put the grasses in a mortar and grind them into dust. The comfortable familiarity of the pestle in my hand eases the strain on my mind, and soon I'm replaying memories from the field and memories from the shore on a loop, over and over again.

Memories of the magic.

Memories of Wolfe.

I'm ashamed that my mind finds refuge in remembering the lines of his face and the feel of his magic, ashamed that when the house is quiet and my parents are asleep, I'm met with thoughts of him in the dark.

It doesn't feel real, the night we had together. It feels like a dream, soft and hazy, already fading away at the edges. It's so far removed from my daily life that I'm almost convinced it didn't happen. And that's good.

Dreams aren't threatening. They can't grab the corners of your world and pull it out from under you. They can't change the course of your ship.

I continue to work the grasses into a fine dust, lost in the motion. "When memories fade and time makes them weak, spray this perfume for the moment you seek."

I don't even realize I'm speaking the spell aloud until the door flies open and my dad rushes in. I stare at him, waiting for any indication that he heard me, trying to formulate an explanation that would make sense, but he doesn't look my way. He quickly closes the door behind him and leans his back against the wood, pushing his palms into it as if an angry mob may come barging through at any moment.

Speaking spells out loud isn't strictly prohibited, but most of us refrain because of the power it gives them. Low magic doesn't require it, and if my father heard me speaking a spell after nineteen years of keeping them in my head, he would have questions.

I silently reprimand myself for my carelessness, for letting my night with Wolfe seep into my days. But it seems my dad didn't notice, and I won't let it happen again.

"Dad?" I ask when he still hasn't looked at me.

"Hey, Tana," he says with a laugh. "I didn't know you were here."

"In a moment of bravery, I decided to come to work today. Then I saw the crowd from the street and snuck in through the back."

Dad nods and walks over to the island. "That was an excellent choice."

"How's it going out there?" I ask.

Dad reaches for his mortar and grabs a bundle of herbs on the side of the island. He gets to work grinding them down as he talks.

"Your mother has it handled," he says. "She could run the whole world. And the good thing about our neighbors is that they feel guilty coming in for gossip without paying for it, so sales have been through the roof."

"Well, that's a silver lining, I suppose."

"I'll be here all night trying to restock our staples."

My eyes drift to the grass in my mortar and the sand beside me, to the wildflowers from the field and the kelp from the shore, and I realize for the first time what I intend to do with it all.

Make a scent for Wolfe. As a gift for helping me.

I suppose it's normal to want to thank the person who saved my life, but I don't want him to think I'm okay with his methods. I don't want him believing that the new coven's most influential daughter is indifferent to the use of dark magic, because nothing could be further from the truth.

But I want to say thank you, and I want him to know I mean it.

"Want some help restocking tonight?" I ask. Helping my dad is a better use of my time than giving gifts to Wolfe, and I know that.

Dad looks up at me. "I'd love some," he says with a smile.

We work in silence, and it's the first time I've felt truly at peace in days, my thoughts quieting and my shame fading with each grind of the pestle. Dad hums to himself, and I work the grass in time to the melody. We look up in unison when the back door opens.

Ivy walks in with three cups of tea. "I come bearing gifts."

"A true hero," I say.

"I've got Energize, Persist, and Invigorate."

"I'll take Persist." Ivy hands me a cup, and steam rises in front of me.

"I'll take Energize," Dad says. Ivy sets the tea down on the island next to his mortar. "Thanks, Ivy. You're a lifesaver. Tana, why don't you take a little break? You'll be here all night."

"Thanks, Dad."

"I'll take this out to Ingrid, though she hardly needs it." He winks at me, then grabs the last cup and walks out into the main store.

"Do you have time to take a break with me, or do your parents need you back at the shop?" I ask Ivy.

"We just got through the midday rush. I'm fine for a few minutes," she says. "Want some fresh air?"

"As long as we don't go down Main, yes."

She holds the back door open for me, and we walk down the path and onto a trail in the surrounding woods.

"What kind of perfume were you making back at the shop? I haven't seen that combination before," Ivy says, and my cheeks flush. I don't say anything and stare intently at the dirt path in front of me.

"What?" Ivy asks.

"It's nothing," I say, keeping my voice casual. "Just a small token for Wolfe."

Ivy stops and raises an eyebrow. "Wolfe?"

"The boy I met on the beach."

"So he has a name," she says, a slight pull to her lips.

"Of course he has a name."

She holds her hands up in defense, and we start walking again.

"What kind of token are you making?"

Embarrassment makes me look away again. "A cologne made from scents of our night together."

"Oh, Tana," Ivy says, her voice sad. "That's a lovely gift. But it's..." She struggles to find the right word.

"Do you think it's too much? I'm not really sure what the etiquette is on thank-you gifts."

Ivy shakes her head, then looks me in the eye. "I think it's dangerous."

The words make my heart race, make dread stir in my stomach, and I force the feeling away and keep my voice even. "That's a bit dramatic, don't you think?"

Ivy doesn't seem fazed, and she loops her arm through mine.

"This boy could break your heart," she says.

"Break my heart?" I ask, laughing. "It's just a gift."

"Is it?" she asks.

"Of course." I want to tell Ivy that he saved my life, that giving him something in return is the least I can do.

We're both quiet for a while, the sounds of our footfalls on the soft earth and the leaves rustling in the autumn breeze filling the air between us.

"You want him to remember you," Ivy says, looking at me with a mix of pity and understanding and sadness, and it frustrates me, seeing those things reflected back at me. I'm stung by her words because it's such a ridiculous thing, but the way my face heats when she says them tells me she's right. She's right, and I hate it.

"You don't need to ascribe meaning where there is none," I

say, defensiveness rising inside me. "He helped me with something, and I just want to say thank you. That's all."

Ivy watches me, considering my words. "How will you even find him?"

"He told me the next time he'll be on the island," I lie, and I'm disgusted by how easily it rolls off my tongue.

"I don't think it's a good idea," she finally says. I'm about to argue when she speaks again. "But you clearly haven't moved on from this, and seeing him once more might give you the closure you need."

"I don't need closure," I say.

"Then why do you want to see him?"

I sigh, and Ivy wraps her arm around my shoulders, leaning her head against mine. Maybe she's right. Maybe I do need closure.

"Listen, if you want to give him a gift, give him a gift. Say whatever it is you need to say, then never see him again."

"You're making this out to be a bigger deal than it is," I say, needing the words to be true.

"I don't blame you for wanting to downplay this, but you've never had a remotely romantic situation with someone before, and that's bound to make you feel things."

"I'm not sure I'd call it romantic."

Ivy laughs. "You swam with a mainlander by the light of the moon. You don't think that's romantic?"

"I don't know. Maybe it was," I finally say. It was necessary and intense, terrifying and relieving. I don't think it was romantic, but I get what Ivy is saying.

"Which brings me back to my last point. Say thank you, then never see him again. Get the closure you need so he is no longer a distraction. That's the best you can hope for."

Hope paves the way for wanting things that were never part of the plan.

"Okay. Never again," I agree.

She studies my face, seemingly trying to figure out how serious I am, then nods as if she's satisfied.

She changes the subject, talking about the tea shop and different brews she's working on. Then, as we make our way back toward Main Street, she says, "Don't hate me."

"Oh no."

"My parents want me to make a new blend... inspired by you and Landon... called Tandon."

"Absolutely not," I say, horrified.

"I told my parents you wouldn't like it, but they insisted."

"And what would you magic it with?"

"Excitement and peace," she says. She lowers her voice and gets a mischievous look on her face. "But I'd add a drop of quiet defiance, just for you."

"Excuse me, when have I ever been defiant?"

"You're defiant every day when you quietly insist on walking the path your parents have laid out for you on your own terms. You're defiant when you're honest with Landon and when you go swimming in your nicest dresses." She pauses. "And you're definitely being defiant by making a boy named Wolfe a memory keeper."

"I never said it was a memory keeper." The spell I spoke earlier rushes back to my mind, and I blush.

"You may as well have," Ivy says, rolling her eyes.

I don't admit to it, but she knows me too well.

We walk back into the shop, and I take off my jacket and head over to the wooden island to finish Wolfe's cologne.

Dad pokes his head into the back. "I thought that was you. Honey, we're going to have to postpone our restock date—I forgot about the council dinner your mother has tonight. Can we do it tomorrow instead?"

Ivy and I exchange a quick glance before I answer, "Sure, Dad, that works."

"Great," he says, slipping back into the store and letting the door swing shut behind him.

"Tana, you can never see him again after tonight. Give him your gift, get your closure, and make sure he's on the last ferry out."

I nod. She's right, so right it makes my chest ache.

"Never," she says.

"I know."

She looks at me, head tilted to the side. "Good," she finally says. Then she gives me a quick hug and leaves.

fifteen

I arrive at the western shore a few minutes before midnight. That's how he told me to reach him: whisper his name into the wind at midnight. If he hears it, he will come.

I won't pretend to understand the way his magic works, and there's a part of me that worries he gave me false instructions just so I'd feel foolish whispering his name on the deserted beach.

And yet, when midnight arrives, I do exactly that. His name falls from my lips and drifts into the velvety black sky.

"Wolfe."

I say it only once. I'm self-conscious enough already, whispering his name while holding the memory keeper I made for him. I know the evening we spent together didn't carry the same weight for Wolfe as it did for me—he saved my life, and I will never forget it. But it also might be the only night that will ever be truly mine, a night off the path I've been walking my entire life.

I watch the waves as they roll onto the shore, and I'm suddenly overcome with an urge to rush into the sea, to call up the wind and float above the water by moonlight. I want to be cradled by the Earth's breath and invite the retreating waves back to where I stand.

I pace along the beach, trying to fight the desire that's rising within me. I stop when Wolfe's words rush back into my mind.

What should scare you most about tonight isn't that you're about to use high magic, Mortana. What should scare you most is that you're going to want to use it again.

I swallow hard and let the realization crawl beneath my skin: I want to practice dark magic again. I didn't know it until I was back on this beach, standing in the same place as before, reminded so vividly of the magic that coursed through my veins. But Wolfe was right, and it terrifies me.

I made a mistake by coming here.

I shove the memory keeper into my pocket and walk back up the beach. I hurry to the road that will lead me to the safety of my large house and dark bedroom, my mother's watchful eyes and Landon's sea glass.

The road that will lead me firmly back to the path I'm destined to walk.

I exhale when my feet leave the unstable rocky beach and touch the secure, steady pavement.

But then I hear his voice.

"Mortana?"

I tell my legs to run, to pick up speed and carry me back home, but they don't listen. I slowly turn to see Wolfe walking up the beach, following my escape route.

"You called for me." He tilts his head to the side but gives nothing away. I can't tell what he's thinking.

"I didn't mean to," I say, cringing at how ridiculous I sound. My eyes drift to the sidewalk.

He takes a step closer to me. "You didn't?"

"I mean, I did, but then I changed my mind." I need to stop talking. "I'm really sorry, but I have to go."

My legs finally respond, and I hurry down the road but stop when his hand touches mine.

"It isn't bad, you know."

I inhale and make the catastrophic mistake of meeting his eyes.

"What isn't?" I ask, already fearing his answer.

"Your pull toward high magic. I wanted you to find me again."

I tense and make my next mistake when I ask him why.

"You have an incredible gift. How could you give that up?"

I take a step back. "Because I don't want anything to do with your magic."

"Then why are you here?" he asks, echoing my words from the last time we saw each other.

I take a deep breath and reach into my pocket. "I just wanted to thank you for what you did for me."

I hand him the memory keeper and look at the clouds passing in front of the moon. I avoid his face as if he's the sun, as if looking directly at him will cause irreparable damage.

I hear him take the cap off and inhale its earthy scent. He releases a single spray into the space between us.

Memories of our night practicing dark magic fill my mind

and overwhelm my senses, the way they must be doing for Wolfe. The way they will anytime he sprays the cologne.

"It's a memory keeper," I say. "Something to remember me by." I want to make myself smaller somehow, and I wrap my arms tightly around my chest and dip my head. Maybe the gift is too much.

Maybe all of this is too much.

"Thank you," he says. I feel the energy shift in the air as he slowly reaches toward me and tips my chin up with his fingers. "But I won't need any help remembering you."

The words are intimate. Special. But he says them as if they're the vilest words he's ever spoken.

"Why are you angry?"

"Because your way of life goes against everything I stand for," he says, shoving a hand through his hair. "Your alliances make us smaller. Your compromises make us weak." He looks out over the water, shaking his head. "I *hate* you. And I want you anyway."

His words spark a flame in my core that spreads through the rest of me, devastating everything in its path. I can't see past it.

I don't *want* to see past it.

"I can't see you again." I'm shocked when the words leave my mouth, when I finally make myself say what I should have said at the very start. I'm shocked by how desperate I am to turn the words into a lie, to turn them into something that results in more nights with him.

Wolfe looks at me for a single breath. "Well, then, let's make tonight count."

He takes my hand and pulls me back to the beach, to the unstable ground where anything can happen. And even as my heart races and my mind tell me to leave, I let him.

He doesn't let go until we are far down the shoreline, ocean to my right and towering evergreens to my left. We are protected here. Safe. Invisible as the rest of the Witchery sleeps.

Wolfe pulls a single moonflower from his pocket and wraps it around my wrist by the stem. "For tradition's sake," he says.

"Where are you finding these?" I ask, looking down at the flower.

"We have them at my house, though the one I saw with you was the first I've seen beyond our gates. It's been said that the very first witch was born on this island in a field of moonflowers, hundreds of them, and that instead of reaching for her mother, the first thing she touched was a blossom. You don't practice magic only during the day because it's more palatable to the mainland; you practice magic during the day because magic is most powerful by the light of the moon. Practicing during the day automatically weakens it."

"I've never heard that," I say. My fingers tremble as they run over the white petals, not understanding how Wolfe's history of the flower is so different from my own. Not understanding why there is no pain, why my life is spared every time I encounter one. This damned flower has pulled on the thread of my life, and if everything unravels, I will know it started that night in the field when a flower fatal to witches proved to be anything but.

"Why doesn't it hurt?" I finally ask, the words so quiet. So vulnerable. I hold my breath as I wait for his reply.

"Because it isn't poisonous to witches." Wolfe's tone is impassive, but he watches me as if my response matters somehow.

"Why does my entire coven believe otherwise?"

Wolfe's jaw tenses, and he looks out over the water as if considering his words. "You should ask your mother about it," he says, and it sounds like a challenge.

"But my mother believes it's poisonous."

Wolfe exhales, a long, heavy sound that makes me nervous. "Just ask her."

"Maybe I will," I say, my fingers brushing the petals on my wrist, my stomach twisting at the thought of mentioning the flower to my mother. But something in Wolfe's tone makes me think it's important, and so I tuck the thought away for later.

"Good. Let's move on. Every living thing has its own heartbeat, its own energy that it pours into the world." Wolfe motions to a fern growing at the base of a tree, its leaves rustling in the wind. "As a witch, that energy is accessible to us, just waiting to form a connection."

He touches his fingers to the plant and closes his eyes. He takes several deep breaths, then moves away from the fern and touches the bare dirt beside it.

"Where once there was one, another." He whispers the words reverently, and a new fern grows from the dirt, full and vibrant and real.

"How did you do that?" I ask, watching in amazement. I move toward the plant, afraid it will vanish if I get much closer. I reach out and gently brush the leaves.

It stays where it is.

Wolfe touches the first plant again, then takes my hand and covers his own with it.

"Close your eyes and focus," he says. "What do you feel?"

The fire in my belly rages at his touch, but I know that's not what he's referring to. I force myself to focus on everything else, everything other than his fingers under mine.

I've worked around plants my whole life, and after several seconds of concentration, I know exactly what he's asking me. A pulsing stream of cool, clean magic waits in his hand. I feel it as clearly as the heat in my gut and the wind in my hair.

"There," he says. "That's it."

Gently, I pull the magic from him. I don't know why I think to do it, how I even know it's possible, but it feels natural to me.

"Where once there was one, another." I take the fern's heartbeat and plant it in the earth.

Another fern grows before us.

I plant more and more of them, watching them sprout from the dirt one after the other. I want to plant hundreds, thousands of them, my own secret meadow I can go to whenever I want.

Another, another, another.

I laugh, utterly delighted by the feel of the plant's energy wrapped up in my own.

It isn't like this with low magic. We add our magic to what already exists: perfume, tea leaves, makeup, dough. But this tangling of my magic with the fern, with the wind and the sea the last time I saw Wolfe—it's intoxicating.

It's how it's meant to be.

As soon as I think it, I scramble to undo it, but it's too late. The thought settles, taking root in my mind like the ferns that surround me.

"Thank you for teaching me," I say. "I'm glad I got to experience this."

"Is that all you want to do tonight?"

I can feel the magic waking in my body, stirring, wanting more. But that is a dangerous feeling.

"Yes."

Wolfe nods. "Then you're welcome."

We walk back toward the main beach, out of the cover of the trees, and I try to ignore the sinking feeling in my stomach.

Then every part of me freezes with panic. Mrs. Wright is walking along the beach, humming to herself, her dog a few yards in front of her. She's on the council with my mother, and I stare in horror as she gets closer. A cloud drifts in front of the moon, shrouding Wolfe and me in darkness.

But soon she will see us.

Suddenly, my body takes over. I sense the breeze over the sea and latch on to it, building it up until it's a strong wind. I send it barreling off the water, sea spray suspended in the air, covering the beach in a hazy mist that moves straight toward Mrs. Wright.

"A breeze to a gale, fresh off the sea, more distance is needed, walk away from me." I frantically whisper the words under my breath over and over, hoping they're enough.

"Oh my," Mrs. Wright says, so close I can hear her.

A few more steps and she'll see us.

I kick up more wind, ready to send her way, but Wolfe collides with me, sending us flying into a thicket of long grass and overgrown shrubs. He lands right on top of me.

"What was that?" I hear Mrs. Wright say. Her dog runs over, sniffing at the grass, but as soon as it gets here, it whines and runs away. Wolfe holds a finger to his lips, and I can feel his chest expanding against my own, our breaths tangling in the space between us.

I push one more strong gust of wind her way, and it's enough to send Mrs. Wright back the way she came. I hear her muttering about unpredictable weather, and then her voice fades to nothing.

My heart beats against my ribs so violently I'm afraid it might break free.

Wolfe is still on top of me, making it hard to breathe.

The clouds continue their march across the sky, and the moon comes out of hiding once again. It pours its pale blue light over Wolfe, over his disheveled hair and gray eyes, illuminating his expression. Illuminating the way his gaze finds my lips.

All I can think about is closing the space between us. I want to know what he feels like; I want to know how he tastes. I want to know all these things that are forbidden to me.

I almost do it. I almost close my eyes and touch my lips to his, but then I think of my parents' expectations and Landon's sea glass, my ancestors' sacrifices and Ivy's belief in me.

And I can't do it.

I want it more than I've maybe ever wanted anything, but I can't do it.

I clear my throat and roll to the side, but I don't stand up. Instead, I stay on my back and look up at the stars.

Wolfe does the same.

"You're not going to like what I'm about to tell you." I turn to him, but he doesn't look at me. He keeps his eyes on the waxing moon, on the sparkling starlight.

"What is it?" I ask, terrified of what he might say. I think about my early days in the perfumery, infusing feelings into scents. I never had to work at it. And I think about how nothing, not even making perfumes, has ever come as easily to me as pulling the wind from the sea.

"What you just did is impossible for a witch of the new order. You shouldn't have been able to do it." He pauses. "Do you know what that tells me?"

I'm silent. I don't move, don't breathe, don't blink. I wait for his answer, afraid it might shatter my whole world.

"You're practicing the wrong magic."

And I'm right. It does.

sixteen

Main Street is bustling with tourists, a sea of scarves blowing in the autumn breeze and gloved hands holding warm beverages. The maples are changing, the green and yellow leaves morphing into shades of deep orange and bloodred. The cobbles are wet from the recent rain, but today is clear and bright, and the sunlight catches the raindrops that rest on the foliage and vines.

Ivy's arm is looped through mine, and we follow my mother as she weaves her way through the tourists. I love seeing the paper bags dangling from their hands, seeing the way our island is thriving, the way our magic is being appreciated. I'm scared by how easily it could fall apart.

You're practicing the wrong magic.

I shake my head and banish the words. The right magic is the magic that protects us. That lets us live freely and openly. That guarantees the safety of our children.

"Hey, where are you?" Ivy asks, bringing me back to the present.

"Sorry, I'm here."

Ivy rolls her eyes. "Give my regards to Wolfe."

"Ivy!" I say, hoping I sound harsh. "Don't say his name anywhere near my mother. And I wasn't thinking about him."

"Whatever you say. Just..." She slows her steps, distancing us from my mom.

I look at her. "Say what you need to say."

"This is your heart on the line, Tana. I just want you to be careful." She doesn't start walking again after she says it. Instead, she swallows and twists her hands.

"And?"

"And it's Landon's heart, too." The words are so quiet I have to lean in to hear them.

"I don't know about that," I say under my breath, then instantly regret the words.

"What do you mean?"

I shake my head and start walking again, but Ivy stops me. "Forget I said anything. It doesn't matter."

"It matters to me."

"It's just something he said about duty mattering more than anything else. He said he couldn't promise me love."

"Did you ask for that?"

"No, of course not," I say. "I just asked that he be open to it. I guess I always thought that once we began our courtship, there would be a spark." I shrug. "I realize how silly that sounds now."

My mother is far ahead of us, and we start walking again, Ivy's arm looped through mine once more.

"It isn't silly. I don't know how anyone could spend an extended amount of time with you and not fall completely in love. He'll be a fool for you one day; just give it time."

I smile at the words, but my stomach is tight, because as much as I want to believe her, I don't think I do. I squeeze her arm; the weight of her next to me feels good, anchoring me to this world and this magic and this life. She's trying to protect me, and I'm grateful for it. We all need protection at some point, and I think this is mine.

Because sometimes, in the middle of the night when the Witchery is sleeping, I feel myself slipping away. Slipping away to darker magic and broken rules, to the western shore and a boy who's sharp and beautiful, like raw crystal pulled from the earth.

And I don't want to slip away. So I cling to Ivy a little tighter than necessary as we catch up to my mother.

"Ready, girls?" she asks, stopping in front of Ms. Talbot's dress shop.

"Let's find a dress," I reply. My mother nods in approval, then sweeps into Satin & Silk like the autumn breeze down Main Street.

"Hello, Ms. Talbot," she says. We have the shop to ourselves. Mom set up a private appointment so that she, Ivy, Ms. Talbot, and me would be the only people to see the dress before the ball. It seems a little excessive to me, but I'm happy to go along with it. I've been looking forward to the ball my whole life.

Every witch has their own ball the night of their twentieth birthday because it is the individual that makes our coven strong.

With each witch who renounces dark magic and commits them-self to the new order, we get stronger. We get more stable. We get closer to the life we're striving for.

And my ball will seal that life with the announcement of my engagement to Landon.

My mother is right: I need the perfect dress.

"Well, Tana, this is very exciting indeed," Ms. Talbot says as she brings out a pot of tea and three teacups.

We sit down on an ivory tufted sofa that faces a raised platform with a wall of mirrors on the other side. The room is immaculate and bright, and sunlight streams in through the floor-to-ceiling windows, making the gilded mirrors glisten.

"What are you looking for, dear?" Ms. Talbot asks, standing in front of me.

My mother begins speaking, but I cut her off. "I'd like some-thing the color of the ocean," I say. "As if I were born of the sea. Train in the back. No lace or frills. I want to look dramatic. Alluring."

"Tana, don't you want something a little brighter? Softer?"

"No."

My mother takes a sip of her tea. "Very well. That sounds lovely."

Ms. Talbot claps her hands, then rushes to the back for fabric samples.

My mind wanders as Ivy and my mom begin talking about Ivy's ball, which will be just a few months after mine. Their conver-sation is easy and smooth—they get excited about the same things and emphasize the same words. They are both such perfect prod-ucts of their environment, put together and warm and powerful.

Wolfe is wrong about low magic. He's wrong that we're cowards and a disgrace to witches. He thinks we're weak because he can't see past his narrow definition of strength.

Strength is shrouding ourselves in a veil of passivity to save the people we love.

Strength is allowing the mainlanders to see our vulnerabilities in order to be accepted.

Strength is swallowing our words when people like Wolfe dare to label us as weak.

I shake my head. God, he's infuriating.

I huff and cross my arms, wanting nothing more than to storm to the western shore and tell him off.

"Tana?" my mother asks, her teacup raised halfway to her mouth.

"Sorry. What did you say?"

She shakes her head and puts her cup down on its saucer, the porcelain rattling. "What is going on with you lately? You're unfocused and aloof. I need you to *be* here, Tana. This is important."

"I'm sorry, Mom. I've just been tired."

She looks at me for a moment, studying my face before finally nodding. "Well, try to get to bed early tonight. We can stop at the Enchanted Cup on the way home and get some of their Sleepful blend."

"That would be nice."

"Ivy, why don't you tell me more about your Covenant plans?" My mother picks up her teacup again and looks at Ivy.

Sometimes I think Ivy is the daughter my mother wishes she had. I don't resent Ivy for it—not at all. If anything, I wish I could be more like her. I have this incredible role to play, and I know I'm doing a poor job of it.

Ivy would be better, and we all know it. But my last name means it is my responsibility, as if a name makes a difference.

The thought startles me. It does matter... doesn't it? When did I start questioning these traditions and values that are pillars of our coven?

But I know the answer: it was the moment I touched the moonflower and it didn't hurt. It was the evening I practiced a magic I was never meant to encounter, and it makes me angry, enraged that I've allowed a single person to plant these ideas in my mind. As I raise my teacup to my lips, I notice the porcelain is trembling in my hand. I quickly put it down, but it's too hard, and it slams into the saucer on the table.

"Tana, be careful!" my mother exclaims. She looks mortified, even though Ms. Talbot is still in the back. "Your behavior is troubling. Please pull yourself together." She shakes her head. "I certainly hope Landon has recovered from his autumnal swim with you. Honestly, Tana, what were you thinking?"

"There was nothing to recover from," I say. "It was his idea."

"Here we are!" Ms. Talbot singsongs as she comes out of the back with folds of fabric draped over her arms. All of them are shades of blue, deep navy and cerulean, stone and azure. The fabric shimmers in the light like the sea beneath a full moon, and I sit up in my seat and reach toward the silk.

"Oh, Shawna, this is gorgeous," my mother says, pulling a piece of fabric from Ms. Talbot.

"That's the one I like best, too," I say. It's the stone silk, a blue-gray fabric that could be mistaken for foaming waves. Mom meets my eyes, a warm smile spreading across her face. "It will look perfect on you," she says, and it somehow fills all the empty spaces inside me.

She's proud of me. I know it even when I set my teacup down too hard and when my mind is elsewhere. I feel it radiating from her, and I wish I were at the perfumery so I could bottle it up in one of our scents, spray it in the air when I need a reminder.

"Tana, that color was made for you," Ivy says.

Ms. Talbot beckons me to the platform and begins taking my measurements. She wears narrow wire-rimmed glasses, and her brown skin is pulled taut at her forehead by the sleek bun atop her head. She bites her lip as she measures, writes down the numbers, then measures again. The dress will be cinched at the chest and will flow down from the waist, but there will be no crinoline or extra fabric beneath the silk. It will trail behind me, and I will glisten just like the water.

I've never had anything like it, such a far cry from the pastels and soft colors of the Witchery. I can't wait to wear it.

My mom comes up behind me and places a gemstone necklace around my neck, heavy with the weight of a dozen sapphires.

My hand drifts up to the necklace, but as I look at myself in the mirror, it doesn't feel right.

"I was hoping I could wear your pearls," I say.

I see the surprised look on my mother's face, followed by the small smile that tugs at her lips. She swallows and pulls the necklace away.

"Of course you may," she says, her eyes meeting mine in the mirror.

When Ms. Talbot is done with my measurements, she tells us to come back in two weeks for my first dress fitting. We finish our tea and walk out onto Main, not as busy now that it's later. The days are getting shorter, and most of the shops have lanterns lit outside that cast a warm amber glow over the cracked stone and climbing vines.

"Why don't I take you girls out to dinner?" my mother asks, pulling Ivy and me in close.

"Just the three of us?" I ask. We eat dinner with Dad almost every night; I don't think Mom has ever taken me out to dinner with a friend.

"Just the three of us."

"I'm free," Ivy says, and I lean into them.

"Sounds perfect."

There are moments when I think I'll be crushed by the weight of expectation and responsibility, when I worry I will never live up to the role I'm meant to play. But then there are moments when I look around the Witchery, at my parents and friends, and I'm filled with a deep pride that runs beneath my skin, nourishing every part of me.

Now is one of those times.

We don't talk about Landon over dinner. We don't talk about the mainland or the Covenant Ball or the proper etiquette when hosting a distinguished visitor. We talk about the small, inconsequential details that make up our lives on this tiny island.

And it's everything.

seventeen

I haven't slept well since my date with Landon, preoccupied with things I shouldn't give space to. I'm frustrated by my lack of understanding and the incessant questions that hammer my mind. I wish I could let the moonflower go, let high magic and Wolfe Hawthorne be carried away by a vicious current, never to be seen again. But I can't, and I'm so angry at myself for that.

Once my parents settle in with their evening tea, I find my harvesting basket and slip outside. I need to clear my head, and I follow the shoreline to the western edge, to the wild coast where I won't be disturbed. I still haven't asked my mother about the moonflower, and I know I need to, that I need to put this to rest. But ever since that first night I met Wolfe in the field, an awful feeling has settled in my stomach; this could change everything, and in some ways, maybe it already has. But I'm trying so hard to stay in control of my life, and I think not asking is my way of doing that, of clinging to the way things were before I missed the rush.

Wolfe would call me a coward. Maybe he's right.

The perfumery is low on violet and narcissus, and I head to the trails where I know I can find more. It's a calm evening, a beautiful twilight settling over the island, and I hum to myself as I fill my basket with flowers. I start imagining the different perfumes I can make, what combinations I'll use and what kind of magic I'll infuse them with. I make perfumes most days, and I never tire of it, never get bored or restless. Using magic for my hair and makeup is nothing more than a convenience for me, but when I'm in the back room of the perfumery, finding the perfect blend of fragrance and magic, I feel completely at home in myself.

At least I did until I met Wolfe. Now I have to ignore a part of my magic that urges me to use more, and I will never forgive him if my low magic no longer feels like enough. I will never get over it.

My basket is overflowing, and instead of heading north, back the way I came, I walk farther south. The southwestern part of the island is heavily wooded, and as I walk through the trees, I start to wonder if maybe there is a home among them, protected by magic. It feels impossible; I've explored every part of this island many times over, and yet I'm learning that there is an abundance of impossibilities that are anything but.

I scan the woods, searching for any clues that point to human life—gardens or smoke or gates that might confirm the things I don't want to believe. If there is a home on this island that none of us know about, it would be in this area, farthest from the houses and shops of the new coven. But I see nothing.

The sky gets darker as I move deeper into the trees, and I

suddenly realize how far from home I've walked. I turn to leave when I hear a branch break in the distance.

I squint into the darkness, but all I see are the shadows of evergreens.

"Who's there?" a voice asks, and I recognize it instantly.

I don't know what comes over me, but I turn the other direction and run, not wanting him to see me. Not wanting him to know I was looking for signs of a magical house or forgotten coven.

It's so dark now, I can barely see where I'm going. My foot catches on an exposed root, and I fall to the earth hard. My basket lands several feet away from me, the flowers scattered across the forest floor.

For a moment, it's painfully quiet.

"Mortana?"

I look up, and Wolfe is standing over me. I try to respond but can't find the words.

"What are you doing out here?" he asks. He offers me his hand, and I slowly take it, ignoring the jolt that moves through me when I do.

"I got lost," I say, getting to my feet, unwilling to meet his eyes.

"You got lost? On this small island where you've spent your entire life?" I'm looking at the ground, but I can hear the mockery in his tone, can imagine the smirk on his face.

"It's dark out," I say weakly.

I walk to my basket and start filling it with my spilled flowers, and Wolfe bends over to help me. When I've retrieved everything I can see, I stand back up.

"Are you hurt?" Wolfe asks.

"No."

He doesn't respond and instead starts walking, picking herbs and plants and adding them to my basket. I follow him slowly, my chest aching as I see the care he takes with each and every plant, the way he gently removes them from the earth and sets them in my basket as if they're glass that might shatter at any moment.

It's difficult to see, but something stains his fingers. I stop and take his hand, pulling it close to my face. "You're bleeding."

"It isn't blood," he says, watching me. "I was painting."

"You paint?"

"Yes." The word is tense, as if he has admitted to something he meant to keep hidden.

"What do you paint?"

Wolfe starts walking again, and I follow behind him. "People, mostly."

"Your coven?"

"Yes, my coven."

"Why?" I ask, wanting him to keep talking, to keep sharing this part of himself with me.

"Because if I don't, how will we be remembered?"

The words take my breath away, the raw honesty of them. I want to say something to ease the anger in his voice, the pain, but there is nothing. My coven doesn't know his exists, a hidden life concealed in magic and the shadows of the trees.

"I will remember."

Wolfe turns to me, putting some cedar in my basket. "And

will you tell your mother? Your future husband? Or am I a secret you will carry to your grave?"

"I—" I stop myself because the answer hurts too much to say out loud. I stare at him, more shadow than person in the dense forest. He knows I can't tell anyone, that our protection and his depends upon the mainland believing that dark magic is gone. But it's a painful truth, one that will claw at my chest for the rest of my life.

I'm stunned when his fingers find my face, gently trailing over my cheek and tucking a piece of hair behind my ear. "That's what I thought."

He turns without another word, but I'm stuck in place, my hand coming to rest where his fingers were just moments ago.

"I need to get home," I finally say, forcing myself to move.

Wolfe slows, putting a narcissus stem in my basket. "What are you really doing out here?" he asks, ignoring my comment entirely.

I turn and follow the sound of the waves, wanting to get to the shoreline, where the moonlight will illuminate my way home. Wolfe falls into step beside me. I don't respond until I've reached the beach and breathed in the salt air, letting it calm me from the inside out.

Finally, I turn to Wolfe.

"I came out to harvest and started thinking about our conversation, and I don't know. I think I subconsciously went searching for proof that what you've told me is true."

"You don't believe me?"

"I didn't say that."

"Then why would you be looking for proof?"

I take a deep breath. "Because I don't want to believe you." I walk closer to the water and sit on the sand, tired and embarrassed and confused.

"Why not?"

"Because it's easier than the alternative."

"And did you find any proof?" he asks, sitting on the ground next to me. His tone gives nothing away, but there's a softness to him that I haven't felt before, and I don't understand why. Maybe he can see all the threads he's torn loose from me.

"Well, I found you. Either you're following me, or you have a magical house on this island that I got a little too close to."

"I'm not following you," he says.

I pause. "I know. So how does it work? How did you know I was out here?"

Wolfe shifts next to me, and I realize he's uncomfortable too, not knowing if he can trust me. Not knowing if he has shared too much or if I'll go home and tell my mother everything I've learned.

"There is a spell on the house that can sense heat signatures in the woods surrounding it. It was originally used to alert the witches to nearby animals. Before their crops began yielding food, the witches needed to eat. We now use it as a kind of security system."

As he speaks, the anger inside me grows, but it's more than that. It's sadness that this place I have loved with every part of me has kept secrets so large they threaten to break everything my coven has worked so hard to build.

"If you hadn't been there to stop me, would I have eventually bumped into your home?"

"No. The magic would keep you walking in a loop through the forest." He watches me as he answers.

"I hate that you have an explanation for everything," I say, but I think what I really mean is that I hate that I believe what he says. I hate that his words have made me ask questions I've never thought to ask.

"I hate that you require so many," he says, and I think what he really means is that he hates that we don't know about the life he lives, as if it isn't *worth* knowing about.

And I don't know what to say, because part of me wishes I didn't know. Part of me wishes I could go back to before the rush and erase everything that came after, because I'm so scared of learning more.

So scared of asking all the questions I want to ask.

So scared.

But past the fear, past the worries and doubts and uncertainty, is the undeniable truth that I want to know him. I want to know what keeps him up at night, the thoughts that pull at his mind, the reason his edges are sharp and his words are tense.

And the thing that makes my eyes burn, that makes my throat ache with the truth of it, is that I want to know Wolfe Hawthorne more than I've ever wanted to know anything in my entire life. And it's devastating.

"Tell me what you're thinking," he says.

I should lie to him, answer with something mundane, but he

has somehow slipped into the cracks in my foundation, he and the moonflower and his magic, slowly breaking it apart.

"You might be the worst thing that's ever happened to me," I say, scared to meet his eyes, scared even to look in his direction.

He exhales, picks up a stone from the beach and tosses it into the waves. "I know that."

"Then why? Why tell me you want to see me again? Why come find me in the woods when you easily could have let me be?"

He turns to me but doesn't speak until I finally look at him, a decision I instantly regret. "Because I'm selfish, and when I see you practice my magic, the world makes sense."

I want to yell at him, tell him how unfair he's being, how incredibly cruel this is. But more than anything, I want to whisper that on those nights, practicing his magic by the light of the moon, my world made sense, too.

It made sense, even as it was torn apart.

eighteen

A week later, Ivy comes over to stay the night. We haven't had a sleepover in so long, and after laughing with her in my room and whispering about things that have nothing to do with benign flowers or dark magic, I'm feeling like myself again. My parents are downstairs, drinking wine in front of the fire. It's dark outside, and the lights in my room are dim.

We're sprawled out on my bed with a bowl of popcorn between us.

"We've already had dozens of preorders for our Tandon tea, by the way," Ivy says.

"Seriously? Who's actually ordering that?"

"Witches on this island who are finally breathing again after years of holding their breath." The words are serious, and I prop myself up on my elbow.

"That's nice," I say, my tone softening. And it is nice. I feel good knowing my relationship with Landon is bringing peace to a coven that was founded on fear.

"Should I put you down for a large bag?"

I laugh. "Sure," I say. "How's the shop doing, anyway?"

"Great. My parents are teaching me more and more. They expect me to be running it by next year. I have a ton of ideas for how to build our business and create more opportunities."

"If you create a wedding tea, I'm going to revolt."

"I will *obviously* be creating a wedding tea, and it will have a ridiculous name like With This Tea, Tandon Weds."

I choke on a piece of popcorn. "The name needs work."

"I've got time."

"Seriously, though, I'm happy for you. The shop will thrive under your management."

"I know," Ivy says with a smile. It isn't arrogance—she knows her strengths and isn't willing to downplay them for the sake of appearances.

It's one of the things I love most about her.

"I've been thinking," Ivy says, rolling onto her side to face me. Her tone shifts, more serious now. "How you met Wolfe doesn't make sense."

A knot forms in my stomach, and my palms begin to sweat. "Do we have to talk about him?"

"No, not for long. I'm just curious how it happened. The mainlanders keep a tally of the visitors who come here each day to ensure everyone returns in the evening. They would have known someone missed the boat and alerted your mom."

The knot gets tighter. Ivy is my best friend, and I want to share this with her. And maybe sharing something with Ivy will ease the worry in my mind demanding that I talk to my mother. Maybe it will help me move on.

I take a breath, deciding I don't owe it to Wolfe to keep his secrets. At least not from Ivy. "I wasn't totally honest with you. I didn't want to scare you, and I was caught off guard by the whole thing." I look at her, but her expression gives nothing away. "He's a witch," I say carefully.

"What family is he from? I've never heard that name before."

I war with myself, knowing that telling this secret could change everything. Our coven believes the old witches are gone, that dark magic is obsolete. I don't know what would happen if people knew the truth. But I also don't want to carry this alone.

"You have to swear you won't say anything," I finally say.

Ivy sits up. "Why?"

"Swear it."

"I swear," she says, her voice uneasy.

I sit up, too, so we're on the same level. "He's a witch from the old coven."

Ivy laughs, exhaling loudly. "You had me worried for a second," she says, lying back down on the bed.

I grab her arm and gently pull her up again. I look her in the eye. "I'm serious, Ivy. The old coven still exists. It's small, but it exists. Wolfe is one of them."

The smile falls from Ivy's lips, and her skin turns ashen. "It's not possible."

"That's what I thought, too, but he proved it."

"How?"

I pause and look down. I can never unsay what I'm about to tell her. "He proved it with magic."

Her mouth drops open and she shakes her head, back and forth and back and forth. "But that means…"

I nod.

"Dark magic?" she says, her voice trembling.

"Well, technically it's called high magic. But yes."

Ivy looks at me as if I'm a stranger, as if we've never met. My heart breaks when I see the betrayal in her eyes.

"And you let him show you? You let him get away with it? We have to tell your mom," she says, pushing herself off the bed.

I grab her arm. "Ivy, no! Please," I beg. "Please just listen."

Ivy looks toward my door, and it's clear that she's torn. Finally, her shoulders relax slightly, and she sits down on the bed.

"It isn't… it isn't evil," I say, choosing my words carefully. "What he showed me. It's based on a connection with the Earth. It's natural."

Ivy stares at me. "It's *dangerous*."

"No," I say, willing her to understand. "I thought so, too, but it wasn't harmful or anything to be afraid of."

Ivy's face is pinched like she ate something sour. "I can understand you having a rendezvous with a boy on a beach, but this? Do you hear yourself? How do you know he isn't using his magic on your mind? How do you know he hasn't charmed you to speak this way?"

"Of course he hasn't," I say before I even have time to think.

He wouldn't.

Would he?

"He saved my life," I say when Ivy doesn't respond.

"What do you mean?"

I sink lower on the bed. "I missed the rush. It was an accident, and Wolfe helped me expel my excess magic so I wouldn't die."

"You *what*?"

"I know, I shouldn't have missed it. But I did, and the only reason I'm still here is because Wolfe helped me."

"But your life is tainted now," Ivy says.

I look at her in disbelief. "At least I'm alive," I counter, my voice rising. "Would you rather I be dead?"

Ivy doesn't respond right away, and it hurts to see her examining the question, trying to find an answer that won't tear us apart. But then she shakes her head slowly. She won't say it out loud, won't dare put voice to it, but it's enough.

I need to show Ivy, make her understand that my life isn't tainted, that what we've been taught to believe isn't accurate. She knows me better than anyone, and I know I can trust her with this. "Let me show you something," I say, pulling her off the bed.

We walk down the back staircase. My parents are still talking in the living room, and I quietly open the back door and lead Ivy outside.

Our lawn is perfectly manicured, a vibrant green circle surrounded by plants and shrubs. Several ferns grow along the base of a maple tree.

"What are we doing out here, Tana?" Ivy asks. Her voice is wary, but I know I can make her understand.

My hands are in my pockets, and when I pull them out, several petals from the moonflower I forgot about are in my palm, remnants from when I gave Wolfe the memory keeper. "See these?" I say, holding them out to Ivy. "These are petals from a moonflower, but I'm able to touch them. They aren't hurting me; why aren't they hurting?" I walk over to a fern and brush my fingers against the rough leaves, close my eyes until the magic inside me recognizes the energy of the plant. It flows to me freely, and I gently take it and tuck it in the dirt close by, whispering the words I used with Wolfe on the beach. Another fern sprouts.

"How could this be dangerous? Isn't this the most natural expression of magic—working with the Earth instead of harming it?"

Ivy's hand drifts to her mouth, and she takes a step away from me. Her eyes are wild, and she stares at the fern before her. "You used dark magic." The words are so quiet, and she says them as if they're a terminal diagnosis, as if she's preparing herself to lose me. It was one thing when she thought Wolfe had used dark magic to save me; it's another thing entirely to know that I've used it, too.

I take a step closer to her. "Don't you see? There's nothing evil about it. Even the way I reach him is beautiful: I say his name at midnight, and if he hears it, he comes."

"That isn't the point, Tana. Of course there's nothing evil about bringing another fern into existence or saying a name at midnight. But the magic that created that fern and enables you to contact Wolfe is the same magic that heals what should not be healed and summons spirits and plays the role of God." Her voice shakes, red-hot fury pouring from her. "It *is* evil, and our ancestors realized that as soon as they gave it up. It poisons you from the inside out. Why do you think we've been able to sustain the new order for so long? It's because we know now that dark magic is rotten. If you think it won't eat you alive, you're a fool." Ivy practically spits the words. "This is the same magic that got our ancestors killed, Tana. If you need a reminder, I'm happy to walk you down to the docks right now so you can stare at the charred planks until you remember that the kind of magic you just displayed almost eradicated us entirely. How have you lost sight of that?"

She glares at me, and I don't know what to say. She's right, but I can't make myself believe it the way I used to. It's heartbreaking to realize I'm doubting things I've never before doubted. I want to believe in our magic. And I do.

But I also believe in the magic I practiced with Wolfe.

I feel as if I'm on my knees, crying out to God about the beauty of the devil.

"I don't know," I finally say.

"It's him," she says. "Wolfe."

I look at the ground, at the fern that just appeared. I want to hate it, to tear it from the earth and toss it far away. I want to be appalled by what I just did, to repent and do better.

I want to be better.

"Tana," Ivy says, my name catching on a sob. I look up and see my best friend's eyes filled with tears for me. "Is he really worth it?"

I want to yell, scream at her that it isn't about him. It's about magic, about what we're giving up to live this life. It's about being told a flower is deadly only to realize it's just a flower, the same as all the others. But even as I think it, Ivy's words settle deep inside me, and I know she's right.

He isn't worth it.

His magic isn't worth it.

I love my life. I love my parents and Ivy and the Witchery. I know my marriage to Landon will be fulfilling in ways I can't even imagine. But Wolfe blew into my life like a tornado, uprooting everything. Destructive and dangerous.

I see that now.

My face falls and my eyes fill with tears. I look down at the white petals in my hand and shove them back into my pocket.

"No," I say. "I'm sorry, Ivy. I'm so sorry."

She watches me for several breaths, and then all the anger melts away and she pulls me into her arms. I hug her back fiercely, so tight, telling myself that this is why the witches before me sacrificed so much. This is why we adhere to the new order and practice low magic.

Ivy is everything to me. I would marry Landon and move across the Passage even if it only protected her, not this entire coven, this whole island.

"I'm sorry," I say again, pulling away and wiping my eyes. "I don't know what I was thinking."

"You wanted something that was yours," she says simply.

I nod. Maybe that is all it was—wanting something solely my own before I bind myself to my coven and marry the man my parents chose for me.

When she puts it like that, it sounds understandable. Reasonable, even.

We walk inside and back up the stairs, and I close my bedroom door behind us. We finish the popcorn and laugh and talk, and I marvel at how easily we fall back into this. Nothing, not even dark magic, can pull us apart.

But while Ivy sleeps soundly beside me, my mind races. It cannot find a place of rest.

"Mortana?"

I lift my head. It sounds like someone is whispering my name. I listen intently, but all I hear is Ivy's even breathing.

I lie back down and close my eyes.

"Mortana?"

My eyes snap open, and I squint into the darkness. There is only one person who uses my full name. When I hear it a third time, I understand what's happening: Wolfe is using his magic, inviting me to the beach.

I lay my head down and force my eyes shut, but even as I do, hot anger blooms in my chest and rises up my neck. My eyes burn, and it hurts to swallow.

He isn't worth it, and I hate that he has put me in this situation, made me question all the things I love.

He says my name one last time before giving up.

Good. I hope he never says my name again.

As soon as I think it, a tear slips down my cheek and drops onto my pillow. I wipe it away, take a deep breath, and try to find sleep.

nineteen

Seven nights. For seven nights, Wolfe tries to reach me, whispering my name on the wind at midnight, beckoning me to the western shore. And every whisper kindles the fire of anger inside me, spreading it through my chest and into my arms, up my neck and over my skin.

All-consuming.

When he says my name tonight, I'm ready. I sneak out of the house and down the empty street, dodging the golden glow of the lanterns above me. I don't stop running until I reach the edge of the island, where Wolfe's back is bathed in moonlight.

It's almost a full moon again.

"What do you want?" I say the words before he even turns around, letting my anger sharpen them.

He twists to face me.

"I want you to stop telling your friends about me."

I stop walking. "Excuse me?"

"There are wind chimes at my home, and their only purpose is to sound when we're in danger of being found out. They went off last week for the first time in years."

"You're *spying* on us?" My anger flares as I take a step toward him. I can't believe I let myself get mixed up with someone like him.

"We can't hear conversations. The wind chimes are magicked, and when certain words or phrases are used, they sound. We can only hear the chimes, not what was said. Regardless, they haven't gone off in years, which leads me to believe you're what set them off. So, once again, stop talking about me."

Embarrassment mixes with anger, which is a terrible combination. I combust.

"I will tell every single witch on this island that you exist if you don't leave me alone."

"I wouldn't have called to you if the chimes hadn't gone off. If you want me to leave you alone, stop talking about me. Stop thinking about me. Stop making me gifts and using my magic as if it's your destiny."

Heat infiltrates my head and clouds my mind, making it hard to think. "I have a destiny, and it has *nothing* to do with your magic."

He steps toward me. "You really think you're fated for the governor's son?"

Sand sprays his chest and face before I even decide to kick the beach. He steps back and wipes at his eyes, a heavy silence falling between us.

The ocean's constant roar isn't enough to cover up the beating of my heart.

"I'm sorry," I say, shocked by my actions. "I didn't mean to get you."

He spits sand from his mouth and blinks several times.

"Don't apologize," he says, his voice stern. "You apologize too much."

"You don't apologize enough," I say.

I can see my breath in the cold autumn air. Wolfe stands so close to me that it touches his face before vanishing.

"What do I have to apologize for?" His tone is challenging and arrogant, and it reignites my anger.

"Everything," I say, gesturing to the ocean as if he'll understand. "You made me miss the rush, forcing me—"

"I saved your life," he says, cutting me off.

"I was forced to use your dark magic and keep seeing you—"

"So we're back to calling it dark magic now?"

"Stop interrupting me!" I scream, momentarily forgetting that no one can know I'm here. The piercing words echo for a breath before being swallowed by the sea. "I was happy before you came along." I can't help the tears that burn my eyes and spill over my lashes. "I was happy."

"You were ignorant."

"What did you say?"

"I said, you were ignorant." Wolfe shakes his head and looks out into the distance, and even though my vision is blurred, I can see how good he looks drenched in moonlight. It doesn't matter; he is nothing to me. He can't be.

"We have the same history. The same stories. The fact that

I chose a different life after hearing all the information doesn't make me ignorant," I say, taking a deep breath and drying my eyes.

"You haven't heard all the information. That's what I'm trying to tell you."

"What are you talking about?" I ask, exasperated.

Wolfe watches me as if he can't decide whether he wants to continue down this path or not, whether he wants to say what's on his mind. I don't move my eyes off his, daring him to speak.

"The moonflower," he finally says. "Have you asked your mother about it?"

"No," I say as a chill moves through the air. I shiver.

"Why not?"

"I know this might be difficult for you to understand, but I don't just sit at home and think about you. I have things going on, big things, and it hasn't crossed my mind."

What I don't tell him is that I have thought about the moonflower many times, but I haven't had the courage to ask my mother about it.

"See, that's the problem!" Wolfe shouts, walking away from me and toward the water. "It should cross your mind every second of every day. You should demand to know the truth. Don't you care at all about that?"

"You know what I care about? Protecting the people I love. Practicing magic out in the open without fear of being killed for it. Seeing this island thrive and knowing our children will have safe and happy lives. I don't care if those things seem foolish or silly to you, Wolfe. I don't. While you're being selfish, putting us all in jeopardy because you don't know what it is to sacrifice, I'm out there putting in the work to protect this island, and that includes you."

"I sacrifice *everything* for this life. I live in a manor covered in a veil of magic, completely invisible to the outside world. I have to travel by water because I can't risk being recognized. I grow my own food that's threatened every day by your currents eating away at my shoreline. I'm desperately clinging to a life you've all decided isn't worth living, and it's hard."

His voice is getting stronger, but it isn't his usual anger. That's there, of course, but there's also a sadness laced into his tone, and it takes my breath away. Devastating.

"No one asked you to do that," I say gently.

"Exactly. No one asked because no one cared to preserve my way of life."

"No, that's where you're wrong. No one asked because no one was willing to die for it."

We watch each other, the tension between us beginning to ease, melting away like snow in the spring. He believes in his life so fiercely he would do absolutely anything for it, same as I believe in mine. For the first time, I realize how similar we are, and I can no longer be angry at him.

He is willing to die for something the rest of us have decided is evil. I wish there was something I could say that would ease his hurt somehow, but there is nothing.

"I was so angry at you when I came here tonight," I say.

"Why?" He takes a deep breath and exhales slowly, as if trying to rid himself of the pain he has shown me.

"Because I blame you for making me question a life I've never before questioned."

"Questions are good, Mortana."

"I know that. And I know it isn't your fault if my choices don't hold up under scrutiny."

He nods and stares out over the ocean. It's the first time I've seen him look tired, utterly spent after showing so much of himself. I want to reach out and touch him, let him collapse in my arms and rest, but he could never find peace there. Not when my last name is Fairchild.

Then I'm struck by an idea, a wild and ridiculous idea he'll probably never agree to, but I want to try.

"Will you do something for me?"

"It depends on what it is."

"You've shown me your magic several times now; I want to show you mine. Will you make a perfume with me?"

"Why would I do that?"

"Because I'm asking nicely?" I say, inviting lightness into my voice, trying to ease the burden of our previous conversation. Trying to ease something in both of us.

"There are moments when I think I might understand you better than I've ever understood another person, and then you suggest something as absurd as making a perfume together, and I'm sure you're the most baffling creature I've ever laid eyes on."

"I'm going to take that as a compliment," I say.

"If you insist."

"Please do this with me. It would mean a lot."

Wolfe watches me, and I can tell he doesn't want to do it, doesn't want to sink to the level of low magic. But then he takes a deep breath and I know I've won.

"Fine. One perfume."

We walk through the woods to the east of the shore, gathering wildflowers, leaves, and herbs. And as we do, we talk. Not about magic or the mainland or sacrifice, but about life, simple daily things we have never spoken about before. He tells me about the manor he lives in, a large home that's located near where he found me in the woods, hidden with magic. He tells me that he enjoys cooking and reading and that he once set the kitchen on fire trying to soften a loaf of bread that had gone stale. He tells me about the portraits he paints, that it is his goal to paint every single member of his coven.

"Who will paint your portrait?" I ask.

"Mine?" He pauses, as if he's genuinely surprised by the question. "I suppose I haven't given it much thought."

"Well then, perhaps I will learn how to paint."

He looks at me, tilting his head to the side as if he doesn't understand the words that I spoke. Something unrecognizable passes in his eyes, and I'm certain there is not an artist alive who could capture the brilliance of this man.

I'm certain I would want to try.

I'm staring, so I look down and change the subject. I tell him about my parents' shop and my love of swimming and that I used to talk to the wildflowers I picked for our perfumes, a habit I am still not entirely rid of. Wolfe smiles when I say that, and I laugh because I know it's absurd, yet it spreads warmth through my body.

I follow Wolfe to the field where we met, and he picks several blades of grass before we head back to the beach. I grab four large rocks, and we sit on the shore as stars twinkle high above us.

"Okay, first we need to bruise the materials we've gathered," I say. I demonstrate by putting the petals of the wildflowers on one of the rocks, then grinding them down with the other. Wolfe does the same, and soon we've gone through everything.

"What do you want the base notes to be? These will be the foundation of the perfume."

"I suppose the grasses, since that's where I met you." He says it casually, but it still makes my heart pick up speed. I set aside enough material for the base notes, and then we move on to the middle and top notes. Once he's made his selections, I measure everything out and bundle it all together.

"Now it's time to spell it," I say. "Is there anything in particular you'd like?"

"You decide," he says.

I place the bundle between us and decide on peace. I didn't understand until tonight that it's something he's missing, something he can't have because he lives in terror of his way of life being destroyed. And while a perfume can't fix that, it can give him moments of respite.

I close my eyes and pour my magic into the flowers, but Wolfe stops me. I look at him.

"Speak it out loud," he says. "I want to hear you."

I swallow hard, his words affecting me in a way I can't name. I can feel it, though, moving through my body, slow and warm, blooming from my center, and I have to look down, scared that he'll see what I'm feeling.

"Okay," I say quietly. I close my eyes and start again. "Worries cease and tensions ease, when he smells this fragrance, surround him with peace." I whisper the words as magic drenches the bundle, infusing it with the spell. Then Wolfe's voice joins mine, and we say the words together, his magic softening, molding itself to the rules of my world. I'm shocked when my eyes begin to burn, and I keep them squeezed shut, pushing down my emotion so Wolfe doesn't see it.

We speak the words many more times than necessary, but I don't want to give it up, this moment that has somehow imprinted itself on the deepest part of me. I know it must end, though, and I go through the words one final time before falling silent.

Wolfe is watching me when I open my eyes. His back is to the shore, and with the moon high above the sea, it's hard to make out his features. But he almost looks overcome, moved by the experience in the same way I am.

"Why did you choose peace?" he asks me.

"Because you deserve it."

He nods, and I pull from my pocket a linen handkerchief that my mother insists I carry around for emergencies. I doubt this qualifies, but I carefully wrap the bundle of flowers and herbs, leaves and grasses with the cloth before handing it to Wolfe. He takes it from me and gently places it in the pocket of his jacket.

"I should go," I say, standing. "When you get home, put that bundle in oil and let it sit for a week or two. Then pour it into a bottle, add some alcohol, and spray it whenever you need. Instant peace."

I think he'll roll his eyes at that last part, but he doesn't. "I will." He says it in a way that makes me believe he'll follow each instruction perfectly.

"Good." I begin my walk up to the road, but something stops me. I turn. Wolfe is still standing where I left him, watching me. "I'll keep your secret," I say. "You have my word." Because as much as it hurts him to be kept a secret, hidden away from the eyes of the mainland, he knows that it's necessary to his survival. To the survival of his coven.

"I believe you."

I nod and try to make myself walk again, but it feels so hard, as if I'm standing in quicksand and can't get out. But I have to. I force myself to move, and when I get to the road, I fight the urge to turn back and see him one more time.

I keep my face forward and make my way home, but I can feel his eyes following me, watching until the road bends and the connection is finally lost.

twenty

I'm exhausted when I wake up the next morning, my head throbbing. Another night of magic no one can ever know about, and I justify it by telling myself we only practiced low magic. But even as I think it, I know it is beyond justification. We were still practicing at night, and Wolfe is still a member of the old coven.

Nothing will change that, not even making something as harmless as a perfume.

When I get downstairs, my dad is fixing breakfast and my mom is nursing a cup of tea. "Morning, baby," she says.

"Late night last night?" Dad asks, and for one awful moment, I think they know. I'm silent, my mind racing, trying to figure out what to say, how to apologize, what to admit to, but then he speaks again. "It isn't like you to sleep in this late."

His voice is casual, teasing, and my whole body relaxes as I realize my secret is safe. Wolfe's secret is safe.

"I was just thinking," I say, making myself a cup of tea, then sitting next to my mother on the couch. She tosses half of her blanket my way, and I curl up under it with her.

"What's on your mind?" she asks. I'm about to say something about my Covenant Ball or the perfumery when Wolfe's words jump into my mind unbidden.

You were ignorant.

You should demand to know the truth.

My heart begins to race as I work over his words, wondering if I can actually summon the courage I need to ask the question that's been plaguing my mind. *Why didn't it hurt?*

My palms are sweaty, and I rest my mug on my thigh so it doesn't shake.

"Have you ever seen a moonflower?" I ask, trying to keep my tone casual. Curious.

"A moonflower? What ever made you think of that?" Mom asks, but she doesn't sound upset or suspicious, so I keep going.

"I thought I saw one on the island," I say. "I was wrong, of course, but that's what made me think of it." I hate lying to her, but I want to have this conversation, need to have it, and the only way is for my mother to believe it's innocent.

Mom leans back on the couch and looks past me. "Once, when I was a young girl. The flowers had been eradicated by that time, but every once in a while, a stray seed would survive in the earth and bloom. That's why we're so adamant about teaching the risks of the flower. It's extremely difficult to get rid of a plant once it's made a home somewhere, and while we've done a very thorough job, it's never a guarantee that they're completely gone."

"What did you do when you saw it?"

"I was with your grandmother, and she noticed it at the same time I did. She roped off the area until an official from the mainland came over and uprooted it. They're beautiful. I wish I could have seen it at night, when it was blooming."

"What if another one appears on the island?"

"Oh, honey, I wouldn't worry about that. The one I saw as a girl was one of the very last sightings. And if you did see one, you would know how to react. You wouldn't touch it, and you'd come to me."

"But what if I did touch it?"

A heavy silence settles in the room. The noise of my dad preparing breakfast has stopped, and my mother looks at me with interest.

"Why would you ask such a thing?" she says as my father slowly steps out of the kitchen, waiting to hear how I'll respond.

"I just want to know what would happen."

"You know what would happen. It would cause you unimaginable pain, and you'd die within the hour. Those flowers are extraordinarily dangerous, and that's why we went to such great lengths to get them off the island."

There is nothing in her tone that sounds off, nothing that makes me think she's being anything but honest, and I realize she doesn't know the truth. She has been told the same thing I have since she was a child, the same lie, and she knows nothing different.

I grasp for some kind of explanation, something to make

sense of a falsehood this far-reaching, but I come up short. My mother has always been a steady foundation for me, has always had the answers, but she doesn't have this one, and it feels like the ground I stand on is beginning to shake.

I blink and bring myself back the present, realizing both my parents are still watching me. "Well, I certainly hope I never come into contact with one, then," I say. I try to make the words sound light, but I don't succeed.

"Your mother's right, sweetheart," Dad says. "You don't have to worry about that. It's a very recognizable flower, so even if one did appear, which is highly unlikely, you'd know it before you ever risked touching it."

My dad believes in me, and it makes my heart break that he's trying to comfort me, trying to assure me that the flower is nothing to worry about. My mother nods in agreement and rests her hand on my knee.

"Thanks, Dad," I say, giving him a small smile.

"Are my girls ready for breakfast?" he asks, moving back into the kitchen.

"Absolutely." I stand up and follow him, grabbing silverware and setting the table. We sit down and talk about the shop and my next date with Landon, and the flower doesn't come up again.

But I still need the truth, need to understand how my mother, the most powerful person on this island, doesn't know about moonflowers. I don't want to be ignorant anymore, and I don't care if the knowledge shatters my foundation, because it's shattering anyway. I feel it as I clear the table and do the dishes and walk with my mother to the perfumery. I feel it the entire day, each step a little less stable than the last.

Ivy walks through the door of the perfumery moments before we close, handing me a leftover scone from the tea shop. It grounds me, this routine of ours, and I breathe just a little deeper.

"What kind did you make today?" I ask.

"Lavender and honey." It's one of my favorites, and I eagerly take a bite.

"Delicious," I say. "How was your day?"

"Busy. Would you like to guess what our current bestseller is?"

"You can't be serious."

"I am. Our Tandon blend is a huge hit."

"Oh, it's delicious," my mother exclaims from behind the register. "Have you tried it yet, honey?"

"Tana won't try it on principle," Ivy says.

"And what principle is that?"

"Well, for starters, it's called Tandon," I say, and Ivy rolls her eyes.

"You'll try it one day," she says.

"I know."

My mom turns off all the lights, and I flip the sign on the door to CLOSED. The three of us head out into the chilly evening air together, and Mom runs a quick errand while I walk home with Ivy. Our houses are only ten minutes apart, and it is so hard to think that one day soon, those ten minutes will stretch to the entire width of the Passage.

"My parents are going out tonight, so I thought I'd harvest

some of our night flowers for a new blend I want to try. Do you want to join me?" Ivy asks.

Usually, I'd accept right away. I love harvesting at night, when the island sleeps and the moon is my guide. But Wolfe was right: I want to know the truth, and if my mother doesn't have it, I need to find it somewhere else.

"I would, but I didn't sleep well last night and have a headache I haven't been able to shake all day. I think I'm going to go to bed early and try to sleep it off." Even though both things are true, the words still turn my stomach sour. I'm not helping Ivy because I'm planning to search for answers in a place she would never approve of. And I can't tell her that.

"I'm sorry you're not feeling well," she says, stopping at her front steps. "Let me know how you feel in the morning, and if your headache is still around, I'll make you a pain reliever."

"You're too good to me," I say, and she wraps her arm around my shoulders.

"I think I'm just good enough." She gives me a quick hug, then heads up her steps. "See you tomorrow," she calls over her shoulder.

I'm thankful for the walk home, for a few minutes to myself before I sit through another meal with my parents. The truth can't possibly be as bad as the not knowing, and once the question is answered, I can move on. Maybe that's what I've needed this whole time—the closure Ivy was so sure I was seeking. Maybe this has nothing to do with Wolfe and everything to do with a toxic flower that didn't hurt to touch.

Mom grabs sandwiches from the deli on the way home, and we have an easy dinner that is free of any tension or concern from my parents.

"Good news," Mom says, looking up from her meal. "We'll be getting our final shipment of lumber from the mainland this week. By this time next month, any trace of the dock fire will be gone."

"That is good news," I say, but replacing the scorched lumber isn't enough to make any of us forget what it was like to see our docks go up in flames—the fear that followed, the absolute terror that time was shifting backward. No one was killed, which was the only good thing about that day.

"Do you think maybe we should keep a single burned plank as a way to remember?" I ask.

My parents look at me. "That's an interesting idea. What are you thinking?"

"I'm not sure. I just think that maybe the reminder is good that we have to look out for ourselves instead of relying entirely on the mainland. Erasing it feels like resignation, like we're okay with the fact that this happened. Just because we practice weaker magic doesn't mean we must be weak."

"We could keep the burned wood in a discreet place, too, so it wouldn't draw the eyes of tourists. But I like your idea, Tana—I'll run it by the council," Mom says.

"Really?"

"Absolutely. There's something to it."

I smile and finish my meal as my parents chat about other things.

Once we're done eating, I clear the dishes and go to my room. I sit on my window seat, looking out at the Passage, rolling Landon's sea glass around in my hand, my fingers used to its sharp edges by now.

I listen as my parents make their way up the steps and into their room, and slowly, the house begins to settle. I throw a thick sweater over my day dress, and when I'm sure my parents are sleeping, I sneak out of the house.

I wish I were harvesting with Ivy right now, seeing all the plants and flowers in the moonlight, a wholly different experience from harvesting under the sun. But I know I will never get the closure I need unless my questions about the moonflower are answered, and so I walk through the darkness to the western shore and call for Wolfe one last time.

twenty-one

Wolfe walks out of the water and slowly makes his way up the shore to where I'm standing. It is almost a full moon again, and I can't believe the ways in which my life has changed since the last one. So many things I didn't know then, so many questions I didn't have.

"Do you always travel by water?" I ask.

"Yes. We can't use the streets." He mutters the word *dry* under his breath, and his soaking-wet clothing dries instantly. He's wearing trousers and a long-sleeved white shirt that hugs his body, and I try not to notice the way the fabric pulls across his chest as he moves.

"Two nights in a row," he says. "To what do I owe the pleasure?"

"I asked my mother about the moonflower," I say. A mild breeze rolls in from the sea, and I wrap my arms around my chest.

"And?"

"She told me the same thing I've been taught my whole life:

that if I were to touch one, I would experience pain like nothing else, and then I'd die."

"And yet, here you are."

"Here I am," I say. "She doesn't know the truth, and I don't want to keep wondering about it. That's why I'm here."

"Do you really believe that?"

"Believe what?"

"That she doesn't know?" He makes it sound like a question, but it's clear it isn't one.

"Yes, I do." I say it with finality, and he looks as if he's going to argue with me but then simply nods. He watches me, and I gather up the rest of my courage to ask the question I've needed to ask since the moment we met.

"Will you tell me the truth?" The words are quiet, my voice shaking. I am painfully aware that things will change after this. But not all change is bad, and that's what I tell myself as I wait for Wolfe's reply.

"Are you sure you want to know?"

I hesitate for one, two, three beats of my heart, and then I answer. "I'm sure."

"Come to the water with me."

I follow him into the shallows and kneel down next to him. The water laps over my knees, and I shiver. "What are we doing?"

"Do you remember the spell you used to pull in the tide?"

"Yes," I say slowly, not understanding. "What does that have to do with anything?"

"Try it now," he says.

"What? Why?"

"Just trust me. Do the spell."

I sigh and shake my head. I close my eyes and focus on the water around me, on the way it feels on my skin, and I call to my magic.

"Gentle tide, waters low, rise to us now, send us below." I speak the words over and over, the same ones I used last time, but nothing happens. My magic doesn't rise within me, and the water doesn't change. It's as if the sea has forgotten me.

"I don't understand," I say, opening my eyes, looking at Wolfe.

He takes off his silver ring and gently slips it onto my thumb. It's heavy, with intricate carvings of waves and moonflowers adorning the metal. I let my fingers brush over it. "Try again," he says.

I give him a questioning look but follow his instructions. I close my eyes and try to form a connection between the magic inside me and the water around me, and this time, my magic surges. I repeat the spell once more, and the tide rushes toward us, slamming into my chest and pushing me backward.

I cough as salt water enters my lungs, and I scramble to my feet. Wolfe is at my side, offering me his hand, and I take it, letting him lead me up the shore. We sit back down, and Wolfe dries our clothing.

"What just happened?"

"Do you remember the story I told you? About the first witch being born in a field of moonflowers?"

I nod.

"It's true. We are all descended from her, and that flower is the source of our power. More specifically, all magic flows from that flower's relationship to the moon. It's what sustains our connection to the Earth and enables us to manipulate the world around us. In the absence of it, magic is not possible." Wolfe reaches out and takes my hand. He keeps his eyes on mine as he slowly removes his ring from my finger and places it back on his own.

"This ring is filled with moonflower petals that I replenish every few days. This is the first time I can remember taking it off." He says the words quietly, as if they're special. Important, somehow.

"So your ring is what enabled me to pull in the tide?"

"The moonflower in my ring, yes."

"But that doesn't make sense. I use my magic every day to make the perfumes in my shop."

Wolfe puts his head in his hands and lets out a heavy breath. "I really wish your mother had told you the truth."

"I told you; she doesn't know."

He looks at me with an expression I can't read—pity or sadness, maybe. He shakes his head. "It's in the water supply." He says the words plainly, void of emotion.

A shiver runs down my spine, and I hug my arms to my chest. "That can't possibly be true."

"It is. It's actually pretty smart. They control exactly how much is in the supply—just enough to make low magic possible, not nearly enough to use high magic. They've all but ensured that high magic is eradicated."

190

"Who's 'they'?"

He sighs. "You know who it is."

I shake my head, back and forth and back and forth. This can't be true. It can't be. "Let me get this straight. You're telling me that the head of the council—my mother—has a private garden of moonflowers that she puts in our water supply to keep our magic going and that she has purposefully lied to our coven about it so dark magic is never used again."

"It didn't start with your mother, of course. But yes, as far as we know, it gets distilled into an oil that is added to the island's drinking water. Moonflower is most potent in its natural form, which is why oil is used instead."

I think back to every time I've practiced dark magic with Wolfe, and sure enough, he always presented me with a moonflower before we began. My whole body starts to shake, as if I can't carry the weight of a lie this big, this sweeping. I'm overwhelmed by it, and my eyes burn and my throat aches as I try to keep it together in front of Wolfe.

What an incredible lie.

I put my head in my hands, not wanting Wolfe to see my undoing. I couldn't make the pieces fit when I thought my mother didn't know the truth, but everything makes more sense if she does. And of course she does. As the pieces fall into place, the ones inside me break apart.

I feel a soft touch on my back. His hand is still for a moment, then he moves it in circles. When I finally feel like I can speak again, I lift my head and take a long breath.

"I'm sorry," Wolfe says, and there is no derision or superiority in his tone. He means it.

"Me too."

I think Wolfe is about to reply, but he just looks out at the water. Finally he says, "They're going to kill me for this," more to himself than to me. He exhales, heavy and slow. "I want to show you something."

"I don't think I have the energy for anything else tonight."

"Please," he says, one of the few times he's ever sounded gentle. "I think it will make you feel better."

"I can't go with you."

"Yes, you can. Just give me this. After tonight, you never have to see me again. I promise. But you're already here, and there's something I want you to see. I think it will make a difference."

"For what?"

"For you."

When I look at him, I don't see deceit or lies. I see sincerity.

"No magic," I say. "I can't do it tonight. I can't."

"No magic," he agrees.

He offers me his hand, and I stare at it for the span of a breath before taking it. I follow him as he walks into the water. By the time it's up to my waist, I'm worried.

"What are we doing?"

"Looking for a current," he says, as if it's obvious.

"A current?"

"Yeah. I'd have found it already, but it's no longer the only current close to the island." I don't miss the accusation in his voice, but for the first time, I don't feel like it's directed at me.

"What do you need a current for?"

He looks at me then, beautiful in the moonlight. "To go home."

The water is freezing, and goose bumps rise along my skin. I'm so cold, but I follow Wolfe even deeper. "I don't understand."

"I wasn't lying when I said we can't use the streets. The only way to reach the manor is through an ocean current that goes directly to our home's shore. So we are technically using magic tonight, since the current itself is magical, but we aren't the ones creating it."

The water is up to my shoulders now. I'm so cold, but there's also a thrill running through me at the knowledge that I'm being taken somewhere no one in my coven has ever been. No one even knows it exists, and I lean into the feeling because it edges out the pain of being lied to. It will still be there waiting for me once I'm home, but for now, I push it aside.

I know I should be terrified. My parents would never find me if something happened, but it feels vital that I go, that I learn about this part of my heritage. That I let myself be uncomfortable and see for myself the life that's been hidden from me.

"Mortana," Wolfe says, turning to face me. The water rolls and moves around us, but my feet are firmly on the sandy ground. I have loved this sea for as long as I've lived, and I will not start fearing it now.

"Yes?"

"I'm trusting you with this. Don't make me regret it."

I swallow hard. "I won't."

He searches my eyes for another breath, then nods. "Good."

Suddenly, I realize I've never seen Wolfe in sunlight—the one time we met during the day, the sky was blanketed in dark clouds—and I wonder if he's as beautiful at noon as he is at midnight. I wonder if the sun loves him as much as the moon does.

He steps closer to me, and we both drift up, moving with a wave that rolls through us.

"This is intense the first time you do it. I need you to hold on to me and not let go for anything. Do you understand?"

"Yes."

"Okay, it's coming for us." He takes both my hands and places them around his neck. Then he gently grabs my hips and pulls me into him. "Wrap your legs around my waist." His voice is low and rough, making my insides roll like the ocean around us.

I let the water lift my legs, drifting from the security of the ocean floor. I wrap them around Wolfe, my entire body touching him.

"Okay?" he asks.

I nod. We both breathe raggedly, watching each other.

"Don't let go," he says, the words more prayer than command.

"I won't."

His eyes are full of some unrecognizable thing—not the usual anger he carries, but something fragile. Delicate.

Then he guides my head onto his shoulder, and I wrap myself around him as tightly as possible. I wonder if he can feel my heartbeat through my chest, if he can sense that this is the biggest adventure I've ever been on.

"Take a deep breath," he says, and I do.

Then we're sucked into a vortex of water, and the only thing I can think about is not drowning. The current brings us into its center, swirling us around and around as if we're leaves in the wind. I feel Wolfe's arms tighten around my waist, holding me firmly against him.

We're pulled away from the western shore, but I can't tell what direction we're going. Water churns all around us, rolling over my head and into my nose, forcing me onto my side and back up again.

I gasp for air and swallow water instead, choking. My impulse is to push away from Wolfe, to kick my legs and thrash my arms and get out of the hungry current. But he is steady, holding me close, letting the current carry us. I feel myself shaking in his arms, feel when his hand drifts to the back of my head.

Another wave swallows us, and all I can hear is the churn of the water. It whips us around, and we tumble through the sea, clinging to each other.

Then something changes. The current slows, pulling us along at a rate that doesn't make me fear for my life. We surface, and Wolfe's rough voice reaches me, his wet lips brushing against my ear. "Breathe," he says.

I do as I'm told, drinking in the briny sea air, filling my lungs with it. But I don't dare let go, keeping my arms and legs wrapped firmly around him, knowing with absolute certainly that I feel safe here.

That I *am* safe here.

The water pulls us along, and my ragged breaths slow down. Deepen. I try to forge it into my memory, the way it feels to be carried by the sea, the way it feels to be wrapped around this mystifying boy in the waters I love so much.

"Almost there," he says, and I feel him start to kick. He moves as if I'm not even here, light in the water even though I'm weighing him down. It isn't until his feet touch the ground that I slowly unwrap myself from him.

My back is to the shore, and I watch in amazement as the current swirls away from us. The water is smooth and calm again, and I feel Wolfe graze my hand.

"Ready?" he asks.

I'm suddenly afraid of what I'll see when I turn around. I close my eyes and take a deep breath, then slowly rotate in the water.

I think about my parents and Ivy and the Eldons asleep in their beds, think of all they've given up and continue to give up to secure our place in the world. I think about how carefully constructed it is, how even one misstep could obliterate the whole thing.

I think about the moonflower and the lie and how grand a deceit it is.

I find Wolfe's hand beneath the water, lacing my fingers through his.

Then I take a deep breath and open my eyes.

twenty-two

I see nothing but forest, dense trees stretching almost all the way to the beach, same as the rest of the western coast. I look to Wolfe, confused.

"Our home is spelled," he says. "Only those who have been invited to see it are able. To everyone else, it looks like a continuation of the woods." He pauses, and his fingers tighten around mine, the only indication he's nervous. "Let her see," he whispers, such a simple sentence that couldn't possibly lift such a powerful spell.

But it does. I blink several times and gasp.

The trees slowly fade, revealing a large brick manor sitting atop a long sloping lawn. There is just enough moonlight to see a silhouette of a steep roofline and multiple spires reaching toward the sky, looming over us. Tall trees surround the manor on both sides, shrouding it in darkness.

"Where are we?" I ask, staring in wonder at the size of the house, completely awed that it has been here, hidden, all these years.

"We're about three miles south of where you do the rush, on the southwestern shore of the island. You were practically in our backyard the night I found you harvesting."

"I had no idea," I whisper, more to myself than Wolfe.

"Yeah, that's kind of the point."

Wolfe leads me out of the water and onto the rocky beach. Three stone steps put us on the lawn, and we follow the path that leads to the main house. "Dry," he whispers, our clothes drying in an instant.

A low layer of clouds settles over the manor, hiding it from the moon. Soft orange light flickers from glass lanterns that hang on either side of the door, illuminating dense ivy that stretches from the earth to the pitched roof. To the side of the house is a garden, a sea of white in an otherwise dark night.

"Are those all moonflowers?" I ask, mesmerized at the sight of so many at once.

"They are."

I've explored every inch of this island and never once seen the manor before me. I'm amazed that this kind of power lives inside Wolfe, magic so strong it can hide an entire manor for years on end. A power that he thinks lives in me, too.

"This is your home?" I ask, taking in the cracked stone pathways and the candlelight flickering on the brick walls.

"It is," he says, looking up at the manor. "We all live here together."

"How many of you are there?"

He pauses. "Seventy-three."

"Seventy-three?" I repeat, shocked. "There are seventy-three witches practicing dark magic on this island?" I feel an immediate urge to run home and tell my mother, tell her that the old coven is alive and well, thriving on our island.

We've been fooled.

All of us.

In this moment, my mother's lie doesn't seem so bad, not when this exists. Not when there is a manor full of dark magic and old witches and powerful spells. She'll be devastated.

"Mortana, you're at my home," Wolfe says. "Do you think you can refrain from using offensive terms while you're here?"

I barely hear him. I think there was a lightness to his voice, but I'm not sure. My mind is racing and the world seems to spin around me. My stomach clenches and my head lolls back. "I don't feel well," I say.

The spinning gets faster. Wolfe's arm catches me around my waist as I collapse. Then, total darkness.

When my eyes open, I'm in a cozy room on a soft bed. Dark mahogany beams stretch across the ceiling, and the same wood makes up the four-poster bed. A large fireplace rises from floor to ceiling on the opposite wall, the logs popping and crackling as they burn. A glass bottle on the bedside table reflects the firelight, and I recognize it as the memory keeper I gave Wolfe. And sitting beside it is a jar of oil with the flowers and herbs we gathered together: his peace perfume.

An ache starts in my chest.

A pile of leather-bound books covers the table on the other side of the bed, and a canvas with a half-finished portrait rests on an easel between two large windows. Wooden brushes sit in jars, and tubes of paint are scattered around them. I don't recognize the person in the portrait, but that makes sense. Theirs is a hidden life, just like Wolfe's. I'm mesmerized by the painting, by the incredible detail it holds, by the hours he must be spending on it to get it exactly right.

I wonder what my portrait would look like if he were to paint me, but a sadness moves through me as soon as I think it. I have no need for one because I will be remembered.

I slowly stand, but I sit back down when I hear voices beyond the door.

"What were you thinking, bringing her here?" a voice says.

"She doesn't see..." I can't make out the rest of Wolfe's reply.

After several more sentences that are too quiet for me to hear, the door opens and Wolfe steps inside. He gently closes it behind him.

"How long was I out?"

Wolfe pauses when he hears my voice. "Long enough for me to get you settled in my room."

My cheeks heat as I wonder how he got me here, how much of this evening I'll spend enveloped in his arms. Wolfe looks at the fire and the flames get stronger, and for half a second I'm stunned. Then I remember where I am.

"I always forget you can use magic at night."

"So can you," he says plainly.

I sigh. "Do we have to argue right now?"

"No," he says. "We can do it later."

He moves closer to me, and I realize it's the first time I've ever seen him indoors. Candlelight flickers against his dark hair and pale skin, and he seems softer here in the refuge of his home. His gray eyes don't hold the same anger they usually do, and the muscle in his jaw isn't tensing every few seconds.

He's still him, but he's comfortable here. Comfortable and perfect.

"You're staring at me," he says.

"You don't look as disagreeable here."

There's a slight tug at the corner of his mouth that worsens the ache in my chest. "I'm flattered."

"I meant it as a compliment." I whisper the words, worried that all seventy-three of the witches living here will hear me otherwise.

Wolfe shakes his head and looks away. "I know you did."

I feel as if I've said the wrong thing, so I don't say anything else.

"How are you feeling?" he asks me.

"Embarrassed." There's something about him that makes me want to tell the truth, and I realize I've felt that way around him from the moment we met. I've shown him my anger and insecurities and wonder and fear, and never once has he said I'm too much.

It feels as if I've been living in the shadows and he's invited me into the light. His dark expressions and dark magic and dark home have lit me up inside, illuminating the things I've been taught to keep hidden.

His eyes find mine. "Trust me when I say you have nothing to be embarrassed about." He pauses. "Not now. Not ever."

We watch each other, and I'm overwhelmed with the urge to reach out to him, to take his hand and pull him close to me. In the current, I wrapped myself around him because I had to. Because I'd drown if I didn't.

But what if I drown right here in the quiet of his room, suffocated by how desperately I want him?

"Do you feel well enough to meet my dad?"

The question catches me off guard, sparing me from my thoughts. It must have been his dad he was speaking with outside the door. "Yes."

He nods, and I slowly scoot off the bed and make sure I feel steady on my feet. Wolfe keeps his hand on my lower back until I'm sure I'm stable, then we walk into the hallway. The same mahogany wood as in Wolfe's room lines the walls and floors, and a long red-and-gold rug runs the length of the hall. Candlesticks in glass sconces adorn the walls.

"Why do you burn so many candles?" I ask.

"How else are we to see?"

I look at him, confused. "You don't have electricity here?"

"It would have been difficult to convince the mainland to extend power to this side of the island, given that we don't exist. Don't you agree?"

My cheeks flush, and I shake my head. "I'm sorry," I say.

"You have nothing to apologize for. Besides, I'm partial to candlelight." He looks at me for another breath before walking again.

His hand is hanging loosely at his side, and I can almost convince myself that it's angled back at me, an invitation, and I fight the urge to reach out and take it. Hushed voices float from behind closed doors, and I startle when a little girl jumps out from behind a potted tree. Her dark hair is braided, and there's a gap in her smile where her front tooth used to be. She slaps Wolfe on the leg and screams, "Tag, you're it!"

Wolfe scoops her into his arms as she shrieks. "Those aren't the rules we agreed upon, now, are they, Lily?"

She giggles and peeks at me from over Wolfe's shoulder. "Who's your friend?" she asks.

"This is Mortana," Wolfe says. "Mortana, this is Lily."

"His *best* friend," Lily says, eyeing me warily.

"Yes, my best friend," Wolfe agrees. He sets Lily back down, and she watches me from behind his leg.

"It's nice to meet you, Lily. I have a best friend, too. Her name is Ivy."

"Do you like to color?" she asks me.

"I love to color."

"Can she come color with me?" Lily asks, seemingly satisfied that I'm not a threat.

"Not right now, Bug. It's late—you should be in bed."

Lily groans. "But I'm not even tired!" she says on top of a yawn.

"I know, I know. But you need to rest up for our game of tag tomorrow," Wolfe says. "Unless you want to lose."

Lily's mouth falls open. "I'm not going to lose!" she says, and then she runs down the hall and slams a door behind her.

"I like your best friend," I say, following Wolfe down the grand staircase, steadying myself with the iron railing.

"She'll be pleased to hear that tomorrow."

When we get to the bottom of the stairs, it's louder. Voices carry from the right side of the manor, which I'm assuming houses the kitchen, and there are several witches in a formal room to the left, practicing spells. There are lit candles all over the room, and the flames get higher and lower with the words the witches speak.

"Hey, Wolfe," someone says from the room, sending a ball of fire into the foyer that circles around us before dying out.

"Show-off," he says in return.

Laughter follows us as we come to a study near the front of the manor. The door is open, but Wolfe knocks anyway.

"Come on in," the voice says.

My heart beats wildly, and my palms are sweaty. I'm not sure why I'm nervous, but my hands tremble as I enter the room.

A man stands behind a large wooden desk. A fire crackles in the stone fireplace, and lanterns flicker along the walls. There are hundreds of leather-bound books sitting on black iron shelves with a ladder that stretches all the way to the top. I can't help it when my fingers drift to the wall and gently touch the old books.

"Are these grimoires?" I ask, amazed. We have new texts that document the new order of magic, but the old books where our ancestors kept all their spells were removed from our coven. When we stopped using dark magic, there was no longer a need for them, but I'm completely in awe, standing in a room with so much magic. So much history.

"They are," Wolfe says.

There's a large old book open on a stand in the middle of the room. The corners are curled and yellowed, but the pages are still legible. It's a spell for transferring life, and my fingers trace the words that explain how to take one life to save another.

I remember Wolfe telling me that magic is all about balance. It makes sense that we can't simply save a life—there are consequences.

Magic stirs inside my belly as I read the words, and it scares me, the undeniable connection I have to this magic.

You're practicing the wrong magic.

"You must be Mortana," the man says, breaking my concentration. I pull my hand from the grimoire, and heat settles in my cheeks.

"I am."

The man looks so much like Wolfe with his sharp jaw and wild dark hair, his eyes that look like the sea during a storm. But he's softer in a way. His pale skin sags just slightly, and he wears wire-rimmed glasses that have slid down his nose. His eyes crinkle at the corners when he smiles at me.

"I'm Galen, Wolfe's father. Welcome to our coven." He extends his hand to me, and I take it, noticing he wears a ring almost identical to Wolfe's.

"Thank you." My words come out quiet and shaky. An entire world has been opened up to me that I know nothing about, and it calls everything into question. My coven is so close to getting what we've always wanted, and the manor I'm standing in threatens to undo it all. How could we not know they exist?

"I'm aware this is a lot to take in," Galen says. "We like to keep ourselves hidden. I'm sure you understand why."

"How long have you been here?"

"Since the new order of magic became the standard. When your coven formed, almost all the witches joined, leaving very few who kept to the old order. We shared the island for a while, but as the years went on, the new witches realized that if the mainland found out high magic was still being practiced, it would compromise everything. So we met with the council and formed a somewhat tenuous alliance. We agreed to remove ourselves from the community of the island and stay hidden, and they agreed to keep our secret. That was generations ago. Over time, the new witches began to think of us more as myth than anything else. But we're still here, practicing high magic."

"Why, though? Why choose to live like this?"

"Where else are we to go? The mainland?"

I'm quiet because he's right. Magic is forbidden on the mainland, and the consequences if anyone found out they were there would be severe. It's safer for them to practice magic on the Witchery, even if it means hiding themselves away.

"How are there so many of you?"

"There used to be a lot more of us," Galen says. He doesn't sound nervous or unsure as he answers my questions, not the way Wolfe does. He is casual and warm with no hint of severity. Their secrets don't seem as hard for him to carry as they are for Wolfe. "We gain new members occasionally; there are still descendants of the original witch on the mainland, and when they realize they have magic, they tend to find their way to us. And when someone from the new coven denounces low magic at their Covenant Ball, we take them in. And of course there are many families within our coven, and they have children. The truth is that we can't survive forever, not without more members joining us, but that is a problem for another day."

How will we be remembered? Wolfe's words enter my mind, and I'm completely overcome by his devotion to his coven, by his dedication to ensuring that each and every one of the witches in this manor will live on in oil and canvas, long after their bodies have perished.

"I thought anyone who didn't accept the new order was banished to the mainland," I say, my voice quiet.

"What else could you assume if you think the old coven no longer exists?"

I nod, feeling foolish that I'm learning more in this dim office than I ever learned in my lessons. "And how do you stave off the illnesses brought on by dark—excuse me—*high* magic?"

"There are no such illnesses," Galen says. "That's a myth to perpetuate the idea that high magic is somehow evil or poisonous. It simply is not true."

"I'm sorry," I say, embarrassed to have asked. Embarrassed that I believed it. "I don't mean to sound insensitive."

Galen watches me and pulls off his glasses, folding them and placing them on an open book on his desk. "You look a lot like your mother."

My mouth gets very dry. I swallow. "You know my mother?" The words stick to my throat as I force them out.

"Of course," Galen says. "This entire island answers to her. It's my job to know who she is."

"I see." I pause before speaking again. "Does she know who you are?"

Galen looks to Wolfe before looking back at me. "It would seem she does not, given your reaction to seeing our home."

I remember fainting, and my cheeks turn a darker shade of red.

"Sit down, both of you." Galen motions to a large black couch next to the fireplace. My heart is calm and my breathing is even, and I'm too distracted to figure out what that means.

"Mortana, I'm glad my son met you. And you're welcome here anytime, but this will get very complicated for you very quickly. Do you understand that?"

"Yes."

Galen settles in a chair across from us, leaning back. "I'm not worried about your coven learning of our existence—our plans require it. But the timing is something I'm sensitive to."

"Plans?"

"As witches, we are stewards of this Earth. We are healers. And your coven is killing the only home we have. We will not stand by and let that happen."

I shift in my seat. "You're talking about the currents," I say, and for some reason my voice sounds relieved.

Galen nods. "We're strong enough to do something about it. But we need your coven's help, and I suspect your mother won't like that."

"I suspect she won't," I say. The ocean is everything to me, and even before I missed the rush, the violent currents often occupied my thoughts, filled me with worry. We have to do something about them, and I've known for a long time that my mother isn't doing enough.

I'm glad someone intends to do something about it. Maybe that makes me a traitor.

"I support you in that," I say, looking at Galen.

"You do?" he asks, raising his brows. Shadows from the fire dance over his face.

"Yes. I won't tell my mother about your existence until you decide to do it yourself." I pause and take a deep breath, looking Galen in the eye. "But if you do anything to hurt a single person I care about, I'll turn the full force of the mainland against you."

Galen watches me for several moments before a large smile spreads across his face. "I believe you. And you have my word."

"Good."

"Well, I'm glad we got that settled, as it seems my son has a hard time staying away from you."

I look down, but Wolfe levels his dad with an icy stare. "Thanks for that."

"Anytime, son," he says, standing. "Mortana, it was a pleasure meeting you." Galen reaches out his hand, and I stand and take it.

"The pleasure was mine."

"I'm looking forward to seeing you again," he says, and the certainty in his voice, his absolute confidence that I'll be back, sends a chill down my spine. "Until then, enjoy the ceremony."

He places a hand on Wolfe's shoulder and walks out of the study, leaving a million questions in his wake.

twenty-three

"What ceremony?" I turn to Wolfe, my voice urgent. My mind is overwhelming me with images of dark rituals and darker magic, urgent chanting and too-powerful spells, and I'm suddenly terrified of what I've walked into. Of what he brought me here for.

"A vow renewal," he says.

"What kind of vow?" My words are angry, accusatory, and panic tightens my chest.

Wolfe raises an eyebrow, amusement tugging at his mouth. "Marital vows."

"What?" I ask, the words not making sense. All the fight drains out of me.

"What were you expecting? Did you think I brought you here for some kind of blood oath, or perhaps a sacrifice? Oh, I know—maybe we were going to reach into the underworld and summon cruel spirits from the pits of hell to stalk the Witchery. Or maybe we were going to plant horrible nightmares in the minds of the mainlanders to make them turn on you for good. Or maybe—"

"Can you do that?" I ask, cutting him off, completely horrified.

Wolfe looks at me as if my face has turned inside out. "Of course not! My god, what are they teaching you over there?"

I shrug, not finding the thought nearly as outlandish as he does. "They don't teach us much about the inner workings of dark magic; it leaves a lot of room for our imaginations to run wild, I suppose." Wolfe closes his eyes and takes a long, deep breath when I use the phrase *dark magic*. "Sorry, *high magic*."

"Mortana, I swear—"

"I said I was sorry," I say, holding my hands up.

There's a knock on the door, and Galen pokes his head in. "We're about to start."

Wolfe nods, and the door shuts, leaving us in private once again.

"You should get ready," Wolfe says.

"I'm not staying. This is an intimate, special thing. I don't want to intrude."

"You aren't intruding. But you are running late," he says.

Flustered, I look down at my clothing. "I don't have time to get ready."

"You don't need time. You need magic."

"But it's after dark," I say, hearing how ridiculous the words sound as they leave my lips. Music starts to play behind the door, and my heart beats faster.

"Mortana, you've pulled in the tide and commanded the wind. I think you can use a little magic to get ready."

"Will you do it for me?" I ask, not wanting to break another rule. I've already done so many unthinkable things, but I don't have to keep saying yes. "Please."

Wolfe looks at me with a frustrated expression, but he nods. "Okay."

Before I can even say thank you, Wolfe's magic surrounds me, smoothing my hair and brushing makeup over my face. He steps out of the study and returns moments later carrying a dress.

"I'll wait outside while you change," he says.

I take the dress and a long silver necklace slides out from the fabric. "Is this for me to wear as well?" I ask, holding it up.

"Yes." It's the only answer he offers before leaving again.

Once the door is closed, I slip into the gray lace dress. It comes down to my calves and has fitted long sleeves that bell slightly at my wrists, and I walk to the ornate gold mirror behind Galen's desk. My eye shadow is dark and smoky, my lips are a deep crimson, and my hair falls loosely down my back. The necklace Wolfe gave me is ornate and silver with an oval black gemstone in the center. The back is perforated, intricate filigree that is somehow delicate and bold at the same time, and I put it on over my head and let my fingers brush the smooth surface of the stone.

"Come in," I say when there's a soft knock on the door.

Wolfe walks in and stops when he sees me, staring as if I'm a meteor shower on a clear night. I shift uncomfortably and walk back to the mirror.

I've always been taught to keep my makeup light and soft. Natural, as my mother puts it. I'm not used to seeing myself like this, but instead of balking at my reflection or asking Wolfe to tone it down, I'm totally entranced. I love it.

"I can change it if you want," Wolfe says. His voice is thick and rough, and heat rises in my core at the sound.

"I like it," I say, turning to face him. "What do you think?"

"I think..." he starts, then stops, shoving a hand through his hair. He looks frustrated again, and he shakes his head. "I think you look perfect."

"Then why do you sound so upset?"

He walks over to me and gently places a moonflower behind my ear. "Because I don't want you to look perfect in my world. I don't want you to fit."

"I don't," I say, forcing the words from my mouth. My throat is dry, my voice barely audible.

"Look again," he says, turning my face to the mirror.

I look for a single breath, then close my eyes and turn away. I don't want to fit here, either.

We're about to leave when a large painting above the fireplace catches my eye. I must have missed it on my way in, so distracted by the grimoires, but it's breathtaking. It's a portrait of a woman with long, dark hair cascading down her sides and a crown of moonflowers on her head. She wears a fitted silver gown with a large black pendant resting against her chest. There is a soft, contented smile on her face, and her hands are folded lightly in her lap.

"Did you paint this?" I ask, amazed.

Wolfe stands next to me, looking up at the portrait. "Yes. My mother," he says.

"She's beautiful. Will I meet her tonight?"

"She died a long time ago." He tenses beside me, and a sharpness enters his voice.

"What happened?" I'm not sure if it's an appropriate question, if it helps or hurts to talk about, but I want to know him. And this is part of him.

"She died in childbirth. She was on the mainland getting supplies that weren't available on the island when she went into labor. There were complications, and my dad couldn't get to her in time. If she had been on the island, she would have lived. My dad could have saved her."

"That's awful," I say, staring up at the painting. "I'm so sorry."

"Is it awful? Your coven would say that her death was the only acceptable outcome, that using magic to save a life is wicked." I turn to face him, and he looks angry. Hurt. "Which is it, Mortana?"

I'm not sure what makes me do it, how I even work up the courage, but I wrap my arms around his neck and pull him close. "It's awful."

He hesitates, remaining still as I hold him. Then slowly, he wraps his arms around my waist.

The music beyond the door gets louder, and Wolfe steps back. "We need to go," he says.

He walks to the door and opens it without another word.

The foyer has been transformed in the time we've been in Galen's study, the large staircase littered with white moonflower petals, the iron railings wrapped in vines of ivy. Black pillar candles line the stairs, and deep, rich music drifts inside from the open doors.

Wolfe takes my arm, the tension he was holding left behind in his father's study. We walk outside to the long sloping lawn that leads to the water's edge. Black wooden chairs face the shore, each one looking hand-carved, and hundreds of white moonflowers float in the water and reflect the moonlight. A large iron arch sits on the beach, wrapped in more ivy and illuminated by candlelight.

I'm stunned at the beauty of it, how alluring and rich it is. I've been to dozens of weddings on the Witchery, but none of them were like this.

A large garden sits to the north of the manor, much larger than the one I saw earlier, but it's too dark for me to make out what's in it.

"That garden is huge," I say.

"We grow most of our own food."

"It's almost like your own little town," I say. The garden stretches so far I can't make out the edge of it in the darkness.

"Our own little town where we can practice our own kind of magic."

At first I think he's mocking me, but he sounds happy when he says it. Content.

"Well, well, well, if it isn't a low-T in our midst." A woman walks over to me, long dark hair hanging to her thighs and streaks of rouge smeared across her cheeks and lips, standing out against her pale skin. She carries a silver glass, her nails painted the same color red as her makeup. I've only ever been allowed to wear sheer polishes in tones of pink and ivory, and I instinctively move my hands behind my back.

"Low-T? Is that what you call us?" I ask, looking at Wolfe.

"A rather unimaginative nickname derived from low tide magic," he says.

"I see."

"You look good," the woman says, an amused expression on her face. "Dark colors suit you."

"I'm sorry, have we met before?"

"You're the most powerful daughter on the Witchery, love. We all know what you look like." She winks at me and drapes an arm around my shoulders. "I'm Jasmine. Let's get you a drink," she says, leading me away from Wolfe.

"Jasmine?" I ask, the name shaking something loose in my brain. "Jasmine Blake?"

She looks at me, raising an eyebrow, and then a smirk pulls at her mouth. "Yes."

"You denounced the new coven." I'm shocked, can't believe I'm standing next to her. "I thought you had..." I trail off, not wanting to offend. I was too young to remember it myself, but I've heard the story.

"You thought I had died on the mainland?"

I nod.

"After denouncing the new order, I came here," she says simply, offering no further explanation. And maybe she doesn't need one; maybe making that choice isn't as complicated as the new coven believes it to be.

She hands me a silver goblet filled with deep red wine, and it reminds me of my mother. My heart starts to race.

"I hear you're quite gifted in the old order," Jasmine says,

"You must be misinformed. I'm a practitioner of low magic," I say, gripping my goblet too tightly.

"Sure you are," she says. "I was, too, many years ago." She clinks her glass against mine and takes a drink, and then someone calls out for her. "It was nice meeting you, Mortana."

I'm left staring after her, her words replaying in my mind. To my knowledge, Jasmine Blake was the last witch to leave the new order, choosing the outside during her Covenant Ball. A choice must be made, and once it is, it's final. That's why the Covenant is so important. Besides the rush, it is the most powerful magic we do, an irrevocable oath that follows us to the grave.

I am too young to remember Jasmine's Covenant Ball, but year after year, our witches choose the new order. It's hard to imagine what a ceremony would look like if someone chose the outside, the kind of anger and chaos it would evoke.

The music stops, and everyone makes their way to their seats. I know Wolfe told me there were more than seventy witches here, but seeing them all in one place, dressed up and laughing and talking, overwhelms me.

Seventy-three, and we had no idea.

"Are you okay?" Wolfe says, and I jump at the sound of his voice. I didn't see him walk over.

"Why did you bring me here?" I ask.

Before he can respond, Galen walks up to the iron arch and

the ceremony begins. I quickly take my seat next to Wolfe, spinning my glass in my hand, nervous energy humming inside me, refusing to move on.

Wolfe reaches over and places his hand on top of mine, stopping the glass in my fingers. He lowers my hand to my lap, his skin cool. My breath catches, and I don't hear a word Galen says, too focused on the way a single touch can be felt in so many places. I've imagined this feeling so many times before, spent so many sleepless nights hoping my life of duty might still create this kind of madness within me, hoping Landon might ignite this kind of fire. But he hasn't, and in this moment, I'm sure he never could.

I swallow hard, and Wolfe removes his hand from mine.

The music starts again, its deep, vibrant tones drifting on the night air. If I heard this anywhere else, I would think it was meant to evoke sadness, such a stark contrast to the fast, lively pieces at our own weddings. But here it isn't sad. It's beautiful and raw and bold. I blink and take a deep breath.

Two women walk down the aisle together, one in a long black gown with a full tulle skirt and fitted bodice, the other in a tight dress covered in black gemstones, her train reflecting the moonlight. Their fingers are woven together, and they stop in front of Galen.

They speak to each other of love and commitment, loyalty and patience, understanding and grace, and I'm overcome by the beauty of it, the emotions I'm experiencing for two people I've never met. The ceremony feels real in a way so many things in my world don't. I raise my hand to my eye, fighting back tears, and I notice Wolfe shift in his chair, moving closer to me.

Closer.

I try to focus on what's happening in front of me, but the music and the ceremony and the waves crashing on the shore fade away, fade to nothing. All I can hear is my blood pulsing in my ears, my shallow breaths, my too-fast heart.

By the time the women kiss, I think I might snap in half from the tension in my body, from the way every single muscle is straining. The women walk hand-in-hand to the water, saying something I can't make out. Then, all at once, the moonflowers rise into the air and rush up the lawn, swirling all around us like autumn leaves. The music gets louder and louder, the women kiss once more, and the flowers vanish.

In unison, the witches around me say, "May your love be as constant as the tide, as powerful as the moonflower, and as patient as the winter seed. Blessings."

Then applause and cheers break out. I stay in my seat, watching as people hug and kiss, as conversations start and laughter flows.

I wonder what my wedding to Landon will look like, if there will be even a fraction of the intimacy and joy I've seen tonight. But as soon as I think it, I know there won't be. The wedding won't be for Landon and me; it will be for show, a production meant for everyone in attendance.

"What are you thinking about?"

I turn to Wolfe, and he's watching me intently. It isn't his fault that doubt has crept into the edges of my mind, that uncertainty is clawing at my insides, that for the first time in my life,

I'm thinking about what I want instead of what's expected. But I take it out on him anyway.

"I'm thinking that I want to go home." I drop my glass to the earth and rush back to Galen's study, tearing off the gray lace dress and replacing it with my own clothes. I need to get out of here, get back to solid ground.

"Get this off," I say when Wolfe finds me, motioning to my face. His hand reaches for mine, and I step away. "Please."

"Okay." My face cools with his magic, and I instantly miss what it felt like to be in his world, to look the part.

"What's wrong?" he asks, but it's an impossible question to answer. *Everything.* Everything is wrong.

I see a large wooden door carved with silhouettes of moon-flowers, and I know I've found my exit. I force it open, the door groaning on its hinges, and hurry out into the night.

twenty-four

Wolfe follows me to the edge of the trees behind the manor. I can see the path in the distance that will lead me home.

"Why did you bring me here tonight?" I ask again, facing him.

He looks at me intently, his eyes never leaving mine. "Because you're trying to force yourself into a box you don't fit in. This is the life you were taught to despise," he says, pointing to the manor behind us, his voice rising. "We aren't a bunch of evil witches chanting in circles and conspiring with the devil. We're a family. We laugh and have hopes and fears and dreams, just like you do. We farm and raise our children and try our best to protect this Earth."

"It isn't that simple—"

"Yes, it is. This is a *life*, Mortana. A vibrant, full life." His words are urgent and loud and angry.

"And what do you want me to do about it?" I yell, at a total loss for what this life could ever mean for me. "There is no place for me here."

Wolfe grabs my hand and closes the space between us. "There is a life for you here, a life where you can be everything you're afraid of being." He looks down at me, his breaths filling the air and colliding with my own. He searches my face, his gaze so intense I can feel it on my skin, feel it in my core.

He permeates everything, every belief and doubt and question I've ever had about myself. When I look at him, I see the person I want to be, the potential of a life lived on my own terms.

And it hurts.

It hurts.

Hot tears prick at my eyes, and I swallow them down. "That's where you're wrong," I say, the words shaking as they come out of my mouth. "There has only ever been one life for me."

Rain starts falling from the black sky, and I'm soaked in seconds. I pull my hand from Wolfe's. "I have to go."

I turn to leave, but Wolfe catches my wrist and pulls me back, and I crash into him just like the first night we met. I'm scared to look up at him but even more scared not to. I lift my gaze, and he puts his hands on either side of my face, his wet fingers weaving into my hair.

"I don't want to lose you," he says.

I put my hands over his and close my eyes, feel the way his breath tickles my skin and his fingers spark a flame that burns all through my body. I imagine pushing my lips against his and practicing his magic and allowing myself to be all the things he thinks I'm capable of being.

Then I pull his hands from my face and take a step back. "I was never yours to lose," I say.

I take the moonflower from my hair and let it fall to the ground. Then I run. I run as fast as I can until I reach the path that will lead me home. I stop to catch my breath and turn to look at the manor in the distance, its magic lifted just for me. It is dark and looming, haunting and eerie, everything the Witchery is not. And it's absolutely beautiful.

I turn my back to it and follow the path around the northern edge of the island, finally making my way to my street, but I stop as soon as I see my house.

It's four o'clock in the morning, but every single light is on. Through the giant windows, I see my father pacing and my mother on the phone behind him. She wraps her arms around my dad, his face wracked with worry.

Guilt seizes me, and I run into the house even though I'm terrified of the storm that's waiting for me.

"I'm here," I shout, jumping up the stairs and rushing into the living room.

"My god, Tana, where have you been?" my dad asks, hurrying over to me and pulling me into his arms. "We've been so worried." He tucks my head under his chin even though I'm soaking wet, and I can't help bursting into tears.

"I'm so sorry," I say, clutching my dad. "I couldn't sleep. My mind was racing, and I thought it might help to take a walk."

My mother hangs up the phone, and I catch her eye from against Dad's chest. Then she sighs, heavy and loud, walks over, and wraps her arms around us, so tight. Too tight.

"What's going on?" I ask, realizing something other than my absence woke them.

My parents exchange a look.

"It's Ivy, honey," my dad says, putting a hand on my shoulder. "She went out tonight to harvest and accidentally unearthed a hive. She was swarmed."

"That sounds miserable," I say. I've been stung only once; I can't imagine how terrible she must be feeling. "We should take her some bath oils to help her rest. Can I go see her?"

"It isn't that simple," Dad says, and his eyes fill with tears. "Ivy is allergic to bees. She had never been stung before, so she didn't know. It looks... it looks like she might not make it through the night."

I step back. "What?"

"Her parents want me to be there. We should all go." My mother's voice is heavy, full of sadness and regret. But her face is composed, and her makeup is perfect.

"No." I take another step back. "No. I just saw her. She's fine," I say, unwilling to believe what they're telling me.

"Oh, honey, how I wish that were true." Mom reaches out to me, but I won't do this. I won't grieve for my best friend, because she's not going anywhere. She can't. I can't do this without her.

I inhale, steadying myself. "Take me to her."

Ivy's house smells like death. I don't know how else to describe it. The air is thick and heavy and foul, as if preparing its inhabitants for what's to come. Mrs. Eldon rushes to my mom, and they embrace.

"Oh, Rochelle," my mom says into her hair.

Dr. Glass is standing in the corner, speaking in hushed tones to Ivy's father. He looks over and nods at me, but they continue their conversation.

"Hi, Tana," Mrs. Eldon says through tears. She holds a handkerchief up to her nose and wipes her face before giving me a gentle hug. "Why don't you go see Ivy while we're finishing up with Dr. Glass? He's just about to leave."

"What do you mean he's leaving?" I ask, my voice rising. "You're just giving up?" I yell at the doctor, not caring that I'm losing it in front of my parents and Ivy's, not caring that I'm coming undone in this room.

"Tana," my mother warns.

I look around, helpless. I want to scream, want to tell them that this isn't normal, that they should be fighting harder. But I don't say a word; I turn away and rush up the stairs. Ivy's room is the first door on the right, and I knock even though I don't expect an answer.

I push the door open. The air smells of sweat even though the window is open. It's as if I can feel the heat radiating off her body from here.

I carefully walk to the bed and sit on the edge. Her chest rises and falls in shallow bursts, a high-pitched wheeze accompanying each breath. Her eyes are closed, and her arms are by her sides, hands open. Her brown skin is covered in welts, her face and neck swollen almost beyond recognition.

Oh, Ivy.

"I'm here," I say, taking her hand. "I'm here."

She doesn't react to my touch or my voice. Her eyes stay closed, and her hand is limp in mine. She's right in front of me, but I can't accept what I'm seeing. She is my rock, my safe place, my refuge. She sees me when everyone else sees only my role. She hears my voice when everyone else hears only my name. How am I supposed to keep talking without her here?

I look around the room at the discarded medicines and healing tea by her bedside. But there is nothing we can do to truly heal her. The new order of magic forbids anything that would meaningfully change the course of someone's life.

We can't help her.

But the thought won't settle in my mind long enough for me to accept it. We *can* help her; we're choosing not to. If we hadn't abandoned who we are, we would know how to save Ivy's life with magic. But instead, we're helpless, watching the life leave her with each shaking breath. Her body is on fire, and our coven is letting it burn.

"I'm so sorry I wasn't here," I say, guilt rolling through me like a flood. I should have said yes when she asked me to harvest with her, should have been there for her when the hive opened up. I imagine Ivy lying on the ground alone, her parents out for the evening, no one to help her. I imagine her terror and panic and pain, and I can't accept this. I refuse to.

"No," I say, my voice trembling. "I won't let you go."

As soon as I say it, a nighthawk takes flight from a nearby tree, its brown-and-white feathers catching the starlight. It lands on Ivy's windowsill and watches us.

My stomach stirs as I remember the grimoire in Galen's office. The nighthawk is giving me a gift.

Before I can talk myself out of it, before I even know what I'm doing, I move to the windowsill and extend my arm. The bird steps onto my wrist, and I bring it into the room.

My magic knows what I'm doing, and it awakens inside me, strong and forceful and ready for whatever I ask of it.

I don't remember everything I read in the grimoire, but I whisper the words that I do, focusing on my connection to the bird. I can hear its heartbeat racing. I focus on the noise, on my magic, on that solid line of life I so desperately need.

"A life for a life, from one to the next, a heart for a heart, restore her breath."

Magic pours from me and encircles the bird, its heart beating slower and slower until finally it stops.

Tears fall from my eyes as I set the bird gently on the windowsill. "Thank you," I whisper, holding its life in my hands, an ivory glow shining all around it.

I rush to the bed and sit beside Ivy. I don't know what I'm doing, but my magic takes over, guiding my words.

I feel it when Ivy's weakened life latches on to my magic, when her body senses the spell and opens itself up to it. I whisper the words frantically, and the bird's heartbeat glows brighter and brighter in my hand.

My voice gets louder, and Ivy's muscles tense as I release the life into her. I watch as it takes hold, as she comes back to life with each second that passes, her body cooling and her welts healing.

She jolts upright in bed, her eyes wild, her hands latching on to me, squeezing too tight.

"What did you do?" Her voice isn't her own. It's monstrous. Her eyes frantically search the room, landing on the nighthawk on the sill.

She turns back to me, her eyes so wide they could fall from her skull.

"What did you *do*?" she says again, and I'm so scared that for a moment, all I can do is violently shake my head.

"I..." I begin, not sure what to say. Terror grabs me as the full weight of my actions comes crashing down on me. "I couldn't let you die," I finally get out.

"That wasn't your choice to make!" Ivy yells, shoving me off the bed.

I land on the floor, knocking into the dresser behind me.

"It was the only choice," I plead, begging her to understand.

"You've ruined me," she says, crying out for her mother.

The door flies open, and Ivy's parents and mine rush into the room.

"Ivy!" Mrs. Eldon shouts, hurrying to the bed.

Ivy sobs, burying her face in her mother's chest. "I shouldn't be here," she cries, her uncontrollable sobs shaking the whole room.

The nighthawk lies peacefully on the windowsill, and one by one, everyone in the room turns to look at me as they realize what I did.

"You didn't," my mother says, her hand covering her mouth.

"I... I didn't know what I was doing. I just acted. It was like my body took over. I'm sorry." The words are all disjointed, a jumbled mess as they fight their way through my tears.

"Get her out of here!" Ivy shouts, clutching her mother.

I scramble to my feet and try to find the words to explain, but Ivy looks at me as if I'm evil incarnate, the most vile thing she's ever seen in her life. "Now!" she shouts.

My dad helps me out of the room, and Ivy's father slams the door behind us, but it isn't enough to block out the sound of Ivy's screams.

They take hold of me until I'm certain I will never stop hearing them, not for a single second, for the rest of my life.

twenty-five

My dad has to drag me home. I claw and yell, desperate to get back to Ivy, desperate to heal what I broke. But once I'm on the couch staring into the fire, I realize I will never be able to fix it. The way she looked at me told me all I need to know.

My mother has stayed behind, presumably to figure out how to get Ivy's parents to keep my secret. If our coven learns that I used dark magic to save Ivy's life, it will create chaos. Witches will demand punishment. My parents will be held accountable for my sins. And our relationship with the mainland will crumble.

All of our progress, erased in the span of a single breath.

But this is Ivy. *Ivy.* My best friend, my soul mate, the love of my life. And even as I sit here with tears in my eyes, I know I would make the same decision again. It's selfish—I know that it is—but I have to learn to be okay with that. I have to learn to accept labels I've lived in fear of my entire life.

Selfish.

Impulsive.

Irresponsible.

I've never let myself be any of those things, and tonight I was all of them rolled into one desperate girl who would do anything to save her best friend. Maybe Ivy will hate me for the rest of her life; maybe her parents will never get over it; maybe I will always wonder if it truly was the right thing to do.

But Ivy is alive, and I can't make myself regret it. I won't.

My dad brings me a mug of tea and sits down on the couch next to me. I pull the thick wool blanket up to my chin as if it's armor, a shield that will save me from whatever's about to come. I watch the flames dancing in the fireplace. Dawn paints the sky beyond our windows, and I know I have to deal with this.

"You have a lot of explaining to do," Dad finally says, breaking the silence.

"I know." I blow on my tea and take a long sip. There is no magic in it, but it still reminds me of Ivy.

Part of me wants to tell him everything about Wolfe and missing the rush and using dark magic. But I promised Galen I wouldn't, and it's important to me to keep my word. Maybe that's foolish after everything that happened tonight, but the last thing I want to do is throw another family's life into upheaval.

One day, I will tell my parents everything that happened. But tonight, I will tell them only some of it. And that will have to do for now.

"I'm still replaying it in my head," I say. Dad shifts on the couch so he's facing me. He doesn't look angry or disappointed;

he looks curious. Patient. "I was holding Ivy's hand, talking to her. And this nighthawk flew to the window and practically offered itself to me. And I don't know... It's like my magic just took over. I don't even remember thinking about what I was about to do; I don't remember making a choice. I just remember doing it."

Wolfe's words about the moonflower suddenly sound in my mind, how it is the source of all magic, but I didn't have one with me. I'm so frustrated I could cry, so sick of not understanding my world, my magic, myself.

Dad is quiet for several moments, taking in my words. "But you shouldn't have known how to do that. Dark magic doesn't just awaken after years of not being used; it has to be coaxed out. Nurtured."

He's right. He's right, because that's exactly what I did with Wolfe that first night—awaken a magic that had been sleeping for nineteen years.

"I know. I can't explain it, Dad. It didn't feel like I was an active participant in what I was doing. I'm not trying to avoid blame, and I accept full responsibility for my actions. I'm just trying to explain how it felt."

Dad looks outside at the sky, growing brighter with the promise of another day. All I want is to sleep.

"We are very close to the rush," Dad says, more to himself than to me. "Which means you have more magic in your system now than at any other point. Maybe the combination of the hawk and Ivy's imminent death sparked something..." He trails off and shakes his head. "It doesn't make any sense."

"Dad," I whisper, my voice trembling. He looks at me. "I'm glad she's still alive." Each word is dressed in terror as it slowly falls from my lips.

"I know, honey," he says. He scoots closer to me and puts his arm around my shoulders, and I collapse into him. He knows, and he still holds me. He knows, and he still made me tea. He knows, and he still loves me.

Guilt claws at my stomach for all the ways I've betrayed my family. All I've ever wanted was to make them proud, and instead I've put our entire way of life in jeopardy, hanging in the balance of how my mother and the Eldons decide to move forward.

I've always known my role, but as soon as I chased that light during the last rush, as soon as my world collided with Wolfe's, I've been in the weeds, so far from the path I've always walked that I wonder if it's too late to find my way back.

I wonder if I even want to.

Selfish.

The front door slams shut, and my mother comes into the living room. Dad doesn't move away from me, and that simple gesture fills me with strength. I can do this. I can find my way back.

"You've made quite the mess," my mother says, sitting in a teal tufted chair beside me. She sinks into it and leans her head back, and I'm struck by how human she looks. How real. Her eyes are tired, and she yawns without covering her mouth, and for some reason it breaks me open.

Right now, Ingrid Fairchild is my mother. She isn't the head of the council or the coven's darling; she's my mother, exhausted by the chaos of her daughter.

It makes me want to cry.

She kicks off her shoes and looks at my tea. "Hon, I could sure use a cup of that."

Dad gets up and kisses her forehead before walking into the kitchen, and for an instant all I can think about is how I want a love like that. I used to think my mom walked all over my dad, but it isn't true. He encourages her leadership and assertiveness, and she encourages his patience and gentleness. They see the strength in each other, and I desperately want the same thing.

Maybe my fascination with Wolfe is tangled up in my love of his magic, so fully entwined I can't separate the two. Or maybe I'm fascinated with the way he sees my strengths before I can see them myself.

Dad walks over and hands Mom her tea, then sits down next to me.

"Are you okay?" she asks.

"You want to know if *I'm* okay?"

"You are my daughter," she says, holding her teacup close to her face.

"I don't know. I don't understand what happened." I pause. "How is Ivy?"

"Ivy had finally fallen asleep by the time I left. She's confused and angry. Her life is tainted with darkness, and it will take time for her to recover from that."

I want to tell her it isn't true, tell her that Wolfe saved my life using the same magic I used on Ivy and it didn't awaken a darkness in me. If anything, it brightened everything, bathed it all in the light of the moon.

"It isn't tainted, though. There was a time when that was the only kind of magic we practiced—"

"And it was poison," my mother says, cutting me off. "Magic was never meant to be used in that way. You know that, and so does Ivy. She might never forgive you."

I nod. I will spend the rest of my life trying to earn her forgiveness. I will. But I also think Ivy will realize she is the same as she has always been, bright and brilliant, and I cling to that hope. "What about her parents?"

"They're in a very tough position. No one wants their child infected with dark magic. They will watch her, constantly worried about the ways it will infiltrate her daily life." Mom takes a big breath, pauses, then slowly exhales. "But right now, Rochelle and Joseph are focusing on the fact that their daughter is alive."

I breathe out. I think it for the hundredth time tonight: *I'm so glad she's alive.*

"Tana," my mother says, the sternness I've been waiting for finally entering her voice, "your actions have consequences." She lets her words hang in the space between us. "Later today, once we've all gotten some rest, we'll discuss what you did tonight and how you knew to do it. And I will not tolerate dishonesty." She rubs her eyes. "Then we will discuss the ramifications of your choices, of which there are many."

She stands up and reaches her hand out to my father. He takes it and stands as well.

"It's been a long night. Get some sleep."

My parents walk to the staircase, but I stop them.

"Mom?"

She turns to look at me.

"If it had been me…" I don't know how to finish the sentence, but my mother seems to understand what I'm asking.

"None of us knows how to use dark magic, Tana. I wouldn't have been able to save you. But if someone else had made that choice for me, the way you did with Ivy?" She shakes her head. "It would be very difficult for me not to feel indebted to that person for the rest of my life."

Tears fill my eyes and I nod.

She turns and heads up the stairs with my father, and I sink back into the couch and watch the sunrise through the large windows.

The last time I watched a sunrise, I was sure I was going to die. The sky came alive with pinks and oranges, and I tried so hard to accept my fate.

But I wasn't successful, and it changed everything.

I've made a spectacular mess of my life, and I don't know how to fix it. I don't know how to pretend my time with Wolfe didn't happen, that it didn't fundamentally change me, altering the atoms and cells in my body until they called back to a different star.

I don't know how to stop wanting him or his magic.

Because what I can never say out loud, can never think of again, is that it felt right, more natural to me than making any perfume or soap. It wrapped me up in its power and whispered *you're home*, just like the depths of the ocean. It made me feel like I was worth something, like I was worth everything. Like all the questions I've ever asked about myself were finally answered.

And I don't know how to come back from that.

That, more than anything else that has happened during this disastrous month, is what terrifies me the most. Because I will be forced to make a choice. I will be forced to look at the life I didn't choose and weigh it against the life I dream about when the Witchery sleeps.

And if this past month has taught me anything, it's that when it comes to Wolfe Hawthorne, I never make the right choice.

It isn't until I'm in my bedroom changing for bed that I notice the long silver necklace Wolfe gave me still hanging from my neck, tucked beneath my dress, resting over my heart. I hold it up, rolling it around in my fingers.

And there, through the filigree, are the white petals of a moonflower.

twenty-six

My mother goes to Ivy's house once we've all slept, but I'm forbidden from coming. Ivy doesn't want to see me. I did everything I could to save her life, gave up everything, and I lost her anyway.

I'm waiting by the door when Mom walks back in. She hangs up her coat and slips off her cashmere gloves, giving me a sideways glance.

"She's back to normal," my mother says. "Whatever you did, it completely healed her." She says it with no emotion, because it isn't something to celebrate. Not to her.

"Will she ever want to see me again?"

I follow her into the kitchen, where Dad is pouring two glasses of wine. I sit at the kitchen island and wait for her to answer.

"I don't know, Tana. She's still torn up over it." She takes a long pull of her wine, then gently sets the glass down. "The good news is that Ivy's parents have agreed to keep this a secret, contingent upon several things. But before we get into that, I need to know exactly what happened last night."

I shift in my seat, turning to face my mother. I tell her exactly what I told my dad, that the nighthawk flew up to the window almost like an offering and something in my gut took over. I wasn't thinking, I was doing.

My dad reiterates what he said to me last night, his theory that the buildup of magic in my system could have contributed to my actions. My mom listens to him thoughtfully, her expression giving nothing away. She tilts her head to the side, looking between Dad and me.

"This can never happen again," she says to me. "It should have never happened in the first place. New witches don't just stumble upon dark magic, Tana. It must be learned." She pauses, seemingly thinking of something else. "Why did you bring up the moonflower yesterday?"

Goose bumps rise along my skin, and for a moment, my mind goes blank. I don't know what to say, so I repeat my words from the day before. "I saw a flower that looked like one," I say. "I was just curious. Why?"

I watch her, Wolfe's words sliding into my mind, unwelcome. *I really wish your mother had told you the truth.*

She shakes her head and says, "It's nothing."

And with those two words, I know that Wolfe was right. She knows. A sob threatens to escape my mouth, and I force it back down, fighting to keep my composure. Her expression never slips, not even a flinch, and it breaks my heart.

I don't say anything.

"If there's more to what happened, I'll find out about

it. You know I will. But for now, we need to talk about the consequences."

I take a breath. "Tell me."

"First, you are to take a hiatus from your magic. At the end of every day, you will pour your magic into the scraps at the shop so it doesn't build up. You will not make any new perfumes or soaps. Your only displays of magic for the foreseeable future will be draining it at the end of every day and during the full moon."

"Mom," I say, her words strangling me, sucking all the air from my lungs. "Please. Please don't take it away. My magic is everything."

"No, sweetie, not anymore." Her eyes are sad—at least, I think they are from what I can see through my tears.

"Second, you will remain under constant supervision by your father or me until the wedding."

I stop breathing. "The wedding?"

"Which brings me to the third contingency. You will announce your engagement to Landon at the harvest celebration."

"But that's next weekend," I say, my voice rising. "It's too soon."

My mother holds her hand up to silence me. "And the wedding will now take place at your Covenant Ball."

I stand up and back away. "No," I say, shaking my head. "No."

"Honey, it's the only way." Her voice is calm and collected, and that might be what hurts more than anything else. "You know what the punishment is for new witches who attempt dark magic."

I nod. It's part of our agreement with the mainland—we

send them across the Passage to be tried. They inevitably miss the rushes while they are held in prison, where their magic eats them from the inside out.

It's a death sentence.

I shake my head and start to cry, covering my face with my hands.

"This is the only way. This is what Ivy's parents require—an alliance with the mainland. That's what their silence is worth to them."

"Give them time, please. You said yourself that you'd feel indebted if someone did for me what I did for Ivy. I know they're glad she's alive, even if they won't say it. They'll keep my secret."

My mom just shakes her head. "They're willing to swear to it with magic, but they want the wedding moved up. And I won't settle for their word, not on this."

"But I'm not ready." The words are weak, barely making it out of my mouth around my tears.

"It's only a few months' difference. All things considered, this is an extremely lenient outcome. You're lucky, Tana."

"When will I get to practice magic again?"

"After the wedding. You won't be able to practice on the mainland, so we'll need to make sure you're using enough magic when you're working in the perfumery to prevent an unhealthy buildup from happening."

I wince. I didn't fully realize until now that magic will no longer be part of my daily life when I move to the mainland. It will no longer be what makes me rise with the sun and dread the night. I will have to bury it for my life with Landon.

My stomach rolls as nausea crawls up my throat. "I'm going to be sick," I manage to get out before rushing to the bathroom. My father is behind me in seconds, rubbing my back and holding my hair. When I'm done, he gets me a cool washcloth to place on my forehead.

I see the worried expression on his face. I wish I could convince him that I'm okay, that this is okay with me. I wish I could squeeze his hand and tell him that I'm going to be fine, that a life with Landon is a new adventure I can't wait to embark on, because seeing him worry this way, seeing the uncertainty in his eyes—it hurts.

Everything hurts.

And it's in this moment, seeing my dad question the life he's built for me, question the life I'm about to begin, that I finally admit it to myself: I'm not okay with it. It isn't the life I want. I want the love my parents have. I want the certainty Ivy has. I want the passion Wolfe has. I want it all, and a life with Landon won't give it to me.

Selfish.

I go lie down while my parents eat dinner. I roll Landon's sea glass around in my fingers, feel every edge and every corner, hold it in my hands and will myself to believe that I can say the words *I do* without regretting them every single day for the rest of my life.

Landon deserves more than that.

And so do I.

There's a soft knock on my door, and my father pokes his head in. "Almost time, sweetheart."

Another rush. Another release of my magic. Another night of wrecking the sea.

I tremble as I get out of bed, change into my rushing gown, and follow my parents to the western shore. I'm terrified of giving my magic over to the sea when there's nothing I can do to rebuild it. My skills will fade and my magic will weaken, and I will be a shadow of the girl I once was.

Landon will marry an echo, a whisper, a slight breeze at his back that makes him feel as if he's being watched.

I walk behind my parents onto the beach and go through the motions of the rush, following my coven into the water once we're all accounted for. I search for Ivy, but she never once looks my way. She's on the far side of the shore, and I know she put herself there on purpose, keeping as much distance from me as possible.

The water is up to my chest. It's a cold, clear night, and a full moon looks down on us from its perch in the sky, illuminating our shame.

It's midnight.

I don't think about it first. I don't feel as if I'm making a choice, but as the rest of my coven pours their magic into the sea, I hold on to mine.

I keep it close.

And I whisper his name.

Over. And over. And over.

Minutes go by, and the last cries of the witches fade into the night. Magic rolls into the water, heavy and thick like oil, damaging instead of healing.

I stare into the distance, beg for Wolfe to appear, but he

doesn't. The witches begin their march out of the water, shoulders slumped and heads hanging, exhausted from another rush.

I slowly turn and make my way up the beach. My parents find me, and we walk toward the road, waiting for all the other witches to leave before we go. No one says anything, too ashamed to speak to one another even though we have all gone through the same thing.

Finally, it's just the three of us. Mom leans into Dad. "Ready?" she asks.

He nods and we start the walk home.

I'm already on the street when I think I hear my name, though it could just be the wind rushing off the waves. It could be nothing at all. Still, I turn.

And there he is.

Standing in the water, bathed in moonlight, whispering my name.

I don't think, I don't hesitate, I don't fear.

I run.

"Tana!" my mother calls behind me, her voice weak from the rush but urgent. Scared. "Tana!"

I don't look back. Wolfe is no longer facing the shore; he's getting ready to dive back into his current. He didn't see me in time.

"Wolfe!" I scream his name as my mother screams mine, chasing after me. "Wolfe!" I scream again.

He stops and turns, his mouth falling open and his eyes growing wide.

I sprint into the water, pushing through it as fast as I can, trying to ignore the sounds of my mother behind me. I can't turn around because if I do, I might shatter.

I push off the ocean floor and launch myself toward Wolfe. He catches me in his arms, and I wrap myself around him, holding on tight, holding on for my life.

"Go!" I shout.

My father is in the water now, swimming toward us, thrashing through the waves even though he's weak from the rush—too weak, and yet he expends every last ounce of what he has left coming after me. He slows, unable to keep up, bobbing helplessly several yards away. I hold on to Wolfe tightly to keep myself from swimming to my father, but I watch him the whole time, and I know this image will stick with me for the rest of my life, no matter how hard I try to erase it. He shouts my name and begins to choke, the sound tearing me in two. My mother finally reaches him and pulls him toward the shore. Tears roll down my face as I tuck my head into Wolfe's shoulder and take a deep breath. He dives into the current, and the image of my father is replaced by dark water rolling over my head, erasing all the light.

Erasing all the love.

Erasing everything.

Wolfe's arms are wrapped tightly around me as we're swept out to sea, but I'm not sure it's the ocean we're in anymore. Maybe it's a buildup of tears and anguish so vast and wide I'll never find my way back out.

Mom calling my name.

Dad thrashing in the water.

I will never recover from this, not if I live a hundred years, a thousand lifetimes. This moment will scar every part of me, and I will never be without it.

I squeeze my arms and legs tighter around Wolfe because I'm afraid if I don't, I'll give up and let the ocean do with me whatever it will. But Wolfe's arms are secure around me, holding me together when I'm sure I'll fall apart.

The current slows, and we surface. We both pull in air, our chests expanding into each other as we breathe. I cling to him as if he's a life preserver, and in this moment, I'm sure that he is.

The water pulls us along. I look toward the shore, but we're far away from the beach where the rush took place, far away from my parents. Far away from my heart.

Wolfe's feet touch the ground, the water pouring over his shoulders, but I don't move. I stay wrapped around him, afraid that as soon as I let go, the weight of my decision will crush me until I'm nothing more than a grain of sand on the beach.

I slowly pull my head back and look at Wolfe, meeting his eyes for the first time tonight.

His breathing picks up, and he moves his hands to either side of my face. Water drips from his dark hair, his eyelashes, his lips. He looks so perfect it physically hurts.

"What did you do?" he asks, his voice rough. Accusatory. He searches my face, frantic, his palms pressed against my cheekbones.

"I became everything I'm afraid of being."

Then I kiss him. His breath catches when my lips touch his, a gasping sound that turns me into something wild. I grasp at his face, his hair, his shoulders, hungrily taking his kisses as if they're air, the only thing keeping me alive.

He opens his mouth and groans when my tongue meets his, the sound moving through my whole body. My legs stay wrapped tightly around his hips, and he moves his hands to my back, pulling me closer.

Closer.

Closer.

I'm crazed, my lips finding his jaw, his neck, his temple. He tips his head back, his eyes closed, moonlight flooding his face. It completely undoes me. This boy has upended every part of my life, set my entire existence on fire.

I came alive when I met him, and I won't pretend that I didn't. I won't pretend he hasn't become vital to me, that he hasn't enabled me to see myself exactly as I want to be seen.

My lips find his again. He tastes like the sea, my own personal ocean. My arms are tight around his neck, my fingers deep in his hair. When I finally pull away, he looks at me as if he's taking in every vulnerability, every insecurity, every fear and hope and doubt. He takes it all in and kisses me once more, accepting everything I have to offer.

He is my daylight, my sun, my hours spent practicing magic. I know that now, and I vow to be the same for him.

But we aren't confined to daylight. Here we can be whoever we want to be.

I watch him, impossibly beautiful in the moonlight.

I press my lips to his.

He comes alive in darkness, so darkness I become.

twenty-seven

Steam rises all around me in the large porcelain bath. I close my eyes, letting the water wash away the salt from the sea and the salt from my tears. But nothing will take away the image of my father frantically trying to reach me in the waves. Nothing.

There's a heavy freedom that comes with what I've done. I've lived my entire life afraid of being selfish, afraid of searching out what I wanted because I knew all along that what I wanted didn't matter. But I always thought I'd have the strength to be who they needed me to be, to disregard my own happiness because I believe so strongly in an alliance with the mainland. I was wrong.

I have a different strength, though, one I didn't know I had. It takes strength to put duty and loyalty above all else, to find happiness in a life that wasn't chosen—Landon's strength. But it also takes strength to disappoint every person I've ever cared about because I've found something I believe in more.

I don't have the kind of strength my coven was relying on,

that *I* was relying on. But I am strong enough to choose something for myself that the rest of my world believes is wrong. And for someone who has lived by the measure of others for far too long, that's an accomplishment.

I doubt I will ever stop caring. I doubt I will ever be fully comfortable with the enemies I've created and the heartache I've caused. But standing in Wolfe's bathroom, knowing he is on the other side of the door, I wouldn't take it back.

When I get out of the bath, a large black robe is waiting for me. I slip into it and wrap the belt around my waist. I towel dry my hair and let it fall down my back, and then I slowly open the door.

Wolfe is sitting in a large wingback chair in front of the fire. His chin is resting on his hand, and he's looking into the flames, lost in thought.

The door creaks and Wolfe turns toward me. It's the first time I've ever seen him look nervous. He swallows as he takes in the sight of me, and I fight the urge to turn away, force myself to stand here in all my vulnerability and let him see it.

Let him see me.

"How was your bath?" he asks.

"It was just what I needed. Thank you." I pull a blanket from the bed and put it on the floor in front of the fire. "Sit with me?"

He nods and sinks to the ground next to me. I lie on my side, propping myself up on my elbow, and he does the same. And for a moment, we just look at each other.

"Tell me what happened," he finally says.

So I do. I tell him about Ivy and the nighthawk and how I saved her life, how something inside me took over and I let it. I tell him about the deal my parents made, the consequences I would have to endure in order to stay on the island and have my secret protected. And I tell him that during the rush, all I could think about was running, but not running away from what I'd done—running toward what I want.

"What you want," he says, repeating the words.

"You. You and your magic."

He looks away, into the fire, and I see his jaw tense. Something flashes across his face that I can't read, and I sit up.

"Did I say something wrong?" I ask.

He sits up, too, but doesn't meet my eyes. He shakes his head, and I'm suddenly worried that I chose something that isn't available to me. My heart races and my throat gets dry.

"No," he finally says. "I'm used to being in control, Mortana." He pauses, looking at the chaotic flames. "But against you I am powerless."

"Is that what you're afraid of?" I ask, the words quiet. "That I make you weak?"

He looks at me then, an intensity in his eyes that sends a chill down my spine. His jaw is tight, his mouth a hard line. "I would set the world on fire just to see your face. That's what I'm afraid of."

I slowly lean into him, my lips brushing against his. "Then we can burn together."

He takes my face in his hands and kisses me with desperation, like we will never have to leave the safety of this room if he kisses me long enough, deep enough, fervently enough. I wrap my arms around his neck and pull him into me, shifting to get closer, angling myself so I can reach more of him.

My robe slides off my shoulder, and Wolfe moves his fingers down my jaw, my neck, my collarbone. I lie on my back and pull him down with me, his lips following the trail his fingers left. He pauses when he's at my sternum, lets his head rest against my chest. His eyes close.

"I can hear your heartbeat."

His mouth finds my rib cage, and he kisses the bones around my heart as if they're sacred, as if they're guarding the most precious thing in the world. I slowly undo my belt and let the robe fall open.

Wolfe hovers over me. I lie perfectly still as his eyes follow the curves of my body, committing them to memory.

"Mortana," he says, his voice like gravel. "You will be the end of me."

His lips are back on mine before I can tell him that he is my beginning, brilliant, beautiful, and new.

The manor looms behind us as Wolfe and I walk down to the shore. I'm wearing a borrowed nightdress and one of his sweaters, but I might never give it back. It smells like him, and I love being wrapped up in it.

Several witches are crowded around a grimoire in the

greenhouse, but otherwise we are the only ones out here. The full moon casts enough light for me to see where I'm walking, and magic stirs in my belly, waiting to see what I'll ask of it.

I'm no longer willing to dump my magic into the sea, unused and dangerous, killing our animals and harming our island. But it has to get out somehow. It might as well be tonight, beneath the glorious moon, next to the boy who changed everything.

"What's your favorite place?" Wolfe asks when we get to the beach.

"The sea."

"Why?"

"Because of its silence. I like the way nothing above the surface matters when I'm submerged in water. I like the way the silence is louder than my thoughts. It's peaceful and slow. It calms me."

"Close your eyes," Wolfe says.

And I do.

Within seconds, the air around me shifts. It gets heavier, in a way. Denser. The sound of the lapping waves recedes into the background until there's perfect silence.

My skin gets cold, and my mind gets quiet. I feel weightless. A thick calm surrounds me, so real I could roll around in it, touch it. My hair floats out around me, and my clothes cling to my skin. Everything feels slower: my movements, my breathing, my heartbeat.

I feel like I'm under the water, fully submerged in my favorite place.

My eyes snap open, and the setting is torn away. I'm back on the beach with Wolfe under a cloudless sky.

"How did you do that?" I ask, breathless.

"I altered your senses until you believed you were someplace else. It's a perception spell."

"Like the one you use when you have to go into town? That makes people think you're a tourist?"

"Exactly."

"Unbelievable," I say. My clothing is dry and my skin is warm, but there's still a part of me that believes I was under the water just seconds ago. "Teach me."

"Our connection to the natural world is what's most powerful about us—it enables everything we do. Just as we have a heightened sensitivity to the world around us, the world has a heightened sensitivity to us. Your intent matters more than anything else in magic. That's why you were able to save Ivy's life using a spell you'd never used before. Think of it like a veil that's woven from your experiences, desires, and understanding of the physical world. That veil can cover anything you choose."

"Even another person," I say.

"Even another person. I created a veil of the sea and covered you in it."

"Amazing," I say.

"Your turn."

I smile. I've been waiting for this since the last time I saw him, aching to discover more of the magic that's living inside me. We use the sea again for my first time, a setting I could recreate over and over.

I weave a veil of cold water and slow movements, of silence that stretches out in every direction like morning fog over the

Passage. The veil forms in front of me, a physical thing I can see and touch. I weave in memories of being wrapped around Wolfe, our wet bodies pressed tightly together.

Then I take the veil and stretch it until it covers both of us.

The world around me vanishes, and I'm back in the water, in Wolfe's arms, with nothing but the perfect silence of the sea.

Magic pours out of me, sustaining the veil, engaging all of my senses until I fully believe the image I've woven. I'm under the water, moving with the motion of the waves, weightless in Wolfe's arms. We are quiet and still and content, holding each other in the belly of the sea.

I pull the veil away, and we're back on the beach. I look at Wolfe and run my fingers through his hair, sure it will be soaked. But it isn't.

"Did it work?" I ask. I know what I felt, but that doesn't mean Wolfe felt it, too.

He nods. "You are much more powerful than you realize," he says. "You could have changed the perception of every witch in this house."

"Why?" I ask. "Why does this come so naturally to me?"

"I don't know," he says, shaking his head. "I think it has to do with all the time you've spent in the water. You are so connected to this place; every time you've accidentally swallowed seawater, every time you've gathered flowers and herbs for the perfumery, all the hours you've spent wandering this island, you've invited this world in, and it has taken root inside you. I think that's why."

The words cause something inside me to break open. I've been scolded most of my life for getting too dirty, swimming too often, preferring trails in the woods to ballrooms and high teas. It is something I've been taught to apologize for, but in Wolfe's world, it's a gift. An extraordinary gift.

We practice more magic, weaving veils of different places and calling the wind from the sea. We create fire from dust and capture the light of the moon in our hands. We use more magic than I would ever expel during a rush, and instead of hurting the Earth, we're delighting in it.

We walk onto the lawn, and I collapse on the grass, exhausted. Wolfe lies beside me, and we watch the stars. The rest of the witches have gone inside, and it feels as if we have the entire world to ourselves, as if the moon and stars are shining just for us.

"Do you know that I've never seen another moonflower on the island since the night we met?" I ask, rolling onto my side. "I've only ever seen them with you. It's like we were fated for each other, like the flower's only purpose was to bring us together."

I lean down and kiss him. He's hesitant at first, his movements slow and unsure. Then he opens his mouth and pulls me into him, weaving his fingers through my hair and kissing me as if he'll never be able to kiss me again.

I move my hand beneath his shirt and trail my fingers over his skin. He inhales sharply, and I'm ravaged by the way he unravels. He breathes my name into my mouth and clutches me tighter, rolling me over so his body is on top of mine, the weight of him anchoring me in this perfect moment.

Then someone calls his name, and he quickly moves off me.

I'm mortified when I register his father's voice, and we both sit up. I wipe my face and smooth my hair, as if that will do anything.

"Get up, you two," Galen calls as he walks down the lawn to meet us.

Wolfe helps me to my feet, and I fidget with my clothing, hoping the darkness is enough to conceal the heat in my face.

"Lovely to see you again, Mortana," Galen says when he reaches us. He sweeps a hand over both of us, and I feel my hair settle and my skin cool. He keeps his back to the manor, watching me, and goose bumps rise along my skin.

Something isn't right.

"Hello, Ingrid." His voice is even.

It feels as if my heart stops and all the blood rushes out of my body.

"Galen," she says in response.

I follow the voice, and there at the top of the hill, with the manor in perfect silhouette behind her, is my mother.

twenty-eight

My mother walks down the hill, and all the air leaves my lungs. I reach out and take Wolfe's hand, holding it tightly. *Don't let go*, I want to say to him, but I can't make the words come out.

I look at the manor, where witches stand at the windows, watching from behind thick curtains. Others tentatively step onto the balcony, and I realize everyone in this house knows exactly who my mother is.

When I first came here with Wolfe, I was amazed, my world cracking open, so much bigger than I ever imagined. But now, as I watch my mother approach, I start to feel as if I've been fooled, as if this manor on this shore has always been known to all but me. I kept this secret and guarded it like a precious gem, only to discover the witches here didn't need my protection.

My grip on Wolfe's hand gets tighter.

"Hi, honey," my mother says when she finally reaches us.

My greeting sticks to the inside of my throat, and I can't get it out. I watch my mother as she meets Galen's eyes, her shoulders back and her chin high, not a single worry creasing her perfect skin.

"It's been a long time," Galen says, looking at my mom.

"It certainly has."

My heart races. I'd give anything for Wolfe's perception spell to send me beneath the water, to take me anywhere but here.

"You two know each other," I manage to say.

"We do," my mother says simply, as if her words don't reveal that she's been lying to me for nineteen years. As if she doesn't keep breaking my heart.

"You said the old coven doesn't exist anymore."

My mother moves her eyes from Galen to me. "I say a lot of things to protect our way of life."

My entire body runs cold, and I shiver. "But I'm your daughter." I hate the way my words get quiet and my voice shakes. I hate even more how calm my mother is, how my words don't affect her.

"Some things are best kept hidden. Even from you."

Wolfe doesn't move. He doesn't speak. But if I listen closely, I can hear his breathing over the sound of the waves, and it's enough. That sound is enough.

"But I was willing to give up a life of my own to protect our coven. I did everything you ever asked of me in service of that goal. Surely I deserved the truth?"

My mother looks to my hand, to my fingers laced with Wolfe's, and her brows knit together. For a single moment, she looks sad. Then it vanishes.

"You're speaking in the past tense," she says.

"I'm staying here." It takes all my strength to get the words out, to make them sound sure and steady.

"Oh, honey," my mother sighs, and it sounds pitying, like she feels sorry for me. Then she looks at Wolfe. "I haven't seen you since you were a child."

"Forgive me, I don't remember." He shifts but meets my mother's eyes.

"It was a long time ago," she says, waving a hand through the air, dismissing his concern. "It seems my daughter is willing to give up an awful lot for you. Why don't you tell her the truth, though, so she has all the facts?"

Wolfe's hand tightens around mine as a thick dread begins in my stomach and spreads through the rest of me.

"We should give them some privacy," Galen says, but my mother stays where she is.

"He didn't tell her when he had the chance, in *private*," she says. "Perhaps he will tell her now."

"Please stop talking about me like I'm not here," I say to them. I turn to Wolfe. "What do you need to tell me?"

He gently releases my hand, and cold air invades the space where his warmth used to be. I shiver, looking down at my empty hand, then back to his face. The muscle in his jaw tightens and doesn't release.

"We sent Wolfe to seek you out." It's Galen who speaks. "We've been trying to get a meeting with the council for the past year to discuss the ocean currents. This is a problem that must be solved soon, and after our last request was denied—"

"Dad, let me," Wolfe says.

Galen nods.

"They sent me to get close to you. To use you to get to your mother, to get her attention some other way."

"The moonflowers?" I ask, my voice a whisper.

"That was me," he says, angrier than I've ever heard him. "I planted them for you to find. I magicked the light you saw to lure you to the field that first night." I hear the way his voice catches on the word *lure*, and my breath does the same thing.

I remember my words from just moments ago, my overwhelming belief that the moonflower was fate, and my cheeks burn with shame.

"You were using me?" I ask, the last of my heart leaving with the words, floating out into the infinite darkness, never to return.

"Yes." Wolfe swallows hard, his stormy eyes never leaving mine. "I've hated your coven my entire life, hated everything you stand for. I didn't care if I had to use you to get what we want. What we need." His hands are in fists at his sides. "And it was easy to use you—you're too trusting, Mortana." The frustration I've grown so comfortable with sharpens his voice and stabs me right in my chest.

I take a step away from him.

"It was easy to use you," he repeats, "and damn near impossible not to fall in love with you."

Tears sting my eyes, and my stomach clenches. I bend at the waist to ease the pain and take several deep breaths, trying so hard to keep myself together. Then I stand up straight and force myself to look at Wolfe. "You love me so much that you couldn't tell me the truth?"

"I wanted to—"

"Then you should have. You didn't even try," I say, taking another step away from him. "I was ready to give up everything for you." I can't help the tears that roll down my cheeks and drop off my chin, can't help the way my body starts to shake, suddenly too cold. "Was any of it real?"

"Yes," Wolfe says without hesitation. "You are more real to me than the waves on the shore or the blood in my veins. How can you not see that?"

"If that were true, you would have been honest with me."

"I just... I needed more time."

"More time?" I ask, realizing what he means, realizing he never got his meeting. "You are the one thing I thought I chose on my own. The one thing," I say, staring at him. "But you chose this for me." I wipe my face and clear my throat, fulfilling the role he wanted me to play. "Mom, will you give them their meeting?"

"I would be happy to meet with them after the wedding, yes."

"You're not seriously considering—" Wolfe begins, but I raise my hand and turn to Galen.

"You have your meeting. Now, please stay away from me." I look at Wolfe. "Both of you."

I start up the hill, but Wolfe follows me. He grabs my arm and I turn around, anger and pain burning through my veins like acid. He reaches for my face, and I hate that my first instinct is to lean into his touch. I am too trusting, just like he said.

"Please," he says, the single word freezing me in place, unable to move or speak. "I can make this right."

And I want him to—I want him to so badly that I can feel it in my muscles and my bones. I want to cover his hand with mine and tell him it's okay, that we'll figure it out together, but how can it ever be okay when I gave him my world and he couldn't even give me the truth?

"She said to stay away from her," my mother says, putting her arm around my shoulders and guiding me inside.

"I'm not talking to you!" Wolfe yells, moving after us. Galen comes up beside him and grips his shoulder, keeping him in place.

"Let her go, son," he says.

"No!" I hear Wolfe struggle against his dad's hold. "Tana!" he shouts, and I pause, the first time I've ever heard my nickname in his mouth. It sounds so beautiful, like I've never really heard it before this moment, like it was only ever meant to be spoken by him. But then my mother pulls me forward, and I start walking again, far away from here. I keep my head down to avoid the eyes that follow us, the witches watching from dark corners and the top of the staircase.

"Bye, Mortana," Lily calls from behind her mother's legs, and it takes all my strength not to break down right here.

"I'm sorry we never got to color together," I say, and then my mother leads me to the door, and I let her.

"Tana!" Another breath. "Dad, let me go," Wolfe pleads, and I can hear the tears in his voice. "Tana!" he shouts again.

Then the door closes behind us, and all I hear is the wind

through the trees and the waves on the shore and all the words he never said.

When we get to the road, I don't turn to look at the manor, because magic or not, I know that it's gone.

Gone—nothing more than a memory. A bitter, heartbreaking memory I will spend my life trying to forget.

My mother doesn't speak to me as we walk home, but she keeps her arm around my shoulders, a tight, firm grip that lets me know she's here. Even after everything, after I used dark magic and ran away, she's here. And I can't bring myself to pull back from her, to set her lies in the space between us, because I don't think I could handle the distance they'd create. There's already so much of that between me and the people I love most. Too much.

When we turn onto our street, my dad is standing in front of the house, waiting. I remember him thrashing in the water, coming after me, desperate to keep me safe, and I can't hold myself together anymore.

I run to him, and he opens his arms wide. He envelops me, tells me it will be okay, tells me that he loves me.

I sob against his chest and repeat the words *I'm sorry* over and over again.

I'm sorry.

I'm sorry.

I never thought I was perfect, but I thought I was better than

BRING ME YOUR MIDNIGHT

this. Better than turning my back on my family, my coven, my magic. Better than falling for a boy I can never have. My heart is broken, but so is everything else. Bodybroken. Soulbroken.

My dad leads me inside and pours me some tea, sitting with me as I cry. My mom covers me in a blanket and kisses my head and tells me nothing has changed.

We don't ever have to speak of what happened tonight.

We can move forward. I can accept the consequences of practicing dark magic, marry Landon, and everything will be right again.

I want to make everything right again.

Wolfe's manor is not the only place that held a lie. This home has them, too, lies so big I'm shocked they even fit. But without Wolfe, without Ivy, without my parents, where would I go?

I finish my tea and get ready for bed. I brush my teeth and wash my face and think about how just hours ago I was in Wolfe's bathroom in front of his mirror, marveling at how I had changed the entire trajectory of my life.

Marveling because I'd fallen in love with someone who saw me for everything except what I was supposed to be.

Marveling because I couldn't hear all the words he wasn't saying.

I crawl into bed. The cold metal of the necklace he gave me presses into my skin, and I rip it off and throw it across the room. There's a soft knock on the door, and my mother steps inside. She comes and pulls the covers up to my chin, then sits down on the edge of the bed.

"How long have you known?" I ask, my voice quiet and unsteady.

"About you and Wolfe?"

I nod.

"I didn't put everything together until earlier tonight, when I saw him in the water," she says. "Then I knew."

My mind is overwhelmed with all the lies, Wolfe's and my mother's and mine.

"I left Wolfe because he lied to me. And you've lied to me, too. If you want me to stay here and continue down this path, you have to tell me all the things you've been keeping from me. You have to, Mom." My head is throbbing, and my eyes beg for sleep. "Tonight, I need to rest. But soon."

"Deal," she says, stroking the quilt over my arm. She kisses my forehead, then stands. Landon's sea glass sits on my bedside table, shiny now from all the hours I've worked it in my fingers. She picks it up and hands it to me.

"Not all love hurts," she says, turning off my bedside lamp. But I wonder if that's true, because what I felt for Wolfe was a physical ache I carried in my chest even before I knew he had used me to get to my mother. And it hurt not because it was bad but because my happiness was no longer my own.

It was dependent upon the survival of another person.

My lungs and my heart had to shift, rearrange themselves to make space for all the love, and even then, it was more than I could hold, a constant pressure against my ribs.

Still, I nod and take the sea glass, roll it around between my fingers. The door clicks behind my mother when she leaves.

Landon is the only one who hasn't lied to me. The only one who has given me the truth and trusted me to handle it, even if it hurt. A life with him won't be so bad. Maybe it will be a relief to be with someone and not have that ache in my chest. Maybe it will be a relief to not feel so much.

I don't know when my hand stills and the sea glass falls onto my quilt, when my mind finally gives up the day and falls into darkness.

But even in sleep, I remember the way Wolfe's voice sounded as he called out for me. I remember the way he struggled against his father to get to me. I remember the anguish in his tone when he said it was impossible not to fall in love with me, like it was the worst thing he'd ever done.

Even in sleep, I remember.

twenty-nine

When I wake up, Ivy is sitting at the bay window that looks out over the Passage. The day is clear and cold, and condensation has beaded on the glass. The oaks and maples are starting to drop their leaves, bare, spindly branches reaching toward the sky. I wipe my eyes and slowly sit up.

"You're here," I say.

"I'm here." She doesn't look at me.

I want to tell her I'm sorry, to fix what I broke between us, but I'm so glad she's here, so relieved. And I can't apologize for what I did, because I'd do it over and over again if it meant waking up to her staring out my bedroom window, angry and hurt.

"I'm so happy to see you." I say it because it's true, and after last night, the truth is all that matters.

She turns to look at me then. "I might never forgive you for what you did."

I nod and look down, scrunching the quilt up in my fingers. "I can live with that. What I can't live without is you."

She raises an eyebrow. "You aren't going to apologize?"

"No," I say, exhaling. "Because I'm not sorry. You're my best friend, Ivy, and I'd use all the dark magic in the world to keep you here. It was selfish of me, and I accept that. But you deserve the truth, and the truth is that I'm not sorry."

Ivy nods slowly, then looks out the window again. "You apologize too much, anyway," she finally says, and it hurts because Wolfe said the same thing to me.

He saw me, the same way Ivy does. I never thought I'd meet another person who saw me for anything more than the role I'm meant to play, but Wolfe did. He saw me and he lied, and I have to find a way to reconcile those truths.

"When I told you about missing the rush and getting help, you said my life was tainted. But it isn't, Ivy. It is full and complicated and terribly messy, but it isn't tainted. I know you don't accept that kind of magic, and you don't have to, but I promise you it hasn't put a stain on your life. Your life is beautiful, just as it was before."

Ivy nods, swallowing hard when her eyes start to glisten. "I was terrified when I woke up. Terrified of you and whatever magic you used to save me. I still am, and I'm still working through it." She pauses and looks down. "But I'm glad Wolfe saved your life. And I understand why you did what you did. I think one day, I might be glad for it." She says it so quietly I have to lean in to hear it, and it breaks my heart that she thinks she needs to feel shame about being alive. That I once felt that way, too.

"I think you will be." Ivy's form at the window blurs, watery and indistinct. But here. Still here.

"Your mom told me what happened." She moves from the window to the side of my bed, and it feels good having her closer. I try to keep my composure because I don't want her to have to comfort me after what I put her through.

"And?"

"And I think you made a hell of a mess."

I nod because she's right. I pull some tissue off my bedside table and blow my nose. "I know."

"Do you love him?" she asks, watching me.

"Yes." As soon as I say it, I know it's the truth. My life has been full of deceit and lies lately, but in the middle of them all is the unwavering truth that I love Wolfe Hawthorne and would have given up everything to be with him.

Maybe I'm a fool, but I'm a fool who believed in something strongly enough to fight for it with everything I had. I scan the floor, looking for the necklace I threw off last night, but it's gone.

"Your mom wants me to convince you to take a memory eraser," Ivy says. "That's why I'm here."

I nod slowly. I'm not surprised, but it makes the ache in my chest scream, a sharp pain where Wolfe laid his head just last night.

"Do you think I should?"

Ivy looks down, and I can see how hard this is for her, how she's warring with herself over what to say. She finally looks at me again, and her eyes are sad. "Yes." Her voice shakes. "You have a lot of big events coming up, huge decisions that impact not only you but all of us. Forgetting Wolfe will allow you to start your new life with a clean slate, with excitement and hope instead of regret and pain." She pauses. "You turned your back on us, Tana. You turned your back on me. But that doesn't have to be the end. You can still do what you need to do."

"You really believe that?"

"Yes," she says. "This is bigger than you. It always has been."

I bring my knees to my chest. Maybe this is my chance at redemption, my chance to make up for all the mistakes I've made and put myself back on the right path. I can still turn this around and bring security and peace to my coven. I can still make this right.

"How does it work?" I ask, my voice quiet.

"We'd make you a tea using something of Wolfe's," she says, eyeing the black sweater hanging off the foot of my bed, the one I wore home last night. It still smells like him, like woodsmoke and salt, and I instinctively reach for it. "The tea will be very specific and target only memories including Wolfe and dark magic—everything else will remain intact. But it won't be perfect. There is a risk your memories will come back at some point. We wouldn't be erasing them so much as suppressing them; they won't come back unbidden, but there are certain events that could trigger them."

That means I would also forget about my mother's lies, because each one is linked to something I learned from Wolfe. I don't want to be okay with forgetting, to settle for ignorance, but

I'll have to if I decide to go through with this. There is no way to untangle my mother's deceit from memories of Wolfe.

"I wouldn't forget anything else? Nothing about you or my parents or the sea? Nothing about Landon?"

She shakes her head. "You'll forget this conversation and any others we've had about Wolfe. If you think back on it after taking the memory eraser, it will feel foggy. You'll remember I was here, but you won't remember what we talked about."

"Is this allowed within the new order?" I ask. "It sounds a lot like dark magic."

"It's a gray area," Ivy admits, and I don't miss the way she flinches at the words *dark magic*. "We'd never offer something like this in the shop, but given that it would be suppressing your memories instead of stripping them, the council granted us approval. The same effect could be produced with wine or spirits—this is just a more intense version. But that's why it isn't perfect, because it's weak enough to fit within the rules."

"But you would still remember all this. Is my mother okay with that?"

"I would never do anything to jeopardize our alliance with the mainland. She knows that."

I suppose it should upset me that Ivy gets to remember things I have to forget, but she's right—she would never do anything to put our coven at risk. She believes in this life more than anyone I know, and if my memories are safe with anyone, it's her.

I breathe out, heavy and long. "How can this be right when the thought of it is devastating?"

I close my eyes and picture Wolfe in the moonlight, remember what it was like to use his magic and feel like myself for the first time in my life. I see him watching me with awe, kissing my skin, touching me as if I was the answer to every question he'd ever asked. I hear the anger in his voice when I don't give myself enough credit, when I apologize for who I am. I taste the salt on his skin from when we clung to each other in the water, holding on as if we could each save the other's life.

And that's when I understand. I won't make the right decision if I remember, if I hold on to these moments with everything I have. If I think for a single second that he might whisper my name at midnight—if I know he's out there, practicing his magic and painting his portraits and doing whatever it takes to ensure the survival of his coven—I won't make the right choice.

We are the same, he and I. We believe in our ways of life, we are loyal to the ones we love, and we would do anything to give them the safety and peace they deserve. And maybe there's beauty in that, knowing we will each be fighting for these things in our own way, doing all that we can to hold on to what we care about most.

Apart, but together.

"Okay," I finally say, looking at Ivy. "I'll take it."

"You're doing the right thing." She meets my eyes when she says it, but there's no fire in her. Not like there used to be. Maybe I put it out when I saved her life with dark magic, or maybe she won't let her guard down around me anymore.

"I'll tell your mother. We should have it ready later today."

She stands and walks to the door, then backtracks, grabbing

Wolfe's sweater from me. She leaves, and the door slams shut behind her.

"Ivy, wait!" I yell, jumping from my bed and rushing out of the room. She's halfway down the stairs when I pull the sweater from her and clutch it in my hands, bringing it to my face so I can smell him again. My tears soak into the fabric and leave tiny wet spots that will soon dry. Maybe they will end up in the memory eraser.

Ivy looks at me as if I'm breaking her heart, but I can't help the way his sweater trembles in my hands, the way I hold on to it as if it's my whole world, the sun and moon and stars.

I shove my face into the fabric, hiding from Ivy and her memory eraser, my entire body shaking.

Then, ever so slowly, Ivy pulls the sweater away from me.

And ever so slowly, I let her.

I'm downstairs with my parents when Ivy returns with a colorful tea tin. She doesn't say a word, just walks to the kitchen and begins preparing the drink. My parents give each other a meaningful look as I watch Ivy's back.

"Tana, just a reminder that Landon and his parents will be joining us on Wednesday to discuss wedding preparations. They're very eager to see you again," my mother says.

I'm not sure why she's bringing this up now, but I nod anyway. "I haven't forgotten."

The words hang in the air between us, illuminating the magic Ivy laced into her tea. She scoops the leaves into a ceramic pot, the sound impossibly loud, screaming Wolfe's name. And suddenly I'm terrified of forgetting him.

I want to believe there are some things that are stronger than magic, that Ivy's tea will be worthless, nothing compared to the bond I have with him. I want to believe I can drink Ivy's tea and that Wolfe will still linger, hidden in the corners and alleys of my mind until I'm ready to remember.

I want to believe.

The kettle whistles and I jump. Ivy pours the boiling water over the tea leaves, and steam rises into the air. She sets a timer and lets the leaves steep, making sure every drop of magic makes it into the teacup.

Makes it into me.

Images of Wolfe flood my mind, and I squeeze my eyes shut, desperate for them to leave. Desperate for them to stay.

What should scare you most about tonight isn't that you're about to use high magic, Mortana. What should scare you most is that you're going to want to use it again.

My mother says something about our upcoming dinner, but I don't hear the words. I barely notice Ivy in the kitchen or my dad watching me with sadness and concern. All I see is the life I fought so hard for slipping through my fingers like grains of sand, impossible to hold.

Do you want to see me again?

Yes.

The timer goes off, and Ivy strains the tea. My parents are quiet, and my stomach twists itself into knots, tighter and tighter, suffocating my insides.

I hate you. And I want you anyway.

I think of the memory keeper I made for Wolfe, how self-conscious I was when I gave it to him. But I'm so glad I did, so glad that memory will linger somewhere outside of my mind, somewhere it will be safe and cared for.

Speak it out loud. I want to hear you.

Ivy puts the teacup on a saucer and brings it over. It clatters against the marble counter when she sets it down in front of me. The liquid is deep amber, the color of the fire reflecting off the walls of his room.

There is a life for you here, a life where you can be everything you're afraid of being.

I gently pick up the teacup and raise it to my mouth. It trembles in my hand. My parents and Ivy watch me, holding their breath, waiting. If this is the right thing, why does my dad look devastated and Ivy look unsure? Why does my chest feel like it's being torn open?

I would set the world on fire just to see your face.

The tea smells earthy and floral. I breathe deeply and pick up subtle notes of woodsmoke and salt. My eyes fill with tears because it smells like him, just like him, and for a moment I don't think I can do this.

It was easy to use you, and damn near impossible not to fall in love with you.

Maybe there's an alternate universe where my coven isn't depending on me for survival. Maybe there's an alternate universe where my wild heart is free to take refuge in Wolfe, to love him as deeply as a person can love.

The thought almost makes me smile, this desperate hope that there's a version of ourselves loving each other, loving and loving and loving to the ends of the Earth.

You saved my life.

I hold the cup to my lips and drink.

thirty

thirty-one

Wolfe

I say her name each night at midnight, but she never comes. I can't take it anymore. I leave the manor and cut through the trees until I'm closer to Main Street and closer to her.

She was vulnerable and honest when she should have been distant and suspicious. She should have protected herself. But she opened herself up like one of my grimoires, and I read every page, every sentence, until she became my favorite book.

I don't want to be angry, but I am. I was supposed to hate her, to feel nothing but disgust. I fell for her despite myself, and now she's all I can think of. If either of us is weak, it's me. Not her.

And it's infuriating.

Mortana takes the long way home from the perfumery. She likes to hear the roar of the ocean and feel the wind on her face. And today, when she walks along the eastern shore, she'll see me.

I shouldn't be here.

I should let her go and move on, like my dad says. Let Mortana marry the governor's son so we can finally have our meeting with the council and figure out a path forward that will save our island and calm the sea.

That's the right thing.

But how can it be right when she's not with me?

I've never put much stake in happiness. Happiness is erratic and fleeting, hardly a worthwhile thing to spend a life chasing. Living isn't about happiness, and it never has been.

Living is about necessity. But she became necessary to me, like air and magic and blood: absolutely vital.

The Witchery is cold, inviting in winter with choppy water and dark clouds. I cross my arms and watch my breath in the air in front of me. It starts to rain.

At first it isn't much, light enough to be mistaken for mist off the Passage. Then the sky opens up, and I'm drenched in seconds.

At least I have the beach to myself.

I should leave. She doesn't want to see me, and I should respect that.

But god, I have to see her.

And like an answered prayer, there she is, walking along the shore. She's looking up at the sky, holding her hands open to touch the rain.

She smiles to herself and laughs out loud, not at all bothered to be out in a downpour. She looks... content.

I want to give her the space she asked for. I tell myself I'll leave before she sees me, but my feet stay planted on the ground, immovable.

She looks perfect in the rain, her hair soaked, water dripping from the ends.

She looks perfect.

I shove my own hair away from my eyes, needing to see her.

She looks up, directly at me. I think my heart stops.

Her steps slow and she tucks her hair behind her ear.

But something isn't right. Her eyes don't spark the way they normally do when she looks at me. I know, because every time it happens I want to sell my soul just to make sure it happens again.

"Quite the weather to get caught in," she says. "Do you know how to find your way back to the ferry?"

I stare at her. All the heat drains from my body. "Mortana?" The word sounds harsh, but I don't mean it that way.

"I'm sorry, have we met?"

I search her face and stumble back when I realize she has no idea who I am. My chest is on fire. I can't get enough air.

"I apologize if I'm being rude. I meet a lot of mainlanders at the shop, and sometimes I forget." She waves her hand through the air and smiles. Polite. Professional.

She apologizes too much.

"No," I say, shaking my head. "Don't apologize. It's nothing."

She nods and looks relieved. "You can find your way back?"

"Yes." The word barely makes it out, and I clear my throat.

I close my eyes and cover her in a veil of magic. I can feel a memory loss spell working inside her, hiding every memory, every fucking moment, in darkness.

My god, she doesn't remember.

I look away. My eyes are burning, and it feels like there's a boulder lodged in my throat. I can't breathe.

"Well, have a nice day," she says, walking away.

I don't respond. I don't move. I just look at her, watch her perfect face as she offers a small smile and passes me by.

She is so close, an arm's length away, but nothing lights in her eyes, not even a ghost of recognition.

I clutch my chest because of the pressure, the pain that's building there. It isn't normal, pain like this. Fuck, it feels like every one of my ribs has fractured and lodged itself directly in my lungs.

I want to know if she took the memory eraser willingly or if it was forced on her. I *need* to know. But if it's the former, I don't think I'd survive it.

She walks up the beach and onto the road, stopping when she gets there. She slowly turns around. I hold my breath as she watches me, her eyes on mine convincing my heart to start beating again. Is there the hint of recognition?

I almost walk right up to her, take her face in my hands and tell her she knows me, that whatever she's sensing in her gut is real. But she shakes her head slightly and turns back to the road, walking away from me. I stand still, watching her until she rounds a corner and I can't see her anymore.

I stay where I am.

It's over. But it can't be over. It can't be.

Would it be wrong to see her again, to try to make her remember me if she willingly chose to forget?

I know that it would. I know it, but I can't let her go.

Then we can burn together.

I pick up a rock and heave it into the ocean, yelling as I do. The pain in my chest gets worse, and my yelling gets louder, but it doesn't fix anything.

God, I'm falling apart. There's no way I'll survive this.

You will be the end of me.

Mortana is gone, and she doesn't remember.

I gasp at the fire in my lungs.

She doesn't remember.

thirty-two

There is a boy on the shore, standing alone in the pouring rain. There's a hard set to his jaw, and his hair is messy and dark. His skin is pale, and his eyes are stormy like the weather today. I'm embarrassed to catch myself staring.

But it's hard not to.

He's soaking wet and absolutely stunning.

I force myself to look past him and ask if he knows how to find his way back to the ferry. He does, but there's a strain in his voice that makes it sound like he's angry.

He says my name, my full name, and something about the word in his mouth makes my insides stir. It reminds me of a dream I've been having of someone whispering my full name on the western shore. It has woken me up every night lately, always at midnight. Such an odd dream. No one on this island uses my full name, and yet he did.

He did, and it looks as if his entire world has been ripped out from under him.

I want to ask him if he needs help, if there's anything I can do, but something stops me. I'm afraid I've offended him by not knowing him when he clearly knows me. But we get so many patrons in the perfumery that it's hard to remember them all.

Though in this case, it surprises me that I don't. He's impossible to look away from—I can't believe I forgot meeting him.

I offer him a smile, but for some reason, it seems to upset him.

I should go.

I walk up the beach to the road, fighting the urge to turn back to him the whole way. When I reach the sidewalk, I finally do.

And when I turn, he's watching me.

My stomach catches in my throat, and I feel weightless, like that first exhilarating moment when I dive beneath the surface of the water. He's magnetic—an invisible force pushes me toward him.

I want to know his story.

I shake my head and force myself to look away.

I have my own story, one that's been written since the day I was born. And something tells me that if I were to read his, it would become my favorite. So instead, I go home and continue to live out the pages my parents have already written for me.

But maybe I'll sneak in one of my own, a single page about a beautiful boy with stormy gray eyes, that is just for me.

thirty-three

"You look beautiful," my mother says as I come down the stairs. I'm wearing a pale pink sheath dress, teardrop earrings, and nude evening shoes. I tug at the dress and smooth it down at the sides, but no matter how I fidget, I can't get comfortable.

I don't want my hair pulled back so tightly it gives me a headache and my dress so starched I'm scared of putting a single wrinkle in it. I want to feel like myself, with my hair unbrushed and wild, with interesting jewelry and clothing that moves with me. I want to wear dark colors instead of the pastels my coven favors.

I want to be myself in a space that feels like it wasn't meant for me.

I shake my head and smile at my mother. I'm just nervous.

"Thanks, Mom," I say.

My dad puts the finishing touches on the table, and it takes my breath away. Candles run the length of it, different heights and shapes, flickering in the dim room. Autumn leaves are crushed and scattered between them with white rose petals sitting on top. The room smells of the roast my dad made, and he puts a bottle of wine over ice just as the doorbell rings.

I jump at the sound of it.

My mother walks to the door and opens it wide. "Marshall, Elizabeth, welcome to our home! It is so lovely to have you here."

Elizabeth and my mother exchange kisses on each cheek and throw compliments at each other as if they're petals being tossed down a wedding aisle. Landon trails behind them, and my mother's smile widens when she sees him.

"And Landon, it's so nice to have you here again."

He hands her a bouquet of flowers and smiles back. "I'm delighted to be here."

I have to hand it to my future husband—he's so charming that I almost believe he chose this. Chose me. But I remind myself it's an act, if a very good one, and that he can promise me many things, but love is not one of them.

"Tana, you're the best thing I've seen all week," he says, walking over to me and handing me a single rose. "I saved the prettiest one for you," he whispers.

"You're quite the charmer," I say, taking the rose from him.

"Is it too much?" he asks, a smile playing on his lips.

He's good at this, and he *knows* he is, but I look at my mother's beaming face and the rose in my hand. "I think it's just enough."

"Good." He leans down and kisses my cheek. My eyes catch his, and all the playfulness is gone. His gaze moves down to my lips, and for a moment I forget we're in the same room as our parents.

I take a breath and look down. "I should put this in water."

I walk into the kitchen, where my dad is getting beverages for everyone. He pops the bottle of sparkling wine and pours each of us a glass, then sets them all on a silver tray that he takes into the other room. I put the rose in water and follow after him, finding my place next to Landon.

"A toast," Dad says, raising his glass. "To family."

Heat floods my face, and every muscle in my body tightens. Elizabeth places her hand on her chest, and both she and Marshall raise their glasses with an emphatic, "To family!"

"To family," Landon says, his voice low enough that only I can hear.

I smile and touch my glass to his, but the wine tastes bitter. I wonder if everyone here feels like I do in my dress, like we're forcing a lie. But I see the happy expressions on my parents' faces and the laughter that rolls so easily off Elizabeth's tongue, and I realize I'm the only one overthinking this.

"Are you okay?" Landon asks me when our parents are deep in conversation.

"Yes, I'm sorry," I say, setting my glass down. "I think I'm just nervous."

"Why?"

"I'm not sure. I want your parents to like me," I say, looking around the room. "I don't want to mess anything up."

"They already like you," he assures me. "And they'll only like you more as our families continue to spend time together."

"You think so?"

"I do," he says, finishing his drink. "It isn't all for show," he adds, as if reading my mind. "I am truly happy to see you."

Something in his words eases the tension I've been carrying. "Thank you for saying that."

"You're welcome."

We all sit down to dinner, and I'm relieved at how easy the conversation is. My parents and Landon's seem to enjoy each other's company, and seeing them together like this reinforces what a good arrangement this is. Not just necessary, not just advantageous, but *good*.

"Tana, tell me about yourself. Landon says you love to swim," Marshall says, looking at me from across the table. His smile is warm, and he sounds like he's genuinely interested, which I suppose is where Landon gets it from.

"I do," I say. "I've always been drawn to the sea. There's something about it that calms me."

Marshall nods. "I was on the swim team all through school. I enjoyed the competition, but practices were my favorite. I'd stay in the pool after my teammates went home and just swim underwater. The way it shuts off the outside world... There's nothing quite like it."

"I always say the same thing."

"Tana loves the ocean," my dad says, winking at me. "She used to think her mother and I couldn't see the salt caked all over her. She's come home many times with seaweed in her hair and her clothes soaking wet."

"Listen, I never said I was subtle," I say, and everyone laughs.

I laugh, too. "Landon even went in with me the last time he was on the island. I think I could have convinced him to stay in longer had it not been for the currents."

I don't realize what I've said until my mother snaps her head up and glares at me. My heart races, and I give her a pleading look. I can't believe I mentioned the currents; it was a total accident.

"What currents?" Marshall asks between bites of his dinner.

"There's a current that's been circling our island for years, and sometimes it gets close to the shore. We've been watching it carefully and don't see much reason for concern." My mother says it with perfect grace, managing to sound casual and decisive at once.

"Well, you just let us know if you ever need our aid. We'd be happy to help," Marshall says. If he knew the extent of the danger, if he knew the root cause, I suspect he wouldn't be so kind.

"Thank you, I'll certainly let you know."

My mother changes the subject, and soon they're talking about the economy of the Witchery and what kind of partnerships with the mainland might make sense. After Landon and I are married, the Witchery will become an official territory of the mainland. They will share their resources with us, their knowledge and their plans. Most importantly, they will protect us as if we're mainlanders. And legally, we will be. But the arrangement goes both ways—we will start paying taxes to the mainland, and they will have a say in how we run our island. It's economically brilliant for the mainland, and it's necessary for us.

Right now, the mainland has no legal authority here, which makes a certain kind of person more willing to act out, as with the dock burning, because they think they can get away with it. And the sad truth is that they can.

Still, I hear the things no one says. The mainland knows we need them to continue accepting us and welcoming us into their world; we are far outnumbered by them. If their government decided to do away with witches, they could. And we know the mainland wants to keep an eye on everything we do, that they're terrified of a resurgence of dark magic, but that they're also eager for a share of our silver.

It's so delicate, a tapestry woven from half-truths and partial trust.

We can be friends and get along and even become family, but there are so many other things at play that it's hard to keep track of them all.

Maybe one day, it won't feel like so much. That's the point of this wedding, after all. Maybe one day, I will look at Landon with utter adoration and forget that his father is keeping his eyes on the Witchery and his hands in our pockets.

"Samuel, that roast was absolutely divine," Elizabeth says. "You didn't use magic, did you?" she asks in a playful tone.

"I'm wounded you would think so," Dad says. "I made this entirely on my own."

"Dad doesn't use magic in the kitchen," I say. "He thinks it weakens his natural ability." I laugh and give him a smile that lets him know how adorable I think it is.

"Well, I'm even more impressed, then," Elizabeth says.

"Why don't we move to the sitting room for some tea before

dessert?" my mother suggests, and everyone stands. "Tana, I bet Landon would love to see the rooftop."

I look at Landon.

"That does sound like something I'd love." His smiles come easily, but it's hard for me to distinguish the ones that are genuine from the ones that are just for show. I've had to work exceptionally hard at hiding how I really feel in favor of how I'm supposed to feel. But I want to know Landon as he truly is, just as I want him to know me.

"The rooftop it is."

I lead him up the stairs, the sounds of our parents' conversation fading away. I feel myself start to relax, the weight of expectation not quite as heavy when it's just the two of us.

I open the door to the rooftop and grab some blankets from the wicker basket. The night is clear, thousands of stars sparkling in the dark sky. The waning moon casts everything in silver light, and the waves on the shore fill the air with their familiar rhythm.

I sit down on the couch with my future husband and hope he can't sense the disquiet in me.

"What are you thinking about?" His words cut through my thoughts, forcing me back to the present.

"I'm sorry," I say. "I don't know where I was." How can I tell him I was thinking about the weight of it all? How can I tell him that the closer we get to the wedding, the more worried I become?

"Well, what if I tell you what I was thinking about?" he says.

I turn to face him. "I'd like that."

"I was thinking about what a good match we are."

The words catch me off guard, and for a moment, I'm speechless. "Why is that?" I finally ask.

"Because you're good, Tana. Sometimes I get the sense that you're trying so hard to be what you think you're supposed to be. And I admire that. I admire that you believe in this so much that you're willing to try."

I'm mortified when tears sting the backs of my eyes. I look away and take a steadying breath, let the chill of the night calm me. The words are kind, and they're coming from a decent person, but all I can think is that I wish I didn't have to try so hard.

I wish this life came as naturally to me as it does to Landon and my mother and Ivy.

"I do believe in it," I finally say. "And I'm hoping that one day, it won't feel like I'm trying."

Landon brushes a piece of hair behind my ear. "I hope so, too. I want you to trust me and trust that I will accept the person you are when you aren't trying. When you're just you."

I shake my head and look off into the distance.

"Did I say something to upset you?" Landon asks.

"No, no, I'm not upset. But I must admit that I'm a little confused."

"About what?"

"Sometimes you say things that make me think you're trying to—" I cut myself off, not sure how to continue.

"Trying to what?" he asks.

"I don't know. Sometimes it sounds like you have genuine feelings for me, and it confuses me because you've made it very clear that you can't promise me love." I pull the blanket closer to my chest, as if it will cover the parts of myself I've just exposed.

Landon exhales and sits up straighter on the couch. "I want to be honest with you, Tana—I can't promise you that. But I've also been thinking about what you said, about allowing space for more than just duty, and I'm willing to try. I *am* trying. So maybe let me, okay?"

"Fair enough," I say. I laugh and cover my face with my hands. "Doesn't it scare you, marrying someone you don't know?" The words are out of my mouth before I can think better of them.

"Honestly, it scares the hell out of me."

It's maybe the best thing he's ever said to me, the most real thing, and for the first time, I see him as just a boy instead of as the governor's son. I want so desperately to be seen for who I am, not solely the role I play, and yet I haven't even tried to do the same for Landon.

"I'm so glad," I say, wanting to laugh and cry in equal measure.

I wipe my eyes, and he catches my hand. "I believe in this life. I believe in the power of the mainland and the Witchery coming together."

"Me too."

Hearing those words helps me commit to this life in a way I haven't been able to since we moved up the date of the wedding. I don't fully understand the reasons that went into that decision, and those questions have created uncertainty in me. But it's okay to be scared and worried and uneasy. I can believe in this path and still wish I could see farther down the road.

"Landon," I say, my voice quiet, "I think I'd like you to kiss me now."

A smile pulls at the corners of his mouth. He gently places his hand under my chin and tips my face up, leaning down to meet me. My eyes close, and his lips brush mine, shy and hesitant and gentle.

At first I don't move, terrified of not wanting him enough or wanting him too much. But his lips are soft and his hand cradles my face, and he is going to be my husband soon. Slowly, I sink into the kiss, move my mouth against his and let myself feel however I'm going to feel.

There aren't dragonflies in my stomach. I don't erupt in a blaze of fire that leaves me desperate for him, but maybe that kind of kiss doesn't exist. Maybe I wouldn't be able to handle it if it did.

But it's nice, the way his mouth feels against mine. It's tender. It's the kind of kiss I can commit to.

He slowly pulls away, taking my hand. "We'll get better at this," he says, and my cheeks flame, wondering if it was bad, wondering if he didn't enjoy it.

"I think it was pretty good for a first time," I say, even though the spark I've always hoped for was absent.

"That's not what I meant," he says, realizing how that sounded. "What I'm trying to communicate—poorly, I should add—is that I think we're starting from a really good place." He squeezes my hand when he says it, giving me a reassuring smile.

"I think so, too."

It isn't the first kiss I've always dreamed of, especially not with the addition of Landon's comment, but I'm learning that dreams are just dreams. They aren't real, don't have any bearing on my life. And it isn't fair for me to continually compare the Landon in front of me to the one I dreamt about growing up.

I know all that, and yet I can't fully let go, can't fully forget about the Landon in my head. That's the problem with dreams: they are so easy to get lost in and so very difficult to give up.

thirty-four

Landon and his parents are gone, and Dad brings in a tray with tea for me and wine for him and Mom. The fire is going, and instrumental music plays softly in the background. The dinner could not have gone better, and I see it in the way my parents look at each other, in their easy posture as they lean together on the couch.

And it fills me with pride to have helped manifest their biggest hopes.

I'm so happy for them.

I am.

But it also feels a lot like sadness.

I don't know when marrying Landon morphed in my mind from a certainty to a choice, from something I always knew I'd do to something I have to convince myself to do. Landon said he could tell that I'm trying, but I don't want to have to try. I don't want to force this life to fit within all the hopes and fears that make me *me*.

Even kissing Landon—it was nice, and I'm glad I did it. But I can't help but wonder what it would be like to kiss someone because I desperately wanted to, to kiss someone because I couldn't possibly go a single moment longer without it.

"What a great night," my mother says, leaning into my dad. "And what a wonderful idea of Landon's to invite you to the mainland before the harvest celebration. That will be a very special day for both of you."

"It will be nice to start learning my way around," I say. "I'm sure it will be fun learning it with Landon."

"You must be thrilled," Mom says, looking at me. "This is what you've always wanted."

"It's what *you've* always wanted." I'm shocked that the words come out of my mouth, grasping for them, wishing I could pull them back. They linger in the space between us, heavy and dark and ugly. I want to take them back, apologize and make it right.

But they're true.

I'm heartbroken that they're true.

A look passes between my parents, and I wish I knew what it means. For a moment, it feels like they're in on something I know nothing about. But they don't look angry or offended. Mom looks worried, but it's Dad's face that makes my heart ache. He looks sad. So sad.

"You're right," my mother finally says, setting down her drink. "This is what I've always wanted. It's what all of us have always wanted—your father and I, and this entire island. Maybe you don't get all the choices your peers do, and maybe the weight of duty feels heavy on your shoulders, and for that I'm sorry. But you will be changing the course of history, making a difference most people could never dream of making. You should be proud."

"I know," I say, because I do know. I've known it every single day of my life. "I know."

"Good. Try not to forget it," she says.

She finishes the rest of her wine in a single gulp, then walks up the stairs without another word.

Several days later, I'm standing on the shore of the mainland, any lingering tension with my mother all but gone now that I'm visiting Landon. The Witchery is bustling with activity in preparation for the harvest celebration tonight, and while I should be with my parents, helping, my mother insisted I come to the mainland instead.

"Have you done much exploring here?" Landon asks, and I pull my gaze from the island.

"Hardly any," I admit. "I've never really wanted to." The words are out before I can think better of them, and I reprimand myself for being so careless.

"Why not?"

I look at Landon, wondering if I should answer honestly. He's always been forthright with me, though; I want to trust that I can be the same with him. "I suppose it's because for my entire life, it has felt like we are trying to earn our place here. Why would I want to visit somewhere that until very recently was still trying to decide if I am worth protecting?"

"Wow," Landon says, looking down, a break in composure that's rare for him. "I've never thought of it that way."

"And why would you? You've never had to."

"You're right," he says, the words strained.

This isn't how I intended to start our day together, and I want to make things better, to ease some of the tightness that has settled on Landon's face. I reach out and gently touch his arm. "Please don't misunderstand me. I'm happy to be here today, with you."

"As am I," he says after a moment, taking my hand in his. "Why don't I show you around?"

"I'd like that."

We leave the shore and step onto a sidewalk, the natural world disappearing, replaced with brick roads and buildings so tall I have to crane my neck to see the tops. It's overcast, and all I can think is that the stone buildings don't have nearly enough windows to let in the light. How gray and dark it must be inside those walls.

When I look at the mainland from the Witchery, it seems stately, always radiating a kind of energy that is both commanding and dynamic. But being in it, surrounded on all sides by brick and stone, it's as if there isn't as much air here, as if my lungs have to fight to get their fair share. I want to love it, want my whole self to come alive in these streets, but it's never going to be that way.

I tell myself I just need to give it time, need to adjust to the change. But hoping I will love this place even a fraction of how much I love the Witchery is an impossibly high aspiration.

We stop at a café for tea and scones, then sit outside while droves of people pass us on the sidewalks. Landon receives a lot of attention, which he handles with ease, but after a quarter of an hour on the street, I've tired of the whispers and stares. I'm glad I've seen this happen, though; Landon is well practiced at being gracious and patient, and I know he will be able to help me adapt to his world.

He takes me to a gallery next, a clean, open room featuring artwork on its walls. "Not a very efficient use of space, is it?" I ask, laughing at how few paintings hang on each wall. The Witchery is a small island, and most of our shops are designed to maximize the space. But here, it seems there is more than enough.

"What do you mean?"

"It's just such an enormous room for so few paintings."

"It would be difficult to appreciate each piece if you were distracted by the artwork on either side," Landon says, as if it's the most obvious thing in the world.

"Of course. And the art is lovely," I say, making sure he knows I'm happy to be here. Happy to get acquainted with my new home.

We continue through the gallery, but goose bumps rise on my skin when I see the final painting. It shows four people on their hands and knees in an open field, sweat on their brows and anguish on their faces, clutching the earth. They are surrounded by hundreds of moonflowers.

The plaque beneath the paining reads TO KNOW FEAR.

My eyes fill with tears. The painting is so detailed and realistic, such a severe reminder of our history with the mainland. The island is our home, the only place that has ever been truly ours. But we will never forget that we're there because the mainland banished magic, that even though the island became our refuge, it still wasn't enough to stop the fear of the mainland from finding us. We still had to fight for the survival of magic.

I turn away and head for the exit, but there are no trees or waves to comfort me when I step outside.

"I apologize," Landon says, reaching for my hand. "I didn't realize the gallery was still showing Pruitt's work."

"Why is it called that?" I ask. "*To Know Fear.* What does it mean?"

"We don't have to talk about it."

"I want to."

Landon sighs. "It is meant to portray the transfer of fear that happened when the witches left the mainland for the island. How after hundreds of years of us fearing magic, it was finally the witches' turn to know fear."

Arriving on an island full of toxic flowers must have been terrifying. My palms sweat, and I try to keep my voice even.

"And you have that hanging in your gallery? Out of all the artwork to give an entire wall to, that is the one you chose?"

"Like I said, I didn't know Pruitt's work was still on display."

"Do you fear magic?" I ask, watching Landon closely.

"That painting is from a moment in history, Tana. It isn't meant to reflect today's sentiments."

We've stopped in the middle of the sidewalk, and people slow down, looking at us as they pass. Even the automobiles brake, passengers craning their necks to get a look at Landon and his future bride. I can't hear myself think, can't calm my racing heart. Landon takes my hand and leads me back to the shore, where there aren't as many observers.

"That doesn't really answer my question." I say it in a soft tone, trying to conceal the hurt in my voice, but it still comes through.

"I think we're all a little afraid of the things we don't understand." Landon takes a deep breath and exhales slowly. "But magic has become a delight for us, and I'm excited for you to help me understand it better. That's what our union is doing, Tana. I believe there will be a day when no one remembers Pruitt's work, when no one fears magic."

My immediate reaction is to be defensive, to tell him that if anyone should be afraid, it was always going to be us. We have magic, but they have numbers far greater than ours. Even the most powerful magic isn't enough when there are only so many witches to wield it, when there is a seemingly infinite number of mainlanders willing to fight it. And fearing something you don't understand is not the same as fearing something because it has proven to be dangerous.

We have always known fear. Landon called the painting a moment in history, but we are announcing our engagement tonight because my coven is still fearful. We have made this arrangement because the mainland wants its eyes on us. Fear is everywhere.

"I look forward to it," I say, the words burning on the way

out. I want to argue and yell and head back to the Witchery alone, but that is not my role. So instead, I smile, loop my arm through his, and walk up the boardwalk and onto the dock to wait for the ferry. I will teach Landon that magic is nothing to fear, and our children will know magic as one thing and one thing only: a gift.

My role may require me to bite my tongue and temper my tone, but there is power in it as well. And I intend to use it.

Landon points out something in the water, but my eye catches on a sign hanging above us. It's large and colorful, proclaiming: EXPERIENCE THE WITCHERY! CALM YOUR NERVES! INCREASE YOUR HAPPINESS! DELIGHT YOUR LOVER! ALL THIS AND MORE FROM A MAGIC SO SUBTLE, YOU'LL HARDLY FEEL IT.

I stare up at the sign, at what our magic has been reduced to. I don't feel proud that the mainland is advertising our island, I feel ill, filled with a thick, gross sludge that spreads out from my gut. My face heats and my palms sweat, and I close my eyes to stop the tears from running down my face.

"Ferry to the Witchery now boarding!" a man calls out.

"Ready for tonight?" Landon asks, a spark in his eye that wasn't there before.

"I can't wait." I smile at him, but it feels forced and tight. He doesn't seem to notice, though, and we walk onto the ferry side by side, heading to an island with a magic so subtle, we'll hardly feel it.

Tragic.

thirty-five

Landon and I stand up on a wooden platform at the harvest celebration, holding hands, surrounded by dozens of candles flickering in the breeze and wisteria hanging from the pergola above us. Most of my coven is here to celebrate the season coming to a close, and at the end of the evening, Landon announces that we are to be wed.

It is as impactful as my mother said it would be. People cry and hug, the band breaks into a celebratory arrangement, and sparkling wine is passed around the festival in crystal goblets that reflect the moonlight.

People congratulate us over and over, and Landon holds my hand, kisses my temple, and plays the part of an enamored fiancé flawlessly.

But the twisting in my stomach has stayed with me since the ferry, and not even Ivy's soothing tea is enough to calm it. The magic so subtle, I hardly feel it.

The next morning, Ivy is leaning against the stone wall of the perfumery when I arrive for my shift. She holds out a cup of tea and
sips her own as I unlock the front door and turn on the lights.

"Thank you," I say, taking it from her.

She nods in response, and it nags at me. Something feels off
between us, but I don't know what it is. It's fuzzy, like I'm looking
at it through clouded glass.

We head into the back room, and I set my tea down and take
off my coat.

"How was dinner with the Yateses? We never got to talk
about it with all the harvest celebration prep."

"It was good," I say, picking up my tea again. "Really good. I
don't think it could have gone any better."

"Then why do you sound like the world has stopped turning?"

I shake my head and look down. "I don't know."

She watches me, and the same look of sadness I saw on my
dad's face after dinner passes across hers as well. I hate that I'm
letting down the people I love most.

"I'll figure it out," I say, my voice too high. "I think I'm just
nervous about the wedding. And Landon and I had an awkward
exchange when I went to the mainland that I'm trying to untangle."

"What about?"

I walk into the storefront and make sure everything is stocked
appropriately. Then I lean against the counter and look down,
remembering my conversation with Landon.

"He said he's afraid of magic."

"What?" Ivy asks, clearly surprised.

"He took me to a gallery with artwork of witches being tortured in a field of moonflowers, and he said everyone is afraid of the things they don't understand." I see my mother walking down Main Street, so I head into the back room with Ivy and shut the door. "The worst part is that I didn't stand up for myself. For our island. I wanted to, Ivy, I really did, but I was terrified of making a scene or saying the wrong thing. Everyone knows him there. Everyone watches."

Ivy looks thoughtful as she takes a long sip of tea. "You're standing up for our island by marrying him," she says, setting her cup down and reaching for my hand. "Don't forget that."

I nod and swallow the lump forming in my throat. Then she suddenly lets go of my hand and walks to the other side of the worktable as if something has upset her. A heavy silence settles between us. "Hey, are we okay?" I ask.

She looks hesitant at first, then gives me a small smile. "Yeah, of course. We're great. I was cleaning up with my parents after the celebration and got to bed late. I'm just tired."

"Okay," I say, even though there's something in her tone that isn't convincing.

Maybe I'm just overthinking everything.

"Landon kissed me," I blurt out, realizing I haven't told her yet. "I almost forgot."

That gets her attention, and she leans over the counter toward me. "That good, huh?"

"No, no, it was... nice. Sweet."

"Nice? Sweet? That's it?"

I sigh. "Yeah, that's it." I hear how flat the words are, and I silently scold myself. Landon is fully committed to this union, and he's trying. He deserves better than this. And yet I can't stop the burn in my eyes, can't stop the tears from rolling down my face as I look at Ivy.

I don't know what's wrong with me. I'm being selfish and immature, and I open my mouth to apologize, but Ivy slams her cup down on the table, stopping me.

"You know what, fuck this," she says, grabbing my hand and pulling me from the store. I've never heard Ivy curse like that, and it unsettles me.

"Ivy? What's going on?" I ask as I stumble after her all the way into the woods in the center of the island, far away from Main Street. "I'm sorry, I know I'm acting like a child—"

"Just stop, Tana," she says, holding up her hand.

I'm silent. I feel unsteady, unsure of my footing. Ivy has been my foundation my whole life, and I wish I could grasp what's happening between us, something in the distance that's just out of reach.

I know it's there, but I can't see it.

"Please tell me what's going on," I plead. I can't take it anymore.

She exhales and looks past me, her stance rigid and tense. "I made a mistake," she says, more to herself than me.

I watch her as fear climbs out of my stomach and crawls throughout the rest of my body. A heavy dread settles on my shoulders and threatens to crush me into the damp earth. I look to Ivy for some kind of reassurance, but there's nothing.

"Ivy?" I ask, my voice trembling.

"I'm going to get in a lot of trouble for this," she says, shaking her head.

"Tell me."

She breathes out and finally meets my eyes. She looks angry, angrier than I've ever seen her, and my heart starts to race. "The reason you've been feeling like things are off is because they are. I'm mad at you for something you don't remember, and I'm not over it yet. I don't know how to get over it."

"What are you talking about?"

"I thought we were doing the right thing, but seeing you like this... I was wrong." She shakes her head and looks off into the distance.

"Ivy, say what you need to say."

"There's a veil over certain things in your mind. You can feel it, right? A haziness you can't explain?"

All the air leaves my lungs. "How do you know that?"

"Because you made a lot of bad choices, so we had you drink a memory eraser." She looks down at the ground, regret and bitterness crossing her face, two things I so seldom see on her. "You took it willingly because I convinced you to. Because you trust me. But it turns out some of those bad choices were good for you."

"Who's 'we'?"

"Your parents and me."

I take a deep breath and keep my voice as calm as possible. "Ivy, start from the beginning. And don't leave anything out."

"It's a long story," she says, motioning to a bench on the trail.

"I like stories."

She nods and sits down next to me. Then she starts to speak. She tells me about a boy I met, a boy who practiced dark magic and put a glimmer in my eyes. She tells me that he taught me some of his magic and that I loved it the way I love the sea. She tells me that she was swarmed by bees and almost died, but I stepped in and used dark magic to save her life. She tells me that she hasn't been able to forgive me fully.

She tells me that I ran away from home to be with the boy—Wolfe, she calls him—and that I chose him over everything else. That I was willing to give up my whole life for him, my parents and Landon and our coven.

She tells me that I found out he'd lied to me and used me to get close to my mother, that his coven sent him to seek me out for that purpose. She tells me that I willingly took a memory eraser to forget the boy so marrying Landon would be easier.

She tells me that the light inside me went out as soon as I drank it and that I haven't been the same since. She tells me that it's been killing her inside, because from the moment I took my first sip of the tea that would steal my memories, she knew it was a mistake.

She cries as she speaks, still so angry with me. But under that anger is a well of love so deep and so wide that I can feel it even when her voice shakes and her eyes cast blame.

The story is wild, so unbelievable, and yet I know it's true because of the ache that builds in my chest with every word she says. I know it's true because I can feel an emptiness inside me where something used to be. Where someone used to be.

I know it's true because I feel myself stitching back together after some unnameable thing tore me apart.

Then I gasp. The boy on the shore. It was him—it had to be him. He looked so tormented, so utterly wrecked, and even though I can't remember the things Ivy tells me, I believe that they happened.

I know that they did.

"I'm so sorry, Tana," Ivy says when she's done, pulling a lace handkerchief from her pocket and wiping her eyes. "It was a mistake."

I'm quiet for a long time, unsure of what to say. How to process all the things she's told me.

I hesitantly reach out to her, not knowing if she'll want me close after what I did. But when my hand touches hers, she squeezes it tight.

"It sounds like I made enough mistakes for the both of us," I say. "Thank you for telling me."

"Are you mad?"

"No. You thought you were doing the right thing, and I took it willingly." I sigh and look down. "Why can't I just be happy with the life I'm meant to lead?"

"Maybe the life you're thinking of isn't the one that's meant for you."

I look at her then. She has always known me, all of me, who I am and who I'm trying to be. She knows me so well that she could see the fog inside me after I drank the memory eraser and decided it wasn't worth it.

I'm so glad she did.

"Ivy," I say, grasping her hand in both of mine. "I have to see him."

She pauses, weighing something in her mind, and I see the exact moment she makes her decision.

"I know," she finally says.

"Will you help me?"

Another pause, and I worry I've asked too much. Then she sets her jaw and grabs her coat. "Yes."

thirty-six

It's hard being in Ivy's home, seeing the way her parents look at me, a cross between fear and gratitude. I want to say something to them, but they think I'm oblivious, that the memory eraser is doing its work and I've been scrubbed clean of any recollection of saving Ivy's life, so I try my best to act like nothing is wrong.

I know I should feel appalled, shocked and surprised by my actions. And I am. But they also somehow fit, somehow feel like mine, even though I can't remember them. I ache for the memories I lost, for the moments that meant enough to me to give up this life and choose something different. What they must have been like, to cause me to act in such a way.

What *he* must have been like.

When Ivy's parents are asleep and the moon is high above us, Ivy walks me to the western shore.

"Say his name at midnight," she says, "and if he hears it, he'll come."

I think of the dream I've been having, of waking up so often thinking I've heard my name whispered on the wind. I swallow hard. "How would he hear it?"

Ivy shakes her head. "Some kind of dark magic. I don't know the details." I don't miss the way her voice sours on the words *dark magic*.

"Okay," I say, my voice quiet. I'm so nervous, my heart racing wildly in my chest. I'm sweating in the cold autumn night even though there are goose bumps all over my skin.

"Do you want me to stay with you?" Ivy asks, and I'm overwhelmed by how much it means for her to offer. How much of herself she's giving up just to ask.

I pull her into a fierce hug and squeeze her tight. She hugs me back, soft at first, then tighter and tighter, and it takes my breath away because I know we're healing. We're going to be okay.

"Thank you," I whisper.

"I'll see you back at my place," she says.

Once she's out of view, I turn to the water. My stomach is twisting into knots, and for a moment I think I'll be sick. I take several deep breaths, and the feeling subsides.

I can do this.

"Wolfe." I say the name, but it's so quiet it barely makes it past my lips. It's so foreign to me.

"Wolfe," I say again, this time stronger. The name slides out like a perfect melody, and I think maybe it isn't so foreign after all.

I sit down on the rocks. They're cold and wet, but I don't mind. I have no idea how long this is supposed to take or if it will even work. It feels absurd, saying a name on the beach at midnight, but if everything Ivy told me is true, if I loved him even a fraction of the amount I've been led to believe, then I have to meet him. I have to see his face and hear his voice.

"Mortana?"

I look up and see the boy from the shore standing in the water. No boat, no raft. It's as if he just appeared, and I wonder if his magic can do that. I slowly get to my feet, wiping my palms on my dress. He pauses where he stands.

"Wolfe?" I ask, walking closer to the water, trying to get a better look at this person who captured so much of me.

He rushes toward me, water splashing around him as he drags himself from the ocean. It doesn't look like he'll stop running until he crashes into me. I take a step back, and he abruptly stops moving.

"You're Wolfe?" I ask again, and I see it on his face, the hurt and pain as he realizes I don't know him. I still don't know him.

His eyes are raging. Something inside me breaks when I notice they are rimmed in red, reflecting the moonlight, shimmering like the surface of the sea. He sniffs and clears his throat, looks away from me. His jaw is clenched so tight I can see it from here.

He looks broken.

"I am," he finally says. "And you're Mortana."

"Yes, that's right."

I study him in the moonlight, the hard line of his mouth and his dark, messy hair. His skin looks silver in this light, like he is magic personified. But he's angry and closed off, carrying so much tension I'm worried he might snap in half right in front of me.

He's heartbreakingly beautiful.

"You're staring at me," he says.

Heat crawls up my neck, but I don't look away. I can't. "I was told that I love you."

"You never said it, but you didn't need to. I know you did."

I watch him in the moonlight, his every move, every rise of his chest and squeeze of his fist. "Did you love me, too?"

His eyes meet mine, focusing on me with an intensity that sends a shiver down my spine. "Yes."

"Do you still?"

He doesn't pause, doesn't even hesitate. "Yes."

I take a tentative step closer. "Then will you tell me what happened between us? Everything?"

He shoves his hand in his pockets and looks at the ground. "What do you remember?"

"Nothing." The word slides through the air like a knife, and I watch as it enters his chest. A fresh rush of tears wells in his eyes, but he blinks them away quickly. He turns his back to me, his shoulders rising and falling rapidly. When his breathing slows, he faces me once more.

"Okay," he finally says.

"Wolfe?" I say, the sound of his name feeling familiar now.

He looks at me, and his eyes are so pleading, so devastated, I'm amazed he doesn't shatter into a million pieces, forever lost on this shore.

"Please don't lie to me," I say.

"I won't." He turns away, and I think that's all he's going to say, but then he speaks again. "I will tell you every single detail until you're convinced that this is something worth fighting for."

I consider him. He's raw and rough, sharp around the edges and angry, but he's willing to share everything with me, knowing it won't make me remember. He's willing to be hurt all over again as he shares details of his life that mean nothing to me and everything to him.

"That's why I'm here," I say, my words quiet and unsteady. "To fight for something I once believed in more than anything else."

"Okay," he says, walking up the shore to a stretch of grass. He sits down, and I sit next to him, watching him as he decides how to start. We're so close, mere inches between us, and I see the way his body tenses at my nearness.

"Can dark magic undo a memory eraser?" I ask quietly, barely a whisper. He has helped me before; maybe he can help me again.

He exhales, and it sounds defeated. "I talked to my dad about it. We spent hours going through grimoires, but the mind is a delicate thing. Any spell we tried would have to interact with the memory eraser in the exact right way, but we don't know what all went into it, which would make crafting a spell to undo it exceedingly difficult. If we got it wrong, it could erase your memory altogether or even create memories that never happened. There would be no way for us to test it beforehand. It's too risky."

I nod, taking in his words. "Thank you for looking into it. You didn't have to do that."

"Yes, I did."

Neither of us speaks, the weight of my forgotten memories heavy between us. Then Wolfe picks up a small stone and heaves it into the water.

"Fuck, Mortana," he says, covering his face with his hands. He takes a violent, shaking breath, and I want to comfort him in some way, say something to stop the pain he's in.

Slowly, so slowly, I pull his hands away from his face. He looks at me, surprised, red splotches on his skin and eyes swollen. My fingers drift to his chin, and I lean into him, close to his ear.

"I want to remember," I whisper. "Help me."

I lean back and keep my eyes on his, wanting him to see the honesty there. The truth in the words I'm saying. My hand shakes when I pull it away from his face.

Wolfe told me he wants me to fight for this, for us, but as I look at him, I realize he's fighting, too. We both are.

He nods, takes a deep breath, and starts speaking.

I'm amazed at his honesty, how open he is about hating my coven and our way of life. It's difficult to listen to, but I know that central belief is what informs everything else. He tells me it didn't bother him to use me at first, but then he fell in love with me, and even though his intentions were cruel in the beginning, he never lied to me about his feelings.

He says that every look, every touch, every word was real. He tells me I surprised him, that my connection to high magic—that's what it's called—is unlike anything he's ever seen. He tells me that I challenged him to look at the world a different way and to consider the strength in my kind of magic, in sacrificing so much to gain security.

I can tell he doesn't believe it's the right choice, that he would never give up that part of himself for any amount of luxury or protection. But he says meeting me forced him to look at our magic in a new light.

He talks about the currents and how irresponsible my mother is being, how my coven is willingly destroying the island. He says it will come back to harm us in irreparable ways if we don't do something soon, and I nod along with his words because I know they're true. I feel it every time I'm in the sea, and I wonder if this was something we bonded over. He tells me about the moonflowers and the lie I've been told my whole life, and I can't help it when tears form in my eyes. It feels as if the wind has been knocked out of me, and I wonder how I will ever look at my mother the same way.

"The moonflowers," I start, remembering the painting I saw with Landon. "I don't understand. I saw a painting on the mainland that depicted witches being tortured with them; it was hundreds of years old. How far back does this lie go?"

Wolfe shakes his head. "If you're thinking of Pruitt's work, that's not what the painting shows; it just happens to fit into the lie well. When the witches moved from the mainland to the island, it didn't ease tensions the way they had hoped. The mainlanders became more and more aggressive, and it all culminated in a raid on the island during which they uprooted every single moonflower they could find. The painting you saw depicts the witches trying to save the flowers."

"So the mainlanders know the truth about the flowers?"

"They used to," Wolfe says. "But the new coven has been stunningly effective at rewriting history, and over the years, they too began to believe that moonflowers were poisonous."

I stare out at the water, completely shocked. I think of the painting, and my eyes burn with the truth of what Wolfe has said. I don't know what to say because nothing feels big enough, so I stay quiet.

Wolfe begins to speak again. I try to set my pain aside, try to fully hear each word he says because it matters. It matters to me so much.

His voice gets lower, rougher, when he tells me about kissing me. He says I kissed him first, and that when I did, he knew he'd give up anything, everything, if it meant being able to kiss me again. We kissed in the ocean, on the floor in his room, under the light of the moon. We offered up parts of ourselves we'd never offered anyone else, trading touches as if they were secrets.

He talks for a long time. He lets me see his anger and frustration and sadness, overwhelming me with his vulnerability. The way he speaks is guarded, and yet he shares everything with me.

I believe it all, every single word.

He's harsh, unpolished and severe, and I'm completely captivated by it. By him.

I still don't remember the things he tells me. I reach for them desperately, searching for any echo of remembrance, but I find nothing. It's almost as if he's reading me a novel about a boy named Wolfe and girl named Tana, one that weaves its way inside me with every sentence. I would read it over and over again.

He reaches the end of the story and stops speaking, and I don't think I've ever been more disappointed. I wish there was more.

I watch him, willing him to keep talking, but he's quiet.

"You're staring at me again," he finally says. "That seems to be a habit of yours." His voice is stony and impassive.

"It's hard not to," I admit, but for some reason, I'm not embarrassed. "You're beautiful. Have I told you that before?"

He swallows hard and blinks several times. "No."

We're quiet for a long time, watching the waves as they roll up the shore. I feel a pull toward him, strong and real, wholly undeniable.

Maybe there's a part of me that remembers after all.

"How did you get here? It looked as if you just appeared in the water." It sounds so trivial after all he's shared, but everything else feels too big to touch.

"What?"

"Why did you arrive in the water?"

He shakes his head. He knows it's a weak question. "Because it's part of the deal we have with your mother. We can live on the island, but our home is hidden by magic, and we are only allowed to use the streets of the Witchery once a month when we need supplies. Even then, we have to use a perception spell. Using the currents is our way around that."

"Clever," I say, even though it hurts to hear about another lie my mother has told me my entire life. Not only did she know of the old coven's existence, but she's also spoken with them. Set rules for them.

"What now?" he asks, keeping his eyes on the shore. I hear the hope in his voice, the way it lightens his words.

But I can't give him what he wants.

"I don't know," I say quietly.

He tenses beside me. When I don't elaborate, he exhales sharply. "You're going to marry him, aren't you?"

I don't reply.

He shoves himself off the ground and throws his arms in the air. "Damn it, Mortana, why did you make me go through this? Why did you insist I tell you everything if it doesn't matter?"

I stand as well and follow him down the beach. "It *does* matter," I say, my voice rising. He won't stop walking, won't turn to face me. "But it doesn't change the fact that I don't remember any of it."

He stops then, looking at me so intensely I almost turn away, but I don't. I force myself to see him, really see him. "This is real, what we have, and I know you can feel it," he says, gesturing between us. He's angry, this visceral, strong reaction that radiates off him and stops me from moving.

He closes the space between us and takes my hand, pressing it firmly over his heart. "I'm right here, Mortana, standing directly in front of you, promising I will recreate every single memory if that's what it takes."

"I believe you," I say, keeping my palm against his chest.

"Then let me. Please."

"It isn't that simple. I have a duty to my family, to my coven."

"That didn't stop you before," he says, tightening his grip on my hand.

"It should have," I whisper.

As soon as I say it, I wish I could take it back. A wall rises between us, and any vulnerability Wolfe was willing to show me is gone. He drops my hand and backs away from me, my arm falling to my side. For some reason, it makes me want to cry.

He nods slowly. I try to read his face, but he gives nothing away. "Got it. Well, let me make it easier for you this time."

And with that, he dives into the sea, leaving me standing alone on the shore.

thirty-seven

I've been here before. Lying in bed when I should be asleep, thinking about a boy I shouldn't be thinking about.

My Covenant Ball, as well as my wedding, is in three days, and all I can think about is how just weeks ago, I was so deeply in love that I was willing to turn my back on both. Wolfe told me how I got there, recounted every detail of our relationship, but I can't *feel* it. And even when I could, I still chose to take the memory eraser; I still chose my coven in the end.

And I know that's for the best.

Wolfe's passion scares me. His willingness to show me his anger and pain, his frustration and vulnerability, is unlike anything I've experienced. He was so desperate for me to remember that he cut himself open so I could watch him bleed, knowing I might never suture the wound.

And I know that if I live a thousand years, no one will ever feel that way for me again.

But it isn't about me, and I don't think I could forgive myself if I turned my back on my family, my duty. I have one role to play, and my happiness, my wants, my desires have never been a factor. They can't be.

When I hear my parents moving around downstairs, I force myself to get up. Another sleepless night. My mother will scold me for the darkness under my eyes and the pallor of my skin, but it's nothing a little magic can't fix.

We're destroying the sea and ruining our island, but at least we can look well rested as we're doing it.

I brush my teeth and wash my face, thankful I don't have to work today. My mother says it will make the wedding more impactful if the rest of the witches don't see me in the week leading up to the ceremony. Everything is for show in one way or another, but I'm thankful for the time away.

"Where's Dad?" I ask when I get downstairs.

Mom looks up from her leather-bound planner and smiles. "Morning, honey. He's harvesting some lilac before heading to the perfumery."

I pour myself a cup of tea and sit down next to her. "Ivy told me about the memory eraser," I say, watching her.

She slowly closes her planner and looks at me. "I had a feeling she might."

"Why?"

She shrugs. "You've been best friends since birth. Keeping secrets from the other isn't a skill either of you possesses." She sounds so calm, and I wish I knew what she's thinking, wish I knew if her mind is a chaotic mess of to-do lists and worries and overreactions or if it's as put together as the rest of her.

Her words grate on me, though. "Not like you, right, Mom?" The words are quiet, and I can't believe I said them. It is so unlike me to question my mother, and I look down.

"Tana, why don't you ask me what you want to know instead of making snide remarks?"

I swallow and nod. "You're right, I'm sorry," I say. "I want to know why you lied to me about the old coven."

She walks into the kitchen to brew more tea. "The simple answer is that we never would have gotten this far if the mainland knew dark magic was still being practiced on the island. They had to believe the old coven had been disbanded if we were to be on solid ground with them. The old witches are selfish and stubborn, but they aren't stupid; they knew that if the mainland was aware of their existence, each and every one of them would be caught. So they vowed to remain hidden if we vowed to perpetuate the belief that they were gone. The council members are the only ones who know the truth." The kettle whistles, and Mom pours the water over the leaves. "And it has worked rather well, up until now."

I feel foolish for believing her lies and even worse for being hurt. I thought giving up a life of my own to marry Landon and protect my coven would grant me the truth, especially from my mother. I thought it would make me important enough to be involved in the inner workings of our coven and our island. But I was wrong.

"I wish you had told me."

RACHEL GRIFFIN

"I know you do, but I couldn't risk it. You're going to marry the governor's son, Tana—what would happen if you let it slip one night? Surely you must see the danger." She refills my tea before sitting back down. "Not that it matters anymore, of course."

"I can handle it."

"You say that now, but keeping a secret that substantial from your husband will weigh on you, especially as the love and trust between you builds. It won't be easy."

"You believe Landon and I will love each other one day?"

Her expression softens at that, and she reaches her hand out and places it on my arm. "Absolutely. I already see it between you. Don't you?"

I can't promise you love.

I think back to our kiss, to the way it felt to be near him in that way. It didn't feel like love, but maybe my definition of the word is too narrow. Maybe there's love like what Wolfe described, passionate and all-consuming and vital, and also more subtle love that takes root and grows over time, slow and steady. "I don't know," I admit. "But I want to."

Mom squeezes my arm. "In time. He's a good man, Tana, and he will love you well."

I nod and smile at her because I don't want her to see that I'm hoping for something I shouldn't hope for. "I'm sure you're right."

Mom leans back in her chair and takes a sip of tea. "What else do you want to know?"

"Why aren't you concerned about the currents? And why wouldn't you meet with the old coven about them?"

328

She sighs and sets down her teacup. "I don't think you under-stand how fragile our relationship with the mainland is. It only works because they believe we're in complete control of the magic we use. It only works because they aren't afraid of us. And even so, our docks were burned just months ago. The moment they learn there is magic in their waters that can't be controlled, their atti-tude toward us will change. And if they're afraid of us, everything collapses." She looks at me then. "Everything."

I think we're all a little afraid of the things we don't understand.

"But the old coven wants to help us. Why not let them?"

"A couple of years back, Marshall Yates let his advisors know this union with our family was on the horizon. He insisted on having representatives from the mainland keep watch over the island, and I agreed to it. Thankfully, all your trysts with Wolfe have been in the middle of the night—if they hadn't been, we'd be having a very different conversation. Now that the wedding is so close, the mainland is packing the island with security staff. And I won't risk a meeting until they're gone and I can ensure our discussions will remain private."

"But it's been a problem for so long. You're really willing to let all this damage occur for the sake of the wedding?"

"Tana," my mother says, leveling me with her gaze, "I remem-ber my mother making me hide as a young girl when people from the mainland would visit. My grandparents almost didn't have children because they were so worried about what might happen to them. Our ancestors gave up their home on the mainland and practiced a new magic, hoping for a future where we could be accepted and safe. I'm willing to let just about anything occur for the sake of the wedding."

The words send a shiver down my spine. "I still don't understand why you wouldn't address the issue of the currents earlier, before the wedding was ever certain."

"If we rely on the old coven to help with the currents, there's no going back from that. Ever. I respect Galen, but I don't trust him not to take advantage of that situation. And if he does, I want to make sure the mainland is allied with us, and the only way to ensure that is with the wedding."

She shifts in her seat and waits until I'm looking at her before she continues. "I'm willing to have these conversations with you, but let me make one thing clear: it doesn't bother me if you don't understand. My role as the leader of this coven is to keep us safe and to secure our place in society. It isn't to make sure my daughter understands every decision I make." She says it as gently as possible, but it still hurts.

I look away. She's my mother, but she's the head of our coven first and foremost, and while it stings to hear her say it, I also admire her for it.

"Okay," I say, finishing my tea, but then I remember what Wolfe said about the flower. "Wait, there's one more thing."

"Go on," she says.

"How can we practice magic if there is no moonflower on the island?" I know it's childish of me to phrase it as a question when I already know the answer, but I want to hear her say it. It feels important to me in a way I can't name to have her trust me with this. I have put my faith in her my whole life, always believed in the path she laid out for me, and I need to know she trusts me to walk it. I need to.

That question, more than anything else I've asked, catches my mother off guard. Her eyes widen and her spine straightens, and I hear the breath she sucks in through her teeth. It unsettles me, seeing her composure slip that way, and I silently tell her it's okay, assure her that she can trust me.

"Moonflower is poisonous to witches. You know that."

My heart sinks. "Is it?" I ask, watching her.

"Let's take a break from the questions for today," she says. "If I promise you I will have this conversation with you later, will you agree to let it go for now? It's a very complicated answer with a very complicated history, and I don't have the time or energy for it right now."

"We have to come back to it later."

"You have my word."

"Okay," I say. My mother always keeps her promises, and even though she has kept many things from me, I know she'll have this conversation with me when we have more time. And the truth is, I'm tired.

"Okay?" she asks.

I nod, and she pulls me into a hug. "I'm proud of you," she says.

I want to ask her why she's proud when I've caused so much stress and pain, but I don't. Instead, I hug her back and soak up her words, because even though I don't know if I deserve them, I need to hear them anyway.

"We're more alike than you think, you know," my mother says when she pulls away.

"We are?"

She nods. "Your father is the absolute love of my life, but he wasn't the first boy I ever loved." She gives me a meaningful look, and my eyes widen.

"No," I say.

"Wolfe looks almost exactly like his father did at that age. It's uncanny."

"You and Galen?"

"We were young, and he was unlike anyone I'd ever met before. We had a strict rule that we never practiced magic together—that was a line I could never cross—but there were other lines I was more than happy to cross with him." Her voice sounds far away, almost happy.

I shake my head, not quite believing what she's telling me. "But how did you even know him?"

"When your grandmother became ill, she began to include me in all her duties, preparing me to take over her role. And those duties involved occasional meetings with the old coven. Galen started attending with his mother, and, well, things progressed." She speaks of him with regard even now, and I struggle to fit this new information into the version of my mother that I know.

"You loved Galen Hawthorne?"

"It was a long time ago," she says, waving her hand through the air as if clearing the memory. "I loved Galen for all the things he wasn't. I knew we didn't have a future together, and so did he, but for one winter we pretended we had all the time in the world."

"And you both accepted that?"

"It wasn't something we had to work to accept. We were just two kids having fun before we inherited our responsibilities. There was never a question about where our loyalties lay."

"You never wondered what a life with him might be like?"

"No," she says, giving me a sad smile. "*This* is the life I believe in. This is the life I want."

"Would you still want this life, want the new order and low magic, if the mainland wasn't watching? If it wasn't dangerous to do high magic?"

She doesn't answer right away, looking off into a faraway place I can't see. I hold my breath and wait for her to show even the slightest sign of doubt, but she never does. "Yes. I don't love the new order only because it gave us our lives back; I love it because it fulfills me in a way nothing else ever has. I love this island and this magic and delighting tourists. I would choose it over and over again, regardless of what was happening across the Passage."

The answer guts me because I can never live up to that. I wish I believed in anything as much as my mother believes in the new order.

You did.

The thought pops into my head unbidden, but it isn't real, isn't something I can grab hold of. I was told that I once believed in something with everything I am, but without the memories, it's just dust on the road.

"Do you ever think about him?" I ask, needing to change the subject.

"Galen? More, recently," she says, eyeing me. "But not often, no. Your father asked me out not long after Galen and I ended things, and I knew from our first date that he was it for me."

"How did you know?"

Her face softens, the way it always does when we talk about Dad.

"I could be myself with him," she says simply. "We believed in the same things, and I didn't have to put on a show or try to be someone I'm not. He accepted me fully, exactly as I am."

"Thank you for telling me that," I say.

My mother smiles and squeezes my arm. "You're welcome. Now, why don't we get Ivy over here and practice your hair and makeup?"

She walks to the phone, and my mind continues to work through our conversation. I'm glad we talked about everything, so glad I finally know the truth, but it doesn't settle me as much as I wish it would. My mother has made choices I know I could never make, and while she told me about Galen to showcase our similarities, it only serves to highlight our differences.

Because apparently, I couldn't accept that my time with Wolfe was limited.

I couldn't accept that his world, his magic, wasn't an option for me. I couldn't accept that *he* wasn't an option for me.

And even though Landon doesn't want me to have to try with him, I do. But I didn't with Wolfe. He told me I did things I know I would never do unless I was fully and truly myself.

My heart races and my palms sweat as I replay my mother's words.

By her standards, Wolfe should be the absolute love of my life.

thirty-eight

The door to the rooftop opens, but I don't turn around to see who's joining me. The sunrise is beautiful today, and I try to stop the lump in my throat, knowing this will be my last sunrise living at home.

My dad sits on the couch next to me, pulling the corner of my blanket so it's covering his legs. For a while, we sit together in silence, watching the sunrise over the island. Dawn has always been my favorite time, when the darkness recedes and the sky turns dusty blue before erupting into a rainbow of color.

I love it because it signals the start of magic, the hours of the day when I feel most alive and content. There is never enough daylight, and the night seems to stretch on forever, but at sunrise, time feels infinite.

I wonder what it would be like to be Wolfe, to know that I could practice magic at any time, day or night. To know that the only restrictions on my magic were the ones I created myself.

It sounds terrifying, that kind of unchecked power.

And absolutely stunning.

"Thinking about the wedding?" my dad asks, bringing me back to the rooftop. I look away as heat fills my face. Just once, I wish I could focus on the right thing.

"I can't believe it's tonight," I say, looking down. I knead the blanket in my hands, but I stop when I notice my dad watching. I smooth the blanket and force myself to remain still.

"It's okay to be nervous," he says, looking out over the Passage. "It's a big night."

"I wish I could do the ceremonies separately," I say, finally meeting his eyes. "I've been excited about my Covenant my whole life. I hate that I have to share it with Landon."

My dad gives me a sympathetic look and places an arm around me. I lean into him, letting my head rest on his shoulder.

"I know, honey. I wish you could have the ball you've always dreamt of. But this is good. It's important for Landon to see this part of you, for him to be included in it. You're combining your lives—he should see you fully, as both a witch and his bride."

"Would you be okay with him watching a rush?" I ask the question quietly, not wanting to be combative. I genuinely want to know what he thinks.

"That kind of display would terrify the mainlanders, and I suspect Landon is no exception." He pauses, and I feel the rise and fall of his chest when he takes a breath. "But I wish it didn't have to be that way."

"Me too," I say.

"I have something for you." Dad pulls away from me and reaches into his pocket, revealing a worn red velvet box that he hands to me.

"What's this for?"

"It's your Covenant gift," he says. "It's been in my family for generations."

I gently lift the lid and gasp. It's a necklace, a long silver chain with a vial hanging from the end. There's water inside the vial, swirling of its own volition. I watch as it rolls inside the glass, lapping up the sides and rushing back into the center.

"This is incredible," I say, all the air leaving my lungs. "How is it doing that?"

"It was created the night of the very first rush, when our ancestors decided the only way to survive was to give up their darkness and work with the mainland. They drained their magic into the ocean, then filled this vial with the magicked water as a constant reminder of what they were working toward. It feels fitting to give it to you now, when their dream is being fully realized."

I lift the necklace with shaking hands. The water is mesmerizing as it swirls around, and I think I could watch it forever. It's the most beautiful piece of jewelry I've ever seen, bold and enchanting, such a far cry from the polished pearls and dainty diamonds of the Witchery today.

"Dad, I don't think I can take this," I say, rolling the vial in my fingers.

"Of course you can. This is your history, Tana. It's who you are. I want you to have it."

"Thank you," I say, the words barely a whisper. Tears well in my eyes, and I blink them away and swallow the lump that's formed in my throat. Everything aches, and I take several deep breaths.

"I love you, honey. You're strong and independent and secure enough to question why you believe what you believe. You're curious and unbridled and sensitive, so many things I admire. I could not have picked a better daughter, not even if I had magicked her myself."

This time, I can't stop the tears that spill over my lashes. "I love you so much," I say, giving my dad a hug, holding on tight, wanting to stay here just a little longer. Stay his little girl instead of Landon's bride.

"I love you, too."

I wonder if he can sense that I'm struggling to let go, that he is the only solid ground I have left.

The door opens, and my mom comes bustling out with a notebook tucked beneath her arm and a large teapot and three teacups sitting on a tray.

"Today's the day," she proclaims, setting everything down and pouring us each a cup of tea. "How are you feeling, sweetheart?"

Her eyes are so bright and her smile so excited that it's hard not to smile back. "Great," I say, slipping the necklace from Dad over my head. "I can't wait."

"Oh, Tana, it looks perfect on you," she says, touching the vial around my neck.

"I love it." I smile at my dad, and he squeezes my shoulder before taking a sip of tea.

"Okay, why don't we go over the schedule for the day? Ivy will be here at noon to get you ready for your Covenant, which will start promptly at four. Mainlanders will be arriving on the island all day for the wedding, but Landon and his parents will be the only ones permitted at your Covenant. Once the ball is over, you'll go back to the main house, where you'll get changed for the wedding. The ceremony will begin promptly at sunset on the eastern shore, followed by the reception."

I nod along with her words, having memorized the schedule from the previous times she's gone over it with me. It sits heavy on me, knowing so much of my life is about to change. By the end of the day, I'll be bound to my coven for life, an irrevocable tie that can never be broken.

And I'll be Landon's wife, binding my coven to the mainland, another tie that can't be undone.

It's terrifying and exciting and monumental, and I hope I can get through both ceremonies with the grace and poise required for such occasions. At least Ivy will be there helping me, gently guiding me when I'm not quite sure what to do.

Between her and my mother, I'll be fine. I know I will be.

"I'm ready," I tell my mom, making sure my nerves don't edge their way into my voice. I want to sound calm and controlled and strong, all the things she would be if she were in my place. All the things she is.

"I know you are, honey," she says, pulling me into a hug.

The three of us drink our tea and watch the sky until it's a vibrant shade of blue, a clear, crisp day that's perfect for vows and promises and change.

When we're finished, I set my teacup on the tray and fold the blanket.

"Now it's time for the best part of the day," my dad says in a mischievous voice. "Cinnamon rolls."

My mom swats him on the shoulder and laughs. "Hardly."

"I don't know, Mom. His cinnamon rolls are pretty excellent," I say, following my parents inside. "I'd bind myself to them for the rest of my life if I could."

They laugh, and I touch the vial hanging from my neck, already a part of me that I never want to be without.

Today will be a good day, one to remember for the rest of my life. History in the making.

I can do this.

I watch nervously through the window as the council readies the lawn for my Covenant. My mom rushes around with a pencil tucked behind her ear and her notebook held firmly in her hands, passing out orders as if they're hors d'oeuvres.

Ivy pulls me away from the window and motions to a pale pink velvet chair. We're in an old manor house that was converted for events years ago, and the entire room is ornate. Gold botanical wallpaper brightens the space, and a white grand piano sits in the corner, reflecting the light from outside. A fire dances in the white marble fireplace, and a large, gilded mirror hangs above the mantel. Dozens of plants line the windowsills and snake down the wall, and I gently take a leaf between my fingers.

"Sit. We aren't done yet," Ivy says, swirling a brush in a rose-colored powder from Mrs. Rhodes's beauty shop. Ivy had me ready hours ago, but she finds applying makeup without magic soothing, much like my dad keeps magic out of the kitchen. I'm overwhelmed by the number of witches who have offered up their goods, wanting to be part of the ceremony in some way. Mrs. Rhodes's makeup and Ms. Talbot's dress and Mr. Lee's shoes and even Ivy's Tandon blend.

"It's actually pretty good," I say, starting on my second cup.

"I told you I wouldn't let you down." She tilts my face toward the window and studies her work. We still haven't talked about the night I saved her life, but it's in the room with us, occupying the moments of heavy silence and empty laughs.

I feel it the same way I feel the shadows where my memories used to be, following me around every second of every day, haunting me for different reasons.

But I know Ivy and I will be okay, because not all the laughs are empty and not all the silence is heavy. We're still us, standing side by side, walking through the aftermath of my decision together.

"How are you?" Ivy asks. She busies herself with my makeup, but I can feel the weight in her words.

I look over at the door, but it's still closed, blocking us off from the rest of the world.

"I'm good," I say, rolling the vial between my fingers. "I feel ready."

"You do?" I can hear the hope in her voice, and it makes my throat ache, the way she only wants me to be happy, even after everything I put her through.

"Yeah, I do. I've been thinking about it a lot, and I'm proud of the role I get to play. Landon will be a good husband."

"He will be," she agrees, and I look at her closely. "I wouldn't say it if I didn't believe it. I want this union to happen as much as your mother and everyone else, but I wouldn't let you do this if I didn't think you'd find happiness in it."

"Thank you," I say. Ivy goes back to applying my makeup, running the brush over my cheeks again. "And thank you for telling me everything, about the memory eraser and Wolfe. It means a lot to me, more than you will ever know."

I feel the brush slow against my skin. "You're welcome," she says hesitantly. "Are you feeling okay? With all that?"

"I think so. I'm glad I know what happened, but I still don't remember any of it. It all feels like something that happened to someone else, like a character in a book. I don't recognize it as my own lived experience."

Ivy nods, but her eyebrows pinch together, and she purses her lips. "Hey," I say, putting my hand on top of hers, moving the brush away from my skin and making her meet my eyes. "It was my decision. I'm the one who took it. I'm the one who made the choices that led up to it. This isn't on you."

She swallows and takes a heavy breath, then gets back to work. "I know. It's just that one day, it might be nice to remember those nights that you fully chose for yourself."

"Maybe," I say, looking up as she applies something under my eyes. "But why make it harder on myself?"

"Is it hard?" Her voice is casual, but it's a loaded question.

"That's not what I meant," I say quickly.

"It's okay if it is."

"It's not."

"Okay," she says, moving to my other side.

She finishes my makeup in silence, then lifts a gold hand mirror from the table and holds it up in front of me.

"You look beautiful," she says, emotion edging its way into her voice.

"Oh, Ivy, it's perfect." She kept my makeup light enough that I still look like myself, but she has rimmed my eyes in black and added deep gray shadow to my lids. I look dramatic and natural and soft and fierce, just like the sea.

"Thank you," I say.

She helps me into my dress, the gray silk sliding over my skin and trailing on the floor behind me. My hair is down in soft waves, and she gently tucks a comb into place, adorned with pearls and crystals that catch the light.

"We are so lucky to have you," Ivy says, giving me a soft hug, careful not to smudge my makeup.

"Don't you dare make me cry. I have a very long day to get through, and if I start now, who knows when I'll stop."

"Fair," she says.

Just then, the door swings open, and my mother rushes in. "Oh, Tana," she says, coming to a halt when she sees me. Her eyes begin to glisten, and she takes a deep breath before moving closer to me. "You look radiant."

"Thanks, Mom."

"Ready?"

I look to Ivy, and she gives me an encouraging smile. "I'm right behind you," she says.

I nod and squeeze her hand. Then I turn to my mother.

"I'm ready."

thirty-nine

The lawn is packed with bodies. Bright conversation and easy laughter fill the space as I wait to make my entrance. Covenant Balls are our most sacred events, more important than almost anything else. Even though a witch hasn't denounced our coven in years, we still celebrate each and every witch who declares themself for us because it's a win for our way of life. It signifies that the new order will continue, that this life is worth protecting. And at the end of the day, it's still a choice.

The music changes, and my mother weaves her way through the garden and onto the lawn. There's a circular wooden platform with three marble pillars on top set up in the middle where the binding spell will take place. A copper basin glints in the sunlight, resting on the first pillar. On the second is a gold knife, and on the third is a shallow crystal dish filled with water. It has been the same for every witch who has come before me, the only ritual we have preserved from the old order.

If my blood enters the copper basin, mixing with the blood of my ancestors, I am bound to my coven for life.

If my blood enters the crystal basin, spreading through the clear water, I am banished from my coven forever.

I wonder what Landon will think when he sees my blood fall from my finger and into the basin. I wonder if it will scare him or intrigue him, if it will make him second-guess our arrangement or make him more eager to marry me.

I wonder if he will shy away from who I am or accept me fully, power and magic and all. I think back to our conversation on the mainland, and my stomach pinches.

My mother steps onto the platform, and all conversation stops. The witches spread out, fully encircling the wooden stage. My heart beats wildly as she raises her hands.

"Presenting Mortana Edith Fairchild this seventeenth of December for consideration by the new order of magic and all of us therein."

My father helps her off the platform, and the music stops. I step onto the lawn, my heart so loud I struggle to hear the ocean. I remind myself to breathe. All I have to do is breathe. My legs shake as I walk toward the platform.

The crowd parts, creating a small aisle for me. I walk down it, unable to make eye contact with anyone. I've been waiting for this ceremony my whole life, but now that it's here, it feels suffocating. When I get to the platform, a hand takes mine, helping me up.

Landon.

It doesn't feel right, him being the one to help me. It should be my parents or Ivy or just me by myself, but I hear the way the crowd murmurs and see my mother's smile, and I take his hand.

I wish the music would start back up again or the ocean would roar behind me—anything to drown out the blood rushing through my veins, the worries swirling in my mind like the currents. I touch the vial my dad gave me and feel the weight of it in my hand. It steadies me.

I look out over the crowd surrounding the stage, my coven, smiling up at me as I give myself to them forever. It's such a beautiful thing, this group of witches supporting me, watching as I go through the same ceremony they all went through in years past.

My parents are in the front row, and they look so proud. So content. Ivy stands just behind them, the uneasiness on her face still present. I lock eyes with her and she grimaces, and it threatens to stop my heart.

I desperately want to know what it means, want to jump from the platform and ask what she's thinking, but it's too late.

Then there's Landon, his eyes curious and his stance rigid. He isn't comfortable here, surrounded by my coven, the first non-witch ever to witness a Covenant Ball. I wish his shoulders would relax and his hands would ease open.

I wish he were a witch.

The thought gives me pause. It's the first time I've ever considered it, that Landon isn't a witch. He will never understand the most important part of me because he has no connection to it, because the aim of his government has always been to dim the magic inside us. And we're about to marry.

It takes my breath away, knowing we will never revel in magic together, never challenge the power inside each other. I will move to his home, and my magic will be all but forgotten, a silly parlor game he'll use to impress his friends.

I shake my head. I'm being unfair. He has never given me any reason to believe that. He has always been honest and open. He has always been kind.

It's time. I swallow my doubts and prepare to speak the words that will bind me to my coven for life.

I walk to the marble pillars. A gold knife with emeralds and rubies along the hilt shines in the sunlight directly between the two basins. I think about how the earliest witches could have their Covenant Balls at night, surrounded by darkness. How no one required them to step into the light, as if the time of day could erase what stirred inside them.

But here we are. In the light.

I take a deep breath and hold my hands over the knife, preparing to begin the spell. I look between the two basins, and something inside the copper bowl catches my eye. There should be nothing except for the blood of the witches before me, still red and fluid, sustained by magic. But poking through the surface is the top of a perfume bottle with a note that says PRESS THIS. And floating next to it is a single moonflower.

I slowly look up, unsure of what to do. It must be from my parents, but they didn't prepare me for this part of the ceremony. I'm supposed to speak the spell, cut my hand, and let the blood run into the basin of my choice, sealing my fate forever. They never said anything about a perfume, and they would never give me this flower.

Slowly, I reach into the basin and press the top of the bottle. A strong scent fills the air, fresh and earthy. It smells like grass and salt and something else I can't quite place.

Then an image appears, and I gasp. I see myself practicing magic at night, standing on the western shore next to Wolfe. I'm pulling in the tide, and he's watching me as if I'm the most stunning thing he's ever seen. The memory consumes me, coming to life in my mind, strong and vivid and real. I search for other memories, but nothing else comes. Just this one.

I watch as water crashes over me and I almost lose myself in it. Then Wolfe pulls me onto the shore and helps me breathe again, saving my life for the second time. We watch the stars and the moon and each other.

It's hard for me to leave him—I can see it in my slow steps and hesitations. I clutch the edges of the basin as the memory plays out in front of me, awakening something I thought I'd put to sleep.

He walks me up the shore and we pause, staring at each other. I ask if he wants to see me again, and he says yes, even though he sounds disgusted with himself when he answers.

I don't even realize my eyes have filled with tears until one rolls down my cheek and falls into the basin, salt water instead of blood.

Do you want to see me again?

Yes.

I remember it. I remember the way the word slid inside my gut and changed me from the inside out. I remember how leaving him felt as impossible as seeing him again. I remember how he made me feel alive, how his magic made me feel alive.

I'm overwhelmed by it.

The scene fades, but I cling to the bowl, desperate to see more. Just one more glimpse, one more second, one more memory.

But nothing comes.

I stare at the bottle, completely devastated by what I've lost. I want back every single moment I spent with him. I want to see it all.

"Tana?" My father whispers my name, jolting me back to the present. Back to this wooden platform, surrounded by my coven and parents and future husband.

I finally let go of the basin, its sharp rim leaving dents in my palms. My dad gives me a questioning look. I try to smile but feel completely lost.

There are too many people watching me, and I feel frozen to this stage, unsure of how I'll ever step down from it.

I take a deep breath, but it only makes me shake. The air tastes salty, just like the cologne. Just like Wolfe.

I look out over the crowd and find Ivy. She's staring at me, her eyes wide. As soon as I see her, my vision blurs and my throat aches. And before I know what's happening, she rushes onto the stage and pulls me into her arms.

"What did you see?" she whispers in my hair, holding me so close no one else can hear.

"A memory. With him."

I can't help the tears falling down my face now, and I tremble in Ivy's arms.

"Listen to me. Do you want out of this? Tell me now." Her words are clear and concise. Urgent.

"Yes."

I feel her magic as it leaves her system, overwhelming me at once. The same soothing magic she puts in her nighttime tea swims in my head. The world spins, my eyelids get heavy, and I can no longer support my weight.

I collapse in Ivy's arms as the world goes black.

I wake up in the same room I got ready in. Ivy is sitting next to me, tapping her polished nails on a porcelain teacup.

"What happened?" I ask, my voice groggy.

The tapping stops.

"You got sick and passed out. At least, that's what everyone thinks."

I slowly sit up. My head is pounding and my throat is dry. Ivy hands me a cup of tea.

The image from the copper basin comes rushing back to me, so vivid and real. I believe what I saw, the way my eyes were wide with wonder, the way my tears fell from amazement. I believe how deeply dark magic spoke to me and how it made me feel completely at home.

I understand why I was willing to give up this life for a

different one. I don't want to walk away from this, from my family and my coven and Ivy. But maybe this was never the life that was meant for me.

"What happens now?"

"Everyone is still out there. Your mother said you didn't eat enough earlier and that the Covenant will happen at the top of the hour."

I strain my eyes to read the clock on the wall. "That's in thirty minutes."

"You need to figure out what you're going to do. You know how it works—you have to go through the Covenant and make your choice. Blood in the basin or blood in the water."

I close my eyes. The Covenant isn't only for show; our magic is bound to it. If we don't go through the ritual, it becomes erratic and violent.

I have to make a choice.

"I know."

My mother walks into the room, relief crossing her face when she sees that I'm awake. "How are you feeling, darling?"

"Better," I say. Then I remember the moonflower floating in the basin, and I know I can't put it off any longer. "Ivy, would you mind getting me a bite to eat? Just something small?"

"Of course, I'll be right back."

I wait until Ivy is out of the room, then look at my mother. "How can we practice magic if there are no moonflowers on the island?"

"Tana," she says, exasperated. "We don't have time for this."

"I need to know." *I need to hear you say it. I need you to trust me.*

My mother considers me for a moment, but I won't back down, and she must know it because she sighs and sits next to me. "Tana, what I'm about to tell you must remain secret. You can never repeat this to a single soul, not to Ivy or Landon or even your father. Do you understand me?"

"I understand."

She closes her eyes, and for a moment I think she's not going to tell me. Then she speaks. "The moonflower is the source of all magic; we cannot practice without it. It's most potent in its natural state, and dark magic is only possible with the physical flower. The council decided years ago, when the new order was formed, that moonflowers would be banished from the island and that we would perpetuate the belief that they are poisonous to witches. If there are no moonflowers on the island and witches believe them to be deadly, there is no chance anyone can practice dark magic."

"But if the flower is required for all magic, how are we able to practice?"

"We keep a low level of moonflower extract in the Witchery's water supply. It isn't strong enough to be used for dark magic, but it's enough to keep the magic going in our veins. It's enough to sustain our way of life."

It's exactly what I wanted to hear, confirming what Wolfe told me, but it doesn't make me feel better the way I hoped it would. It doesn't make me feel trusted or like I'm part of the inner workings of my island. It makes me feel foolish because I believed her lies.

"Dad doesn't know?" I ask, hating the way my voice shakes.

"No. Three of the seven council members know, including myself, and now you. That's it, and that's how it must stay."

"Does the governor know?"

"Absolutely not. The mainlanders believe the flowers are deadly to witches, and it is imperative that they continue to believe that."

I want to argue, to dive in and ask how she could perpetuate such a lie, ask why she doesn't trust our coven to make the right choices if she believes in this life so much, but the words get lost somewhere inside me.

I sit up straighter, nod, and look at my mother. "I will not share this with anyone—I swear it. Thank you for telling me."

"You're welcome. I know my obligations to this coven have made certain aspects of our relationship difficult at times, and for that I'm sorry. But out of every role I've ever played, being your mother is my favorite." She squeezes my hand then clears her throat, the moment passing by me too soon. "Now, let's move on to your Covenant. Are you ready to proceed?"

"I am," I say.

She gives me a tight hug, then leaves the room, passing Ivy on her way out.

Ivy sets down a porcelain plate filled with tea sandwiches, but I'm too nauseated to eat. I walk to the window and look at everyone standing on the lawn, drinking and chatting as if all is well. "Ivy, I know you just got back, but would you mind sending Landon in here?"

She raises an eyebrow. "Why, what happened? What are you about to do?"

"Just send him in."

She watches me for a breath, then leaves, and a moment later, the door creaks open. "You gave us all quite the scare," Landon says as he gently shuts the door behind him. He sounds nervous.

"I'm sorry. Other than being embarrassed, I'm fine."

"I'm glad to hear it."

I motion him over, and Landon sits down on the couch beside me. I lightly take his hand, and he looks down at it with a confused expression.

"Landon, I can't marry you." Once the words are out of my mouth, the heaviness I've been carrying begins to ease. I take a deep breath.

He studies me as if trying to discern how serious I am. "Why not?"

"Because I don't want to worry that you will fear me our whole marriage. I don't want you to have to try to love me."

"I value honesty; that's why I said those things. But this marriage has never been about love. It has always been about duty, and that comes first. It must come first."

I look down, because he's voicing something I used to believe about myself, that duty mattered more than anything else. I was wrong. "But it doesn't come first. Not for me."

Landon shakes his head, pulling his hand from mine. "Tana, I will treat you well. I will do right by you and our families. I will swim with you and teach you to ride and help you build a life on the mainland. You and I have been walking the same path our entire lives, carrying the same expectation. We understand each other. This is a foundation we can build a fulfilling life upon."

"I know you would treat me well. That has never been a question," I say. "You think you understand me because of the role I'm meant to play, but I'm more than that. I want to be more than that."

He exhales, heavy and loud. "What more is there?"

The memory surges in my mind, images of powerful magic and intense glances and fragile touches, a love so strong it broke every restraint I'd ever put on myself. "So much more."

Landon stands and begins to pace. "There are things in life that are bigger than the individual. Bigger than you and bigger than me. This is one of those things. Don't ruin everything our families have worked to build."

"It doesn't have to be ruined. Your father is the most powerful person on the mainland. You could find another suitable match, someone from one of our coven's original families. I'm the most obvious choice, but I'm not the only one." I stand and gently touch his hand. "You could choose who to spend your life with, Landon. Someone who believes in the same things you do."

He looks at me then. "I thought you were that person."

My gaze falls to the floor. "I did, too."

We're both quiet for a moment, standing in the truth that I am unable to do the one thing I was meant for. Then Landon speaks. "My father will never agree to this. I cannot force you into a marriage, nor would I want to, but you must know what this will do to our alliance."

I look out the window at the waves hitting the shore in the distance. "What if you put the blame on me? Told your father you've discovered something that would make me an unsuitable wife? You can control the narrative, and I will not contradict you. This alliance can still happen."

"You would risk your reputation for this?"

"I already am," I say. "I will be extraordinarily disliked before the day is out. Nothing you come up with will hurt as much as that."

"I don't understand," Landon says, looking out at all the witches waiting for my Covenant to begin. "But I won't press you any further. I want this alliance, and I will ensure my father believes that you are not the appropriate wife to forge it with."

I nod. "You may speak of me however you need to."

"If you'll excuse me, I'm going to leave before your Covenant." He walks to the door, pauses, and looks back at me. "I hope you find what you're looking for."

"Take care of yourself, Landon."

He nods once, exiting the room without another word. A moment later, Ivy enters.

"He looks like he's leaving," she says, her eyes following Landon.

"He is."

She rushes over to me, and her voice shakes when she speaks. "What did you do?"

"Something my parents will be very unhappy about."

Ivy stares at me, her eyes wide and hurt and scared. "Are you sure about this?"

I take her hands in mine. "I wish I were as selfless as you are, Ivy. I wish I believed in this life as much as you do. But there's something out there I believe in more, and I know it isn't right, but I can't ignore it. I wish I could."

Her eyes fill with tears, and she squeezes my hands. "I'm so mad at you," she says, the words coming out on top of a sob. "What am I going to do without you?"

The words put me back together, stitch me up, prove to me that love is the strongest magic of all. Not high or low, not old or new. Love.

She pulls me close, holding me so tight I ache. "You're about to create absolute chaos," she says.

"I know."

She looks at me for one more breath, then walks back outside just as my mother finds her way to the platform, repeating her words from earlier. Presenting me once more.

I close my eyes and replay the memory from the bottle over and over again. There is only one person who could have put that bottle there, one person who saw the life that's meant for me long before I saw it myself. That life has been waiting in the shadows all these years, patient, and as I step from the house and make my way to the platform, I'm finally ready to claim it.

forty

I'm standing on the platform again, my heart slamming against my ribs. I take a deep breath and look between the basins, between the two paths laid out before me. The perfume no longer sits in the copper bowl, and the moonflower from earlier is gone. I wonder if my mother saw it and removed it or if Wolfe did, waiting and watching from a distance.

I slowly pick up the knife, its golden blade reflecting the light of the sun. It feels heavy in my hand. Sacred.

The ocean waves roll onto the shore, and my coven is silent around me. Landon is gone, and Ivy looks up at me with expectant, anxious eyes. I'm not sure if my parents have noticed Landon's absence, but they stand with their heads high, looks of pride on their faces.

I touch the vial around my neck with my free hand, letting the feel of it calm my racing heart. Then I begin.

I place the blade against my right palm and slowly slide the

BRING ME YOUR MIDNIGHT

metal down my hand. It leaves a perfect cut that fills with blood, running down my skin like a river.

Then I speak the words that will determine the rest of my life.

"Blade of gold,
witch's blood,
pour from me as though a flood.
Copper basin,
crystal bowl,
determine who will hold my soul.
Just one choice,
seal my fate,
this covenant will never break.
Year to year
forever remain,
until I meet my dying day."

I reach my hand out in front of me as my blood starts to drip. My parents watch me, a sea of affection in their eyes, and my hand wavers to the left, toward the copper basin. I love them so much. All I've ever wanted was to make them proud.

I always thought that would be enough, and I'm heartbroken that it isn't.

I close my eyes and force my hand over the crystal bowl, my blood dropping into the water and spreading out for my entire coven to see.

Gasps fill the air, and my mother cries out. She collapses into my father, sobbing, as loud voices and angry shouts rise up all around me. I'm frozen where I stand, shocked by the choice I made.

Irrevocable.

Witches start rushing the platform, banging on the wood with their fists. I should run, but I can't make myself move, completely stuck to the floor beneath me.

They know what I've given up. They know my choice affects them all, that I'm not only turning my back on their way of life but on their safety as well.

My arm is still outstretched in front of me, my fist shaking. I can't believe I actually did it.

Ivy jumps onto the platform and grabs my arm, dragging me off the other side. She holds me close to her as she pushes through the crowd, forcing me to move, pulling me far away. Shouts of "Traitor!" follow us, but Ivy remains steady next to me. She never falters and only stops running when we enter the woods, when the shouts aren't quite as loud. She pulls me behind a towering evergreen, the trunk large enough to hide us both.

"Go," she says, her voice urgent.

"Ivy," I start, tears running down my face.

"I know," she says, pulling me into her. "I love you, too."

We hold each other through tears and the sound of the ocean and loud voices getting louder.

"Forever," I say, crying into her hair.

"Forever."

We clutch each other for another breath, and then Ivy pulls back, pushing me away from her. "Go," she says again.

I run from the crowd, deeper into the trees bordering the lawn, unsure of where I'm going. Angry shouts follow me, and I keep running until they fade away, until I can no longer hear the desperate cries and outraged voices. I'm completely alone, banished from my coven with nowhere to go.

I keep moving, and when I'm far enough away that I'm sure I won't be found, I sink to the forest floor and bury my face in my hands. I wish I could forget the sound of my mother's cries, the way she looked as she collapsed into my father. My hand drifts to the vial he gave me just this morning, and a new wave of tears finds me. I should never have accepted it, though I can't quite imagine being without it.

I know I'll see my parents again when the chaos of my Covenant Ball has calmed and I can go home, be with them in private. But I can't live there anymore. I'm no longer one of them. No longer allowed.

I force myself to breathe. I inhale deeply and wait for my tears to stop and my heart to slow.

I can't believe I went through with it. But even as I sit here, scared and alone, I don't regret it. I know it was the right choice for me. The wrong choice for everyone else, but the right choice for me.

Selfish.

Selfish and right.

"Mortana?"

I jump and look up, my eyes adjusting to the darkness in the trees as the sun sets.

Wolfe is standing in front of me, tense and unreadable. I push myself up from the ground, my gray silk dress damp from the earth, and meet his eyes. He hands me a moonflower, and I take it, brushing the petals lightly with my fingertips.

"Do you remember?" he asks me.

"No."

He breathes out. "You don't remember, and you walked away?"

"Yes."

"Why?" He sounds angry, but I realize it isn't anger at all. He's protecting himself, not allowing any of his vulnerability to show. He's scared.

"Because I believe you," I say. "I used the memory keeper and knew I would never be happy if I wasn't standing on the shore with you, practicing magic at night."

His eyes get red and his jaw tenses. He nods several times and looks away, as if he's embarrassed.

"Can I touch you?" I ask hesitantly.

He exhales and looks at me. "Mortana," he says, his voice shaking, "the answer to that question will always be yes."

I slowly close the space between us, wrapping my arms around him, holding on tight. He hesitates for a single breath, and then his arms are around my waist and his head is against my neck, his breath sending goose bumps all along my skin.

I thought it would feel odd, hugging this boy I barely know, but it doesn't. I think my body remembers him, remembers the way it felt to be wrapped up in him.

He feels like home.

We hold each other for a long time, breathing each other in. I feel safe in his arms, peaceful and calm, even though I don't remember. Even though I left such an unimaginable mess behind me. This is where I'm meant to be. Right here.

I finally pull away from him. "Take me home?"

He nods, holding his hand out to me.

And I take it, letting him lead the way.

Wolfe and I are sitting on a boulder that overlooks the eastern shore, watching as the sky changes from velvet blue to black. The stars are out tonight, and the half-moon shines brightly, reflecting off the water of the Passage. Lightning flashes in the darkness, and a few moments later, thunder rumbles in the distance. Then the sky opens up over the channel separating us from the mainland, drenching it in rain.

Landon's boat is halfway across the water, the *Emerald Princess* sign lit up on the back of the ship. Small globe lights hang along the railings, slightly illuminating the silhouette of a person walking inside from the stern. I watch as it pulls farther away from the Witchery, and I wonder what kind of conversations he's having with his parents, what he said to them after we spoke. I can't deny the relief I feel as his boat gets farther away, knowing how close I was to being on it with him.

I've said goodbye to so many things today. I'm glad this island isn't one of them.

The lights on the ship move in the distance, jerking to the right, and I sit up, straining my eyes to get a better look.

They swing back to the left.

"Oh my god," I breathe, getting to my feet.

"What is it?" Wolfe asks, placing his hand on my back.

At first, I think it's the storm battering the ship, but the swells aren't big enough to jolt it like that. It's something else. "The boat," I say. "It's caught in a current."

For a moment, I just stare, mesmerized by the way the ship tips and thrashes as if it's weightless. It starts spinning around and around, and I can hear the groaning and breaking of wood from here.

"We have to do something," I say, rushing into the water, braiding the moonflower into my hair so I don't lose it.

Wolfe follows me, conjuring a thick cloud of magic that fully immerses me. I feel it working, entering my lungs and flowing into the water, overwhelmed by its power.

"We'll use a current to get there quickly. You'll be able to stay underwater for minutes as long as you stay close to me."

I nod, then put my hand in his and dive into the water. We're immediately caught in the current he created, but instead of spinning us around, it drags us out into the Passage. I kick my legs and reach with my arms as we're carried closer and closer to the ship.

The groaning of metal and wood punctuates the stormy night, and I kick harder when I hear yelling. An awful crack splits the air, followed by a large wave that rushes toward us.

It pushes us back several yards, but the current finds us again quickly. My formal gown drags in the water around me, and my body shakes from the cold as we're pulled farther out to sea. Another bolt of lightning cuts through the darkness, and rain pelts us as we swim.

When we finally get close enough to see the ship in detail, Wolfe slows the current, and we tread water.

"Do you know how many people are on board?" he asks, breathing heavy.

I shake my head. "Landon and his parents for sure. Probably a captain, maybe some staff?"

Wolfe works beside me, his magic rising around us. This time, it stretches to the heavens, and I'm amazed when his palm lights up with a silver-blue glow.

"Is that moonlight?" I ask, completely amazed.

"It will help us see underwater."

A scream pulls my eyes from the moonlight, and I recognize the voice immediately as Landon's. He's in the water now, thrashing around with all the debris of his broken ship. His scream is swallowed by the Passage as he's pulled under.

"I'm going," I yell, forcing myself underwater and begging my eyes to adjust. Wolfe follows, stretching his moonlight into the depths, turning the black water a soft shade of gray. The current swirls in front of us, violently stirring the sea.

I see a body drifting down to the ocean floor, completely still. I tap Wolfe on the arm and point, letting some air out of my lungs in order to sink deeper and deeper. The water is cold and sharp against my skin, but even in the midst of the chaos, the quiet here is comforting.

Wolfe's moonlight illuminates the body, and I panic when I realize it isn't Landon. I get closer, but I don't recognize the man. Maybe the captain. I wrap my arms around his waist and kick upward, Wolfe's light going off in another direction. We surface, and I see a boat from the Witchery rushing toward us, taking advantage of Wolfe's current. It stops a safe distance away, and I flip onto my back and swim with the body, kicking as hard as I can.

When I finally reach the boat, it's my father's arms that reach over and pull the body inside.

"Tana, are you hurt?" he asks, and the words take me a moment to process.

"No," I say.

"Get in the boat. It's not safe," he says, reaching for me.

"I'll be okay. Wolfe is here; he's helping."

My dad realizes what I'm saying, that it's Wolfe's magic that is enabling me to help. Wolfe's magic that is saving Landon and his family. He tenses, but he doesn't argue.

"Okay. There's nothing we can do until that current moves on. Help as much as you can, and we'll be here, standing by." He's soaking wet, the rain unrelenting, the inside of the boat drenched, but they're safe where they are.

Dad reaches over and rests his hand against the side of the boat. I quickly squeeze it, then dive beneath the surface and search for Wolfe. His light is coming toward me, and I rush to meet him. He's carrying another person, Landon's mother, but she's moving, kicking her legs along with Wolfe.

Watching him, carrying the light of the moon and riding a current he created, I see just how powerful high magic is. If there's a manor full of witches who can do what Wolfe is doing now—if this is the baseline of what they're capable of—I can only imagine what they could do with more magic.

An idea forms in my mind, fuzzy at first but growing in clarity.

"What's wrong?" Wolfe shouts at me, and I realize I've been treading water, staring at the sea.

"I know how to fix the currents," I say, stunned. Then the trance is broken; Landon is still missing. "Get her to the boat," I yell.

Wolfe transfers his light to me, and I'm amazed when it doesn't go out, doesn't even flicker. I feel my magic rush to meet it, sustaining it in my hand and guiding my path as I dive deeper into the Passage. A shadow moves above me, and I look up to see a person swimming away from the wreckage.

I quickly surface to see Landon's father swimming toward my parents' boat.

"Can you make it on your own?" I call after him.

He treads water and looks back at me, blood running down his face from a large gash on his forehead.

"Is Landon on the boat?" he asks, his voice frantic.

"Not yet. I'm going to find him now. How many of you were aboard?"

"Four of us. Our family plus the captain."

"Get to the boat. I'll find your son."

I dive back beneath the water and head toward the current. It begins to shift, slowly releasing the wreckage from its hold, debris surfacing and sinking, wooden shards everywhere. Landon is trapped somewhere in this mess, and my heart slams against my chest, desperate to find him.

I cast my light as far out in front of me as it will go, and finally, *finally*, I see him, his suit jacket caught on a large piece of debris dragging him down, down, down.

He settles on the Passage floor before I can get to him, totally lifeless. His arms and legs drift from side to side, moving with the sea. I follow after him, kicking my legs and thrashing my arms, letting air out of my lungs to swim deeper.

Light comes from behind me, and I know Wolfe is close by, bringing more moonlight with him. When I finally reach Landon, his eyes are closed and his lips are blue. His skin looks gray, all the life in him gone.

I try to pull him off the seafloor, but he's stuck, his jacket pinned beneath the debris. I struggle to get him free, worried I won't be able to do it in time, but then Wolfe is by my side, holding Landon up. There's blood all over his white shirt, a deep red circle that seeps out in all directions. My lungs burn. When he's finally clear of his jacket, I wrap my arms around Landon's torso, careful to avoid his injury, and begin to kick.

I gasp for air when we pop out of the water. Wolfe surfaces a second later, and he reverses the current he created, sending us sailing back to my parents with Landon's limp body.

"Mom! Dad!" I yell as we get closer, and both of them lean

over the side of the boat, stretching out their arms. "He's hurt," I say when we finally reach them.

They lift Landon out of the water, and I pull myself into the boat, desperate to help. Elizabeth is standing out of the way with a blanket wrapped around her, and the captain is sitting on the bench seat with his face in his hands.

Landon's father begins CPR, pressing on Landon's chest and then breathing air into his lungs. Wolfe climbs over the edge of the boat and kneels on the floor next to Landon, holding his hands over the injury.

"I can help him," Wolfe says, his voice urgent.

My mother reaches out her hand, fear on her face. "He's speaking of magic."

"Do it," Marshall says without hesitation, and it's clear he doesn't understand what kind of magic he has agreed to.

Wolfe closes his eyes and whispers a spell so fast and low I can't make it out. His hands are covered in red. I stand off to the side and, without thinking, reach for my mother's hand.

She doesn't pull away from me. She doesn't take a step back. Instead, she takes my hand and squeezes it tight. "He's going to be okay," she says in that calm tone of hers that makes me feel as if everything in the world will be well.

Another crack of thunder tears through the night sky, and I jump.

Wolfe opens Landon's shirt, and I watch in wonder as the blood stops seeping and his skin begins to heal itself. My mother turns away, but Elizabeth has her eyes fixed on Wolfe. High magic wraps around Landon and moves through his body, healing him in a way that shouldn't be possible. The captain's mouth hangs open, and Marshall's hands form fists at his sides as he watches Wolfe use a magic he thought had been eradicated.

Everyone is too quiet, too still, too rigid.

Then, finally, Landon breathes.

forty-one

We drop Landon and his family off on the mainland, where an ambulance is waiting to take him to the hospital. Whatever Landon told his parents about me seems to have worked, because I've gotten several judgmental glances, but I'm glad for it. If they believe I'm personally the problem, they will still pursue the alliance. It can still be achieved.

"Wait," my mother says before anyone gets off the boat. She turns to Wolfe. "Erase their memories of the current and your magic. They need to believe the storm is what sank their ship."

"I beg your pardon?" Elizabeth says, reaching for Marshall's hand.

"You are forbidden from doing that," Marshall says, giving my mother a look that sends a chill down my spine. "We're leaving."

"Do it now," my mother says, her voice rising.

"If I do this, you will work with my coven to stop the currents. Otherwise I refuse."

My mother gapes at Wolfe, stunned that he would negotiate at a time like this, but she regains her composure quickly. "Agreed. Do it."

Then, all at once, Marshall, Elizabeth, Landon, and the boat captain are looking at Wolfe as he rewrites their memories. They will think the storm capsized their ship. They won't remember Wolfe or his magic. The secret of the old coven will be safe.

It doesn't take long, and soon the Yateses are climbing out of the boat, thanking my parents for rescuing them. I get one more cold glance from Landon's father, and then they're gone. My mother goes with them to the hospital, offering support and making sure their questions are answered appropriately. She hugs me before she leaves, a promise that we aren't through, that I don't have to live with her or be part of her coven to remain her daughter.

Wolfe and I stay on the boat with my dad, and we sail back to the Witchery in silence. The storm has passed, and the Passage is quiet again. Dad docks the boat, but he doesn't move to step out, so neither do I. Wolfe and I are sitting on the bench seat in the back, wrapped in blankets and towels. My silk gray dress is torn and ruined, and I lost my shoes along the way, but the necklace my father gave me sits firmly in place. My hand drifts up to it, and I roll the vial between my fingers.

My father paces back and forth for several seconds, then finally stops and extends his hand to Wolfe.

"I don't believe we've been properly introduced. I'm Samuel, Tana's father."

Wolfe stands and takes my father's hand. "I'm Wolfe Hawthorne."

"Hawthorne?" my dad asks, and I wonder if he knows about my mother's relationship with Galen. An odd expression passes over his face, something between amusement and understanding, and I realize he does.

"That's right."

"Well, Wolfe, thank you for what you did tonight. If you don't mind, I'd like a few minutes alone with my daughter."

"Of course." Wolfe takes off his blanket and wraps it around my shoulders, then jumps onto the dock and waits for me on the shore.

My dad stands in front of me, looking into my eyes. "Tana, what you did tonight was unimaginable. I truly didn't think I'd ever see that happen again."

I'm having a hard time reading him. His words don't sound like condemnation, not really. He sounds surprised more than anything else.

I almost apologize. I *am* sorry, sorry for not warning him beforehand and making a choice that reflects poorly on him and Mom. Sorry for blowing up the arrangement we had with Landon and straying from the path they worked so hard to lay down for me.

But I'm not sorry that I'll get to spend my life with a boy who sees my wildness and a magic that makes me come alive.

"It was the hardest decision I've ever made." I'm still playing with the necklace, and my dad's eyes go to it. I don't want to lose it, but this necklace belongs to him, not to a daughter who has defied everything he believes in. "Here, Dad. I'm sure you want this back."

He looks pained, his brows pinching together and his mouth turning downward. "Put that back on." He says it with conviction, as if he's giving a sermon. "That belongs to you, and I'm proud for you to wear it." His voice shakes at the end.

"Dad?"

He sits down next to me and takes my hands in his. "You believe in something strongly enough that you gave up all the comforts of this life in search of something different. You are brave and loyal to yourself," he says, pulling me into him. "It won't be easy, but if you believe in this life half as much as I believe in mine, you're going to do well."

I had accepted that there would always be a gap between my parents and me, that from now on I'd be seen as a traitor and an embarrassment. I had never let myself hope that they might understand, and I'm completely overwhelmed by it.

"And if you and that boy continue to look at each other the way you did tonight, I suspect you'll be very happy."

"Thank you, Dad," I say, holding him tight.

We walk onto the dock and meet Wolfe on the beach. I almost ask my dad if I can go home with him, if I can spend another night in my bedroom with the comfort of his presence nearby. But I've made my choice, and I gave up that option when I cast my blood into crystal instead of copper.

"Let's plan for a meeting in two days at the perfumery. Wolfe, bring your father. We have much to discuss, and we ought to do it privately before the councils get involved."

Wolfe agrees, and my dad gives me another smile before turning and walking toward home. I try not to dwell on the image of him walking away, on the way it hurts my insides like a punch to the gut. But I can ache for the loss of my previous life while delighting in all the wonders that are yet to come.

Wolfe and I walk in the direction opposite my dad, to the wild part of the island where anything is possible. When we finally get to the manor, a man is waiting for us outside. Wolfe offered to magic me into dry clothing while we were on the boat, but I didn't want to use more magic than necessary in front of my parents. I look horrid, though, and now I wish I had agreed to it. I self-consciously smooth my hand over my dress and try to fix my messy braid.

The man smiles, and his expression tells me he isn't at all surprised to see me here.

"I'm Galen, Wolfe's father," he says, even though it's obvious—they look so much alike.

"Have we met before?" I ask, reaching for a memory of him that I can't find.

"Several times."

"I'm sorry, I don't remember." I look down, but Galen reacts as if it's nothing.

"Not at all. I heard about what you did tonight."

I suppose it makes sense that he already knows—he probably keeps tabs on the island more than my mother realizes—but it still catches me off guard.

I start to explain myself, say I understand if he doesn't want me here, but he holds up his hand, and I stop speaking.

"Welcome home, Mortana." Then he pulls me into a hug. I'm stunned by his kindness, but it helps to ease the ache in my heart, and I'm sure that I'll be happy here.

"Thank you."

"I know you've had a long day, so I'll let you get settled. But tomorrow, if you're feeling up to it, the rest of the coven would love to meet you."

"How many of you are there?"

"Seventy-three," he says.

Seventy-three. The number astounds me, and I'm amazed that I went my entire life without knowing of their existence. But I can't help the excitement that rises inside me as I realize I will have a home here. A family.

It will be different from the life I have always envisioned for myself. But it will be wholly and completely my own.

"I'm looking forward to meeting them."

Galen offers a warm smile, then turns to Wolfe and squeezes his shoulder. His eyes look glassy, tears pooling in them as he looks at his son. Then he walks inside, leaving Wolfe and me alone.

Wolfe turns toward me and extends his hand. "Do you want to see your new home?" I can hear the heaviness in his voice, the weight of my decision wrapping around us both. It's a good weight, a calming one, binding us together.

I look at the manor, its steep pitched roof reaching toward the heavens. Lanterns cast a soft, warm glow on the stone wall and illuminate the climbing vines that crawl along the exterior. Smoke drifts into the clear night sky from a large chimney, and the soft sound of a piano filters out into the cold.

"Yes." I take his hand in mine, but a shock runs through me, a flash of something I can't place, and I pull away.

There is a life for you here.

"What did you say?" I ask him, stepping closer.

"I didn't say anything." He watches me. "Are you okay?"

"I could have sworn I heard something," I say. "It was a long day. I guess I'm just tired."

"Then let's get you inside."

Wolfe offers his hand to me once more, and I take it.

I don't want to lose you.

My grip tightens as an image rushes into my mind: the two of us in this same place, standing in the woods outside the manor on a cold autumn night. He had just shown me his home for the first time, opened his entire life up to me so I could envision something different for myself. And I ran away.

I squeeze my eyes shut as the memory takes hold of my brain and my chest and my heart, digging its roots into me, ensuring I never forget it again.

"I've been here before," I whisper. "With you. Right here. You told me there is a life for me here."

Wolfe doesn't say anything, but when I meet his eyes, they're red. He nods and his jaw tenses. "Yes."

Then it's a flood.

A moonflower and a light. Crashing into Wolfe in a field.

Missing the rush. Learning dark magic. Going to the western shore over and over, hoping to see the boy who changed everything.

I can hear your heartbeat.

Clutching him in the sea.

Touching him by the fire.

Kissing him on the shore.

I'm overwhelmed, drowning in an ocean of memory, an unfathomable depth of feeling I didn't know I was capable of. I'm completely shocked by the way my love for him took hold of every part of me, masked itself as an impossible choice when the truth was that I could only ever choose him.

From that very first night, my fate was sealed.

Queen of the dark.

I rush to him, crashing into him with my whole body, squeezing him with all my might. Tears run down my face, and I close my eyes and press my lips to his ear. "I remember."

His body shakes as he takes a breath, so strong it's as if it's the first time his lungs have ever met the air, breathing in the life he almost lost.

"I remember," I say again, my voice louder, making sure he hears it. Making sure he trusts it. Making sure he knows.

"I missed you." His words are quiet and rough and beautiful.

I kiss his neck and jaw before finding his lips, already wet with saltwater tears. His movements are slow and hesitant, as if he's ensuring that I'm real, ensuring that I won't disappear as soon as he lets his guard down.

"I'm here," I whisper against his lips.

I feel the moment his walls crumble between us, crashing to the earth.

"Tana," he breathes, opening his mouth and clutching my face between his hands, kissing me as if he's making up for all the kisses we lost, hungry from the time we spent apart.

His fingers are restless, sliding down my face and lingering on my jaw, trailing down my neck and moving over my collarbones. A shiver runs down my spine, and my breath hitches. "Take me upstairs," I say.

He kisses me again and finds my hand, leading me through the manor and up to his room. He keeps looking back at me as if it isn't enough to feel my fingers laced with his. He needs to *see* me, needs to make sure I'm still here, and I love it.

He opens his bedroom door, and I walk inside, the light from the fire casting the room in copper shadows that dance across the floor and up the walls. There is no other light.

I slowly walk to the bed and turn to face him.

"Wolfe?" I say, letting the thin straps of my dress fall from my shoulders.

He swallows hard. "Yes?" His voice is like sandpaper, coarse and uneven, and I hear the vulnerability in it, the fear that this might all be a dream, that he might wake up to a girl with no memory of him.

"I'm right here," I say. "Touch me until you're convinced this is real."

He doesn't move. He stares at me, frozen in place, completely still.

"Please."

He finally closes the space between us and takes my head in his hands, kissing me until I'm breathless. I tug at his shirt and pull it over his head before letting it fall to the floor. He slowly undoes the buttons of my dress, the gray silk sliding down my body and pooling around my feet, his fingers trailing the length of my spine.

I lean back onto the bed and bring Wolfe with me, never letting go of him. He kisses my mouth and eyelids and neck, desperate at first, then slower, as if with every touch he's assuring himself this will not be the last time. He slides his hand down my side and over my hip, all the way to my knee before pausing and slowly trailing his fingers back up. I clutch at his shoulders as he follows the curve of my thigh, gasping when he finds what he's looking for, my entire body responding. I am lost in him. Completely lost in him.

I shove my hands into his hair and arch into his touch, whispering his name against his mouth. "More," I say.

He brings his hands to my ribs and his hips between my legs, his breath catching in his throat as he begins to move, closer to me than he's ever been. The closest he can get, and yet it doesn't feel close enough. I grasp his back and feel his weight on me, pulling and pulling and pulling, and maybe he isn't the only one who's terrified he's dreaming.

I savor every sigh, every kiss, every touch, feeling him in ways I've never felt anyone, listening to his breaths as they stall and hitch, as they get heavier and faster. We build together, nearing a cliff I'm desperate to jump from. He pauses, catching my mouth in his. Then we leap together, and the intimacy of seeing him so out of control takes my breath away. He is magic to me, and I realize that at some point, I stopped being able to distinguish between the two.

He has always seen me, not as a role but as the center of my life, forcing me to find my own truths. And in the midst of it all, I found him. He is my truth, and there are not enough lies in the world to convince me otherwise.

He whispers my name, breathing with me and slowing with me until the fire dies down to nothing more than ash.

Then we sleep, each knowing that tomorrow, the other will be here when we wake.

forty-two

Two days later, Galen, Wolfe, and I meet with my parents. We wait until the sun has set before leaving the manor, sticking to the trails that wind through the forest so we aren't seen. My mother has much to discuss with the council, but those conversations won't start until she knows where the old witches stand. She never shares anything until she has a thorough answer for every possible question. And she makes sure she knows everything that happens on her island so she's never surprised.

She does not like being surprised.

We meet in the back room of the perfumery, long after the shops have closed for the day. Main Street is empty, and yet I can't help craning my neck as we pass the Eldons' tea shop, hoping to catch a glimpse of Ivy. But the shop is dark.

My parents are already there when we get to the perfumery. My father is grinding down herbs with his mortar and pestle as if it's a normal day at the shop. His hands still when I walk into the room, and a small smile pulls at his lips and brightens his eyes.

"Hi, Dad," I say, walking over and hugging him tight. It's only been two days, but I miss the way his cooking fills the house with the clanging of pots and mouthwatering smells. I miss the way he hums to himself and how he always has a cup of tea ready when I need one. The vial he gave me hangs from my neck and digs into my sternum when I tighten the hug.

My mother is watching us when I pull away, and I don't know what to expect from her. When I saw her on the water, she was completely focused on Landon and his parents. Now that she has had time to sit with the events of my Covenant, I'm not sure how things have changed. I don't know if she will treat me like a threat or an enemy or the person who ruined the plans she so painstakingly laid.

But when my eyes meet hers, she pulls back her shoulders and lifts her chin, then takes a long, deep breath. She's trying not to cry. "Hi, sweetie," she says.

"Hi, Mom." And before I can think better of it, I cross the room and give her a tight hug, the kind that will mess up her hair and rumple her blouse. She doesn't pull away, though. She sinks into it and clutches me tight, a mother hugging her only child.

When she pulls away, she smooths her hair and clears her throat. "I believe this belongs to you," she says, handing me the silver necklace that Wolfe gave me the night I first visited the manor. I had completely forgotten about it, and I run my fingers over the smooth black stone. It must have taken so much for her to give this back to me when it goes against everything she has worked for, and I don't trust myself to speak. I look at her, and she blurs in my vision.

"Thank you," I manage to get out.

"You're welcome." She brushes my cheek with the back of her hand, then looks at Wolfe. "There are many things we don't agree on, but you're part of our family now. I hope you'll learn to think of us as such."

"Thank you," he says. "That shouldn't be too difficult—I've had plenty of practice disagreeing with my dad."

My mother's mouth quirks at his words, and she looks at Galen as she answers. "I don't doubt it."

"Some habits refuse to die," Galen says.

"Speaking of disagreeing," my mother says, motioning to the chairs they've set out, "we have a lot to discuss."

We sit down, a clear delineation between our chairs and hers. We might be family, but right now we're also opposing forces who must try to find some common ground.

I watch as my mother slips into her role as coven leader, narrowing her eyes and straightening her spine. "Here is your meeting, Galen. Say what you need to say."

"Actually, Tana's going to take this one, if that's okay with you."

She slowly turns her gaze to me, one eyebrow arching in surprise. She nods. "Of course. The floor is yours, Tana."

I shift in my seat and fold my hands together to keep from fidgeting. My dad's grinding stops, and the room fills with weighted silence. I take a deep breath and think back to that moment in the water, watching Wolfe and his magic, when the idea took root inside me.

"The mainlanders believe their ship was sunk by the storm, which will buy you a little time," I say. "But as soon as something else happens with the currents, they will realize what happened and blame you for the near loss of Landon and his family. Any trust they had in you will fade, and it could take years to rebuild the relationship—if they decide they're open to it in the first place."

My mother tilts her head to the side as she listens. "Yes, that's all true. If you have something helpful to propose, I'm open to hearing it, but I don't need you to recount the things I already know."

I pause before continuing. She'll hate what I'm about to say, but I don't see any other way out. "You can't keep rushing your magic into the sea. Give it to us instead."

She takes a sharp breath, then exhales slowly. "Explain to me exactly what you mean."

"Rush your magic to us. We're strong enough to hold it. There aren't enough of us to undo the damage the rushes have caused with our magic alone, but with your excess magic as well, we'd be able to. We could fix the currents and heal the island. And the mainlanders would never know that your magic is what nearly killed their ruling family."

"This was your idea?" Her tone is sharp and pointed, and my chest hurts as I recognize what's in her voice: betrayal. She feels betrayed. By me.

"Yes."

"Absolutely not." She says it with finality, strong words that land heavy in the space separating us. My father is staring off into the distance the way he does when he's deep in thought. His hand is still firmly around his pestle, but he hasn't started working again.

He's considering what I said.

"Ingrid," Galen says from beside me, "this would work. It's a smart idea, one I wish I had come up with on my own."

"It's a smart idea for *you*," my mother says. "It would make your coven significantly stronger. You could use that power for anything. It's off the table."

They stare each other down, and I realize how tenuous their relationship is. The new coven protects the old coven by keeping their existence a secret. If the mainland knew about us, they would do everything in their power to eradicate the use of high magic. And my mother is right—if the new coven rushed their excess magic to us, the power dynamics would shift dramatically.

We'd be strong enough to put up a fight, far stronger than we are today. If we weren't careful with all that magic, we could accidentally get the attention of the mainland, and that would completely destroy the relationship the new coven has spent generations working to build.

"What if we spelled it?" I say, and my mother and Galen both turn to look at me. "What if we bound the excess magic to the full moon, ensuring we could only use it once a month? We would meet you at your rushes, and you would know exactly when and how the magic was being used because you could watch us do it."

"That would give them an awful lot of power over us," Galen says.

"Not really," I counter. "You'd still be stronger than you are now. You could make the currents worse if you were dissatisfied with how you were being treated. The magic would be bound to the moon, but you could still use it for whatever you wanted. It would just make it difficult for you to hide anything from the new coven."

Galen isn't looking at me, though. He's looking at my mother. They watch each other, neither of them saying a word.

"The mainland protects the new coven. The new coven protects us. And we protect the earth." As soon as I say it, I'm sure this is how it's supposed to be. I'm completely overcome, realizing that the path I gave up, the life I turned my back on, was all in service of something bigger than me. Bigger than Landon and bigger than the new coven and bigger than high magic.

My mother is considering my words—I know she is—and it's more progress than Galen ever could have made on his own.

This is my role, and I feel my roots take hold in this soil and drink of its nourishment until I punch through the earth and bloom.

Wolfe takes my hand in his. "She's right, Dad," he says, his voice sure. Steady.

"I know she is," Galen says. "What do you say, Ingrid?"

My mother doesn't respond. She leans back in her chair and looks past us, thinking things over. "I say it's worth trying," she finally says. "We'll have to set clear boundaries before we begin, and given that my coven thinks yours no longer exists, we will have to get on the same page before presenting this idea, making it clear that you are as much a surprise to me as you are to them. And there is the matter of ensuring this stays hidden from the mainland. We can go over the details once we've both had time to consider the arrangement and speak with our councils. And we will of course stop rushing our magic to you at once if you do anything that is even slightly questionable. But it's worth trying."

Everyone stands, and my dad walks over to me and wraps his arm around my shoulders, pulling me close. "I'm proud of you," he says.

"Me too," I say.

He looks down at me and smiles. "That's all I've ever wanted for you."

My mother walks to the other side of my dad and leans into him. "What a wholly unexpected turn of events," she says.

"She's your daughter."

She looks at me then, a small smile pulling at her lips. "Yes, she is."

She squeezes my hand as she passes by me. "Lock up when you leave," she says, and then she and my dad are out the door, hugging each other as they go.

It's such a casual request, something she's said to me hundreds of times. *Lock up when you leave.* And it fills my chest with all the things I've been too afraid to hope for. There will be clashes between the covens as we figure out this new relationship, and it will unquestionably change things, but not all change is bad.

There is growth in change.

Beauty and fulfillment.

Joy.

"If you ever doubted your place in the world, Tana, I hope those voices have been quieted," Galen says. "I'll meet you back at the manor."

When the door closes behind Galen, Wolfe pulls me into him and buries his face in my neck. "Now that everyone else is gone, I have a few demands of my own," he says, his lips moving against my skin, sending a shiver down my spine.

"Tell me."

He lifts his head and meets my eyes as a seriousness takes over his expression. "Let me love you," he says, his voice quiet and soft, pouring over me like a hot bath on a winter's night. "Let me love you until you're sure it's magic."

And before I have time to respond, he kisses me, his lips soft and slow against my own. I pull him closer, backing into the wooden island in the center of the room. My dad's pestle falls to the floor, but I don't move away.

Wolfe brings his hands to my hips and lifts me onto the counter, kissing me as he does. I wrap my arms around his neck and my legs around his waist, hugging him close as his lips trail down my skin and onto my chest.

My head falls back, and I whisper his name, hoping he hears that I'm already sure. Hoping he knows that to me, he is magic, a spell I will practice over and over for the rest of my life.

I am bewitched, every part of me.

And as long as he says my name and touches my skin and exists on this beautiful Earth, I always will be.

forty-three

It's a cold winter night. The sky is clear, and stars shine brightly overhead. The full moon is tomorrow, and it will be the first time the new coven rushes their magic to us. The manor is alive with anticipation, a thrill I can almost see moving through the air.

But I know the anticipation we feel is likely a mirror of the dread the new coven feels. That my parents and Ivy feel. Giving us more power goes against everything they believe in, and it will take a lot of time to build trust between us.

Maybe one day, the new coven won't feel the need to watch us use their magic. Maybe they will see the healing island and the calmer seas and know we're being faithful to our word.

It's that thought that gets me excited, a future I believe in with the entirety of my being. And I will work for it as hard as I possibly can.

I wrap my arms around my chest and watch my breath drift out in front of me before vanishing. The waves roll onto the shore, one after the other, the constant harmony to my life. The noise is still with me regardless of what side of the island I'm on or what kind of magic I practice.

A flash catches my eye, and I turn to see a small, circular light dancing at the periphery of the woods. As soon as I spot it, it dashes into the forest, and I jump up and follow it.

It's dark under the cover of the trees, the canopy so dense the moonlight has to fight to get through. I slow my steps and walk carefully as the light darts ahead of me, casting a soft glow that cuts through the shadows.

After minutes of leading me, the light rushes into a clearing and tumbles through the air before vanishing. When I step out from the woods, a small, private beach is revealed.

Wolfe stands in the middle of the shore, and for a moment I stop breathing, still completely taken by the way he looks bathed in the moon's light. It's truly a wonder I get anything done, living in the same manor as him.

"Well, Mr. Hawthorne, you've successfully lured me here. What will you do now that you have me?"

His mouth pulls up on one side as he reaches a hand out to me. "You'll see."

I take his hand, and he leads me to an outgrowth of tall grasses with a narrow dirt trail running through them. A small wooden gate blocks the path, and it creaks when I push it open, its weather-worn wood splintered and faded.

The salty sea air is tinged with sweetness, and I look around to see dozens of flowers surrounding me, growing tall and wild.

Evening primrose and black hellebores bask in the moonlight, and a single white moonflower grows amidst the night-blooming flowers.

"I was in this garden the first time you said my name at midnight," Wolfe says. "When I heard it, my heart started racing, and I dove into the water thinking of only one thing: getting to you. And that's all I've thought of since."

"Wolfe," I say, lingering over his name, saying it slowly so I can savor the way it feels in my mouth. I take a step closer to him.

"Wolfe."

Another step toward him, this time close enough to touch. I grab him by his collar and pull him into me, brushing my lips against his ear. "Wolfe."

He shudders as I say his name.

"You're distracting me," he says, his voice low, as if it hurts him to say it.

I raise my hands in the air in mock apology. "You're easily distracted."

"Only by you." He says it in that way of his where he sounds angry, but I know it's just that he's frightened by how much he loves me. Everyone on this island knows his weakness now, and it's a liability he never intended to have.

Perhaps the most unfair thing of all is that I find immeasurable strength in being the only thing that's ever brought him to his knees. It is my openness, my vulnerability that cracked the exterior of this jagged boy, qualities only the foolish say are weak.

But I know better.

"I vow to use my power only for good." I say it as a joke, but it's wrapped in spools of truth.

Wolfe leans into me, his warm breath colliding with the cold air, sending a shiver down my spine. "Use it however you want," he says, his words causing my insides to stir with desire. "I trust you."

"I know you do."

"Good."

We watch each other for several breaths, and then Wolfe grabs my hand and leads me farther into the garden. He picks the moonflower and hands it to me, the petals brushing my lips when I raise it to my face.

"Every queen needs a castle," he says, pushing through another gate and releasing my hand. I step through and gasp as I take in my surroundings. An entire field of moonflowers stretches out before me as far as I can see, thousands of them in bloom despite the winter chill. Their petals shimmer with moonlight and move in the breeze, a rolling sea of white in the darkness.

"Did you do all this?" I ask, unable to fully take in what I'm seeing. There are so many.

"I did."

I turn to face him, still holding the flower he gave me. "It's unbelievable," I say. "Thank you."

I slowly sink to the earth, pulling him down with me. His mouth is on mine in an instant, his breath warming me from the inside out, making me forget that it's winter. He could kiss me as many times as there are flowers in this field and it would never be enough.

I lie down and he follows, and I commit to memory the way it feels to have his body on top of mine, the way his breaths respond when I touch him.

"Wolfe," I say, refilling my lungs with the air he stole, "Do you want to swim with me?"

"Yes."

I rush to the water's edge with Wolfe right behind me, laughing into the midnight sky as I go. I close my eyes and think of the sun, think of all the hours I spent practicing magic during the day, and I pour it into the waves, heating them just enough make swimming tolerable.

I don't bother taking off my nightdress. Instead, I dive in headfirst, swimming out far enough that I have to tread water to stay afloat. We swim together by the light of the moon, telling stories and using magic and living. Fully living.

And as we do, I marvel at what it feels like to practice magic at night.

Wolfe starts to make his way back to the shore, but I tell him to wait. I swim up next to him and wrap my arms around his neck, kissing him with all the joy and passion and wonder of the moment. And as I do, I call up my magic. It rises with excitement, getting stronger with each passing moment.

With my lips still on Wolfe's, I release my magic into the water. Our feet stay planted on the ocean floor as the waves rise up on either side of us, surrounding us in a vortex of salt water and magic and midnights. Infinite midnights.

"High or low, the moon's rhythmic phase; surround us in wonder for all of our days."

Wolfe pulls back and watches in awe as it spins around us, dark water perfectly controlled by darker magic.

Slowly, I let my magic ease. The water drains back to the ocean floor, lifting us up as it does, and together we swim to the beach. Wolfe takes my hand and gives me a meaningful look.

"I think it's time to head back to the manor." His gaze lingers on my lips before finding my eyes.

"I think you're right."

I lace my fingers through his, but before we leave, I turn back to the water one more time. It looks so perfect with the moonlight glinting on its surface, a thing of beauty and power, heavy silence and deceptive calm.

A force that recognizes the magic inside me and yields to it because it knows I'll keep it safe.

A home that has unfailingly let my wild heart be free.

I used to believe that I belonged to the sea.

But I was wrong.

The sea belongs to me.

acknowledgments

This book is extremely special to me, and from the moment the initial idea sparked in my mind, all I have wanted was to share it with readers. If you have picked it up, read it, or talked about it, thank you. Thank you so much.

There are many brilliant people who helped me get *Bring Me Your Midnight* from idea to finished book, and I feel very fortunate that my stories are touched by their wisdom, support, and enthusiasm.

First, to Pete Knapp, my literary agent. Thank you for your belief in me and my stories and for being such an incredible advocate for my work. You make me feel like anything is possible, and I know my hopes and ambitions are in the best of hands.

Thank you to Annie Berger, my incredible editor. You saw the magic in this story before it was even on the page and helped me find it when I lost the thread. Thank you for loving this book and helping me turn it into the best version of itself. I am so lucky to work with you.

To the entire Sourcebooks Fire team, thank you for the amazing work you do to get my stories out into the world. Karen Masnica, Madison Nankervis, and Rebecca Atkinson, thank you for making readers aware of this book in the coolest, most exciting of ways. Thank you to Liz Dresner for designing the most striking cover of all time, Elena Masci for bringing it to life so beautifully, and Tara Jaggers for the gorgeous internal design. Thank you to Erin Fitzsimmons for the case and end papers of my dreams and to Sveta Dorosheva for the most stunning map I've ever seen. Thea Voutiritsas, Alison Cherry, and Carolyn Lesnick, thank you for putting the finishing touches on this book and for polishing it until it shined. Gabbi Calabrese, thank you for your help in making this process smooth and seamless. Margaret Coffee, Valerie Pierce, and Caitlin Lawler, thank you for your tireless work to put my books on the radar of as many booksellers, educators, and librarians as possible. Ashlyn Keil, you are an events rockstar. Thank you for everything you do to connect me with readers. Sean Murray, I have seen my book on so many shelves because of the work you do—thank you. And finally, thank you to my publisher, Dominique Raccah. I love being a Sourcebooks author.

To the entire Park & Fine team, I am so grateful to have your collective brilliance behind me and my books. Andrea Mai and Emily Sweet, thank you for the strategy and enthusiasm you bring. Stuti Telidevara, thank you for keeping me organized amidst the chaos. Kat Toolan and Ben Kaslow-Zieve, thank you for your work to get my books into the hands of readers all around the world.

To Debbie Deuble Hill and Alec Frankel, thank you for being such excellent guides on all things television and film.

To Marta Courtenay, thank you for your creativity, enthusiasm, and for the hours of work you save me.

To Elana Roth Parker, thank you for helping make this book happen.

To the authors who so generously read this book early and sent along such wonderful blurbs—thank you. Your enthusiasm makes me so excited to send this book out into the world.

Adalyn Grace, thank you for the hours you spent on the other side of my screen, drafting with me. May our schedules forever align. Diya Mishra, you read this book first, and your enthusiasm and excessive use of the f-word fueled my love for it from the very start. Thank you. Julia Ember, Miranda Santee, Tyler Griffin, Heather Ezell, Kristin Dwyer, and Rosiee Thor, thank you for not only being some of my very favorite people, but for also reading this book early and providing such invaluable insight. Rachel Lynn Solomon, Adrienne Young, Isabel Ibañez, and Tara Tsai, I wouldn't want to be on this journey without you.

Angela Davis, you gave me permission to imagine a path for myself that was truly mine. Thank you for helping me find my happiness.

To my dog, Doppler, who keeps me company day after day as I write these stories and who gets me out of my office when I might not otherwise leave.

Chip, I can't really describe the peace that settled over me when you came into our family. Thank you for your heart.

Mom, thank you for your constant encouragement and support as I navigate this career. You have always believed in my writing, and I'm so thankful. Dad, you have never once made me doubt your love, and in the hardest moments of my life, you have been my safe haven and harbor during the storm. I love you both so much.

Mir, I am only able to do this because of you. The way you support me, encourage me, and love me completely blows me away, and I could not ask for a more perfect person to be totally dependent on. The truth is that I'm in awe of you. I love you to the ends of the earth.

Ty, you are my one and only, my epic love, my very best friend. I would go on any journey, no matter how difficult, if it meant finding you at the end. Thank you for believing in me and supporting me as I pursue dream after dream; I hope you know that out of them all, you are my greatest dream come true. I love you so much.

And finally, to Jesus. Thank for loving me through all my questions and doubts—especially then.

about the author

Rachel Griffin is the *New York Times* bestselling author of *The Nature of Witches* and *Wild is the Witch*. Born and raised in the Pacific Northwest, she has a deep love of nature and hopes more vampires settle down in her beloved state of Washington. When she isn't writing, you can find her wandering in the woods, reading by the fire, or drinking copious amounts of coffee and tea. She lives with her husband, small dog, and growing collection of houseplants. Visit her on Instagram @TimesNewRachel or online at rachelgriffinbooks.com.